MEMOIRS OF A CAVALIER

DANIEL DEFOE

MEMOIRS OF A CAVALIER

OR A Military Journal Of
The Wars in Germany, And the Wars in England;
From the Year 1632, to the Year 1648.
Written Threescore Years Ago by an
English Gentleman,
who served first in the Army of Gustavus Adolphus,
the glorious King of Sweden, till his Death;
and after that, in the
Royal Army of King Charles the First,
from the Beginning of the Rebellion,
to the End of that War.

EDITED WITH AN INTRODUCTION BY
JAMES T. BOULTON

OXFORD UNIVERSITY PRESS
1978

Oxford University Press, Walton Street, Oxford OX2 6DP

OXFORD LONDON GLASGOW
NEW YORK TORONTO MELBOURNE WELLINGTON
IBADAN NAIROBI DAR ES SALAAM LUSAKA CAPE TOWN
KUALA LUMPUR SINGAPORE JAKARTA HONG KONG TOKYO
DELHI BOMBAY CALCUTTA MADRAS KARACHI

Introduction, Notes, Bibliography, and Chronology
© *Oxford University Press 1972*

First published as an Oxford English Novel 1972
First issued as an Oxford University Press Paperback 1978

Printed in Great Britain
at the University Press, Oxford
by Vivian Ridler
Printer to the University

CONTENTS

INTRODUCTION

The following Historical Memoirs are writ with so much Spirit and good Sense, that there is no doubt of their pleasing all such as can form any just Pretentions to either. However, as upon Reading of a Book, 'tis a Question, that naturally occurs, *Who is the Author?* . . . Some have imagin'd the whole to be a Romance; if it be, 'tis a Romance the likest to Truth that I ever read. It has all the Features of T[r]uth, 'tis cloath'd with her Simplicity, and adorn'd with her Charms . . . I am fully perswaded our Author whoever he was, had been early concerned in the Actions he relates.

James Lister, the Leeds publisher of the second (undated) edition of the *Memoirs of a Cavalier*, raised two issues which have disturbed readers presumably since the book first appeared, anonymously, in 1720.

'*Who is the Author?*' Lister believed him to be Andrew (1623–99), the second son of Sir Richard Newport; so confident was he that he inserted the name of the Newport family home, High Ercall in Shropshire, into the text. Many later editions (including Sir Walter Scott's in 1810 and Bohn's in 1854) perpetuated Lister's emendation. A tradition was born and it died hard. Newport was under ten when the Cavalier was serving Gustavus Adolphus; manifestly he could not have been the memorialist; but, by ignoring chronology, a plausible hypothesis could be formulated. It frequently was. The edition of 1792 carried the title: *Memoirs of the Honourable Col. Andrew Newport, a Shropshire Gentleman.*

Defoe's name was first publicly associated with the

Memoirs on the title-page of the 1784 edition published by Francis Noble. Noble was evidently unsure about Defoe's rôle: was he merely the 'editor' of a manuscript (as Noble describes him in an addendum to the Preface), or the author of the entire piece? Each subsequent editor and commentator has faced this question. As late as 1924 Paul Dottin in his *Defoe et ses Romans* postulated a manuscript source for the European section of the book; but Aitken in 1895 and Maynadier in 1903 pointed to the now generally accepted view: that it is unnecessary to assume 'any manuscript basis for even a page of the *Memoirs*.'[1] The case for Defoe as sole author was finally argued with the authority that rests on full documentary proof by Arthur W. Secord in *Robert Drury's Journal and Other Studies* (1961).[2]

The other issue raised by Lister is closely allied: if Defoe (as we now know) was the sole author, how did he, born later than the events so vividly related, achieve 'all the Features of Truth' so as to convince his readers that the narrator was 'concerned in the Actions he relates'? It was, of course, this verisimilitude which led early editors to credit the circumstantial account of a manuscript in the Preface. (They apparently failed to notice, or preferred to ignore, the conflict between the assertion that the manuscript was discovered 'at, or after, the Fight at *Worcester*', in 1651, and the reference in the text to the Restoration of 1660.) It was the same capacity for fabricating personal history that was later to deceive the sceptical intelligence of Samuel Johnson into accepting the veracity of the *Memoirs of an English Officer* (1728): 'he found in it such an air of Truth, that he could not doubt of its authenticity.'[3] Neither Lister nor Johnson was aware of the cumulative experience of the man responsible for such works as *The Shortest-Way*

---

[1] G. H. Maynadier, *Works of Defoe* (1903), v. xxi.

[2] John C. Major, in *The Role of Personal Memoirs in English Biography and Novel* (1935), had advanced a similar argument but without the weight of evidence presented by Secord.

[3] Boswell, *Life of Johnson*, ed. Hill and Powell (1934–50), iv. 333–4.

with the Dissenters (1702), *A True Relation* (1706), and a
series of pamphlets published in 1713, in which Defoe
brilliantly impersonated a Tory High-Churchman, a witness
to the appearance of the ghostly visitor Mrs. Veal, and a
bigoted Jacobite respectively. Of each work—as well as the
series of fictional memoirs he produced just prior to creating
the Cavalier—he could justly claim: the 'relation is . . .
attended with such Circumstances as may induce any
Reasonable Man to believe it.'[1]

Secord demonstrated (what Scott had begun to prove in
his edition) that the verisimilitude which compelled Lister's
admiration was the fruit of extensive research. It is worth
remark that of the 193 names listed in the Biographical
Index to this edition, 187 are those of identifiable historical
persons; six cannot be identified but some even of these may
be authentic. Such fidelity to historical fact in the personae of
the *Memoirs* is reflected in Defoe's account of events. Of
course he makes errors; but more remarkable is his closeness
to historical truth both in broad outline and in the detail.
Moreover, the Cavalier purports to write not as an historian
but as a participant 'in the Actions he relates', one who
'embellished with particulars' what can be found in the works
of historians.

Yet, as the Cavalier observes, there is truth in 'an old
English proverb, *That Standers-by see more than the Gamesters.*'[2] If he was the 'gamester', Defoe was the informed
'stander-by'. The Cavalier's experiences with the French in
Savoy mainly derive from Tom Brown's translation (1695)
of Jean Le Clerc's *Life of the Famous Cardinal—Duke de
Richlieu* (a misspelling adopted by Defoe); for his career
with the Swedish army in Germany up to 1632, Defoe's
source was unquestionably *The Swedish Intelligencer* (Parts
I–III, 1632–3); and for his adventures during the English
Civil War, the novelist relied principally on Clarendon's

---

[1] Preface to *A True Relation of the Appearance of one Mrs. Veal; Defoe*, ed.
James T. Boulton (1965), p. 134.
[2] p. 29.

History of the Rebellion (1702–4), Edmund Ludlow's *Memoirs* (1698–9), and Sir Bulstrode Whitelocke's *Memorials of the English Affairs* (1682).[1] Defoe may have read other relevant works about the campaigns in question. Echard's *History of England* (1707–18), Sprigg's *Anglia Rediviva* (1654), Richelieu's *Letters to Lewis 13th* (1698), Sir T. Fairfax's *Short Memorials* (1699), and many Civil War tracts appear in the sale catalogue which included Defoe's library.[2] Nor should we overlook the investigations he carried out in preparing such an earlier work as *The Scots Nation and Union Justified* (1714). In this (pp. 25–8) he lists a number of Scottish officers who were to reappear in *Memoirs of a Cavalier*. But detailed comparison between Defoe's text and the works confidently named as his sources establishes his undoubted reliance on them.[3] However, Defoe was not content merely to borrow from these: facts were selected, imaginatively adapted, and presented in a style appropriate to the character of the supposed narrator.

Defoe's debt to Le Clerc, to take one example, can be pin-pointed. It begins with the appointment of Richelieu as 'General of the King's Forces';[4] Le Clerc's version is: the King 'gave him the Title of *Lieutenant General, representing the person of the King*, which was never before given to any whatsoever' (*i.* 330). Characteristically, Defoe felt free to adapt his source-material at will: he retains Le Clerc's detail about 'six thousand men' (*i.* 341) raised in Switzerland for the French Army; he follows him in describing the French King's visit to Grenoble; but he fuses the two. He shows Louis in Grenoble reviewing 'a Body of 6000 *Swiss* Foot.' Again, where Le Clerc estimates the French forces

---

[1] See Secord, *Robert Drury*, pp. 84–130.

[2] See *The Libraries of Daniel Defoe and Phillips Farewell: Oliver Payne's Sales Catalogue* (1731), ed. H. Heidenreich (Berlin, 1970), items 120, 157, 200, 914, 961, 1026, 1412 etc. Regrettably the two libraries were not listed separately in the catalogue: it is therefore no more than a (fairly confident) conjecture that the books mentioned belonged to Defoe and not Farewell.

[3] For selected evidence see *infra*, Explanatory Notes and Appendix.

[4] p. 14.

in Savoy as 'eighteen thousand Foot, and two thousand Horse' (*i.* 342), Defoe's version is 'not above 22000 Men'. Le Clerc refers casually to 'a Commotion at *Lyons*, although the Queen were present, the People refusing to pay the new Taxes' (*i.* 342); for his part Defoe gives a circumstantial account of a mob-riot and the Queen-Mother's skill in quelling it. Similarly, Le Clerc's brief report of the battle between the Savoyards and the French under 'Thoiras' trapped in 'a Defile' becomes, in Defoe's hands, lengthy, vivid and packed with the kind of detail available to an alleged participant. Indeed Le Clerc—in these and other ways—proved invaluable for providing a framework of historical fact; his *Richlieu* had been rifled—one can track Defoe in his snow; but, to adapt Dryden on Jonson, what would be theft in others is victory in Defoe.

Adapting the *Swedish Intelligencer* presented few difficulties. The author of the *Intelligencer*, W. Watts, was himself capable of writing vividly; he shared Defoe's admiration for Gustavus Adolphus—'that incomparable Conqueror who was alone worth 2 Armies' (*iii.* 154); Defoe would sympathize with his intention to portray 'this *Great Deliverer*' (*iii.* 155) bringing 'some *ease and consolation* to the miserably afflicted *Churches* of *Germany*' (*ii*[ii]); and with his literary ambitions, '*Truth* and *Plainenesse*' (*iii.*[iii]). Watts declared that he had eschewed fine phrases and coined words—'the presumptions of an over-bold fancy' (*ii.*[vi])—but not appropriate military terms even though they might occasionally be obscure to some readers. The remark might well have been Defoe's.

Curiosity about Swedish affairs had revived just before Defoe wrote the *Memoirs*, largely owing to the recent death (in 1718) of Gustavus Adolphus's grandnephew, Charles XII; his frequent appearance in eighteenth-century literature testifies to the fascination he exerted on Defoe's contemporaries. Defoe could, then, assume that Gustavus would be an object of concern. But he had to maintain a proper balance between the claims of the Cavalier as an independent character to the sympathetic interest of his audience, and those of the historical persons portrayed by the Cavalier. Defoe satisfied both. Passages quoted in Appendix I below allow this assertion to be verified.

When the Cavalier becomes caught up in English affairs Defoe's manner of handling his narrator and source-material does not change. Passages in the Notes and Appendix II prove this. Whitelocke, Clarendon, and Ludlow are pressed into service when they are relevant; their errors as well as their accurate facts show through; but the Cavalier is no mere pasteboard figure. He is an independent, vital character. In Part I Defoe had already added numerous authenticating details; he had also freely invented, as in the vivid description of the Cavalier's resourceful handling of the sortie and ambush outside Augsburg, or in his account of the dragoon-sergeant's skill in out-witting Tilly's sentries before the crossing of the river Lech.[1] Now, in the English situation, the Cavalier in flight after Marston Moor, masquerading as a peasant in enemy Leeds, and leading his men over unknown, forbidding countryside to join the Royalist army, is given an existence totally independent of facts derived from historians and yet in complete harmony with them.[2] Whether at Augsburg or in the Yorkshire Dales, the Cavalier is a consistent character. He displays shrewd common sense, courage (though also a capacity for fear), initiative, loyalty, and gratitude,[3] concern for others, pragmatic intelligence, and devotion to principle. These same qualities are found in some leading historical figures such as Gustavus Adolphus or Fairfax; they also form the standard by which others like Charles I or Prince Rupert are assessed and found wanting.

The narrator's style is a warranty for his trustworthiness; its characteristics have a direct relation to his moral qualities.

---

[1] pp. 88-9, 94-6.

[2] pp. 204-18.

[3] 'Gratitude and Fidelity are inseparable from an honest Man': *An Appeal to Honour and Justice*, in *Defoe*, ed. Boulton, p. 172.

Defoe himself believed in this. He remarked in the *Serious Reflections of Robinson Crusoe*: 'plainness . . . both in style and method seems to me to have some suitable analogy to the subject, honesty . . . honesty shows the more beautiful, and the more like honesty, when artifice is dismissed.'[1] Hence the significance of 'easy, plain and familiar language' (recommended by Defoe in *The Complete English Tradesman*) to the Cavalier. His reliability must be unquestioned. Thus he must avoid 'Stiffness and Affectation, hard Words, and long unusual Coupling of *Syllables*, and Sentences' which Defoe associated with lawyers, physicians, and divines.[2] (These are the professions for which the Cavalier explicitly declares himself unfitted.[3]) No parade of learning then, but not the ignorance of the common soldier; the Cavalier is, after all, a student of history and geography, fluent in Dutch and with some command of Latin and French.[4]

It is all of a piece that the Cavalier 'never designed to write a Book';[5] we are invited to trust in him as a 'natural', though not unsophisticated, writer. Thus his easy command of military terminology is important; so are the language and imagery appropriate to a man whose experience has proved the value of proverbial wisdom accessible to all his readers. He draws similes from the common stock: soldiers fight 'like lions' on at least six occasions, 'like Furies' or 'Mad Men'; the enemy is cut down 'like Grass before a Scyth'; shot flies 'like Hail'; the Cavalier is 'as ravenous as a Hound'; and Montrose 'rowling like a Snow Ball, spread all over Scotland.' The paucity of imaginative resource is not damaging; this is an author who is patently not out to deceive by stylistic contrivance. He experiences and records simply and (Defoe would have us believe) without any falsifying intermediary. Thus he reports Hepburn's remark,

---

[1] *Works*, ed. Maynadier, iii. 26–7.
[2] *An Essay upon Projects*, in *Defoe*, ed. Boulton, p. 29.
[3] p. 8.
[4] pp. 8, 12, 58.
[5] p. 32.

'*Tilly* has a great Army of old Lads that are used to boxing';
when he meets Gustavus Adolphus the king 'was leaning on
his Elbow in the Window'; and, properly in character, he
muses 'what signifies Reason to the Drum and the Trumpet'?[1] Stylistic evidence of a memorialist's integrity is
essential: the Cavalier provides it.

If Defoe's whole design is to succeed, we should also
sympathize with the narrator's motives and, if possible,
accept his values. The reader of 1720 would find this
relatively easy. With recent experience of the 1715 rebellion
and the increase of political factions (which caused Swift so
much concern), he would warm to a writer who both felt
'an Aversion to popular Tumults' and approved of a firm
ruler who understood 'the Management of Politicks and the
Clamours of the People.'[2] The Cavalier is also consistently
opposed to all tyranny whether of 'the House of *Austria*' or,
in England, 'when Law and Justice was under the Feet of
Power; the Army ruled the Parliament, the private Officers
their Generals, the common Soldiers their Officers, and Confusion was in every Part of the Government.'[3] He is moreover, no religious bigot; indeed he confesses that he 'had
not much Religion in [him] at that time.'[4] Nevertheless such
religious leanings as he has are—judging from his comments
on the priestly regimen in Italy—distinctly Protestant.
Hence his (and, from references in Defoe's *Review*, his
creator's) admiration for Gustavus Adolphus's devotion to
'Liberty and Religion'. And his motives in the Civil Wars
would gain immediate approval in 1720: 'to suppress the
exorbitant Power of a Party, to establish our King in his just
and legal Rights; but not with a Design to destroy the
Constitution of Government, and the Being of Parliament.'[5]
The Cavalier is in fact in many ways a scaled-down version

---

[1] pp. 56, 57, 194.
[2] p. 21.
[3] pp. 112, 270.
[4] p. 165 Cf. p. 32.
[5] p. 166.

of Defoe's hero (bracketed at least on one occasion in the *Review* with Gustavus),[1] William III. Above all, the *Memoirs* leaves with all 'Sober and Impartial Men' an implicit warning which is reinforced by the sum of the Cavalier's experiences as well as by his integrity and honest mien. Defoe had expressed it well five years earlier in his *Appeal to Honour and Justice*:

It cannot be pleasant or agreeable, and, I *think*, it cannot be safe to any just Prince to Rule over a divided People, split into incens'd and exasperated Parties: Tho' a skilful Mariner may have Courage to master a Tempest, and goes fearless thro' a Storm, yet he can never be said to delight in the Danger; a fresh fair Gale, and a quiet Sea, is the pleasure of his Voyage, and we have a Saying worth Notice to them that are otherwise minded, *Qui amat periculum peribit in illo*.[2]

---

[1] *Review* (16 Oct. 1707), iv. 106.
[2] In *Defoe*, ed. Boulton, p. 167.

ACKNOWLEDGEMENTS

I wish to acknowledge the kindness of the following in helping to identify certain historical persons mentioned by Defoe: Dr. O. von Feilitzen, Kungliga Biblioteket, Stockholm; Dr. Ian Roy, King's College, London; and the Librarians of Newark, Newcastle-upon-Tyne, Pontefract, the County of Buckinghamshire, and the National Library of Scotland. I am indebted to Miss J. Darden, my research assistant at Hofstra University, New York, and, for devoted secretarial assistance, to Miss J. Wootton. For professional advice from the General Editor, my colleague Professor James Kinsley, I am particularly grateful. Finally no editor of the *Memoirs of a Cavalier* could fail to recognize his debt to the scholarship of the late Arthur W. Secord.

NOTE ON THE TEXT

Memoirs of a Cavalier was first published in 1720, the only edition to appear in Defoe's lifetime. The present text is that of 1720, printed from a xerox reproduction of the copy in the British Museum. The long 's' of the first edition has been eliminated; obvious errors of the press have been silently corrected.

SELECT BIBLIOGRAPHY

Memoirs of a Cavalier appeared in six editions after the first, in the eighteenth century: James Lister's (n.d.) in Leeds; in Edinburgh, 1759 and 1766; in Newark 1782; by Francis Noble in London, 1784; and in London 1792. It was reprinted in all the major collections of Defoe's novels: by Sir Walter Scott, 1810; Tegg, 1840; Hazlitt, 1840–3; Bohn, 1854–6; Aitken, 1895; Maynadier, 1903; and Blackwell, 1927–8.

BIBLIOGRAPHY. The standard work is John Robert Moore's *Checklist of the Writings of Daniel Defoe* (1960).

BIOGRAPHY AND CRITICISM. The chief biographies are William Lee's *Defoe: Life and Recently Discovered Writings*, 3 vols. (1869); Paul Dottin, *Defoe et ses Romans* (1924); James Sutherland, *Defoe* (1937); John Robert Moore, *Defoe: Citizen of the Modern World* (1958). Three studies of Defoe's use of original source-material in his fiction are Arthur W. Secord's *Studies in the Narrative Method of Defoe* (1924) and *Robert Drury's Journal and Other Studies* (1961), and John C. Major's *The Role of Personal Memoirs in English Biography and Novel* (1935). General critical works on Defoe's novels include A. D. McKillop, *Early Masters of English Fiction* (1956), Ian Watt, *The Rise of the Novel* (1957), and James Sutherland, *Defoe* (1972). For the historical background to the Cavalier's story see the works by C. V. Wedgwood, *The Thirty Years War* (1938), *The King's Peace* (1955), and *The King's War* (1958).

A CHRONOLOGY OF DANIEL DEFOE

THE PREFACE

As an Evidence that 'tis very probable these Memorials were written many Years ago, the Persons now concerned in the Publication, assure the Reader, that they have had them in their Possession finished, as they now·appear, above twenty Years: That they were so long ago found by great Accident, among other valuable Papers in the Closet of an eminent publick Minister, of no less Figure than one of King *William*'s Secretaries of State.

As it is not proper to trace them any farther, so neither is there any need to trace them at all, to give Reputation to the Story related, seeing the Actions here mentioned have a sufficient Sanction from all the Histories of the Times to which they relate, with this Addition, that the admirable Manner of relating them, and the wonderful Variety of Incidents, with which they are beautified in the Course of a private Gentleman's Story, add such Delight in the reading, and give such a Lustre, as well to the Accounts themselves, as to the Person who was the Actor; and no Story, we believe, extant in the World, ever came abroad with such Advantages.

It must naturally give some Concern in the reading, that the Name of a Person of so much Gallantry and Honour, and so many Ways valuable to the World, should be lost to the Readers: We assure them no small Labour has been thrown away upon the Enquiry, and all we have been able to arrive to of Discovery in this Affair is, that a *Memorandum* was found with this Manuscript, in these Words, but not signed by any Name, only the two Letters of a Name, which

gives us no Light into the Matter, which Memoir was as
follows.

Memorandum,
I found this Manuscript among my Father's Writings, and
I understand that he got them as Plunder, at, or after,
the Fight at *Worcester*, where he served as Major of ———'s
Regiment of Horse on the Side of the Parliament.

L.K.

As this has been of no Use but to terminate the Enquiry
after the Person; so, however, it seems most naturally to
give an Authority to the Original of the Work, (*viz.*) that it
was born of a Soldier, and indeed it is thro' every Part,
related with so Soldierly a Stile, and in the very Language
of the Field, that it seems impossible any Thing, but the very
Person who was present in every Action here related, could
be the Relator of them.

The Accounts of Battles, the Sieges, and the several
Actions of which this Work is so full, are all recorded in the
Histories of those Times; such as the great Battle of *Leipsick*,
the Sacking of *Magdeburgh*, the Siege of *Nurembergh*, the
passing the River *Leck* in *Bavaria*; such also as the Battles
of *Keynton*, or *Edge-Hill*; the Battles of *Newberry*, *Marston-
Moor*, and *Naseby*, and the like: They are all, we say,
recorded in other Histories, and written by those who lived
in those Times, and perhaps had good Authority for what
they wrote. But do those Relations give any of the beautiful
Ideas of things formed in this Account? Have they one half
of the Circumstances and Incidents of the Actions themselves, that this Man's Eyes were Witness to, and which his
Memory has thus preserved? He that has read the best
Accounts of those Battles, will be surprized to see the
Particulars of the Story so preserved, so nicely, and so
agreeably describ'd; and will confess what we alledge, that
the Story is inimitably told; and even the great Actions of
the glorious King *GUSTAVUS ADOLPHUS*, receive a
Lustre from this Man's Relations, which the World was

never made sensible of before, and which the present Age has much wanted of late, in Order to give their Affections a Turn in Favour of his late glorious Successor.[1]

In the Story of our own Country's unnatural Wars, he carries on the same Spirit. How effectually does he record the Virtues and glorious Actions of King *Charles* the First, at the same Time that he frequently enters upon the Mistakes of his Majesty's Conduct, and of his Friends, which gave his Enemies all those fatal Advantages against him, which ended in the Overthrow of his Armies, the Loss of his Crown and Life, and the Ruin of the Constitution?

In all his Account he does Justice to his 'Enemies,' and honours the Merit of those whose Cause he fought against; and many Accounts recorded in his Story, are not to be found even in the best Histories of those Times.

What Applause does he give to the Gallantry of Sir *Thomas Fairfax*, to his Modesty, to his Conduct, under which he himself was subdued, and to the Justice he did the King's Troops when they laid down their Arms?

His Description of the *Scots* Troops in the beginning of the War, and the Behaviour of the Party under the Earl of *Holland*, who went over against them, are admirable; and his Censure of their Conduct, who push'd the King upon the Quarrel, and then would not let him fight, is no more than what many of the King's Friends, tho' less knowing (as Soldiers, have often complained of.)

In a Word, this Work is a Confutation of many Errors in all the Writers upon the Subject of our Wars in *England*, and even in that extraordinary History written by the Earl of *Clarendon*;[2] but the Editors were so just, that when near twenty Years ago, a Person who had written a whole Volume in Folio, by Way of Answer to, and Confutation of *Clarendon's* History of the Rebellion, would have borrowed the Clauses in this Account, which clash with that History, and confront it: We say the Editors were so just as to refuse them.

There can be nothing objected against the general Credit

of this Work, seeing its Truth is established upon universal History; and almost all the Facts, especially those of Moment, are confirmed for their general Part by all the Writers of those Times, if they are here embellished with Particulars, which are no where else to be found, that is the Beauty we boast of; and that it is that must recommend this Work to all the Men of Sense and Judgment that read it.

The only Objection we find possible to make against this Work is, that it is not carried on farther; or, as we may say finished, with the finishing the War of the Time; and this we complain of also: But then we complain as a Misfortune to the World, not as a Fault in the Author; for how do we know but that this Author might carry it on, and have another Part finished which might not fall into the same Hands, or may still remain with some of his Family, and which they cannot indeed publish, to make it seem any Thing perfect, for want of the other Part which we have, and which we have now made publick? Nor is it very improbable, but that if any such farther Part is in Being, the publishing these Two Parts may occasion the Proprietors of the Third to let the World see it; and that by such a Discovery, the Name of the Person may also come to be known, which would, no doubt, be a great Satisfaction to the Reader, as well as us.

This, however, must be said, that if the same Author should have written another Part of this Work, and carried it on to the End of those Times; yet as the Residue of those melancholly Days, to the Restoration, were filled with the Intrigues of Government, the Political Management of illegal Power, and the Dissentions and Factions of a People, who were then even in themselves but a *FACTION*, and that there was very little Action in the Field; it is more than probable that our Author, who was a Man of Arms, had little Share in those Things, and might not care to trouble himself with looking at them.

But besides all this, it might happen that he might go abroad again, at that Time, as most of the Gentlemen of

Quality, and who had an Abhorrence for the Power that then govern'd, here did. Nor are we certain that he might live to the End of that Time, so we can give no Account whether he had any Post in the subsequent Actions of that Time.

'Tis enough that we have the Authorities above to recommend this Part to us that is now published; the Relation, we are perswaded, will recommend it self, and nothing more can be needful, because nothing more can invite than the Story it self, which when the Reader enters into, he will find it very hard to get out of, 'till he has gone thro' it.

PART I

I T MAY suffice the Reader, without being very inquisitive after my Name, that I was born in the County of *SALOP*, in the Year 1608; under the Government of what Star I was never Astrologer enough to examine; but the Consequences of my Life may allow me to suppose some extraordinary Influence affected my Birth. If there be any thing in Dreams also, my Mother, who was mighty observant that Way, took Minutes, which I have since seen in the first Leaf of her Prayer Book, of several strange Dreams she had while she was with Child of her second Son, which was myself. Once she noted that she dreamed she was carried away by a Regiment of Horse, and delivered in the Fields of a Son, that as soon as it was born had two Wings came out of its Back, and in half an Hour's Time flew away from her: And the very Evening before I was born, she dreamed she was brought to Bed of a Son, and that all the while she was in Labour a Man stood under her Window beating on a Kettle-Drum, which very much discomposed her.

My Father was a Gentleman of a very plentiful Fortune, having an Estate of above 5000 Pounds *per Annum*, of a Family nearly allied to several of the principal Nobility, and lived about six Miles from the Town: And my Mother being at—on some particular Occasion, was surprized there at a Friend's House, and brought me very safe into the World.

I was my Father's second Son, and therefore was not altogether so much slighted as younger Sons of good Families generally are. But my Father saw something in my

Genius also which particularly pleased him, and so made him take extraordinary Care of my Education.

I was taught therefore, by the best Masters that could be had, every Thing that was needful to accomplish a young Gentleman for the World; and at seventeen Years old my Tutor told my Father an Academick Education was very proper for a Person of Quality, and he thought me very fit for it: So my Father entered me of—College in *Oxford*, where I continued three Years.

A Collegiate Life did not suit me at all, though I loved Books well enough. It was never designed that I should be either a Lawyer, Physician or Divine; and I wrote to my Father, that I thought I had staid there long enough for a Gentleman, and with his Leave I desired to give him a Visit.

During my Stay at *Oxford*, though I passed through the proper Exercises of the House,[1] yet my chief reading was upon History and Geography, as that which pleased my Mind best, and supplied me with Ideas most suitable to my Genius: By one I understood what great Actions had been done in the World; and by the other I understood where they had been done.

My Father readily complied with my Desire of coming home; for besides that he thought, as I did, that three Years time at the University was enough, he also most passionately loved me, and began to think of my settling near him.

At my Arrival I found my self extraordinarily caressed by my Father, and he seemed to take a particular Delight in my Conversation. My Mother, who lived in a perfect Union with him, both in Desires and Affection, received me very passionately: Apartments were provided for me by my self, and Horses and Servants allowed me in particular.

My Father never went a Hunting, an Exercise he was exceeding fond of, but he would have me with him; and it pleased him when he found me like the Sport. I lived thus, in all the Pleasures 'twas possible for me to enjoy, for about a Year more; when going out one Morning with my Father to hunt a Stag, and having had a very hard Chase, and

gotten a great Way off from home, we had Leisure enough
to ride gently back: And as we returned, my Father took
Occasion to enter into a serious Discourse with me concerning the Manner of my settling in the World.

He told me, with a great deal of Passion, that he loved me
above all the rest of his Children, and that therefore he
intended to do very well for me; that my eldest Brother being
already married and settled, he had designed the same for
me, and proposed a very advantageous Match for me with a
young Lady of very extraordinary Fortune and Merit, and
offered to make a Settlement of 2000 *l. per Annum* on me,
which he said he would purchase for me without diminishing
his paternal Estate.

There was too much Tenderness in this Discourse not to
affect me exceedingly. I told him, I would perfectly resign
my self unto his Disposal. But, as my Father had, together
with his Love for me, a very nice Judgment in his Discourse,
he fixed his Eyes very attentively on me; and though my
Answer was without the least Reserve, yet he thought he
saw some Uneasiness in me at the Proposal, and from
thence concluded that my Compliance was rather an Act of
Discretion than Inclination; and, that however I seemed
so absolutely given up to what he had proposed, yet my
Answer was really an Effect of my Obedience rather than
my Choice: So he returned very quick upon me, *Look you,
Son, though I give you my own Thoughts in the Matter, yet
I would have you be very plain with me; for if your own
Choice does not agree with mine, I will be your Adviser, but
will never impose upon you; and therefore let me know your
Mind freely. I don't reckon my self capable, Sir,* said I, with
a great deal of respect, *to make so good a Choice for my self as
you can for me; and though my Opinion differed from yours,
its being your Opinion would reform mine, and my Judgment
would as readily comply as my Duty. I gather at least from
thence,* said my Father, *that your Designs lay another Way
before, however they may comply with mine: And therefore
I would know what it was you would have asked of me if I had*

*not offered this to you; and you must not deny me your Obed-
ience in this, if you expect I should believe your Readiness in
the other.*

Sir, said I, *'twas impossible I should lay out for my self just
what you have proposed; but if my Inclinations were never so
contrary, though at your Command you shall know them, yet
I declare them to be wholly subjected to your Order: I confess
my Thoughts did not tend towards Marriage or a Settlement;
for though I had no Reason to question your Care of me, yet
I thought a Gentleman ought always to see something of the
World before he confined himself to any part of it: And if I had
been to ask your Consent to any Thing, it should have been to
give me leave to Travel for a short Time, in order* [to] *qualifie my
self to appear at home like a Son to so good a Father.*

In what Capacity would you Travel, replied my Father?
*You must go abroad either as a private Gentleman, as a
Scholar, or as a Soldier. If it were in the latter Capacity, Sir*,
said I, returning pretty quick, *I hope I should not misbehave
my self; but I am not so determined as not to be ruled by your
Judgment. Truly*, replied my Father, *I see no War abroad at
this Time worth while for a Man to appear in, whether we talk
of the Cause or the Encouragement; and indeed, Son, I am
afraid you need not go far for Adventures of that Nature, for
Times seem to look as if this Part of* Europe *would find us
Work enough.* My Father spake then relating to the Quarrel
likely to happen between the King of *England* and the
Spaniard,* for I believe he had no Notions of a Civil War
in his Head.

In short, my Father perceiving my Inclinations very
forward to go abroad, gave me Leave to Travel, upon
Condition I would promise to return in Two Years at
farthest, or sooner, if he sent for me.

While I was at *Oxford* I happened into the Society of a
young Gentleman, of a good Family, but of a low Fortune,
being a younger Brother, and who had indeed instilled into
me the first Desires of going abroad, and who I knew
passionately longed to Travel, but had not sufficient Allow-

---

* Upon the Breach of the Match between the King of *England* and the Infanta of
Spain;[1] and particularly upon the old Quarrel of the King of *Bohemia* and the
Palatinate.

ance to defray his Expences as a Gentleman. We had contracted a very close Friendship, and our Humours being
very agreeable to one another, we daily enjoyed the Conversation of Letters. He was of a generous free Temper,
without the least Affectation or Deceit, a handsome proper
Person, a strong Body, very good Mien, and brave to the
last Degree: His Name was *Fielding*,[1] and we called him
Captain, though it be a very unusual Title in a College; but
Fate had some Hand in the Title, for he had certainly the
Lines of a Soldier drawn in his Countenance. I imparted to
him the Resolutions I had taken, and how I had my Father's
Consent to go abroad; and would know his Mind, whether
he would go with me: He sent me Word, he would go with
all his Heart.

My Father, when he saw him, for I sent for him immediately to come to me, mightily approved my Choice; so
we got our Equipage ready, and came away for *London*.

'Twas on the 22nd of *April* 1630, when we embarked at
Dover, landed in a few Hours at *Calais*, and immediately
took Post for *Paris*. I shall not trouble the Reader with a
Journal of my Travels, nor with the Description of Places;
which every Geographer can do better than I; but these
Memoirs being only a Relation of what happened either to
our selves, or in our own Knowledge, I shall confine my self
to that Part of it.

We had indeed some diverting Passages in our Journey to
Paris; as first, the Horse my Comrade was upon fell so very
lame with a Slip that he could not go, and hardly stand:
And the Fellow that rid with us Express, pretended to ride
away to a Town five Miles off to get a fresh Horse, and so
left us on the Road with one Horse between two of us: We
followed as well as we could, but being Strangers, missed
the Way, and wandered a great Way out of the Road.
Whether the Man performed in reasonable Time, or not,
we could not be sure; but if it had not been for an old Priest,
we had never found him. We met this Man, by a very good
Accident, near a little Village whereof he was Curate: We

spoke *Latin* enough just to make him understand us, and he did not speak it much better himself; but he carried us into the Village to his House, gave us Wine and Bread, and entertained us with wonderful Courtesie: After this he sent into the Village, hired a Peasant, and a Horse for my Captain, and sent him to guide us into the Road. At parting he made a great many Compliments to us in *French*, which we could just understand; but the Sum was, to excuse him for a Question he had a mind to ask us. After leave to ask what he pleased, it was, if we wanted any Money for our Journey, and pulled out two Pistoles,[1] which he offered either to give or lend us.

I mention this exceeding Courtesie of the Curate, because, though Civility is very much in Use in *France*, and especially to Strangers, yet 'tis a very unusual thing to have them part with their Money.

We let the Priest know, first, that we did not want Money, and next that we were very sensible of the Obligation he had put upon us; and I told him in particular, if I lived to see him again, I would acknowledge it.

This Accident of our Horse, was, as we afterwards found, of some use to us: We had left our two Servants behind us at *Calais* to bring our Baggage after us, by reason of some Dispute between the Captain of the Pacquet and the Custom-House Officer which could not be adjusted; and we were willing to be at *Paris*: The Fellows followed as fast as they could, and as near as we could learn, in the Time we lost our Way were robbed, and our Portmanteaus opened. They took what they pleased; but as there was no Money there, but Linen and Necessaries, the Loss was not great.

Our Guide carried us to *Amiens*, where we found the Express and our two Servants, who the Express meeting on the Road with a spare Horse, had brought back with him thither.

We took this for a good Omen of our successful Journey, having escaped a Danger which might have been greater to us than it was to our Servants; for the Highway-Men in

France do not always give a Traveller the Civility of bidding him Stand and Deliver his Money, but frequently Fire upon him first, and then take his Money.

We staid one Day at *Amiens*, to adjust this little Disorder, and walked about the Town, and into the great Church, but saw nothing very remarkable there; but going cross a broad Street near the great Church, we saw a Crowd of People gazing at a Mountebank Doctor who made a long Harangue to them with a thousand antick Postures, and gave out Bills this Way, and Boxes of Physick that Way, and had a great Trade, when on a sudden the People raised a Cry,* *Larron*, *Larron*, on the other side the Street, and all the Auditors ran away from Mr. Doctor, to see what the matter was— Among the rest, we went to see; and the case was plain and short enough. Two *English* Gentlemen, and a *Scotch-Man*, Travellers as we were, were standing gazing at this prating Doctor, and one of them catched a Fellow picking his Pocket: The Fellow had got some of his Money, for he dropt two or three Pieces just by him, and had got hold of his Watch; but being surprized, let it slip again: but the Reason of telling this Story, is for the Management of it. This Thief had his Seconds so ready, that as soon as the *English-Man* had seized him, they fell in, pretended to be mighty zealous for the Stranger, takes the Fellow by the Throat, and makes a great Bustle; the Gentleman not doubting but the Man was secured, let go his own Hold of him, and left him to them: The Hubbub was great, and 'twas these Fellows cried *Larron*, *Larron*; but with a Dexterity peculiar to themselves, had let the right Fellow go, and pretended to be all upon one of their own Gang. At last they bring the Man to the Gentleman, to ask him what the Fellow had done? who, when he saw the Person they seized on, presently told them that was not the Man: Then they seemed to be in more Consternation than before, and spread themselves all over the Street, crying *Larron*, *Larron*, pretending to search for the Fellow; and so one one Way, one another, they were all gone, the Noise went over, the

* In English, *Thief*, *Thief*.

Gentlemen stood looking one at another, and the bawling Doctor began to have the Crowd about him again.

This was the first *French* Trick I had the Opportunity of seeing; but I was told they have a great many more as dextrous as this.

We soon got Acquaintance with these Gentlemen, who were going to *Paris* as well as we; so the next Day we made up our Company with them, and were a pretty Troop of five Gentlemen and four Servants.

As we had really no Design to stay long at *Paris*, so indeed, excepting the City it self, there was not much to be seen there. Cardinal *Richlieu*, who was not only a supreme Minister in the Church, but prime Minister in the State, was now made also General of the King's Forces, with a Title never known in *France* before nor since, *viz.* Lieutenant-General *au Place du Roy*,[1] in the King's stead, or as some have since translated it, representing the Person of the King.

Under this Character he pretended to execute all the Royal Powers in the Army without Appeal to the King, or without waiting for Orders: and having parted from *Paris* the Winter before, had now actually begun the War against the Duke of *Savoy*; in the process of which, he restored the Duke of *Mantua*, and having taken *Pignerol* from the Duke, put it into such a state of Defence, as the Duke could never force it out of his hands, and reduced the Duke, rather by Manage[2] and Conduct than by Force, to make Peace without it; so as annexing it to the Crown of *France*, it has ever since been a Thorn in his Foot, that has always made the Peace of *Savoy* lame and precarious: and *France* has since made *Pignerol* one of the strongest Fortresses in the World.

As the Cardinal, with all the Military part of the Court, was in the Field; so the King, to be near him, was gone with the Queen and all the Court, just before I reached *Paris*, to reside at *Lyons*. All these considered, there was nothing to do at *Paris*: the Court looked like a Citizen's House when the Family was all gone into the Country: and I thought the whole City looked very melancholy, compared to all the fine things I had heard of it.

The Queen Mother and her Party were chagrin at the Cardinal, who, tho' he owed his Grandeur to her immediate Favour, was now grown too great any longer to be at the Command of Her Majesty, or indeed in her Interest; and therefore the Queen was under Dissatisfaction, and Her Party looked very much down.

The Protestants were every where disconsolate; for the Losses they had received at *Rochel*, *Nismes*, and *Montpelier*, had reduced them to an absolute Dependence on the King's Will, without all possible hopes of ever recovering themselves, or being so much as in a Condition to take Arms for their Religion; and therefore the wisest of them plainly foresaw their own entire Reduction, as it since came to pass: and I remember vere well, that a Protestant Gentleman told me once, as we were passing from *Orleans* to *Lyons*, That the *English* had ruined them; and therefore, says he, I think the next Occasion the King takes to use us ill, as I know 'twill not be long, before he does, we must all fly over to *England*, where you are bound to maintain us for having helped to turn us out of our own Country. I asked him what he meant by saying the *English* had done it?[1] He returned short upon me; I do not mean, says he, by not relieving *Rochel*, but by helping to ruin *Rochel*, when you and the *Dutch* lent Ships to beat our Fleet, which all the Ships in *France* could not have done without you.

I was too young in the World to be very sensible of this before, and therefore was something startled at the Charge; but when I came to discourse with this Gentleman, I soon saw, the Truth of what he said was undeniable, and have since reflected on it with regret, that the Naval Power of the Protestants, which was then superior to the Royal, would certainly have been the Recovery of all their Fortunes, had it not been unhappily broke by their Brethren of *England* and *Holland*, the former lending seven Men of War, and the latter twenty, for the Destruction of the *Rocheller*'s Fleet;

and by those very Ships the *Rocheller*'s Fleet were actually beaten and destroyed, and they never afterward recovered their Force at Sea, and by consequence sunk under the Siege, which the *English* afterwards in vain attempted to prevent.

These things made the Protestants look very dull, and expected the Ruin of all their Party; which had certainly happened had the Cardinal lived a few Years longer.

We stayed in *Paris* about three Weeks, as well to see the Court, and what Rarities the Place afforded, as by an Occasion which had like to have put a short Period to our Ramble.

Walking one Morning before the Gate of the *Louvre*, with a Design to see the *Swiss* Drawn up, which they always did, and Exercised just before they Relieved the Guards; a Page came up to me, and speaking *English* to me, Sir, says he the Captain must needs have your immediate Assistance. I that had not the knowledge of any Person in *Paris* but my own Companion, whom I called Captain, had no room to question, but it was he that sent for me; and crying out hastily to him, Where, followed the Fellow as fast as 'twas possible: he led me thro' several Passages which I knew not, and at last thro' a Tennis-Court, and into a large Room where three Men, like Gentlemen, were Engaged very briskly, two against one: the Room was very dark, so that I could not easily know them asunder; but being fully possessed with an Opinion before of my Captain's Danger, I ran into the Room with my Sword in my Hand: I had not particularly Engaged any of them, nor so much as made a Pass at any, when I received a very dangerous Thrust in my Thigh, rather occasioned by my hasty running in, than a real Design of the Person; but enraged at the Hurt, without examining who it was hurt me, I threw my self upon him, and run my Sword quite thro' his Body.

The Novelty of the Adventure, and the unexpected Fall of the Man by a Stranger come in no Body knew how, had becalmed the other two, that they really stood gazing at me. By this Time I had discovered that my Captain was not there, and that 'twas some strange Accident brought me thither. I could speak but little *French*, and supposed they could speak no *English*; so I stepped to the Door to see for the Page that brought me thither: but seeing no body there, and the Passage clear, I made off as fast as I could, without speaking a Word; nor did the other two Gentlemen offer to stop me.

But I was in a strange Confusion when coming into those Entries and Passages which the Page led me thro', I could by no means find my way out; at last seeing a Door open that looked through a House into the Street, I went in, and out at the other Door; but then I was at as great a Loss to know where I was, and which was the way to my Lodging. The Wound in my Thigh bled apace, and I could feel the Blood in my Breeches. In this Interval came by a Chair, I called, and went into it, and bid them, as well as I could, go to the *Louvre*; for tho' I knew not the Name of the Street where I lodged, I knew I could find the way to it when I was at the *Bastile*. The Chair-Men went on their own Way, and being stopp'd by a Company of the Guards as they went, set me down till the Souldiers were marched by; when looking out I found I was just at my own Lodging, and the Captain was standing at the Door looking for me; I beckoned him to me, and whispering told him I was very much hurt, but bid him pay the Chairmen, and ask no Questions but come to me.

I made the best of my Way up Stairs, but had lost so much Blood that I had hardly Spirits enough to keep me from swooning till he came in: He was equally concerned with me to see me in such a bloody Condition, and presently called up our Landlord, and he as quickly called in his Neighbours, that I had a Room full of People about me in a quarter of an Hour. But this had like to have been of worse Consequence to me than the other; for by this Time there was great enquiring after the Person who killed a Man at the Tennis-Court. My Landlord was then sensible of his Mistake, and came to me, and told me the Danger I was in, and very honestly offered to convey me to a Friend's of his, where I should be very secure; I thanked him, and suffered my self to be carried at Midnight whither he pleased; he visited me very often till I was well enough to walk about, which was not in less than ten Days, and then we thought fit to be gone, so we took Post for *Orleans*; but when I came upon the Road I found my self in a new Error, for my Wound opened again with riding, and I was in a worse Condition than before, being forced to take up at a little Village on the Road, called   about   Miles from *Orleans*, where there was no Surgeon to be had, but a sorry Country Barber, who nevertheless dressed me as well as he could, and in about a Week more I was able to walk to *Orleans* at three times.[1]

Here I staid till I was quite well, and then took Coach for *Lyons*, and so through *Savoy* into *Italy*.

I spent near two Years Time after this bad beginning in travelling through *Italy*, and to the several Courts of *Rome*, *Naples*, *Venice* and *Vienna*.

When I came to *Lyons* the King was gone from thence to *Grenoble* to meet the Cardinal, but the Queens were both at *Lyons*.

The *French* Affairs seemed at this Time to have but an indifferent Aspect; there was no Life in any Thing but where the Cardinal was, he pushed on every Thing with extraordinary Conduct, and generally with Success; he had taken *Suza* and *Pignerol* from the Duke of *Savoy*, and was preparing to push the Duke even out of all his Dominions.

But in the mean Time every where else Things looked ill; the Troops were ill paid, the Magazines empty, the People mutinous, and a general Disorder seized the Minds of the Court; and the Cardinal, who was the Soul of every Thing, desired this Interview at *Grenoble*, in order to put Things into some better Method.

This politick Minister always ordered Matters so, that if there was Success in any Thing the Glory was his; but if Things miscarried it was all laid upon the King. This Conduct was so much the more Nice, as it is the direct contrary to the Custom in like Cases, where Kings assume the Glory of all the Success in an Action; and when a Thing miscarries make themselves easie by sacrificing their Ministers and Favourites to the Complaints and Resentments of the People; but this accurate refined Statesman got over this Point.

While we were at *Lyons*, and as I remember, the third Day after our coming thither, we had like to have been involved in a State Broil,[1] without knowing where we were; it was of a *Sunday* in the Evening, the People of *Lyons*, who had been sorely oppressed in Taxes, and the War in *Italy* pinching their Trade, began to be very tumultuous; we found the Day before the Mob got together in great Crouds, and talked oddly; the King was every where reviled, and spoken disrespectfully of, and the Magistrates of the City either winked at, or durst not attempt to meddle, lest they should provoke the People.

But on *Sunday* Night, about Midnight, we was waked by a prodigious Noise in the Street; I jumpt out of Bed, and running to the Window, I saw the Street as full of Mob as it could hold, some armed with Musquets and Halbards, marched in very good Order; others in disorderly Crouds, all shouting and crying out *du Paix*[2] *le Roy*, and the like: One that led a great Party of this Rabble carried a Loaf of Bread upon the Top of a Pike, and other lesser Loaves, signifying the Smallness of their Bread, occasioned by Dearness.

By Morning this Croud was gathered to a great Heighth, they run roving over the whole City, shut up all the Shops, and forced all the People to join with them from thence; they went up to the Castle, and renewing the Clamour, a strange Consternation seized all the Princes.

They broke open the Doors of the Officers, Collectors of the new Taxes, and plundered their Houses, and had not the Persons themselves fled in time they had been very ill treated.

The Queen Mother, as she was very much displeased to

see such Consequences of the Government, in whose Management she had no Share, so I suppose she had the less Concern upon her. However, she came into the Court of the Castle and shewed her self to the People, gave Money amongst them, and spoke gently to them; and by a Way peculiar to her self, and which obliged all she talked with, she pacified the Mob gradually, sent them home with Promises of Redress and the like; and so appeased this Tumult in two Days, by her Prudence, which the Guards in the Castle had small Mind to meddle with, and if they had, would, in all Probability, have made the better Side the worse.

There had been several Seditions of the like Nature in sundry other Parts of *France*, and the very Army began to murmur, though not to mutiny, for want of Provisions.

This Sedition at *Lyons* was not quite over when we left the Place, for, finding the City all in a Broil, we considered we had no Business there, and what the Consequence of a popular Tumult might be, we did not see, so we prepared to be gone. We had not rid above three Miles out of the City but we were brought as Prisoners of War, by a Party of Mutineers, who had been abroad upon the Scout, and were charged with being Messengers sent to the Cardinal for Forces to reduce the Citizens: With these Pretences they brought us back in Triumph, and the Queen Mother being by this Time grown something familiar to them, they carried us before her.

When they enquired of us who we were, we called our selves *Scots*; for as the *English* were very much out of Favour in *France* at this Time, the Peace having been made not many Months, and not supposed to be very durable, because particularly displeasing to the People of *England*; so the *Scots* were on the other Extreme with the *French*. Nothing was so much caressed as the *Scots*, and a Man had no more to do in *France*, if he would be well received there, than to say he was a *Scotchman*.

When we came before the Queen Mother she seemed to

receive us with some Stiffness at first, and caused her Guards to take us into Custody; but as she was a Lady of most exquisite Politicks, she did this to amuse the Mob, and we were immediately after dismissed; and the Queen her self made a handsome Excuse to us for the Rudeness we had suffered, alledging the Troubles of the Times; and the next Morning we had three Dragoons of the Guards to convoy us out of the Jurisdiction of *Lyons*.

I confess this little Adventure gave me an Aversion to popular Tumults all my Life after, and if nothing else had been in the Cause, would have byassed me to espouse the King's Party in *England*, when our popular Heats carried all before it at home.

But I must say, that when I called to mind since the Address, the Management, the Compliance in shew, and in general the whole Conduct of the Queen Mother with the mutinous People of *Lyons*, and compared it with the Conduct of my unhappy Master the King of *England*, I could not but see that the Queen understood much better than King *Charles*, the Management of Politicks, and the Clamours of the People.

Had this Princess been at the Helm in *England*, she would have prevented all the Calamities of the Civil War here, and yet not have parted with what that good Prince yielded in order to Peace neither; she would have yielded gradually, and then gained upon them gradually; she would have managed them to the Point she had designed them, as she did all Parties in *France*; and none could effectually subject her, but the very Man she had raised to be her principal Support; I mean the Cardinal.

We went from hence to *Grenoble*, and arrived there the same Day that the King and the Cardinal, with the whole Court, went out to view a Body of 6000 *Swiss* Foot, which the Cardinal had wheedled the Cantons to grant to the King to help ruin their Neighbour the Duke of *Savoy*.

The Troops were exceeding fine, well accoutred, brave, clean-limbed, stout Fellows indeed. Here I saw the Cardinal;

there was an Air of Church Gravity in his Habit, but all the Vigor of a General, and the Sprightliness of a vast Genius in his Face; he affected a little Stiffness in his Behaviour, but managed all his Affairs with such Clearness, such Steddiness, and such Application, that it was no Wonder he had such Success in every Undertaking.

Here I saw the King, whose Figure was mean, his Countenance hollow, and always seemed dejected, and every Way discovering that Weakness in his Countenance that appeared in his Actions.

If he was ever sprightly and vigorous it was when the Cardinal was with him; for he depended so much on every Thing he did, that he was at the utmost Dilemma when he was absent, always timorous, jealous and irresolute.

After the Review the Cardinal was absent some Days, having been to wait on the Queen Mother at *Lyons*, where, as it was discoursed, they were at least seemingly reconciled.

I observed while the Cardinal was gone there was no Court, the King was seldom to be seen, very small Attendance given, and no Bustle at the Castle; but as soon as the Cardinal returned the great Councils were assembled, the Coaches of the Ambassadors went every Day to the Castle, and a Face of Business appeared upon the whole Court.

Here the Measures of the Duke of *Savoy*'s Ruine were concerted, and in Order to it the King and the Cardinal put themselves at the Head of the Army, with which they immediately reduced all *Savoy*, took *Chamberry* and the whole Dutchy except *Montmelian*.

The Army that did this was not above 22000 Men, including the *Swiss*, and but indifferent Troops neither, especially the *French* Foot, who compared to the Infantry I have since seen in the *German* and *Swedish* Armies, were not fit to be called Soldiers. On the other hand, considering the *Savoyards* and *Italian* Troops, they were good Troops; but the Cardinal's Conduct made amends for all these Deficiencies.

From hence I went to *Pignerol*, which was then little more

than a single Fortification on the Hill near the Town called
St. *Bride's*; but the Situation of that was very strong: I
mention this because of the prodigious Works since added
to it, by which it has since obtained the Name of the Right
Hand of *France*; they had begun a New Line below the Hill,
and some Works were marked out on the Side of the Town
next the Fort; but the Cardinal afterwards drew the Plan of
the Works with his own Hand, by which it was made one of
the strongest Fortresses in *Europe*.

While I was at *Pignerol* the Governor of *Milan* for the
Spaniards came with an Army and sat down before *Casal*.
The Grand Quarrel and for which the War in this Part of
Italy was begun, was this; the *Spaniards* and *Germans*
pretended to the Dutchy of *Mantua*; the Duke of *Nevers*, a
French Man, had not only a Title to it, but had got Posses-
sion of it, but being ill supported by the *French*, was beaten
out by the *Imperialists*, and after a long Siege the *Germans*
took *Mantua* it self, and drove the poor Duke quite out of the
Country.

The taking of *Mantua* elevated the Spirits of the Duke of
Savoy, and the *Germans* and *Spaniards* being now at more
Leisure, with a compleat Army came to his Assistance, and
formed the Siege of *Montferrat*.

For as the *Spaniards* pushed the Duke of *Mantua*, so the
French by Way of Diversion lay hard upon the Duke of
Savoy; they had seized *Montferrat*, and held it for the Duke
of *Mantua*, and had a strong *French* Garrison under *Thoiras*,
a brave and experienced Commander; and thus Affairs
stood when we came into the *French* Army.

I had no Business there, as a Soldier, but having passed
as a *Scotch* Gentleman with the Mob at *Lyons*, and after with
her Majesty, the Queen Mother, when we obtained the
Guard of her Dragoons; we had also her Majesty's Pass,
with which we came and went where we pleased; and the
Cardinal, who was then not on very good Terms with the
Queen, but willing to keep smooth Water there, when two
or three times our Passes came to be examined, shewed a

more than ordinary Respect to us on that very account, our Passes being from the Queen.

Casal being besieged, as I have observed, began to be in Danger, for the Cardinal, who 'twas thought had formed a Design to ruin *Savoy*, was more intent upon that than upon the Succour of the Duke of *Mantua*; but Necessity calling upon him to deliver so great a Captain as *Thoiras*, and not to let such a Place as *Casal* fall into the Hands of the Enemy, the King, or Cardinal rather, order'd the Duke of *Momorency* and the Mareschal D'*Effiat*, with 10000 Foot and 2000 Horse, to march and joyn the Mareschals *De la Force* and *Schomberg*, who lay already with an Army on the Frontiers of *Genoa*, but too weak to attempt the raising the Siege of *Casal*.

As all Men thought there would be a Battle between the *French* and the *Spaniards*, I could not prevail with my self to lose the Opportunity, and therefore by the Help of the Passes abovementioned, I came to the *French* Army under the Duke of *Momorency*; we marched through the Enemy's Country with great Boldness and no small Hazard, for the Duke of *Savoy* appeared frequently with great Bodies of Horse on the Rear of the Army, and frequently skirmished with our Troops, in one of which I had the Folly, *I can call it no better, for I had no Business there*, to go out and see the Sport, as the *French* Gentlemen called it; I was but a raw Soldier, and did not like the Sport at all, for this Party was surrounded by the Duke of *Savoy*, and almost all killed, for as to Quarter, they neither asked nor gave; I run away very fairly one of the first, and my Companion with me, and by the Goodness of our Horses got out of the Fray, and being not much known in the Army, we came into the Camp an hour or two after, as if we had been only riding abroad for the Air.

This little Rout made the General very cautious, for the *Savoyards* were stronger in Horse by 3 or 4000, and the Army always marched in a Body, and kept their Parties in or very near Hand.

I 'scaped another Rub in this *French* Army about five Days after, which had liked to have made me pay dear for my Curiosity.

The Duke *de Momorency* and the Mareschal *Schomberg* joined their Army above four or five Days after, and immediately, according to the Cardinal's Instructions, put themselves on the March for the Relief of *Casal*.

The Army had marched over a great Plain, with some marshy Grounds on the Right, and the *Po* on the Left, and as the Country was so well discovered that 'twas thought impossible any Mischief should happen, the Generals observed the less Caution. At the End of this Plain was a long Wood, and a Lane or narrow Defile thro' the Middle of it.

Thro' this Pass the Army was to march, and the Van began to file through it about four a Clock; by three Hours Time all the Army was got through, or into the Pass, and the Artillery was just entred when the Duke of *Savoy*, with 4000 Horse and 1500 Dragoons, with every Horse-man a Foot-man behind him; whether he had swam the *Po*, or passed it above at a Bridge, and made a long March after, was not examined, but he came boldly up the Plain and charged our Rear with a great deal of Fury.

Our Artillery was in the Lane, and as it was impossible to turn them about, and make way for the Army, so the Rear was obliged to support themselves, and maintain the Fight for above an Hour and a half.

In this Time we lost abundance of Men, and if it had not been for two Accidents all that Line had been cut off; one was, that the Wood was so near that those Regiments which were disordered presently sheltred themselves in the Wood; the other was, that by this Time the Mareschal *Schomberg*, with the Horse of the Van, began to get back through the Lane, and to make good the Ground from whence the other had been beaten, till at last by this Means it came to almost a pitched Battle.

There were two Regiments of *French* Dragoons who did

excellent Service in this Action, and maintained their Ground till they were almost all killed.

Had the Duke of *Savoy* contented himself with the Defeat of five Regiments on the Right, which he quite broke and drove into the Wood, and with the Slaughter and Havock which he had made among the rest, he had come off with Honour, and might have called it a Victory; but endeavouring to break the whole Party, and carry off some Cannon, the obstinate Resistance of these few Dragoons lost him his Advantages, and held him in play till so many fresh Troops got through the Pass again, as made us too strong for him; and had not Night parted them he had been entirely defeated.

At last finding our Troops encrease and spread themselves on his Flank, he retired and gave over, we had no great Stomach to pursue him neither, tho' some Horse were ordered to follow a little Way.

The Duke lost above a thousand Men, and we almost twice as many, and but for those Dragoons, had lost the whole Rear-guard and half our Cannon. I was in a very sorry Case in this Action too, I was with the Rear in the Regiment of Horse of *Perigoort*, with a Captain of which Regiment I had contracted some Acquaintance; I would have rid off at first, as the Captain desired me, but there was no doing it, for the Cannon was in the Lane, and the Horse and Dragoons of the Van eagerly pressing back through the Lane, must have run me down, or carried me with them: As for the Wood, it was a good Shelter to save ones Life, but was so thick there was no passing it on Horseback.

Our Regiment was one of the first that was broke, and being all in Confusion, with the Duke of *Savoy*'s Men at our Heels, away we ran into the Wood; never was there so much Disorder among a Parcel of Runaways as when we came to this Wood, it was so exceeding bushy and thick at the Bottom there was no entring it, and a Volley of small Shot from a Regiment of *Savoy's* Dragoons poured in upon us at our breaking into the Wood made terrible Work among our Horses.

For my Part I was got into the Wood, but was forced to quit my Horse, and by that means with a great deal of Difficulty got a little farther in, where there was a little open Place, and being quite spent with labouring among the Bushes, I sat down resolving to take my Fate there, let it be what it would, for I was not able to go any farther; I had twenty or thirty more in the same Condition came to me in less than half an Hour, and here we waited very securely the Success of the Battle, which was as before.

It was no small Relief to those with me to hear the *Savoyards* were beaten, for otherwise they had all been lost; as for me, I confess, I was glad as it was, because of the Danger, but otherwise I cared not much which had the better, for I designed no Service among them.

One Kindness it did me, that I began to consider what I had to do here, and as I could give but a very slender Account of my self for what it was I run all these Risques, so I resolved they should fight it out among themselves, for I would come among them no more.

The Captain with whom, as I noted above, I had contracted some Acquaintance in this Regiment, was killed in this Action, and the *French* had really a great Blow here, though they took Care to conceal it all they could; and I cannot, without smiling, read some of the Histories and Memoirs of this Action, which they are not ashamed to call a Victory.

We marched on to *Saluces*, and the next Day the Duke of *Savoy* presented himself in Batallia on the other Side of a small River giving us a fair Challenge to pass and engage him: We always said in our Camp that the Orders were to fight the Duke of *Savoy* where-ever we met him; but tho' he braved us in our View, we did not care to engage him, but we brought *Saluces* to surrender upon Articles, which the Duke could not relieve without attacking our Camp, which he did not care to do.

The next Morning we had News of the Surrender of *Mantua* to the *Imperial* Army; we heard of it first from the

Duke of *Savoy*'s Cannon, which he fired by way of Rejoycing, and which seemed to make him Amends for the loss of *Saluces*.[1]

As this was a Mortification to the *French*, so it quite damped the Success of the Campaign, for the Duke *de Momorency* imagining that the *Imperial* General would send immediate Assistance to the Marquis *Spinola*, who besieged *Casal*, they call'd frequent Councils of War what Course to take, and at last resolved to halt in *Piedmont*.

A few Days after their Resolutions were changed again, by the News of the Death of the Duke of *Savoy*, *Charles Emanuel*, who died, as some say, agitated with the Extreams of Joy and Grief.

This put our Generals upon considering again, whether they should march to the Relief of *Casal*, but the Chimera of the *Germans* put them by, and so they took up Quarters in *Piedmont*; they took several small Places from the Duke of *Savoy*, making Advantage of the Consternation the Duke's Subjects were in on the Death of their Prince,[2] and spread themselves from the Sea-side to the Banks of the *Po*.

But here an Enemy did that for them which the *Savoyards* could not, for the Plague got into their Quarters and destroyed abundance of People, both of the Army and of the Country.

I thought then it was Time for me to be gone, for I had no manner of Courage for that Risque; and I think verily I was more afraid of being taken sick in a strange Country, than ever I was of being killed in Battle. Upon this Resolution I procured a Pass to go for *Genoa*, and acordingly began my Journey, but was arrested at *Villa Franca* by a slow lingring Fever, which held me about five Days, and then turned to a burning Malignancy, and at last to the Plague:[3] My Friend, the Captain, never left me Night nor Day; and though for four Days more I knew no Body, nor was capable of so much as thinking of my self, yet it pleased God that the Distemper gathered in my Neck, swelled and broke; during the Swelling I was raging mad with the Violence of

Pain, which being so near my Head, swelled that also in Proportion, that my Eyes were swelled up, and for twenty four Hours my Tongue and Mouth; then, as my Servant told me, all the Physicians gave me over, as past all Remedy, but by the good Providence of God the Swelling broke.

The prodigious Collection of Matter which this Swelling discharged, gave me immediate Relief, and I became sensible in less than an Hour's Time; and in two Hours, or thereabouts, fell into a little Slumber which recovered my Spirits, and sensibly revived me. Here I lay by it till the Middle of *September*, my Captain fell sick after me, but recovered quickly; his Man had the Plague, and died in two Days; my Man held it out well.

About the Middle of *September* we heard of a Truce[1] concluded between all Parties, and being unwilling to winter at *Villa Franca*, I got Passes, and though we were both but weak began to travel in Litters for *Milan*.

And here I experienced the Truth of an old *English* Proverb,[2] *That Standers-by see more than the Gamesters.*

The *French*, *Savoyards* and *Spaniards* made this Peace or Truce all for separate and several Grounds, and every one were mistaken.

The *French* yielded to it because they had given over the Relief of *Casal*, and were very much afraid it would fall into the Hands of the Marquiss *Spinola*. The *Savoyards* yielded to it because they were afraid the *French* would winter in *Piedmont*; the *Spaniards* yielded to it because the Duke of *Savoy* being dead, and the Count *de Colalto*, the *Imperial* General, giving no Assistance, and his Army weakened by Sickness and the Fatigues of the Siege, he foresaw he should never take the Town, and wanted but to come off with Honour.

The *French* were mistaken, because really *Spinola* was so weak, that had they marched on into *Montferrat* the *Spaniards* must have raised the Siege; the Duke of *Savoy* was mistaken, because the Plague had so weakened the *French* that they durst not have staid to winter in *Piedmont*; and *Spinola* was mistaken, for tho' he was very slow, if he had staid before the Town one Fortnight longer *Thoiras* the Governour must have surrendred, being brought to the last Extremity.

Of all these Mistakes the *French* had the Advantage, for *Casal* was relieved, the Army had Time to be recruited, and the *French* had the best of it by an early Campaign.

I past through *Montferrat* in my Way to *Milan* just as the Truce was declared, and saw the miserable Remains of the *Spanish* Army, who by Sickness, Fatigue, hard Duty, the Sallies of the Garrison, and such like Consequences, were reduced to less than 2000 Men, and of them above 1000 lay wounded and sick in the Camp.

Here were several Regiments which I saw drawn out to their Arms that could not make up above 70 or 80 Men, Officers and all, and those half starved with Hunger, almost naked, and in a lamentable Condition. From thence I went into the Town, and there Things were still in a worse Condition, the Houses beaten down, the Walls and Works ruined, the Garrison, by continual Duty, reduced from 4500 Men to less than 800, without Clothes, Money, or Provisions. The brave Governour weak with continual Fatigue, and the whole Face of things in a miserable Case.

The *French* Generals had just sent them Thirty Thousand Crowns for present Supply, which heartened them a little, but had not the Truce been made as it was, they must have surrendred upon what Terms the *Spaniards* had pleased to make them.

Never were two Armies in such Fear of one another with so little Cause; the *Spaniards* afraid of the *French* whom the Plague had devoured, and the *French* afraid of the *Spaniards* whom the Siege had almost ruined.

The Grief of this Mistake, together with the Sense of his Master, the *Spaniards*, leaving him without Supplies to compleat the Siege of *Casal*, so affected the Marquess *Spinola* that he died for Grief, and in him fell the last of that rare breed of *Low Country* Soldiers who gave the World so great and just a Character of the *Spanish* Infantry as the best

Soldiers of the World; a Character which we see them so very much degenerated from since, that they hardly deserve the Name of Soldiers.

I tarried at *Milan* the rest of the Winter, both for the Recovery of my Health, and also for Supplies from *England*.

Here it was I first heard the Name of *Gustavus Adolphus*, the King of *Sweden*, who now began his War with the Emperor; and while the King of *France* was at *Lyons*, the League[1] with *Sweden* was made, in which the *French* contributed 1200000 Crowns in Money, and 600000 *per An.* to the Attempt of *Gustavus Adolphus*: About this Time he landed in *Pomerania*, took the Towns of *Stetin*[2] and *Straelsund*, and from thence proceeded in that prodigious Manner, of which I shall have Occasion to be very particular in the Prosecution of these Memoirs.

I had indeed no Thoughts of seeing that King, or his Armies, I had been so roughly handled already that I had given over the Thoughts of appearing among the fighting People, and resolved in the Spring to pursue my Journey to *Venice*, and so for the rest of *Italy*.

Yet I cannot deny, that as every Gazette gave us some Accounts of the Conquests and Victories of this glorious Prince, it prepossessed my Thoughts with secret Wishes of seeing him, but these were so young and unsettled, that I drew no Resolutions from them for a long while after.

About the Middle of *January* I left *Milan* and came to *Genoa*, from thence by Sea to *Leghorn*, then to *Naples*, *Rome* and *Venice*, but saw nothing in *Italy* that gave me any Diversion.

As for what is modern, I saw nothing but Lewdness, private Murthers, stabbing Men at the Corner of a Street, or in the dark, hiring of Bravoes, and the like; all the Diversions here ended in Whoring, Gaming and Sodomy, these were to me the modern Excellencies of *Italy*; and I had no Gust[3] to Antiquities.

'Twas pleasant indeed when I was at *Rome* to say here stood the Capitol, there the Colossus of *Nero*, here was the

Amphitheatre of *Titus*, there the Aqueduct of——here the Forum, there the Catacombs, here the Temple of *Venus*, there of *Jupiter*, here the Pantheon, and the like; but I never designed to write a Book, as much as was useful I kept in my Head; and for the rest, I left it to others.

I observed the People degenerated from the ancient glorious Inhabitants, who were generous, brave, and the most valiant of all Nations, to a vicious Baseness of Soul, barbarous, treacherous, jealous and revengeful, lewd and cowardly, intolerably proud and haughty, bigotted to blind, incoherent Devotion, and the grossest of Idolatry.

Indeed I think the Unsuitableness of the People made the Place unpleasant to me, for there is so little in a Country to recommend it when the People disgrace it, that no Beauties of the Creation can make up for the Want of those Excellencies which suitable Society procure the Defect of; this made *Italy* a very unpleasant Country to me, the People were the Foil to the Place, all manner of hateful Vices reigning in their general Way of living.

I confess I was not very religious my self, and being come abroad into the World young enough, might easily have been drawn into Evils that had recommended themselves with any tolerable Agreeableness to Nature and common Manners; but when Wickedness presented it self full grown in its grossest Freedoms and Liberties, it quite took away all the Gust to Vice that the Devil had furnished me with, and in this I cannot but relate one Scene which passed between no Body but the Devil and my self.

At a certain Town in *Italy*, which shall be nameless, because I won't celebrate the Proficiency of one Place more than another, when I believe the whole Country equally wicked, I was prevailed upon rather than tempted, *a la Courtezan*.

If I should describe the Woman I must give a very mean Character of my own Virtue to say I was allured by any but a Woman of an extraordinary Figure; her Face, Shape, Mein, and Dress, I may, without Vanity, say, the finest that

I ever saw: When I had Admittance into her Apartments, the Riches and Magnificence of them astonished me, the Cupboard or Cabinet of Plate, the Jewels, the Tapestry, and every Thing in Proportion, made me question whether I was not in the Chamber of some Lady of the best Quality;——— but when after some Conversation I found that it was really nothing but a Courtezan, in *English*, a common Street Whore, a Punk of the Trade, I was amazed, and my Inclination to her Person began to cool; her Conversation exceeded, if possible, the best of Quality, and was, I must own, exceeding agreeable; she sung to her Lute, and danced as fine as ever I saw, and thus diverted me two Hours before any Thing else was discoursed of;—but when the vicious Part came on the Stage, I blush to relate the Confusion I was in, and when she made a certain Motion by which I understood she might be made use of, either as a Lady, or as—I was quite Thunder-struck, all the vicious Part of my Thoughts vanished, the Place filled me with Horror, and I was all over Disorder and Distraction.

I began however to recollect where I was, and that in this Country these were People not to be affronted; and though she easily saw the Disorder I was in, she turned it off with admirable Dexterity, began to talk again *a la Gallant*, received me as a Visitant, offered me Sweetmeats and some Wine.

Here I began to be in more Confusion than before, for I concluded she would neither offer me to eat or to drink now *without Poison*, and I was very shy of tasting her Treat, but she scattered this Fear immediately, by readily, and of her own accord, not only tasting but eating freely of every Thing she gave me; whether she perceived my Wariness, or the Reason of it, I know not, I could not help banishing my Suspicion, the obliging Carriage and strange Charm of her Conversation had so much Power of me, that I both eat and drank with her at all Hazards.

When I offered to go, and at parting presented her five Pistoles, I could not prevail with her to take them, when she spoke some *Italian* Proverb which I could not readily understand, but by my Guess it seemed to imply, that *she would not take the Pay, having not obliged me otherwise*: At last I laid the Pieces on her Toilet, and would not receive them again; upon which she obliged me to pass my Word to visit her again, else she would by no Means accept my Present.

I confess I had a strong Inclination to visit her again, and besides thought my self obliged to it in Honour to my Parole; but after some Strife in my Thoughts about it, I resolved to break my Word with her, when going at Vespers one Evening to see their Devotions, I happened to meet this very Lady very devoutly going to her Prayers.

At her coming out of the Church I spoke to her, she paid me her Respects with a *Seignior Inglese*, and some Words she said in *Spanish* smiling, which I did not understand; I cannot say here so clearly as I would be glad I might, that I broke my Word with her; but if I saw her any more I saw nothing of what gave me so much Offence before.

The End of my relating this Story is answered in describing the Manner of their Address, without bringing my self to Confession; if I did any Thing I have some Reason to be ashamed of, it may be a less Crime to conceal it than expose it.

The Particulars related however, may lead the Reader of these Sheets to a View of what gave me a particular Disgust at this pleasant Part of the World, as they pretend to call it, and made me quit the Place sooner than Travellers use to do that come thither to satisfy their Curiosity.

The prodigious stupid Bigottry of the People also was irksome to me; I thought there was something in it very sordid, the entire Empire the Priests have over both the Souls and Bodies of the People, gave me a Specimen of that Meanness of Spirit which is no where else to be seen but in *Italy*, especially in the City of *Rome*.

At *Venice* I perceived it quite different, the Civil Authority having a visible Superiority over the Ecclesiastick; and the Church being more subject there to the State than in any other Part of *Italy*.

For these Reasons I took no Pleasure in filling my Memoirs of *Italy* with Remarks of Places or Things, all the Antiquities and valuable Remains of the *Roman* Nation are done better than I can pretend to by such People who made it more their Business; as for me, I went to see, and not to write, and as little thought then of these Memoirs, as I ill furnished my self to write them.

I left *Italy* in *April*, and taking the Tour of *Bavaria*, though very much out of the Way, I passed through *Munick*, *Passaw*, *Lints*, and at last to *Vienna*.

I came to *Vienna* the 10th of *April* 1631, intending to have gone from thence down the *Danube* into *Hungary*, and by Means of a Pass which I had obtained from the *English* Ambassador[1] at *Constantinople*, I designed to have seen all those great Towns on the *Danube* which were then in the Hands of the *Turks*, and which I had read much of in the History of the War between the *Turks* and the *Germans*; but I was diverted from my Design by the following Occasion.

There had been a long bloody War in the Empire of *Germany* for 12 Years, between the Emperor, the Duke of *Bavaria*, the King of *Spain*, and the Popish Princes and Electors on the one Side, and the Protestant Princes on the other; and both Sides having been exhausted by the War, and even the Catholicks themselves beginning to dislike the growing Power of the House of *Austria*, 'twas thought all Parties were willing to make Peace.

Nay, Things were brought to that Pass that some of the Popish Princes and Electors began to talk of making Alliances with the King of *Sweden*.

Here it is necessary to observe, that the two Dukes of *Mecklenburgh* having been dispossessed of most of their Dominions by the Tyranny of the Emperor *Ferdinand*, and being in danger of losing the rest, earnestly sollicited the King of *Sweden* to come to their Assistance; and that Prince, as he was related to the House of *Mecklenburgh*,[2] and especially as he was willing to lay hold of any Opportunity to break with the Emperor, against whom he had laid up an implacable Prejudice, was very ready and forward to come to their Assistance.

The Reasons of his Quarrel with the Emperor were grounded upon the *Imperialists* concerning themselves in the War of *Poland*, where the Emperor had sent 8000 Foot and 2000 Horse to join the *Polish* Army against the King, and had thereby given some Check to his Arms in that War.

In Pursuance therefore of his Resolution to quarrel with the Emperor, but more particularly at the Instance of the Princes above-named, his *Swedish* Majesty had landed the Year before at *Straelsund* with about 12000 Men, and having joined with some Forces which he had left in *Polish Prussia*, all which did not make 30000 Men, he began a War with the Emperor, the greatest in Event, filled with the most famous Battles, Sieges and extraordinary Actions, including its wonderful Success and happy Conclusion, of any War ever maintained in the World.

The King of *Sweden* had already taken *Stetin*, *Straelsund*, *Rostock*, *Wismar*, and all the strong Places on the *Baltick*, and began to spread himself in *Germany*; he had made a League with the *French*, as I observed in my Story of *Saxony*, he had now made a Treaty[1] with the Duke of *Brandenburg*, and, in short, began to be terrible to the Empire.

In this Conjuncture the Emperor called the General Diet of the Empire to be held at *Ratisbon*, where, as was pretended, all Sides were to treat of Peace and to join Forces to beat the *Swedes* out of the Empire. Here the Emperor, by a most exquisite Management, brought the Affairs of the Diet to a Conclusion, exceedingly to his own Advantage and to the farther Oppression of the Protestants; and in particular, in that the War against the King of *Sweden* was to be carried on in such Manner as that the whole Burthen and Charge would lie on the Protestants themselves, and they be made the Instruments to oppose their best Friends. Other Matters also ended equally to their Disadvantage, as the Methods resolved on to recover the Church-Lands, and to prevent the Education of the Protestant Clergy; and what remained was referred to another General Diet to be held at *Frankfort au Main*, in *August* 1631.

I won't pretend to say the other Protestant Princes of *Germany* had never made any Overtures to the King of *Sweden* to come to their Assistance, but 'tis plain they had entred into no League with him; that appears from the Difficulties which retarded the fixing the Treaties afterward, both with the Dukes of *Brandenburgh* and *Saxony* which unhappily occasioned the Ruine of *Magdenburgh*.

But 'tis Plain the *Swede* was resolved on a War with the Emperor; his *Swedish* Majesty might and indeed could not but foresee that if he once shewed himself with a sufficient Force on the Frontiers of the Empire, all the Protestant Princes would be obliged by their Interest or by his Arms to fall in with him, and this the Consequence made appear to be a just Conclusion; for the Electors of *Brandenburgh* and *Saxony* were both forced to join with him.

First, They were willing to join with him, at least they could not find in their Hearts to join with the Emperor, of whose Power they had such just Apprehensions; they wished the *Swedes* Success, and would have been very glad to have had the Work done at another Man's Charge; but like true *Germans* they were more willing to be saved than to save themselves, and therefore hung back and stood upon Terms.

Secondly, They were at last forced to it; the first was forced to join by the King of *Sweden* himself, who being come so far was not to be dallied with; and had not the Duke of *Brandenburgh* complied as he did, he had been ruined by the *Swede*; the *Saxon* was driven into the Arms of the *Swede* by Force, for Count *Tilly* Ravaging his Country made him comply with any Terms to be saved from Destruction.

Thus Matters stood at the End of the Diet at *Ratisbon*; the King of *Sweden* began to see himself leagued against at the Diet both by Protestant and Papist; and, *as I have often heard his Majesty say since*, he had resolved to try to force them off from the Emperor, and to treat them as Enemies equally with the Rest if they did not.

But the Protestants convinced him soon after, that tho' they were tricked into the outward Appearance of a League against him at *Ratisbon*, they had no such Intentions; and by their Ambassadors to him let him know, that they only wanted his powerful Assistance to defend their Councils, when they would soon convince him that they had a due Sense of the Emperor's Designs, and would do their utmost for their Liberty; and these I take to be the first Invitations the King of *Sweden* had to undertake the Protestant Cause as such, and which entitled him to say he fought for the Liberty and Religion of the *German* Nation.

I have had some particular Opportunities to hear these Things from the Mouths of some of the very Princes themselves, and therefore am the forwarder to relate them; and I place them here, because previous to the part I acted on this bloody Scene, 'tis necessary to let the Reader into some Part of the Story, and to shew him in what Manner and on what Occasions this terrible War began.

The Protestants, alarmed at the Usage they had met with at the former Diet, had secretly proposed among themselves to form a general Union or Confederacy, for preventing that Ruin which they saw, unless some speedy Remedies were applied, would be inevitable. The Elector of *Saxony*, the Head of the Protestants, a vigorous and politick Prince, was the first that moved it; and the Landgrave of *Hesse*, a zealous and gallant Prince, being consulted with, it rested a great while between those two, no Method being found practicable to bring it to pass; the Emperor being so powerful in all Parts, that they foresaw the petty Princes would not dare to negotiate an Affair of such a Nature, being surrounded with the *Imperial* Forces, who by their two Generals, *Wallestein* and *Tilly*, kept them in continual Subjection and Terror.

This Dilemma had like to have stifled the Thoughts of the Union as a Thing impracticable, when one *Seigensius*,[1] a *Lutheran* Minister, a Person of great Abilities, and one

whom the Elector of *Saxony* made great Use of in Matters
of Policy as well as Religion, contrived for them this excellent
Expedient.

I had the Honour to be acquainted with this Gentleman
while I was at *Leipsick*; it pleased him exceedingly to have
been the Contriver of so fine a Structure as the *Conclusions
of Leipsick*, and he was glad to be entertained on that Subject;
I had the Relation from his own Mouth, when, but very
modestly, he told me he thought 'twas an Inspiration darted
on a sudden into his Thoughts, when the Duke of *Saxony*
calling him into his Closet one Morning, with a Face full of
Concern, shaking his Head and looking very earnestly,
What will become of us, Doctor? said the Duke, *we shall all
be undone at* Frankfort au Main. *Why so, please your Highness?* says the Doctor, *Why they will fight with the King of*
Sweden *with our Armies and our Money*, says the Duke, *and
devour our Friends and our selves, by the help of our Friends
and our selves: But what is become of the Confederacy then*,
said the Doctor, *which your Highness had so happily framed
in your Thoughts, and which the Landgrave of* Hesse *was so
pleased with? Become of it*, says the Duke, *'tis a good Thought
enough, but 'tis impossible to bring it to pass among so many
Members of the Protestant Princes as are to be consulted with,
for we neither have Time to treat, nor will half of them dare
to negotiate the Matter, the* Imperialists *being quarter'd in
their very Bowels. But may not some Expedient be found out*,
says the Doctor, *to bring them all together to treat of it in a
General Meeting? 'Tis well proposed*, says the Duke, *but in
what Town or City shall they assemble where the very Deputies
shall not be besieged by* Tilly *or* Wallestein *in* 14 *Days Time,
and sacrificed to the Cruelty and Fury of the Emperor* Ferdinand? *Will your Highness be the easier in it*, replies the Doctor,
*if a way may be found out to call such an Assembly upon other
Causes, at which the Emperor may have no Umbrage, and
perhaps gives his Assent? You know the Diet at* Frankfort *is
at Hand ; 'tis necessary the Protestants should have an Assembly
of their own, to prepare Matters for the General Diet, and it*

may be no difficult Matter to obtain it. The Duke, surprized with Joy at the Motion, embraced the Doctor with an extraordinary Transport, *Thou hast done it, Doctor*, said he, and immediately caused him to draw a Form of a Letter to the Emperor, which he did with the utmost Dexterity of Style, in which he was a great Master, representing to his *Imperial* Majesty, that in order to put an End to the Troubles of *Germany*, his Majesty would be pleased to permit the Protestant Princes of the Empire to hold a Diet to themselves, to consider of such Matters as they were to treat of at the General Diet, in order to conform themselves to the Will and Pleasure of his *Imperial* Majesty, to drive out Foreigners, and settle a lasting Peace in the Empire; he also insinuated something of their Resolutions unanimously to give their Suffrages in favour of the King of *Hungary* at the Election of a King of the *Romans*, a thing which he knew the Emperor had in his Thought, and would push at with all his Might at the Diet. This Letter was sent, and the Bait so neatly concealed, that the Electors of *Bavaria* and *Mentz*, the King of *Hungary*, and several of the Popish Princes, not foreseeing that the Ruin of them all lay in the bottom of it, foolishly advised the Emperor to consent to it.

In consenting to this the Emperor signed his own Destruction, for here began the Conjunction of the *German* Protestants with the *Swede*, which was the fatalest blow to *Ferdinand*, and which he could never recover.

Accordingly the Diet was held at *Leipsick*, *Feb.* 8, 1630, where the Protestants agreed on several Heads for their mutual Defence, which were the Grounds of the following War; these were *the Famous Conclusions of Leipsick*, which so alarmed the Emperor and the whole Empire, that to crush it in the Beginning, the Emperor commanded Count *Tilly* immediately to fall upon the Landgrave of *Hesse*, and the Duke of *Saxony*, as the principal Heads of the Union; but it was too late.

The Conclusions were digested into ten Heads;

1. That since their Sins had brought God's Judgments

upon the whole Protestant Church, they should command Publick Prayers to be made to Almighty God for the diverting the Calamities that attended them.

2. That a Treaty of Peace might be set on Foot, in order to come to a right Understanding with the Catholick Princes.

3. That a Time for such a Treaty being obtained, they should appoint an Assembly of Delegates to meet preparatory to the Treaty.

4. That all their Complaints should be humbly represented to his *Imperial* Majesty, and the Catholick Electors, in order to a peaceable Accommodation.

5. That they claim the Protection of the Emperor, according to the Laws of the Empire, and the present Emperor's solemn Oath and Promise.

6. That they would appoint Deputies who should meet at certain Times to consult of their common Interest, and who should be always empoured to conclude of what should be thought needful for their Safety.

7. That they will raise a competent Force to maintain and defend their Liberties, Rights and Religion.

8. That it is agreeable to the Constitution of the Empire, concluded in the Diet at *Ausburg* to do so.

9. That the arming for their necessary Defence shall by no Means hinder their Obedience to his *Imperial* Majesty, but that they will still continue their Loyalty to him.

10. They agree to Proportion their Forces, which in all amounted to 70000 Men.

The Emperor, exceedingly startled at the Conclusions, issued out a severe Proclamation or Ban against them, which imported much the same Thing as a Declaration of War, and commanded *Tilly* to begin, and immediately to fall on the Duke of *Saxony* with all the Fury imaginable, as I have already observed.

Here began the Flame to break out; for upon the Emperor's Ban, the Protestants send away to the King of *Sweden* for Succour.

His *Swedish* Majesty had already conquered *Mecklenburgh*, and Part of *Pomerania*, and was advancing with his victorious Troops, encreased by the Addition of some Regiments raised in those Parts, in order to carry on the War against the Emperor, having designed to follow up the *Oder* into *Silesia*, and so to push the War home to the Emperor's Hereditary Countries of *Austria* and *Bohemia*, when the first Messengers came to him in this Case; but this changed his Measures, and brought him to the Frontiers of *Brandenburgh*, resolved to answer the Desires of the Protestants: But here the Duke of *Brandenburgh* began to halt, making some Difficulties and demanding Terms which drove the King to use some Extremities with him, and stopt the *Swedes* for a while, who had otherwise been on the Banks of the *Elbe*, as soon as *Tilly* the *Imperial* General had entred *Saxony*, which if they had done, the miserable Destruction of *Magdenburgh* had been prevented, as I observed before.

The King had been invited into the Union, and when he first came back from the Banks of the *Oder* he had accepted it, and was preparing to back it with all his Power.

The Duke of *Saxony* had already a good Army, which he had with infinite Diligence recruited, and mustered them under the Cannon of *Leipsick*. The King of *Sweden* having, by his Ambassador at *Leipsick*, entred into the Union of the Protestants, was advancing victoriously to their Aid, just as Count *Tilly* had enter'd the Duke of *Saxony*'s Dominions. The Fame of the *Swedish* Conquests, and of the Hero who commanded them, shook my Resolution of travelling into *Turkey*, being resolved to see the Conjunction of the Protestants Armies, and before the Fire was broke out too far to take the Advantage of seeing both sides.

While I remained at *Vienna*, uncertain which Way I should proceed, I remember I observed they talked of the King of *Sweden* as a Prince of no Consideration, one that they might let go on and tire himself in *Mecklenbergh*, and thereabout, till they could find Leisure to deal with him, and then might be crushed as they pleased; but as 'tis never safe to despise an Enemy, so this was not an Enemy to be *despised*, as they afterwards found.

As to the Conclusions of *Leipsick*, indeed at first they gave the *Imperial* Court some Uneasiness, but when they found the *Imperial* Armies began to fright the Members out of the Union, and that the several Branches had no considerable Forces on Foot, it was the general Discourse at *Vienna*, that the Union at *Leipsick* only gave the Emperor an Opportunity to crush absolutely the Dukes of *Saxony*, *Brandenburgh*, and the Landgrave of *Hesse*, and they looked upon it as a Thing certain.

I never saw any real Concern in their Faces at *Vienna*, 'till News came to Court that the King of *Sweden* had entered into the Union; but as this made them very uneasie, they began to move the powerfullest Methods possible to divert this Storm; and upon this News *Tilly*[1] was hastened to fall into *Saxony* before this Union could proceed to a Conjunction of Forces. This was certainly a very good Resolution, and no Measure could have been more exactly concerted had not the Diligence of the *Saxons* prevented it.

The gathering of this Storm, which from a Cloud began to spread over the Empire, and from the little Dutchy of *Mecklenburgh* began to threaten all *Germany*, absolutely determined me, as I noted before, as to travelling; and laying aside the Thoughts of *Hungary*, I resolved, if possible, to see the King of *Sweden*'s Army.

I parted from *Vienna* the middle of *May*, and took post for *Great Glogau* in *Silesia*, as if I had purposed to pass into *Poland*, but designing indeed to go down the *Oder* to *Custrin* in the Marquisate of *Brandenburgh*, and so to *Berlin*; but when I came to the Frontiers of *Silesia*, tho' I had Passes I could go no farther, the Guards on all the Frontiers were so strict; so I was obliged to come back into *Bohemia*, and went to *Prague*.

From hence I found I could easily pass through the *Imperial* Provinces to the *Lower Saxony*, and accordingly took Passes for *Hamburgh*, designing however to use them no farther than I found Occasion.

By Virtue of these Passes I got into the *Imperial* Army, under Count *Tilly*, then at the Siege of *Magdenburgh*, *May* the 2d.

I confess I did not foresee the Fate of this City, neither I believe did County *Tilly* himself expect to glut his Fury with so entire a Desolation, much less did the People expect it. I did believe they must capitulate, and I perceived by Discourse in the Army, that *Tilly* would give them but very indifferent Conditions; but it fell out otherwise; the Treaty of Surrender was as it were begun, nay some say concluded, when some of the Out-guards of the *Imperialists* finding the Citizens had abandoned the Guards of the Works, and looked to themselves with less Diligence than usual, they broke in, carried an Half-Moon Sword in Hand with little Resistance; and tho' it was a Surprize on both Sides, the Citizens neither fearing, nor the Army expecting the Occasion, the Garrison, with as much Resolution as could be expected under such a Fright, flew to the Walls, twice beat the *Imperialists* off, but fresh Men coming up, and the Administrator of *Magdenburgh*[1] himself being wounded and taken, the Enemy broke in, took the City by Storm, and entred with such terrible Fury, that without Respect to Age or Condition, they put all the Garrison and Inhabitants, Man, Woman and Child, to the Sword, plundered the City, and when they had done this, set it on Fire.

This Calamity sure was the dreadfullest Sight that ever I saw; the Rage of the *Imperial* Soldiers was most intolerable, and not to be expressed; of 25000, some said 30000 People, there was not a Soul to be seen alive, till the Flames drove those that were hid in Vaults and secret Places to seek Death in the Streets, rather than perish in the Fire: Of these miserable Creatures some were killed too by the furious Soldiers, but at last they saved the Lives of such as came out of their Cellars and Holes, and so about 2000 poor desperate Creatures were left: The exact Number of those that perished in this City could never be known, because those the Soldiers had first butcher'd, the Flames afterwards devour'd.

I was on the other Side the *Elbe* when this dreadful Piece of Butchery was done; the City of *Magdenburgh* had a Sconce or Fort over against it, called the Toll-House, which joined to the City by a very fine Bridge of Boats.

This Fort was taken by the *Imperialists* a few Days before, and having a Mind to see it, and the rather because from thence I could have a very good View of the City, I was gone over *Tilly*'s Bridge of Boats to view this Fort; about 10 a Clock in the Morning I perceived they were storming by the firing, and immediately all ran to the Works, I little thought of the taking the City, but imagined it might be some Out-work attacked, for we all expected the City would surrender that Day, or next, and they might have capitulated upon very good Terms.

Being upon the Works of the Fort, on a sudden I heard the dreadfullest Cry raised in the City that can be imagined, 'tis not possible to express the Manner of it, and I could see the Women and Children running about the Streets in a most lamentable Condition.

The City Wall did not run along the Side where the River was with so great a Heighth but we could plainly see the Market-Place and the several Streets which run down to the River: In about an Hour's Time after this first Cry all was Confusion; there was little shooting, the Execution was all cutting of Throats and meer House Murthers; the resolute Garrison, with the brave Baron *Falconberg*, fought it out to the last, and were cut in Pieces, and by this Time the *Imperial* Soldiers having broke open the Gates and entred on all Sides, the Slaughter was very dreadful, we could see the poor People in Crowds driven down the Streets, flying from the Fury of the Soldiers who followed butchering them as fast as they could, and refused Mercy to any Body; 'till driving them to the River's Edge, the desperate Wretches would throw themselves into the River, where Thousands of them perished, especially Women and Children; several

Men that could swim got over to our Side, where the Soldiers not heated with Fight gave them Quarter, and took them up, and I cannot but do this Justice to the *German* Officers in the Fort, they had five small flat Boats, and they gave leave to the Soldiers to go off in them, and get what Booty they could, but charged them not to kill any Body, but take them all Prisoners.

Nor was their Humanity ill rewarded, for the Soldiers wisely avoiding those Places where their Fellows were employed in the butchering the miserable People, rowed to other Places, where Crouds of People stood crying out for help, and expecting to be every Minute either drowned or murdered; of these at sundry Times they fetched over near Six hundred, but took Care to take in none but such as offered them good Pay.

Never was Money or Jewels of greater Service than now, for those that had any Thing of that sort to offer were soonest helped.

There was a Burgher of the Town, who seeing a Boat coming near him, but out of his Call, by the help of a speaking Trumpet, told the Soldiers in it he would give them 20000 Dollers to fetch him off; they rowed close to the Shore, and got him with his Wife and six Children into the Boat, but such Throngs of People got about the Boat that had like to have sunk her, so that the Soldiers were fain to drive a great many out again by main Force, and while they were doing this, some of the Enemies coming down the Street desperately drove them all into the Water.

The Boat however brought the Burgher and his Wife and Children safe, and though they had not all that Wealth about them, yet in Jewels and Money he gave them so much as made all the Fellows very rich.

I cannot pretend to describe the Cruelty of this Day, the Town by five in the Afternoon was all on a Flame; the Wealth consumed was inestimable, and a Loss to the very Conqueror. I think there was little or nothing left but the great Church, and about 100 Houses.

This was a sad Welcome into the Army for me, and gave me a Horror and Aversion to the Emperor's People, as well as to his Cause. I quitted the Camp the third Day after this Execution, while the Fire was hardly out in the City; and from thence getting safe Conduct to pass into the *Palatinate*, I turned out of the Road at a small Village on the *Elbe*, called *Emerfield*, and by Ways and Town I can give but small Account of, having a Boor for our Guide, who we could hardly understand. I arrived at *Leipsick* on the 17th of *May*.

We found the Elector intense upon the strengthening of his Army, but the People, in the greatest Terror imaginable, every Day expecting *Tilly* with the *German* Army, who by his Cruelty at *Magdeburg* was become so dreadful to the Protestants, that they expected no Mercy where-ever he came.

The Emperor's Power was made so formidable to all the Protestants, particularly since the Diet at *Ratisbon* left them in a worse Case than it found them, that they had not only formed the Conclusions of *Leipsick*, which all Men looked on as the Effect of Desperation rather than any probable Means of their Deliverance, but had privately implored the Protection and Assistance of foreign Powers, and particularly the King of *Sweden*, from whom they had Promises of a speedy and powerful Assistance. And truly if the *Swede* had not with a very strong Hand rescued them, all their Conclusions at *Leipsick* had served but to hasten their Ruin. I remember very well when I was in the *Imperial* Army they discoursed with such Contempt of the Forces of the Protestants, that not only the *Imperialists* but the Protestants themselves gave them up as lost: the Emperor had not less than 200000 Men in several Armies on Foot, who most of them were on the back of the Protestants in every Corner. If *Tilly* did but write a threatning Letter to any City or Prince of the Union, they presently submitted, renounced the Conclusions of *Leipsick*, and received *Imperial* Garrisons, as the Cities of *Ulm* and *Memingen*, the Dutchy of *Wirtemberg*, and several others, and almost all *Suaben*.

Only the Duke of *Saxony* and the Landgrave of *Hesse* upheld the drooping Courage of the Protestants, and refused all Terms of Peace; slighted all the Threatnings of the *Imperial* Generals, and the Duke of *Brandenburgh* was brought in afterward almost by Force.

The Duke of *Saxony* mustered his Forces under the Walls of *Leipsick*, and I having returned to *Leipsick* two Days before, saw them pass the Review. The Duke, gallantly mounted, rode through the Ranks, attended by his Field Marshal *Arnheim*, and seemed mighty well pleased with them, and indeed the Troops made a very fine Appearance; but I that had seen *Tilly*'s Army, and his old Weather-beaten Soldiers, whose Discipline and Exercises were so exact, and their Courage so often tried, could not look on the *Saxon* Army without some Concern for them, when I considered who they had to deal with; *Tilly*'s Men were rugged surly Fellows, their Faces had an Air of hardy Courage, mangled with Wounds and Scars, their Armour shewed the Bruises of Musquet Bullets, and the Rust of the Winter Storms; I observed of them their Cloaths were always dirty, but their Arms were clean and bright; they were used to camp in the open Fields, and sleep in the Frosts and Rain; their Horses were strong and hardy like themselves, and well taught their Exercises; the Soldiers knew their Business so exactly that general Orders were enough; every private Man was fit to command, and their Wheelings, Marchings, Counter-marchings and Exercises were done with such Order and Readiness that the distinct Words of Command were hardly of any use among them; they were flushed with Victory, and hardly knew what it was to fly.

There had passed some Messages between *Tilly* and the Duke, and he gave always such ambiguous Answers as he thought might serve to gain Time; but *Tilly* was not to be put off with Words, and drawing his Army towards *Saxony*, sends four Propositions to him to sign, and demands an immediate Reply, the Propositions were positive.

1. To cause his Troops to enter into the Emperor's

Service, and to march in Person with them against the King of *Sweden*.

2. To give the *Imperial* Army Quarters in his Country, and supply them with necessary Provisions.

3. To relinquish the Union of *Leipsick*, and disown the 10 Conclusions.

4. To make Restitution of the Goods and Lands of the Church.

The Duke being pressed by *Tilly*'s Trumpeter for an immediate Answer, sat all Night, and part of the next Day in Council with his Privy Councillors, debating what Reply to give him, which at last was concluded, in short, that he would live and die in Defence of the Protestant Religion, and the Conclusions of *Leipsick*, and bad *Tilly* Defiance.

The Dye being thus cast, he immediately decamped with his whole Army for *Torgau*, fearing that *Tilly* should get there before him, and so prevent his Conjunction with the *Swede*. The Duke had not yet concluded any positive Treaty with the King of *Swedeland*, and the Duke of *Brandenburgh* having made some Difficulty of joining, they both stood on some Niceties till they had like to have ruined themselves all at once.

Brandenburgh had given up the Town of *Spandau* to the King by a former Treaty to secure a Retreat for his Army, and the King was advanced as far as *Frankfort* upon the *Oder*, when on a sudden some small Difficulties arising *Brandenburgh* seems cold in the Matter, and with a sort of Indifference demands to have his Town of *Spandau* restored to him again. *Gustavus Adolphus*, who began presently to imagine the Duke had made his Peace with the Emperor, and so would either be his Enemy, or pretend a Neutrality, generously delivered him his Town of *Spandau*; but immediately turns about, and with his whole Army besieges him in his Capital City of *Berlin*. This brought the Duke to know his Error, and by the Interposition of the Ladies, the Queen of *Sweden* being the Duke's Sister, the Matter was accommodated, and the Duke joined his Forces with the King.

But the Duke of *Saxony* had like to have been undone by this Delay, for the *Imperialists*, under Count *de Furstemburgh*, were entred his Country, and had possessed themselves of *Hall*, and *Tilly* was on his March to join him, as he afterwards did, and ravaging the whole Country laid Siege to *Leipsick* it self; the Duke driven to this Extremity rather flies to the *Swede* than treats with him, and on the second of *September* the Duke's Army joined with the King of *Sweden*.

I had not come to *Leipsick* but to see the Duke of *Saxony*'s Army, and that being marched as I have said for *Torgau*, I had no Business there; but if I had, the approach of *Tilly* and the *Imperial* Army was enough to hasten me away, for I had no Occasion to be besieged there; so on the 27th of *August* I left the Town, as several of the principal Inhabitants had done before, and more would have done had not the Governor published a Proclamation against it; and besides they knew not whether to fly, for all Places were alike exposed, the poor People were under dreadful Apprehensions of a Siege, and of the merciless Usage of the *Imperial* Soldiers, the Example of *Magdeburgh* being fresh before them, the Duke and his Army gone from them, and the Town, though well furnished, but indifferently fortified.

In this Condition I left them, buying up Stores of Provisions, working hard to scour their Moats, set up Palisadoes, repair their Fortifications, and preparing all Things for a Siege; and following the *Saxon* Army to *Torgau*, I continued in the Camp till a few Days before they joined the King of *Sweden*.

I had much ado to persuade my Companion from entring into the Service of the Duke of *Saxony*, one of whose Collonels, with whom we had contracted a particular Acquaintance, offering him a Commission to be Cornet in one of the old Regiments of Horse; but the Difference I had observed between this new Army and *Tilly*'s old Troops had made such an Impression on me, that I confess I had yet no manner of Inclination for the Service; and therefore persuaded him to wait a while till we had seen a little further into Affairs, and particularly till we had seen the *Swedish* Army, which we had heard so much of.

The Difficulties which the Elector Duke of *Saxony* made of joining with the King were made up by a Treaty concluded with the King on the 2d of *September* at *Coswig*, a small Town on the *Elbe*, whither the King's Army was arrived the Night before; for General *Tilly* being now entered into the Duke's Country, had plundered and ruined all the lower part of it, and was now actually besieging the Capital City of *Leipsick*. These Necessities made almost any Conditions easy to him, the greatest Difficulty was that the King of *Sweden* demanded the absolute Command of the Army, which the Duke submitted to with less good Will than he had Reason to do, the King's Experience and Conduct considered.

I had not Patience to attend the Conclusions of their particular Treaties, but as soon as ever the Passage was clear I quitted the *Saxon* Camp, and went to see the *Swedish* Army: I fell in with the Out-guards of the *Swedes* at a little Town called *Beltsig*, on the River *Wersa*, just as they were relieving the Guards, and going to march, and having a Pass from the *English* Ambassador[1] was very well received by the Officer who changed the Guards, and with him I went back into the Army; by nine in the Morning the Army was in full March, the King himself at the Head of them on a gray Pad, and riding from one Brigade to another, ordered the March of every Line himself.

When I saw the *Swedish* Troops, their exact Discipline, their Order, the Modesty and Familiarity of their Officers, and the regular living of the Soldiers, their Camp seemed a well ordered City; the meanest Country Woman with her *Market Ware* was as safe from Violence as in the Streets of *Vienna*: There was no Regiments of Whores and Rags as followed the *Imperialists*; nor any Women in the Camp, but such as being known to the Provosts to be the Wives of the Soldiers, who were necessary for washing Linen, taking Care of the Soldiers Cloaths, and dressing their Victuals.

The Soldiers were well clad, not gay, furnished with excellent Arms, and exceeding careful of them; and though they did not seem so terrible as I thought *Tilly*'s Men did when I first saw them, yet the Figure they made, together with what we had heard of them, made them seem to me invincible: The Discipline and Order of their Marchings, Camping and Exercise was excellent and singular, and which was to be seen in no Armies but the King's, his own Skill, Judgment and Vigilance having added much to the general Conduct of Armies then in use.

As I met the *Swedes* on their March I had no Opportunity to acquaint my self with any Body 'till after the Conjunction of the *Saxon* Army, and then it being but four Days to the great Battle of *Leipsick*, our Acquaintance was but small, saving what fell out accidentally by Conversation.

I met with several Gentlemen in the King's Army who spoke *English* very well, besides that there were 3 Regiments of *Scots* in the Army, the Collonels whereof I found were extraordinarily esteemed by the King, as the Lord *Rea*, Collonel *Lumsdell*, and Sir *John Hepburn*: The latter of these, after I had by an Accident become acquainted with, I found had been for many Years acquainted with my Father, and on that Account I received a great deal of Civility from him, which afterwards grew into a kind of intimate Friendship; he was a compleat Soldier indeed, and for that Reason so well beloved by that gallant King, that he hardly knew how to go about any great Action without him.

It was impossible for me now to restrain my young Comrade from entring into the *Swedish* Service, and indeed every Thing was so inviting that I could not blame him. A Captain in Sir *John Hepburn*'s Regiment had picked Acquaintance with him, and he having as much Gallantry in his Face as real Courage in his Heart, the Captain had persuaded him to take Service, and promised to use his Interest to get him a Company in the *Scotch* Brigade. I had made him promise me not to part from me in my Travels without my Consent, which was the only Obstacle to his Desires of entring in the *Swedish* Pay; and being one Evening in the Captain's Tent with him, and discoursing very freely together, the Captain asked him very short but friendly, and looking earnestly at me, *Is this the Gentleman, Mr.* Fielding, *that has done so much Prejudice to the King of* Sweden'*s Service?* I was doubly surprized at the Expression, and at the Collonel, Sir *John Hepburn*, coming at that very Moment into the Tent; the Collonel hearing something of the Question, but knowing nothing of the Reason of it, any more than as I seemed a little to concern my self at it; yet after the Ceremony due to his Character was over, would needs know what I had done to hinder his Majesty's Service. *So much truly*, says the Captain, *that if his Majesty knew it he would think himself very little beholding to him. I am sorry, Sir*, says I, *that I should offend in any Thing, who am but a Stranger; but if you would please to inform me, I would endeavour to alter any Thing in my Behaviour that is prejudicial to any one, much less to his Majesty's Service. I shall take you at your Word, Sir*, says the Captain; *the King of* Sweden, *Sir, has a particular Request to you. I should be glad to know two Things, Sir*, said I, *First, How that can be possible, since I am not known yet to any Man in the Army, much less to his Majesty? And, Secondly, What the Request can be? Why, Sir, his Majesty desires you would not hinder this Gentleman from entring into his Service, who it seems desires nothing more, if he may have your Consent to it. I have too much Honour for his Majesty*, return'd I, *to deny any Thing which he pleases to command me; but methinks 'tis some Hardship, you should make that the King's Order, which 'tis very probable he knows nothing of.* Sir *John Hepburn* took the Case up something gravely, and drinking a Glass of *Leipsick* Beer to the Captain, said, *Come, Captain, don't press these Gentlemen; the King desires no Man's Service but what is purely Voluntier.* So we entred into other Discourse, and the Collonel perceiving by my Talk that I had seen *Tilly*'s Army, was mighty curious in his Questions, and seemed very well satisfied with the Account I gave him.

The next Day the Army having pass'd the *Elbe* at *Wittemberg*, and joyn'd the *Saxon* Army near *Torgau*[1] his Majesty caused both Armies to draw up in Battalia, giving every Brigade the same Post in the Lines as he purposed to fight in: I must do the Memory of that glorious General this Honour, that I never saw an Army drawn up with so much Variety, Order, and exact Regularity since, tho' I have seen many Armies drawn up by some of the greatest Captains of the Age; the Order by which his Men were directed to flank and relieve one another, the Methods of receiving one Body of Men if disordered into another, and rallying one Squadron, without disordering another was so admirable; the Horse every where flank'd, lin'd and defended by the Foot, and the Foot by the Horse, and both by the Cannon, was such, that if those Orders were but as punctually obey'd, 'twere impossible to put an Army so modell'd into any Confusion.

The View being over, and the Troops return'd to their Camps, the Captain with whom we drank the Day before meeting me, told me I must come and sup with him in his Tent, where he would ask my Pardon for the Affront he gave me before. I told him he needed not put himself to the Trouble; I was not affronted at all, that I would do my self the Honour to wait on him, provided he wou'd give me his Word not to speak any more of it as an Affront.

We had not been a quarter of an Hour in his Tent but Sir *John Hepburn* came in again, and addressing to me, told me he was glad to find me there; that he came to the Captain's Tent to enquire how to send to me; and that I must do him the Honour to go with him to wait on the King, who had a Mind to hear the Account I could give him of the *Imperial* Army from my own Mouth. I must confess I was at some Loss in my Mind how to make my Address to his Majesty; but I had heard so much of the conversible Temper of the King, and his particular Sweetness of Humour with the meanest Soldier, that I made no more Difficulty, but having paid my Respects to Collonel *Hepburn*, thank'd

him for the Honour he had done me, and offer'd to rise and
wait upon him: Nay, says the Collonel, we will eat first, for
I find *Gourdon*, which was the Captain's Name, has got
something for Supper, and the King's Order is at seven a
Clock: So we went to Supper, and Sir *John* becoming very
friendly, must know my Name; which, when I had told him,
and of what Place and Family, he rose from his Seat and
embracing me, told me he knew my Father very well, and
had been intimately acquainted with him; and told me several
Passages wherein my Father had particularly obliged him.
After this we went to Supper, and the King's Health being
drank round, the Collonel moved the sooner because he had
a Mind to talk with me; when we were going to the King,
he enquired of me where I had been, and what Occasion
brought me to the Army. I told him the short History of my
Travels, and that I came hither from *Vienna* on purpose to
see the King of *Sweden* and his Army; he ask'd me if there
was any Service he could do me, by which he meant,
whether I desired an Employment; I pretended not to take
him so, but told him the Protection his Acquaintance would
afford me was more than I could have ask'd, since I might
thereby have Opportunity to satisfie my Curiosity, which was
the chief End of my coming abroad. He perceiving by this
that I had no Mind to be a Soldier, told me very kindly I
should command him in any thing; that his Tent and
Equipage, Horses and Servants should always have Orders
to be at my Service: But that as a Piece of Friendship, he
would advise me to retire to some Place distant from the
Army, for that the Army wou'd march to morrow, and the
King was resolved to fight General *Tilly*, and he wou'd not
have me hazard my self; that if I thought fit to take his
Advice, he wou'd have me take that Interval to see the Court
at *Berlin*, whither he would send one of his Servants to wait
on me: His Discourse was too kind not to extort the tenderest
Acknowledgement from me that I was capable of; I told
him his Care of me was so obliging, that I knew not what
Return to make him, but if he pleased to leave me to my

Choice I desired no greater Favour than to trail a Pike under his Command in the ensuing Battle. I can never answer it to your Father, says he, to suffer you to expose your self so far. I told him my Father would certainly acknowledge his Friendship in the Proposal made me; but I believ'd he knew him better than to think he wou'd be well pleas'd with me if I should accept of it; that I was sure my Father would have rod[e] Post 500 Miles to have been at such a Battle under such a General, and it should never be told him that his Son had rod[e] 50 Miles to be out of it: He seem'd to be something concern'd at the Resolution I had taken, and replied very quickly upon me, that he approved very well of my Courage; but, says he, no Man gets any Credit by running upon needless Adventures, nor loses any by shunning Hazards which he has no Order for. 'Tis enough, says he, for a Gentleman to behave well when he is commanded upon any Service; I have had fighting enough, says he, upon these Points of Honour, and I never got any thing but Reproof for it from the King himself. Well, Sir, said I, however if a Man expects to rise by his Valour, he must shew it somewhere; and if I were to have any Command in an Army, I wou'd first try whether I could deserve it; I have never yet seen any Service, and must have my Induction some time or other: I shall never have a better Schoolmaster than your self, nor a better School than such an Army. Well, says Sir *John*, but you may have the same School and the same teaching after this Battle is over; for I must tell you before-hand, this will be a bloody Touch;[1] *Tilly* has a great Army of old Lads that are used to boxing; Fellows with Iron Faces, and 'tis a little too much to engage so hotly the first Entrance into the Wars: You may see our Discipline this Winter, and make your Campaign with us next Summer, when you need not fear but we shall have fighting enough, and you will be better acquainted with Things: We do never put our common Soldiers upon Pitcht Battles the first Campaign, but place our new Men in Garrisons and try them in Parties first. Sir, said I with a little more Freedom,

I believe I shall not make a Trade of the War, and therefore need not serve an Apprenticeship to it: 'Tis a hard Battle where none escapes: If I come off, I hope I shall not disgrace you, and if not, 'twill be some Satisfaction to my Father to hear his Son died fighting, under the Command of Sir *John Hepburn* in the Army of the King of *Sweden*, and I desire no better Epitaph upon my Tomb. Well, says Sir *John*, and by this time we were just come to the King's Quarters, and the Guards calling to us interrupted his Reply; so we went into the Court Yard where the King was lodg'd, which was in an indifferent House of one of the Burghers of *Debien*, and Sir *John* stepping up, met the King coming down some Steps into a large Room which looked over the Town-Wall into a Field where Part of the Artillery was drawn up. Sir *John Hepburn* sent his Man presently to me to come up, which I did; and Sir *John* without any Ceremony carries me directly up to the King, who was leaning on his Elbow in the Window: The King turning about, this is the *English* Gentleman, says Sir *John*, who I told your Majesty had been in the *Imperial* Army. How then did he get hither, says the King, without being taken by the Scouts? At which Question Sir *John* saying nothing; By a Pass, and please your Majesty, from the *English* Ambassador's Secretary at *Vienna*, said I, making a profound Reverence. Have you then been at *Vienna*, says the King? Yes, and please your Majesty, said I; upon which the King folding up a Letter he had in his Hand, seemed much more earnest to talk about *Vienna*, than about *Tilly*: And pray what News had you at *Vienna*? Nothing, Sir, said I, but daily Accounts one in the Neck of another of their own Misfortunes, and your Majesty's Conquests, which makes a very melancholy Court there. But pray, said the King, what is the common Opinion there about these Affairs? The common People are terrified to the last Degree, said I, and when your Majesty took *Frankfort* upon *Oder*, if your Army had march'd but 20 Miles into *Silesia*, half the People wou'd have run out of *Vienna*, and I left them fortifying the City. They need not, reply'd the

King smiling, I have no Design to trouble them, 'tis the
Protestant Countries I must be for: Upon this the Duke of
Saxony entred the Room, and finding the King engag'd,
offer'd to retire; but the King beckoning with his Hand
call'd to him in *French*, Cousin, says the King, this Gentleman has been travelling and comes from *Vienna*, and so
made me repeat what I had said before; at which the King
went on with me, and Sir *John Hepburn* informing his
Majesty that I spoke high *Dutch*, he changed his Language,
and ask'd me in *Dutch* where it was that I saw General
Tilly's Army; I told his Majesty at the Siege of *Magdeburgh*.
At *Magdeburgh*. said the King shaking his Head, *Tilly* must
answer to me one Day for that *City*, and if not to me to a
greater King than I: Can you guess what Army he had with
him, said the King? He had two Armies with him, said I,
but one I suppose will do your Majesty no harm: Two
Armies! said the King. Yes Sir, he has one Army of about
26000 Men, said I, and another of above 15000 Whores and
their Attendants; at which the King laughed heartily; Ay,
ay, says the King, those 15000 do us as much Harm as the
26000; for they eat up the Country, and devour the poor
Protestants more than the Men; Well, says the King, do
they talk of fighting us? They talk big enough, Sir, said I,
but your Majesty has not been so often fought with as
beaten in their Discourse. I know not for the Men, says the
King, but the old Man is as likely to do it as talk of it, and
I hope to try them in a Day or two: The King enquired after
that, several Matters of me about the *Low Countries*, the
Prince of *Orange*, and of the Court and Affairs in *England*;
and Sir *John Hepburn* informing his Majesty that I was the
Son of an *English* Gentleman of his Acquaintance, the King
had the Goodness to ask him what Care he had taken of me
against the Day of Battle. Upon which Sir *John* repeated to
him the Discourse we had together by the Way; the King
seeming particularly pleased with it, began to take me to
Task himself: You *English* Gentlemen, says he, are too
forward in the Wars, which makes you leave them too soon

again. Your Majesty, reply'd I, makes War in so pleasant a Manner, as makes all the World fond of fighting under your Conduct. Not so pleasant neither, says the King, here's a Man can tell you that sometimes 'tis not very pleasant. I know not much of the Warrior, Sir, said I, nor of the World, but if always to conquer be the Pleasure of the War, your Majesty's Soldiers have all that can be desired. Well, says the King, but however considering all Things, I think you would do well to take the Advice Sir *John Hepburn* has given you. Your Majesty may command me to any Thing, but where your Majesty and so many gallant Gentleman hazard their Lives, mine is not worth mentioning; and I should not dare to tell my Father at my return into *England* that I was in your Majesty's Army, and made so mean a Figure that your Majesty would not permit me to fight under that Royal Standard. Nay, replied the King, I lay no Commands upon you, but you are young. I can never dye, Sir, said I, with more Honour than in your Majesty's Service; I spake this with so much Freedom, and his Majesty was so pleased with it, that he asked me how I would choose to serve, on Horseback or on Foot; I told his Majesty I should be glad to receive any of his Majesty's Commands, but if I had not that Honour I had purpos'd to trail a Pike under Sir *John Hepburn*, who had done me so much Honour as to introduce me into his Majesty's Presence. Do so then, reply'd the King, and turning to Sir *John Hepburn*, said, and pray do you take Care of him; at which overcome with the Goodness of his Discourse I could not answer a Word, but made him a profound Reverence and retired.

The next Day but one, being the Seventh of *September*, before Day the Army march'd from *Dieben* to a large Field[1] about a Mile from *Leipsick*, where we found *Tilly*'s Army in full Battalia in admirable Order, which made a shew both glorious and terrible. *Tilly*, like a fair Gamster, had taken up but one Side of the Plain, and left the other free, and all the Avenues open for the King's Army; nor did he stir to the Charge 'till the King's Army was compleatly drawn up and advanced towards him: He had in his Army 44000 old Soldiers, every Way answerable to what I have said of them before; and I shall only add, a better Army I believe never was so soundly beaten.

The King was not much inferior in Force, being joined with the *Saxons*, who were reckoned 22000 Men, and who drew up on the Left, making a main Battle and two Wings, as the King did on the Right.

The King placed himself at the right Wing of his own Horse; *Gustavus Horn* had the main Battle of the *Swedes*, the Duke of *Saxony* had the main Battle of his own Troops, and General *Arnheim* the right Wing of his Horse.

The second Line of the *Swedes* consisted of the two *Scotch* Brigades, and three *Swedish*, with the *Finland* Horse in the Wings.

In the beginning of the Fight, *Tilly*'s right Wing charg'd with such irresistible Fury upon the Left of the King's Army where the *Saxons* were posted, that nothing could withstand them; the *Saxons* fled amain, and some of them carried the News over the Country that all was lost, and the King's Army overthrown; and indeed it passed for an Oversight with some, that the King did not place some of his old Troops among the *Saxons* who were new raised Men; the *Saxons* lost here near 2000 Men, and hardly ever shew'd their Faces again all the Battle, except some few of their Horse.

I was posted with my Comrade, the Captain, at the Head of three *Scottish* Regiments of Foot, commanded by Sir *John Hepburn*, with express Directions from the Collonel to keep by him: Our Post was in the second Line, as a Reserve to the King of *Sweden*'s main Battle, and which was strange, the main Battle, which consisted of four great Brigades of Foot, were never charged during the whole Fight; and yet we, who had the Reserve, were obliged to endure the whole Weight of the *Imperial* Army; the Occasion was, the right Wing of the *Imperialists* having defeated the *Saxons*, and being eager in the Chace, *Tilly*, who was an old Soldier, and

ready to prevent all Mistakes, forbids any Pursuit; let them
go, says he, but let us beat the *Swedes*, or we do nothing.
Upon this the victorious Troops fall in upon the Flank of
the King's Army, which the *Saxons* being fled lay open to
them; *Gustavus Horn* commanded the left Wing of the
Swedes, and having first defeated some Regiments which
charged him, falls in upon the Rear of the *Imperial* right
Wing, and separates them from the Van, who were advanced
a great Way forward in pursuit of the *Saxons*; and having
routed the said Rear or Reserve, falls on upon *Tilly's* main
Battle, and defeated Part of them, the other Part was gone in
Chase of the *Saxons*, and now also returned, fell in upon the
Rear of the left Wing of the *Swedes*, charging them in the
Flank; for they drew up upon the very Ground which the
Saxons had quitted. This changed the whole Front, and
made the *Swedes* face about to the Left, and make a great
Front on their Flank to make this good; our Brigades, who
were placed as a Reserve for the main Battle, were by special
Order from the King, wheeled about to the Left, and placed
for the Right of this new Front to charge the *Imperialists*;
they were about 12 Thousand of their best Foot, besides
Horse; and flusht with the Execution of the *Saxons*, fell on
like Furies: The King by this time had almost defeated the
Imperialist's left Wing; their Horse with more Haste than
good Speed, had charged faster than their Foot could follow,
and having broke into the King's first Line, he let them go;
where, while the second Line bears the Shock, and bravely
resisted them; the King follows them on the Crupper with
13 Troops of Horse, and some Musqueteers, by which
being hemm'd in, they were all cut down in a Moment as it
were, and the Army never disordered with them. This fatal
Blow to the left Wing, gave the King more Leisure to defeat
the Foot which followed, and to send some Assistance to
Gustavus Horn in his left Wing, who had his Hands full with
the main Battle of the *Imperialists*.

But those Troops who, as I said, had routed the *Saxons*,
being called off from the Pursuit, had charged our Flank,

and were now grown very strong, renewed the Battle in a
terrible Manner: Here it was I saw our Men go to Wrack;
Collonel *Hall*, a brave Soldier, commanded the Rear of the
Swedes left Wing; he fought like a Lion, but was slain, and
most of his Regiment cut off, tho' not unrevenged; for they
entirely ruined *Furstemberg*'s Regiment of Foot: Collonel
Cullembach with his Regiment of Horse, was extreamly over-
laid also, and the Collonel and many brave Officers killed,
and in short all that Wing was shattered, and in an ill
Condition.

In this Juncture came the King, and having seen what
Havock the Enemy made of *Cullembach*'s Troops, he comes
riding along the Front of our three Brigades, and himself
led us on to the Charge; the Collonel of his Guards, the
Baron *Dyvel*, was shot dead just as the King had given him
some Orders: When the *Scots* advanced, seconded by some
Regiments of Horse which the King also sent to the Charge,
the bloodiest Fight began that ever Man beheld, for the
Scotish Brigades giving Fire three Ranks at a Time over
one anothers Heads, pour'd in their Shot so thick, that the
Enemy were cut down like Grass before a Scyth; and following into the thickest of their Foot with the Clubs of their
Musquets, made a most dreadful Slaughter, and yet was
there no flying; *Tilly*'s Men might be killed and knocked
down, but no Man turned his Back, nor would give an Inch
of Ground, but as they were wheel'd, or marched, or retreated by their Officers.

There was a Regiment of Cuirassiers, which stood whole
to the last, and fought like Lions, they went ranging over the
Field when all their Army was broken, and no Body cared
for charging them; they were commanded by Baron *Cronenburgh*, and at last went off from the Battle whole. These
were armed in black Armour from Head to Foot, and they
carried off their General;[1] about Six a Clock the Field was
cleared of the Enemy, except at one Place on the King's
Side, where some of them rallied, and though they knew all
was lost would take no Quarter, but fought it out to the last

Man, being found dead the next Day in Rank and File as they were drawn up.

I had the good Fortune to receive no Hurt in this Battle, excepting a small Scratch on the side of my Neck by the push of a Pike; but my Friend received a very dangerous Wound when the Battle was as good as over; he had engaged with a *German* Collonel whose Name we could never learn, and having killed his Man, and pressed very close upon him so that he had shot his Horse, the Horse in the fall kept the Collonel down, lying on one of his Legs, upon which he demanded Quarter, which Captain *Feilding* granting, helped him to quit his Horse, and having disarmed him, was bringing him into the Line, when the Regiment of Cuirassiers, which I mentioned, commanded by Baron *Cronenburgh*, came roving over the Field, and with a flying Charge saluted our Front with a Salvo of Carabin-shot, which wounded us a great many Men, and among the rest the Captain received a Shot in his Thigh, which laid him on the Ground, and being separated from the Line, his Prisoner got away with them.

This was the first Service I was in, and indeed I never saw any Fight since maintained with such Gallantry, such desperate Valour, together with such Dexterity of Management, both Sides being composed of Soldiers fully tried, bred to the Wars, expert in every Thing, exact in their Order, and uncapable of Fear, which made the Battle be much more bloody than usual. Sir *John Hepburn*, at my Request, took particular Care of my Comrade, and sent his own Surgeon to look after him; and afterwards when the City of *Leipsick* was retaken, provided him Lodgings there, and came very often to see him; and indeed I was in great Care for him too, the Surgeons being very doubtful of him a great while; for having lain in the Field all Night among the Dead, his Wound, for want of dressing, and with the Extremity of Cold, was in a very ill Condition, and the Pain of it had thrown him into a Fever. 'Twas quite dusk before the Fight ended, especially where the last rallied Troops fought so long, and therefore we durst not break our Order to seek out our Friends, so that 'twas near seven o'Clock the next Morning before we found the Captain, who though very weak by the loss of Blood, had raised himself up, and placed his Back against the Buttock of a dead Horse; I was the first that knew him, and running to him, embraced him with a great deal of Joy: He was not able to speak, but made Signs to let me see he knew me, so we brought him into the Camp, and Sir *John Hepburn*, as I noted before, sent his own Surgeons to look after him.

The Darkness of the Night prevented any Pursuit, and was the only Refuge the Enemy had left; for had there been three Hours more Day-light, ten Thousand more Lives had been lost, for the *Swedes* (and *Saxons* especially) enraged by the Obstinacy of the Enemy, were so thoroughly heated that they would have given Quarter but to few; the Retreat was not sounded 'till seven o'Clock, when the King drew up the whole Army upon the Field of Battle, and gave strict Command that none should stir from their Order;[1] so the Army lay under their Arms all Night, which was another reason why the wounded Soldiers suffered very much by the Cold; for the King, who had a bold Enemy to deal with, was not ignorant what a small Body of desperate Men rallied together might have done in the Darkness of the Night, and therefore he lay in his Coach all Night at the Head of the Line, though it froze very hard.

As soon as the Day began to peep the Trumpets sounded to Horse, and all the Dragoons and Light Horse in the Army were commanded to the Pursuit; the Cuirassiers and some commanded Musqueteers advanced some Miles, if need were, to make good their Retreat, and all the Foot stood to their Arms for a Reserve; but in half an Hour Word was brought to the King, that the Enemy was quite dispersed, upon which Detachments were made out of every Regiment to search among the Dead for any of our Friends that were wounded; and the King himself gave a strict Order, that if any were found wounded and alive among the Enemy none should kill them, but take Care to bring them into the Camp: A Piece of Humanity which saved the Lives of near a Thousand of the Enemies.

This Piece of Service being over, the Enemy's Camp was seized upon, and the Soldiers were permitted to plunder it; all the Cannon, Arms, and Ammunition was secured for the King's Use, the rest was given up to the Soldiers, who found so much Plunder that they had no Reason to quarrel for Shares.

For my share, I was so busie with my wounded Captain that I got nothing but a Sword, which I found just by him when I first saw him; but my Man brought me a very good Horse with a Furniture on him, and one Pistol of extraordinary Workmanship.

I bad him get upon his Back and make the best of the Day for himself, which he did, and I saw him no more till three Days after, when he found me out at *Leipsick* so richly dressed that I hardly knew him; and after making his Excuse for his long Absence, gave me a very pleasant Account where he had been: He told me, that according to my Order being mounted on the Horse he had brought me, he first rid into the Field among the Dead, to get some Clothes suitable to the Equipage of his Horse, and having seized on a laced Coat, a Helmet, a Sword, and an extraordinary good Cane, was resolved to see what was become of the Enemy, and following the Track of the Dragoons, which he could easily do by the Bodies on the Road, he fell in with a small Party of 25 Dragoons, under no Command but a Corporal, making to a Village where some of the Enemies Horse had been quartered; the Dragoons taking him for an Officer by his Horse, desired him to command them, told him the Enemy was very rich, and they doubted not a good Booty: He was a bold brisk Fellow, and told them, with all his Heart; but said he had but one Pistol, the other being broke with firing, so they lent him a pair of Pistols, and a small Piece they had taken, and he led them on. There had been a Regiment of Horse and some Troops of *Crabats*[1] in the Village, but they were fled on the first Notice of the Pursuit, excepting three Troops, and these on Sight of this small Party, supposing them to be only the first of a greater Number, fled in the greatest Confusion imaginable; they took the Village and about 50 Horses, with all the Plunder of the Enemy, and with the Heat of the Service he had spoiled my Horse, he said, for which he had brought me two more; for he passing for the Commander of the Party, had all the Advantage the Custom of War gives an Officer in like Cases.

I was very well pleased with the Relation the Fellow gave me, and laughing at him, *Well, Captain*, said I, *and what Plunder have ye got? Enough to make me a Captain, Sir*, says he, *if you please, and a Troop ready raised too; for the Party of Dragoons are posted in the Village by my Command, till they have farther Orders.* In short, he pulled out 60 or 70 Pieces of Gold, 5 or 6 Watches, 13 or 14 Rings, whereof 2 were diamond Rings, one of which was worth 50 Dollars; Silver as much as his Pockets would hold, besides that he had brought three Horses, two of which were laden with Baggage, and a Boor he had hired to stay with them at *Leipsick* till he had found me out. *But I am afraid Captain*, says I, *you have plundered the Village instead of plundering the Enemy. No indeed not we*, says he, *but the* Crabats *had done it for us, and we light of*[1] *them just as they were carrying it off. Well*, said I, *but what will you do with your Men; for when you come to give them Orders, they will know you well enough? No, no*, says he, *I took Care of that; for just now I gave a Soldier five Dollars to carry them News that the Army was marched to* Moersburgh, *and that they should follow thither to the Regiment*.

Having secured his Money in my Lodgings, he asked me if I pleased to see his Horses, and to have one for my self? I told him I would go and see them in the Afternoon; but the Fellow being impatient goes and fetches them: There was three Horses, one whereof was a very good one, and by the Furniture was an Officer's Horse of the *Crabats*, and that my Man would have me accept, for the other he had spoiled, as he said; I was but indifferently horsed before, so I accepted of the Horse, and went down with him to see the rest of his Plunder there; he had got three or four pair of Pistols, two or three Bundles of Officers Linen and Lace, a Field-Bed and a Tent, and several other Things of Value; but at last coming to a small Fardel, and this, says he, I took whole from a *Crabat* running away with it under his Arm, so he brought it up into my Chamber; he had not looked into it, he said, but he understood 'twas some Plunder the Soldiers had made, and finding it heavy took it by Consent; we opened it and found 'twas a Bundle of some Linen, 13 or 14 Pieces of Plate, and in a small Cup three Rings, a fine Necklace of Pearl, and the Value of 100 Rix-dollars[1] in Money. The Fellow was amazed at his own good Fortune, and hardly knew what to do with himself: I bid him go take Care of his other Things, and of his Horses, and come again; so he went and discharged the Boor that waited, and packed up all his Plunder, and came up to me in his old Clothes again. *How now, Captain,* says I, *what have you altered your Equipage already? I am no more ashamed, Sir, of your Livery,* answered he, *than of your Service, and nevertheless your Servant for what I have got by it. Well,* says I to him, *but what will you do now with all your Money? I wish my poor Father had some of it,* says he, *and for the rest I got it for you, Sir, and desire you would take it.* He spoke it with so much Honesty and Freedom that I could not but take it very kindly; but however, I told him I would not take a Farthing from him, as his Master; but I would have him play the good Husband with it now he had such good Fortune to get it: He told me he would take my Directions in every Thing. *Why then,* says I, *I'll tell you what I would advise you to do, turn it all into ready Money, and convey it by Return home into* England, *and follow your self the first Opportunity, and with good Management you may put your self in a good Posture of living with it.* The Fellow, with a sort of Dejection in his Looks, asked me, if he had disobliged me in any Thing?

Why, says I: That I was willing to turn him out of his Service. *No*, George, (that was his Name) says I, *but you may live on this Money without being a Servant. I'd throw it all into the* Elbe, says he, *over* Torgaw *Bridge, rather than leave your Service; and besides*, says he, *can't I save my Money without going from you? I got it in your Service, and I'll never spend it out of your Service, unless you put me away. I hope my Money won't make me the worse Servant, if I thought it would, I'd soon have little enough. Nay*, George, says I, *I shall not oblige you to it, for I am not willing to lose you neither: come then*, says I, *let us put it all together, and see what it will come to.* So he laid it all together on the Table, and by our Computation he had gotten as much Plunder as was worth about 1400 Rix-dollars, besides 3 Horses with their Furniture, a Tent, a Bed, and some wearing Linen. Then he takes the Necklace of Pearl, a very good Watch, a Diamond Ring, and 100 Pieces of Gold, and lays them by themselves, and having according to our best Calculation valued the Things, he put up all the rest, and as I was going to ask him what they were left out for, he takes them up in his Hand, and coming round the Table, told me, that if I did not think him unworthy of my Service and Favour, he begged I would give him leave to make that Present to me; that it was my first thought, his going out; that he had got it all in my Service, and he should think I had no Kindness for him if I should refuse it. I was resolved in my Mind not to take it from him, and yet I could find no Means to resist his Importunity; at last I told him, I would accept of Part of his Present, and that I esteemed his Respect in that as much as the whole; and that I would not have him importune me farther, so I took the Ring and Watch with the Horse and Furniture as before, and made him turn all the rest into Money at *Leipsick*, and not suffering him to wear his Livery, made him put himself into a tolerable Equipage, and taking a young *Leipsicker* into my Service, he attended me as a Gentleman from that Time forward.

The King's Army never entred *Leipsick* but proceeded to

Moersburg, and from thence to *Hall* and so marched on into
Franconia, while the Duke of *Saxony* employed his Forces
in recovering *Leipsick* and the driving the *Imperialists* out of
his Country. I continued at *Leipsick* 12 Days, being not
willing to leave my Comrade 'till he was recovered; but Sir
John Hepburn so often importuned me to come into the
Army, and sent me Word that the King had very often
enquired for me, that at last I consented to go without him;
so having made our Appointment where to meet and how to
correspond by Letters, I went to wait on Sir *John Hepburn*,
who then lay with the King's Army at the City of *Erfurt* in
Saxony. As I was riding between *Leipsick* and *Hall* I observed
my Horse went very aukwardly and uneasy, and sweat very
much, though the Weather was cold, and we had rid but
very softly; I fancied therefore that the Saddle might hurt
the Horse, and calls my new Captain up; *George* say I, I
believe this Saddle hurts the Horse; so we alighted and
looking under the Saddle found the Back of the Horse
extreamly galled; so I bid him take off the Saddle, which
he did, and giving the Horse to my young *Leipsicker* to lead,
we sat down to see if we could mend it, for there was no
Town near us; Says *George*, pointing with his Finger, if you
please to cut open the Pannel there, I'll get something to
stuff into it which will bear it from the Horse's Back; so
while he look'd for something to thrust in, I cut a Hole in
the Pannel of the Saddle, and following it with my Finger
I felt something hard, which seemed to move up and down;
again as I thrust it with my Finger, here's something that
should not be here, says I, not yet imagining what afterwards
fell out, and calling, run back, bad him put up his Finger;
whatever 'tis, says he, 'tis this hurts the Horse, for it bears
just on his Back when the Saddle is set on; so we strove to
take hold on it, but could not reach it; at last we took the
upper Part of the Saddle quite from the Pannel, and there
lay a small Silk Purse wrapt in a Piece of Leather, and full
of Gold Ducats; thou art born to be rich, *George*, says I to
him, here's more Money, we opened the Purse and found

in it 438 small Pieces of Gold, there I had a new Skirmish with him whose the Money should be; I told him 'twas his, he told me no, I had accepted of the Horse and Furniture and all that was about him was mine, and solemnly vow'd he wou'd not have a Penny of it: I saw no Remedy but put up the Money for the Present, mended our Saddle, and went on; we lay that Night at *Hall*, and having had such a Booty in the Saddle, I made him search the Saddles of the other two Horses; in one of which, we found Three *French* Crowns, but nothing in the other.

We arrived at *Erfurt* the 28th of *September*, but the Army was removed,[1] and entred into *Franconia*, and at the Siege of *Koningshoven* we came up with them. The first thing I did, was to pay my Civilities to Sir *John Hepburn*, who received me very kindly, but told me withal, that I had not done well to be so long from him; that the King had particularly enquired for me, had commanded him to bring me to him at my return: I told him the Reason of my Stay at *Leipsick*, and how I had left that Place and my Comrade, before he was cured of his Wounds, to wait on him according to his Letters. He told me the King had spoken some Things very obliging about me, and he believed would offer me some Command in the Army, if I thought well to accept of it; I told him I had promised my Father not to take Service in an Army without his Leave; and yet if his Majesty should offer it, I neither knew how to resist it, nor had I an Inclination to any thing more than the Service, and such a Leader; tho' I had much rather have serv'd as a Volunteer at my own Charge, (which as he knew was the Custom of our *English* Gentlemen) than in any Command. He replied, do as you think fit; but some Gentlemen would give 20000 Crowns to stand so fair for Advancement as you do.

The Town of *Koningshoven* capitulated that Day,[2] and Sir *John* was ordered to treat with the Citizens, so I had no farther Discourse with him then; and the Town being taken, the Army immediately advanced down the River *Main*, for the King had his Eye upon *Frankfort* and *Mentz*, two great

Cities, both which he soon became Master of, chiefly by the prodigious Expedition of his March; For within a Month after the Battle, he was in the lower Parts of the Empire, and had passed from the *Elb* to the *Rhine*, an incredible Conquest; had taken all the Strong Cities, the Bishopricks of *Bambergh*, of *Wirtsburgh*, and almost all the Circle of *Franconia*, with Part of *Schawberland*; a Conquest large enough to be seven Year a making by the common Course of Arms.

Business going on thus, the King had not Leisure to think of small Matters, and I being not thoroughly resolved in my Mind, did not press Sir *John* to introduce me; I had wrote to my Father with an Account of my Reception in the Army, the Civilities of Sir *John Hepburn*, the Particulars of the Battle, and had indeed press'd him to give me Leave to serve the King of *Sweden*: To which Particular I waited for an Answer, but the following Occasion determined me before an Answer cou'd possibly reach me.

The King was before the Strong Castle of *Marienburgh*, which commands the City of *Wurtsburgh*; he had taken the *City*, but the Garrison and richer Part of the Burghers were retir'd into the Castle, and trusting to the Strength of the Place, which was thought impregnable, they bad the *Swedes* do their worst; twas well provided with all Things, and a strong Garrison in it; so that the Army indeed expected 'twould be a long Piece of Work. The Castle stood on a high Rock, and on the Steep of the Rock was a Bastion, which defended the only Passage up the Hill into the Castle; the *Scots* were chose out to make this attack, and the King was an Eye Witness of their Gallantry: In the Action Sir *John* was not commanded out, but Sir *James Ramsey* led them on, but I observed that most of the *Scotch* Officers in the other Regiments prepared to serve as Volunteers for the Honour of their Countrymen, and Sir *John Hepburn* led them on: I was resolved to see this Piece of Service, and therefore joined my self to the Volunteers; we were armed with Partizans, and each Man two Pistols at our Belt; it was a Piece of Service that seemed perfectly desperate, the

Advantage of the Hill, the Precipice we were to mount, the height of the Bastion, the resolute Courage and Number of the Garrison, who from a compleat Covert made a terrible Fire upon us, all joined to make the Action hopeless; but the Fury of the *Scots* Musqueteers was not to be abated by any Difficulties; they mounted the Hill, scaled the Works like Madmen, running upon the Enemies Pikes, and after two Hours' desperate Fight in the midst of Fire and Smoke, took it by Storm, and put all the Garrison to the Sword. The Voluntiers did their part, and had their Share of the Loss too, for 13 or 14 were killed out of 37, besides the wounded, among whom I received a Hurt more troublesome than dangerous, by a Thrust of a Halberd into my Arm, which proved a very painful Wound, and I was a great while before it was thoroughly recovered.

The King received us as we drew off at the Foot of the Hill, calling the Soldiers *his brave Scots*, and commending the Officers by Name. The next Morning the Castle was also taken by Storm, and the greatest Booty that ever was found in any one Conquest in the whole War; the Soldiers got here so much Money that they knew not what to do with it and the Plunder they got here and at the Battle of *Leipsick* made them so unruly, that had not the King been the best Master of Discipline in the World they had never been kept in any reasonable Bounds.

The King had taken Notice of our small Party of Voluntiers, and though I thought he had not seen me, yet he sent the next Morning for Sir *John Hepburn*, and asked him if I were not come to the Army? *Yes*, says Sir *John*, *he has been here two or three Days:* And as he was forming an Excuse for not having brought me to wait on his Majesty, says the King interrupting him, *I wonder you would let him thrust himself into such a hot Piece of Service as storming the* Port Graft: *Pray let him know I saw him, and have a very good Account of his Behaviour.* Sir *John* returned with this Account to me, and pressed me to pay my Duty to his Majesty the next Morning; and accordingly, though I had but an ill Night with the Pain of my Wound, I was with him at the Levee in the Castle.

I cannot but give some short Account of the Glory of that Morning; the Castle had been cleared of the dead Bodies of the Enemies, and what was not pillaged by the Soldiers, was placed under a Guard. There was first a Magazine of very good Arms for about 18 or 20000 Foot, and 4000 Horse, a very good Train of Artillery of about 18 Pieces of Battery, 32 brass Field-pieces and four Mortars. The Bishop's Treasure, and other publick Monies not plundered by the Soldiers, was telling out by the Officers, and amounted to 400000 Florins in Money; and the Burghers of the Town in solemn Procession, bareheaded, brought the King three Tun of Gold as a Composition to exempt the City from Plunder. Here was also a Stable of gallant Horses which the King had the Curiosity to go and see.[1]

When the Ceremony of the Burghers was over the King came down into the Castle Court, walked on the Parade (where the great Train of Artillery was placed on their Carriages) and round the Walls, and gave Order for repairing the Bastion that was stormed by the *Scots*; and as at the Entrance of the Parade Sir *John Hepburn* and I made our Reverence to the King, *Ho, Cavalier*, said the King to me, *I am glad to see you*, and so passed forward; I made my bow very low, but his Majesty said no more at that Time.

When the View was over the King went up into the Lodgings, and Sir *John* and I walked in an Anti-Chamber for about a Quarter of an Hour, when one of the Gentlemen of the Bed-Chamber came out to Sir *John*, and told him the King ask'd for him; he staid but a little with the King and came out to me, and told me the King had ordered him to bring me to him.

His Majesty, with a Countenance full of Honour and Goodness interrupted my Compliment, and asked me how I did; at which answering only with a bow, says the King, *I am sorry to see you are hurt, I would have laid my Commands on you not to have shewn your self in so sharp a Piece of Service, if I had known you had been in the Camp. Your Majesty does me too much Honour*, said I, *in your Care of a Life that has yet done nothing to deserve your Favour.* His Majesty was pleased to say something very kind to me relating to my Behaviour in the Battle of *Leipsick*, which I have not Vanity enough to write; at the Conclusion whereof, when I replyed very humbly, that I was not sensible that any Service I had done or could do could possibly merit so much Goodness; he told me he had ordered me a small Testimony of his Esteem, and withal gave me his Hand to kiss: I was now conquered, and with a sort of Surprize, told his Majesty, I found my self so much engaged by his Goodness, as well as my own Inclination, that if his Majesty would please to accept of my Devoir I was resolved to serve in his Army, or wherever he pleased to command me. *Serve me*, says the King, *why so you do, but I must not have you be a Musketeer; a poor Soldier at a Dollar a Week will do that. Pray*, Sir John, says the King, *give him what Commission he desires. No Commission, Sir*, says I, *would please me better than Leave to fight near your Majesty's Person, and to serve you at my own Charge till I am qualified by more Experience to receive your Commands. Why then it shall be so*, said the King, *and I charge you*, Hepburn, says he, *when any Thing offers that is either fit for him, or he desires, that you tell me of it*, and giving me his Hand again to kiss I withdrew.

I was followed before I had passed the Castle-Court by one of the King's Pages, who brought me a Warrant directed to Sir *John Hepburn* to go to the Master of the Horse for an immediate delivery of Things ordered by the King himself for my Account, where being come, the Querry produced me a very good Coach with four Horses, Harness and Equipage, and two very fine Saddle-Horses out of the Stable of the Bishop's Horses, afore-mentioned; with these there was a List for three Servants, and a Warrant to the Steward of the King's Baggage to defray me, my Horses and Servants at the King's Charge till farther Order. I was very much at a Loss how to manage my self in this so strange freedom of so great a Prince, and consulting with Sir *John Hepburn*, I was proposing to him whether it was not proper to go immediately back to pay my Duty to his Majesty and acknowledge his Bounty in the best Terms I could; but while we were resolving to do so, the Guards stood to their Arms, and we saw the King go out at the Gate in his Coach to pass into the City, so we were diverted from it for that Time. I acknowledge the Bounty of the King was very surprising, but I must say it was not so very strange to me when I afterward saw the Course of his Management; Bounty in him was his natural Talent, but he never distributed his Favours but where he thought himself both loved and faithfully served, and when he was so, even the single Actions of his private Soldiers he would take particular Notice of himself, and publickly own, acknowledge and reward them, of which I am obliged to give some Instances.

A private Musqueteer at the storming the Castle of *Wurtzberg*, when all the Detachment was beaten off, stood in the Face of the Enemy and fired his Piece, and though he had 1000 shot made at him, stood unconcerned, and charged his Piece again, and let fly at the Enemy, continuing to do so three Times, at the same Time beckoning with his Hand to his Fellows to come on again, which they did, animated by his Example, and carried the place for the King.

When the Town was taken the King ordered the Regiment to be drawn out, and calling for that Soldier, thanked him before them all for taking the Town for him, gave him 1000 Dollars in Money, and a Commission with his own Hand for a Foot Company, or Leave to go home, which he would; the Soldier took the Commission on his Knees, kissed it, and put it into his Bosom, and told the King, he would never leave his Service as long as he lived.

This Bounty of the King's, timed and suited by his Judgment, was the Reason that he was very well served, intirely beloved, and most punctually obeyed by his Soldiers, who were sure to be cherished and encouraged, if they did well, having the King generally an Eye-witness of their Behaviour.

My Indiscretion rather than Valour had engaged me so far at the Battle of *Leipsick*, that being in the Van of Sir *John Hepburn*'s Brigade, almost three whole Companies of us were separated from our Line, and surrounded by the Enemies Pikes; I cannot but say also that we were disengaged rather by a desperate Charge Sir *John* made with the whole Regiment to fetch us off, than by our own Valour, though we were not wanting to our selves neither, but this Part of the Action being talked of very much to the Advantage of the young *English* Voluntier, and possibly more than I deserved, was the Occasion of all the Distinction the King used me with ever after.

I had by this Time Letters from my Father, in which, though with some Reluctance, he left me at Liberty to enter into Arms if I thought fit, always obliging me to be directed, and, as he said, commanded by Sir *John Hepburn*; at the same Time he wrote to Sir *John Hepburn*, commending his Son's Fortunes, as he called it, to his Care; which Letters Sir *John* shewed the King, unknown to me.

I took Care always to acquaint my Father of every Circumstance, and forgot not to mention his Majesty's extraordinary Favour, which so affected my Father that he obtained a very honourable mention of it in a Letter from King *Charles* to the King of *Sweden*, written by his own Hand.

I had waited on his Majesty with Sir *John Hepburn*, to give him Thanks for his magnificent Present, and was received with his usual Goodness, and after that I was every Day among the Gentlemen of his ordinary Attendance; and if his Majesty went out on a Party, as he would often do, or to view the Country, I always attended him among the Voluntiers of whom a great many always followed him; and he would often call me out, talk with me, send me upon Messages to Towns, to Princes, free Cities, and the like, upon extraordinary Occasions.

The first Piece of Service he put me upon had like to have

embroiled me with one of his favourite Collonels; the King was marching through the *Bergstract*, a low Country on the edge of the *Rhine*, and, as all Men thought, was going to besiege *Heidelberg*, but on a sudden orders a Party of his Guards, with five Companies of *Scots*, to be drawn out; while they were drawing out this Detachment the King calls me to him, *Ho, Cavalier*, says he, *that was his usual Word, you shall command this Party*; and thereupon gives me Orders to march back all Night, and in the Morning, by break of Day, to take Post under the Walls of the Fort of *Oppenheim*, and immediately to entrench my self as well as I could: *Grave Neels*, the Collonel of his Guards, thought himself injured by this Command, but the King took the Matter upon himself, and *Grave Neels* told me very familiarly afterwards, We have such a Master, says he, that no Man can be affronted by: I thought my self wronged, says he, when you commanded my Men over my Head; and for my Life, says he, I knew not which way to be angry.

I executed my Commission so punctually that by break of Day I was set down within Musquet-shot of the Fort, under covert of a little Mount, on which stood a Wind-mill, and had indifferently fortified my self, and at the same Time had posted some of my Men on two other Passes, but at farther Distance from the Fort, so that the Fort was effectually block'd up on the Land-side; in the Afternoon the Enemy sallied on my first Entrenchment, but being covered from their Cannon, and defended by a Ditch which I had drawn cross the Road, they were so well received by my Musqueteers that they retired with the loss of 6 or 7 Men.

The next Day Sir *John Hepburn* was sent with two Brigades of Foot to carry on the Work, and so my Commission ended; the King expressed himself very well pleased with what I had done, and when he was so was never sparing of telling of it, for he used to say that publick Commendations were a great Encouragement to Valour.

While Sir *John Hepburn* lay before the Fort, and was preparing to storm it, the King's Design was to get over the

Rhine, but the *Spaniards* which were in *Oppenheim* had sunk all the Boats they could find; at last the King being informed where some lay that were sunk caused them to be weighed with all the Expedition possible, and in the Night of the 7th of *December* in three Boats passed over his Regiment of Guards, about three Miles above the Town, and as the King thought secure from Danger; but they were no sooner landed and not drawn into Order but they were charged by a Body of *Spanish* Horse, and had not the Darkness given them Opportunity to draw up in the Enclosures in several little Parties, they had been in great Danger of being disordered, but by this Means they lined the Hedges and Lanes so with Musqueteers, that the remainder had Time to draw up in Battalia, and saluted the Horse with their Musquets so that they drew farther off.

The King was very impatient, hearing his Men engaged, having no Boats nor possible Means to get over to help them; at last, about Eleven a Clock at Night the Boats came back, and the King thrust another Regiment into them, and though his Officers dissuaded him, would go over himself with them on Foot, and did so. This was three Months that very Day when the Battle of *Leipsick* was fought, and winter Time too, that the Progress of his Arms had spread from the *Elbe*, where it parts *Saxony* and *Brandenburgh*, to the *Lower Palatinate* and the *Rhine*.

I went over in the Boat with the King, I never saw him in so much Concern in my Life, for he was in Pain for his Men; but before we got on shore the *Spaniards* retired, however the King landed, ordered his Men, and prepared to entrench, but he had not Time; for by that Time the Boats were put off again, the *Spaniards*, not knowing more Troops were landed, and being reinforced from *Oppenheim*, came on again, and charged with great Fury; but all Things were now in Order; and they were readily received and beaten back again: They came on again the third Time, and with repeated Charges attacked us; but at last finding us too strong for them they gave it over. By this Time another

Regiment of Foot was come over, and as soon as Day appeared the King with the three Regiments marched to the Town, which surrendred at the first Summons, and the next Day the Fort yielded to Sir *John Hepburn*.

The Castle at *Oppenheim* held out still with a Garrison of 800 *Spaniards*, and the King leaving 200 *Scots* of Sir *James Ramsey*'s Men in the Town, drew out to attack the Castle; Sir *James Ramsey* being left wounded at *Wurtsburgh* the King gave me the Command of those 200 Men, which were a Regiment, that is to say, all that were left of a Gallant Regiment of 2000 *Scots* which the King brought out of *Sweden* with him, under that Brave Collonel; there was about 30 Officers, who having no Soldiers were yet in Pay, and served as Reformadoes with the Regiment, and were over and above the 200 Men.

The King designed to storm the Castle on the lower side by the Way that leads to *Mentz*, and Sir *John Hepburn* landed from the other Side and marched up to storm on the *Rhine* Port.

My Reformado *Scots* having observed that the Town Port of the Castle was not so well guarded as the rest, all the Eyes of the Garrison being bent towards the King and Sir *John Hepburn*; came running to me, and told me, they believed they could enter the Castle Sword in Hand if I would give them Leave; I told them I durst not give them Orders, my Commission being only to keep and defend the Town; but they being very importunate, I told them they were Voluntiers, and might do what they pleased, that I would lend them 50 Men and draw up the rest to second them, or bring them off, as I saw Occasion, so as I might not hazard the Town; this was as much as they desired, they sallied immediately, and in a trice the Voluntiers scaled the Port, cut in Pieces the Guard and burst open the Gate, at which the 50 entered: finding the Gate won I advanced immediately with 100 Musqueteers more, having locked up all the Gates of the Town but the Castle-Port, and leaving 50 still for a Reserve just at that Gate; the Townsmen too seeing the

Castle as it were taken, run to Arms, and followed me with above 200 Men; the *Spaniards* were knocked down by the *Scots* before they knew what the Matter was, and the King and Sir *John Hepburn* advancing to storm, were surprized, when instead of Resistance, they saw the *Spaniards* throwing themselves over the Walls to avoid the Fury of the *Scots*; few of the Garrison got away, but were either killed or taken, and having cleared the Castle, I set open the Port on the King's Side, and sent his Majesty Word the Castle was his own.[1] The King came on, and entered on Foot, I received him at the Head of the *Scots* Reformadoes, who all saluted him with their Pikes. The King gave them his Hat, and turning about, *Brave* Scots, *Brave* Scots, says he smiling, *you were too quick for me*; then beckoning to me, made me tell him how and in what Manner we had managed the Storm, which he was exceeding well pleased with, but especially at the Caution I had used to bring them off if they had miscarried, and secure the Town.

From hence the Army marched to *Mentz*, which in 4 Days Time capitulated,[2] with the Fort and Citadel, and the City paid his Majesty 300000 Dollars to be exempted from the Fury of the Soldiers; here the King himself drew the Plan of those invincible Fortifications which to this Day makes it one of the strongest Cities in *Germany*.

Friburg, Koningstien, Niustat, Keiser-Lautern, and almost all the *Lower Palatinate*, surrendered at the very Terror of the King of *Sweden*'s Approach, and never suffered the Danger of a Siege.

The King held a most Magnificent Court at *Mentz*, attended by the Landgrave of *Hesse*, with an incredible Number of Princes and Lords of the Empire, with Ambassadors and Residents of Foreign Princes; and here his Majesty staid till *March* when the Queen, with a great Retinue of *Swedish* Nobility came from *Erfurt* to see him. The King attended by a gallant Train of *German* Nobility went to *Frankfort*, and from thence on to *Hoest*, to meet the Queen,[3] where her Majesty arrived *Feb.* 8th.

During the King's stay in these Parts, his Armies were not idle, his Troops on one side under the *Rhinegrave*, a brave and ever-fortunate Commander, and under the Landgrave of *Hesse*, on the other, ranged the Country from *Lorrain* to *Luxemburgh*, and past the *Moselle* on the West, and the *Weser* on the North. Nothing could stand before them, the *Spanish* Army which came to the Relief of the Catholick Electors was every where defeated and beaten quite out of the Country, and the *Lorrain* Army quite ruined; 'twas a most pleasant Court sure as ever was seen, where every Day Expresses arrived of Armies defeated, Towns surrendered, Contributions agreed upon, Parties routed, Prisoners taken, and Princes sending Ambassadours to sue for Truces and Neutralities, to make Submissions and Compositions, and to pay Arrears and Contributions.

Here arrived, *Febr.* 10th, the King of *Bohemia* from *England*, and with him my Lord *Craven*, with a Body of *Dutch Horse*, and a very fine Train of *English* Voluntiers, who immediately, without any stay, marched on to *Hoest* to wait upon his Majesty of *Sweden*, who received him with a great deal of Civility, and was treated at a Noble Collation, by the King and Queen, at *Frankfort*. Never had the Unfortunate King so fair a Prospect of being restored to his Inheritance of the *Palatinate* as at that Time, and had King *James*, his Father-in-Law, had a Soul answerable to the Occasion, it had been effected before, but it was a strange Thing to see him equipped from the *English* Court with one Lord and about 40 or 50 *English Gentlemen* in his Attendance, whereas had the King of *England* now, as 'tis well known he might have done, furnished him with 10 or 12000 *English* Foot, nothing could have hindered him taking a full Possession of his Country; and yet even without that Help did the King of *Sweden* clear almost his whole Country of *Imperialists*, and after his Death, reinstal his Son in the Electorate, but no Thanks to us.

The Lord *Craven* did me the Honour to enquire for me by Name, and his Majesty of *Sweden* did me yet more by presenting me to the King of *Bohemia*, and my Lord *Craven* gave me a Letter from my Father, and speaking something of my Father having served under the Prince of *Orange* in the Famous Battle of *Neuport*,[1] the King smiling returned, *And pray tell him from me his Son has served as well in the warm Battle of* Leipsick.

My Father being very much pleased with the Honour I had received from so great a King, had ordered me to acquaint his Majesty, that if he pleased to accept of their Service he would raise him a Regiment of *English* Horse at his own Charge to be under my Command, and to be sent over into *Holland*; and my Lord *Craven* had Orders from the King of *England* to signify his Consent to the said Levy. I acquainted my old Friend Sir *John Hepburn* with the Contents of the Letter, in order to have his Advice, who being pleased with the Proposal, would have me go to the King immediately with the Letter, but present Service put it off for some Days.

The taking of *Creutznach* was the next Service of any Moment; the King drew out in Person to the Siege of this Town; the Town soon came to a Parly, but the Castle seemed a Work of Difficulty; for its Situation was so strong and so surrounded with Works behind and above one another, that most People thought the King would receive a Check from it; but it was not easy to resist the Resolution of the King of *Sweden*.

He never battered it but with two small Pieces, but having viewed the Works himself, ordered a Mine under the first Ravelin, which being sprung with Success, he commands a storm; I think there was not more commanded Men than Voluntiers, both *English*, *Scots*, *French* and *Germans*: My old Comrade was by this Time recovered of his Wound at *Leipsick*, and made one. The first Body of Voluntiers of about 40, were led on by my Lord *Craven*, and I led the second, among whom were most of the Reformado *Scots* Officers who took the Castle of *Oppenheim*; the first Party was not able to make any Thing of it, the Garrison fought with so much Fury that many of the Voluntier Gentlemen being

wounded, and some killed, the rest were beaten off with
Loss. The King was in some Passion at his Men, and rated
them for running away, as he called it, though they really
retreated in good Order, and commanded the Assault to be
renewed. 'Twas our Turn to fall on next; our *Scots* Officers
not being used to be beaten, advanced immediately, and my
Lord *Craven*, with his Voluntiers, pierced in with us,
fighting gallantly in the Breach with a Pike in his Hand, and
to give him the Honour due to his Bravery, he was with the
first on the Top of the Rampart, and gave his Hand to my
Comrade, and lifted him up after him; we helped one another up, till at last almost all the Voluntiers had gained the
Height of the Ravelin, and maintained it with a great Deal
of Resolution, expecting when the commanded Men had
gained the same Height to advance upon the Enemy, when
one of the Enemies Captains called to my Lord *Craven*, and
told him if they might have honourable Terms they would
capitulate, which my Lord telling him he would engage for,
the Garrison fired no more, and the Captain leaping down
from the next Rampart came with my Lord *Craven* into the
Camp, where the Conditions were agreed on, and the
Castle surrendered.[1]

After the taking of this Town, the King hearing of *Tilly*'s
Approach, and how he had beaten *Gustavus Horn*, the
King's Field Marshal out of *Bamberg*, began to draw his
Forces together, and leaving the Care of his Conquests in
these Parts to his Chancellor *Oxenstern*, prepares to advance
towards *Bavaria*.

I had taken an Opportunity to wait upon his Majesty with
Sir *John Hepburn*, and being about to introduce the Discourse of my Father's Letter, the King told me he had
received a Compliment on my account in a Letter from
King *Charles*: I told him his Majesty had by his exceeding
Generosity bound me and all my Friends to pay their
Acknowledgements to him, and that I supposed my Father
had obtained such a mention of it from the King of *England*
as Gratitude moved him to; that his Majesty's Favour had

been shewn in me to a Family both willing and ready to serve him, that I had received some Commands from my Father, which if his Majesty pleased to do me the Honour to accept of, might put me in a Condition to acknowledge his Majesty's Goodness in a Manner more proportioned to the Sense I had of his Favour; and with that I produced my Father's Letter, and read that Clause in it which related to the Regiment of Horse, which was as follows.

I Read with a great deal of Satisfaction the Account you give of the great and extraordinary Conquests of the King of Sweden, *and with more his Majesty's Singular Favour to you, I hope you will be careful to value and deserve so much Honour; I am glad you rather chose to serve as a Voluntier at your own Charge, than to take any Command, which for want of Experience you might misbehave in.*

I have obtained of the King that he will particularly Thank his Majesty of Sweden *for the Honour he has done you, and if his Majesty gives you so much Freedom, I could be glad you should in the humblest Manner thank his Majesty in the Name of an old broken Soldier.*

If you think your self Officer enough to command them, and his Majesty pleased to accept them, I would have you offer to raise his Majesty a Regiment of Horse, which I think I may near compleat in our Neighbourhood with some of your old Acquaintance who are very willing to see the World. If his Majesty gives you the Word, they shall receive his Commands in the Maes, *the King having promised me to give them Arms, and transport them for that Service into* Holland; *and I hope they may do his Majesty such Service as may be for your Honour and the Advantage of his Majesty's Interest and Glory,*

Your loving Father.

'*Tis an Offer like a Gentleman and like a Soldier*, says the King, *and I'll accept of it on two Conditions; first*, says the King, *that I will pay your Father the Advance Money for the raising the Regiment; and next, that they shall be landed in the*

Weser *or the* Elbe, *for which if the King of* England *will not,*
I will pay the Passage, for if they land in Holland, *it may*
prove very difficult to get them to us when the Army shall be
marched out of this Part of the Country.

I returned this Answer to my Father, and sent my Man
George into *England* to Order that Regiment, and made him
Quarter-Master; I sent blank Commissions for the Officers,
signed by the King, to be filled up as my Father should think
fit; and when I had the King's Order for the Commissions,
the Secretary told me I must go back to the King with them.
Accordingly I went back to the King, who opening the
Packet, laid all the Commissions but one upon a Table before
him, and bad me take them, and keeping that one still in his
Hand, *Now*, says he, *you are one of my Soldiers*, and there-
with gave me his Commission, as Collonel of Horse in
present Pay. I took the Commission kneeling, and humbly
thanked his Majesty; *But*, says the King, *there is one Article*
of War I expect of you more than of others. Your Majesty can
expect nothing of me which I shall not willingly comply with,
said I, *as soon as I have the Honour to understand what it is.*
Why it is, says the King, *that you shall never fight but when*
you have Orders; for I shall not be willing to lose my Collonel
before I have the Regiment. I shall be ready at all Times, Sir,
returned I, *to obey your Majesty's Orders.*

I sent my Man Express with the King's Answer, and the
Commission to my Father, who had the Regiment compleated
in less than 2 Months time, and 6 of the Officers with a List
of the rest came away to me, who I presented to his Majesty
when he lay before *Neurenburg*, where they kissed his Hand.

One of the Captains offered to bring the whole Regiment
travelling as private Men into the Army in six Weeks Time,
and either to transport their Equipage, or buy it in *Germany*;
but 'twas thought impracticable; however, I had so many
came in that Manner that I had a compleat Troop always
about me, and obtained the King's Order to muster them
as a Troop.

On the 8th of *March* the King decampt, and marching up
the River *Mayn*, bent his Course directly for *Bavaria*,
taking several small Places by the Way, and expecting to
engage with *Tilly*, who he thought would dispute his
Entrance into *Bavaria*, kept his Army together; but *Tilly*
finding himself too weak to encounter him, turned away, and
leaving *Bavaria* open to the King, marched into the *Upper
Palatinate*. The King finding the Country clear of the
Imperialists, comes to *Norimberg*, made his Entrance into
that City the 21st of *March*, and being nobly treated by the
Citizens, he continued his March into *Bavaria*; and on the
26th sat down before *Donawert*: The Town was taken the
next Day by Storm, so swift were the Conquests of this
invincible Captain. Sir *John Hepburn*, with the *Scots* and
the *English* Voluntiers at the Head of them, entred the Town
first, and cut all the Garrison to Pieces, except such as
escaped over the Bridge.

I had no Share in the Business of *Donawert*, being now
among the Horse, but I was posted on the Roads with five
Troops of Horse, where we picked up a great many Stragglers of the Garrison, who we made Prisoners of War.

'Tis observable, that this Town of *Donawert* is a very
strong Place and well fortified, and yet such Expedition did
the King make, and such Resolution did he use in his first
Attacks, that he carried the Town without putting himself
to the Trouble of formal Approaches; 'twas generally his
way when he came before any Town with a Design to
besiege it; he never would encamp at a Distance and begin
his Trenches a great Way off, but bring his Men immediately
within half Musquet-shot of the Place, there getting under
the best Cover he could, he would immediately begin his
Batteries and Trenches before their Faces; and if there was
any Place possible to be attacked, he would fall to storming
immediately: By this resolute way of coming on he carried
many a Town in the first heat of his Men, which would have
held out many Days against a more Regular Siege.

This March of the King broke all *Tilly*'s Measures, for

now was he obliged to face about, and leaving the *Upper Palatinate*, to come to the Assistance of the Duke of *Bavaria*; for the King being 20000 strong, besides 10000 Foot and 4000 Horse and Dragoons which joined him from the *Duringer Wald*, was resolved to ruin the Duke, who lay now open to him, and was the most powerful and inveterate Enemy of the Protestants in the Empire.

Tilly was now joined with the Duke of *Bavaria*, and might together make about 22000 Men, and in Order to keep the *Swedes* out of the Country of *Bavaria*, had planted themselves along the Banks of the River *Lech*, which runs on the Edge of the Duke's Territories; and having fortified the other Side of the River, and planted his Cannon for several Miles at all the convenient Places on the River, resolved to dispute the King's Passage.

I shall be the longer in relating this Account of the *Lech*, being esteemed in those Days as great an Action as any Battle or Siege of that Age, and particularly famous for the Disaster of the gallant old General *Tilly*; and for that I can be more particular in it than other Accounts, having been an Eye-witness to every part of it.

The King being truly informed of the Disposition of the *Bavarian* Army, was once of the Mind to have left the Banks of the *Lech*, have repassed the *Danube*, and so setting down before *Ingolstat*, the Duke's Capital City, by the taking that strong Town to have made his Entrance into *Bavaria*, and the Conquest of such a Fortress, one entire Action; but the Strength of the Place, and the Difficulty of maintaining his Leaguer in an Enemy's Country, while *Tilly* was so strong in the Field, diverted him from that Design; he therefore concluded that *Tilly* was first to be beaten out of the Country, and then the Siege of *Ingolstat* would be the easier.

Whereupon the King resolved to go and view the Situation of the Enemy; his Majesty went out the 2d of *April* with a strong Party of Horse, which I had the Honour to command; we marched as near as we could to the Banks of the

River, not to be too much exposed to the Enemy's Cannon, and having gained a little Height, where the whole Course of the River might be seen, the King halted, and Commanded to draw up. The King alighted, and calling me to him, Examined every Reach and Turning of the River by his Glass, but finding the River run a long and almost a straight Course, he could find no Place which he liked, but at last turning himself North, and looking down the stream, he found the River fetching a long Reach, doubles short upon it self, making a round and very narrow Point, *There's a Point will do our business*, says the King, *and if the Ground be good I'll pass there, let* Tilly *do his worst*.

He immediately ordered a small Party of Horse to view the Ground, and to bring him Word particularly how high the Bank was on each Side and at the Point; and he shall have 50 Dollars, says the King, that will bring me Word how deep the Water is. I asked his Majesty Leave to let me go, which he would by no Means allow of; but as the Party was drawing out, a Serjeant of Dragoons[1] told the King, if he pleased to let him go disguised as a Boor, he would bring him an Account of every Thing he desired. The King liked the Motion well enough, and the Fellow being very well acquainted with the Country, puts on a Ploughman's Habit, and went away immediately with a long Pole upon his Shoulder; the Horse lay all this while in the Woods, and the King stood undiscerned by the Enemy on the little Hill aforesaid. The Dragoon with his long Pole comes down boldly to the Bank of the River, and calling to the Centinels which *Tilly* had placed on the other Bank, talked with them, asked them, if they could not help him over the River, and pretended he wanted to come to them; at last being come to the Point, where, as I said, the River makes a short Turn, he stands parlying with them a great while, and sometimes pretending to wade over, he puts his long Pole into the Water, then finding it pretty Shallow he pulls off his Hose and goes in, still thrusting his Pole in before him, till being gotten up to his middle, he could reach beyond him, where it was too

deep, and so shaking his Head, comes back again. The
Soldiers on the other Side laughing at him, asked him if he
could swim? He said, No. Why you Fool you, says one of
the Centinels, the Channel of the River is 20 Foot deep.
How do you know that? says the Dragoon. Why our Engineer, says he, measured it Yesterday. This was what he
wanted, but not yet fully satisfied; Ay but, says he, may be it
may not be very broad, and if one of you would wade in to
meet me till I could reach you with my Pole, I'd give him
half a Ducat to pull me over. The innocent way of his
Discourse so deluded the Soldiers, that one of them immediately strips and goes in up to the Shoulders, and our
Dragoon goes in on this Side to meet him; but the Stream
took the other Soldier away, and he being a good Swimmer,
came swimming over to this Side. The Dragoon was then in
a great deal of Pain for fear of being discovered, and was
once going to kill the Fellow, and make off; but at last
resolved to carry on the Humour, and having entertained the
Fellow with a Tale of a Tub,[1] about the *Swedes* stealing his
Oats, the Fellow being a cold wanted to be gone, and he as
willing to be rid of him, pretended to be very sorry he could
not get over the River, and so makes off.

By this however he learned both the Depth and Breadth
of the Channel, the Bottom and Nature of both Shores, and
every Thing the King wanted to know; we could see him
from the Hill by our Glasses very plain, and could see the
Soldier naked with him: Says the King, he will certainly be
discovered and knocked on the Head from the other Side:
He is a Fool, says the King, he does not kill the Fellow and
run off; but when the Dragoon told his Tale, the King was
extremely well satisfied with him, gave him 100 Dollars, and
made him a Quarter-master to a Troop of Cuirassiers.

The King having farther examined the Dragoon, he gave
him a very distinct Account of the Shore and the Ground on
this Side, which he found to be higher than the Enemy's by
10 or 12 Foot, and a hard Gravel.

Hereupon the King resolves to pass there, and in order

to it gives, himself, particular Directions for such a Bridge as I believe never Army passed a River on before nor since.

His Bridge was only loose Plank laid upon large Tressels in the same homely Manner as I have seen Bricklayers raise a low Scaffold to build a Brick Wall; the Tressels were made higher than one another to answer to the River as it become deeper or shallower, and was all framed and fitted before any Appearance was made of attempting to pass.

When all was ready the King brings his Army down to the Bank of the River, and plants his Cannon as the Enemy had done, some here and some there, to amuse them.

At Night *April* 4th, the King commanded about 2000 Men to march to the Point, and to throw up a Trench on either Side, and quite round it with a Battery of six Pieces of Cannon, at each End besides three small Mounts, one at the Point and one of each Side, which had each of them two Pieces upon them. This Work was begun so briskly, and so well carried on, the King firing all the Night from the other Parts of the River, that by Day-light all the Batteries at the new Work were mounted, the Trench lined with 2000 Musqueteers, and all the Utensils of the Bridge lay ready to be put together.

Now the *Imperialists* discovered the Design, but it was too late to hinder it, the Musqueteers in the great Trench, and the five new Batteries, made such continual Fire that the other Bank, which, as before, lay 12 Foot below them, was too hot for the *Imperialists*; whereupon *Tilly*, to be provided for the King at his coming over, falls to work in a Wood right against the Point, and raises a great Battery for 20 Pieces of Cannon, with a Breast-Work, or Line, as near the River as he could, to cover his Men, thinking that when the King had built his Bridge he might easily beat it down with his Cannon.

But the King had doubly prevented him, first by laying his Bridge so low that none of *Tilly*'s Shot could hurt it; for the Bridge lay not above half a Foot above the Water's edge, by which Means the King, who in that shewed himself an excellent Engineer, had secured it from any Batteries to be made within the Land, and the Angle of the Bank secured it from the remoter Batteries, on the other Side, and the continual Fire of the Cannon and small Shot beat the *Imperialists* from their station just against it, they having no Works to cover them.

And in the second Place, to secure his Passage he sent over about 200 Men, and after that 200 more, who had Orders to cast up a large Ravelin on the other Bank, just where he designed to land his Bridge; this was done with such Expedition too, that it was finished before Night, and in a Condition to receive all the Shot of *Tilly*'s great Battery, and effectually covered his Bridge. While this was doing the King on his Side lays over his Bridge. Both Sides wrought hard all Day and all Night, as if the Spade, not the Sword, had been to decide the Controversy, and that he had got the Victory whose Trenches and Batteries were first ready; in the mean while the Cannon and Musquet Bullets flew like Hail, and made the Service so hot, that both Sides had enough to do to make their Men stand to their Work; the King in the hottest of it, animated his Men by his Presence, and *Tilly*, to give him his Due, did the same; for the Execution was so great, and so many Officers killed, General *Attringer* wounded, and two Sergeant Majors killed, that at last *Tilly* himself was obliged to expose himself, and to come up to the very Face of our Line to encourage his Men, and give his necessary Orders.

And here about one a Clock, much about the Time that the King's Bridge and Works were finished, and just as they said he had ordered to fall on upon our Ravelin with 3000 Foot, was the Brave old *Tilly* slain with a Musquet Bullet in the Thigh; he was carried off to *Ingolstat*, and lived some Days after, but died of that Wound the same Day as the King had his Horse shot under him at the Siege of that Town.

We made no question of passing the River here, having brought every Thing so forward, and with such extraordinary Success, but we should have found it a very hot Piece of Work if *Tilly* had lived one Day more; and if I may give my Opinion of it, having seen *Tilly*'s Battery and Breastwork, in the Face of which we must have passed the River, I must say, that whenever we had marched, if *Tilly* had fallen in with his Horse and Foot, placed in that Trench, the whole Army would have passed as much Danger *as in the Face of a strong Town in the storming a Counterscarp.* The King himself, when he saw with what Judgment *Tilly* had prepared his Works, and what Danger he must have run, would often say, that Day's Success was every way equal to the Victory of *Leipsick.*

Tilly being hurt and carried off, as if the Soul of the Army had been lost, they begun to draw off; the Duke of *Bavaria* took Horse and rid away as if he had fled out of Battle for his Life.

The other Generals, with a little more Caution, as well as Courage, drew off by Degrees, sending their Cannon and Baggage away first, and leaving some to continue firing on the Bank of the River to conceal their Retreat; the River preventing any Intelligence, we knew nothing of the Disaster befallen them; and the King, who looked for Blows, having finished his Bridge and Ravelin, ordered to run a Line with Palisadoes to take in more Ground on the Bank of the River, to cover the first Troops he should send over: This being finished the same Night, the King sends over a Party of his Guards to relieve the Men who were in the Ravelin, and commanded 600 Musqueteers to Man the new line out of the *Scots* Brigade.

Early in the Morning a small Party of *Scots*, commanded by one Captain *Forbes*, of my Lord *Reas* Regiment, were sent out to learn something of the Enemy, the King observing they had not fired all Night; and while this Party were abroad, the Army stood in Battalia; and my old Friend Sir *John Hepburn*, whom of all Men the King most depended upon for any desperate Service, was ordered to pass the Bridge with his Brigade, and to draw up without the Line, with Command to advance as he found the Horse who were to second him came over.

Sir *John* being passed without the Trench, meets Captain *Forbes* with some Prisoners, and the good News of the Enemy's Retreat; he sends him directly to the King, who was by this Time at the Head of his Army, in full Battalia ready to follow his Vanguard, expecting a hot Day's Work of it. Sir *John* sends Messenger after Messenger to the King, intreating him to give him Orders to advance; but the King would not suffer him; for he was ever upon his Guard, and would not venture a Surprize; so the Army continued on this Side the *Lech* all Day, and the next Night. In the Morning the King sent for me, and ordered me to draw out 300 Horse, and a Collonel with 600 Horse, and a Collonel with 800 Dragoons, and ordered us to enter the Wood by 3 Ways, but so as to be able to relieve one another; and then ordered Sir *John Hepburn* with his Brigade to advance to the edge of the Wood to secure our Retreat; and at the same Time commanded another Brigade of Foot to pass the Bridge, if need were, to second Sir *John Hepburn*, so warily did this prudent General proceed.

We advanced with out Horse into the *Bavarian* Camp, which we found forsaken; the plunder of it was inconsiderable, for the exceeding Caution the King had used gave them Time to carry off all their Baggage; we followed them three or four Miles and returned to our Camp.

I confess I was most diverted that Day with viewing the Works which *Tilly* had cast up, and must own again, that had he not been taken off, we had met with as desperate a Piece of Work as ever was attempted. The next Day the rest of the Cavalry came up to us, commanded by *Gustavus Horn*, and the King and the whole Army followed; we advanced through the Heart of *Bavaria*, took *Rain* at the first Summons, and several other small Towns, and sat down before *Ausburg*.[1]

Ausburg, though a Protestant City, had a popish *Bavarian* Garrison in it of above 5000 Men, commanded by a *Fugger*

a great Family in *Bavaria*.The Governour had posted
several little Parties as out Scouts at the Distance of two
Miles and half, or three Miles from the Town. The King,
at his coming up to this Town, sends me with my little
Troop, and 3 Companies of Dragoons to beat in these out
Scouts; the first Party I light on was not above 16 Men, who
had made a small Barricado cross the Road, and stood
resolutely upon their Guard; I commanded the Dragoons
to alight, and open the Barricado, which while they resolutely
performed, the 16 Men gave them 2 Volleys of their Musquets, and through the Enclosures made their Retreat to
a Turn-pike about a quarter of a Mile farther. We past their
first Traverse, and coming up to the Turn-pike, I found it
defended by 200 Musqueteers: I prepared to attack them,
sending word to the King how strong the Enemy was, and
desired some Foot to be sent me. My Dragoons fell on, and
tho' the Enemy made a very hot Fire, had beat them from
this Post before 200 Foot, which the King had sent me, had
come up; being joined with the Foot, I followed the Enemy,
who retreated fighting, till they came under the Cannon of a
strong Redoubt, where they drew up, and I could see another
Body of Foot of about 300 join them out of the Works; upon
which I halted, and considering I was in View of the Town,
and a great way from the Army, I faced about and began to
march off; as we marched I found the Enemy followed, but
kept at a Distance, as if they only designed to observe me;
I had not marched far, but I heard a Volly of small Shot,
answered by 2 or 3 more, which I presently apprehended to
be at the Turn-pike, where I had left a small Guard of 26
Men, with a Lieutenant. Immediately I detached 100
Dragoons to relieve my Men, and secure my Retreat,
following my self as fast as the Foot could march. The
Lieutenant sent me back word the Post was taken by the
Enemy, and my Men cut off; upon this I doubled my Pace,
and when I came up I found it as the Lieutenant said; for
the Post was taken and manned with 300 Musqueteers, and
three Troops of Horse; by this Time also I found the Party

in my Rear made up towards me, so that I was like to be charged in a narrow Place, both in Front and Rear.

I saw there was no Remedy but with all my Force to fall upon that Party before me, and so to break through before those from the Town could come up with me; wherefore commanding my Dragoons to alight, I ordered them to fall on upon the Foot; their Horse were drawn up in an enclosed Field on one Side of the Road, a great Ditch securing the other Side, so that they thought if I charged the Foot in Front they would fall upon my Flank, while those behind would charge my Rear; and indeed had the other come in Time, they had cut me off; my Dragoons made three fair Charges on their Foot, but were received with so much Resolution, and so brisk a Fire that they were beaten off, and sixteen Men killed: Seeing them so rudely handled, and the Horse ready to fall in, I relieved them with 100 Musqueteers and they renewed the Attack, at the same Time with my Troop of Horse, flanked on both Wings with 50 Musqueteers, I faced their Horse, but did not offer to charge them; the Case grew now desperate, and the Enemy behind were just at my Heels with near 600 Men; the Captain who commanded the Musqueteers who flanked my Horse came up to me, says he, if we do not force this Pass all will be lost; if you will draw out your Troop and 20 of my Foot, and fall in, I'll engage to keep off the Horse with the rest. With all my Heart, says I.

Immediately I wheel'd off my Troop, and a small Party of the Musqueteers followed me, and fell in with the Dragoons and Foot, who seeing the Danger too, as well as I, fought like Mad Men; the Foot at the Turn-pike were not able to hinder our Breaking through, so we made our way out, killing about 150 of them, and put the rest into Confusion.

But now was I in as great a Difficulty as before how to fetch off my brave Captain of Foot, for they charged home upon him; he defended himself with extraordinary Gallantry, having the Benefit of a Piece of a Hedge to cover him; but he lost half his Men, and was just upon the Point of being defeated, when the King, informed by a Soldier that escaped from the Turn-pike, one of 26, had sent a Party of 600 Dragoons to bring me off; these came upon the Spur, and joined with me just as I had broke through the Turn-pike; the Enemy's Foot rallied behind their Horse, and by this Time their other Party was come in, but seeing our Relief they drew off together.

I lost above 100 Men in these Skirmishes, and kill'd them about 180; we secured the Turn-pike, and placed a Company of Foot there with 100 Dragoons, and came back well beaten to the Army. The King, to prevent such uncertain Skirmishes, advanced the next Day in View of the Town, and according to his Custom, sits down with his whole Army within Cannon-shot of their Walls.

The King won this great City by Force of Words, for by two or three Messages and Letters to and from the Citizens, the Town was gained, the Garrison not daring to defend them against their Wills. His Majesty made his publick Entrance into the City on the 14th of *April*, and, receiving the Compliments of the Citizens, advanced immediately to *Ingolstat*, which is accounted, and really is the strongest Town in all these Parts.

The Town had a very strong Garrison in it, and the Duke of *Bavaria* lay entrenched with his Army under the Walls of it, on the other Side of the River. The King, who never loved long Sieges, having viewed the Town, and brought his Army within Musquet-shot of it, called a Council of War, where it was the King's Opinion, in short, that the Town would lose him more than 'twas worth, and therefore he resolved to raise his Siege.

Here the King going to view the Town had his Horse shot with a Cannon-bullet from the Works, which tumbled the King and his Horse over one another, that every Body thought he had been killed, but he received no Hurt at all; that very Minute, as near as could be learnt, General *Tilly* died in the Town of the Shot he received on the Bank of the *Lech* as aforesaid.[1]

I was not in the Camp when the King was hurt, for the
King had sent almost all the Horse and Dragoons, under
Gustavus Horn, to face the Duke of *Bavaria*'s Camp, and
after that to plunder the Country, which truly was a Work
the Soldiers were very glad of, for it was very seldom they
had that Liberty given them, and they made very good use
of it when it was; for the Country of *Bavaria* was rich and
plentiful, having seen no Enemy before during the whole War.

The Army having left the Siege of *Ingolstat*, proceeds to
take in the rest of *Bavaria*; Sir *John Hepburn* with 3 Brigades
of Foot, and *Gustavus Horn* with 3000 Horse and Dragoons,
went to *Landshut*, and took it the same Day; the Garrison
was all Horse, and gave us several Camisadoes at our
Approach, in one of which I lost two of my Troops, but
when we had beat them into close Quarters, they presently
capitulated. The General got a great Sum of Money of the
Town besides a great many Presents to the Officers: And
from thence the King went on to *Munick*, the Duke of
Bavaria's Court; some of the General Officers would fain
have had the plundering of the Duke's Palace; but the
King was too generous, the City paid him 400000 Dollars;
and the Duke's Magazine was there seized, in which was
140 Pieces of Cannon, and small Arms for above 20000 Men.
The great Chamber of the Duke's Rarities was preserved
by the Kings special Order with a great deal of Care. I
expected to have staid here some Time, and to have taken
a very exact Account of this curious Laboratory; but being
commanded away, I had not Time, and the Fate of the War
never gave me Opportunity to see it again.[1]

The *Imperialists* under the Command of Comissary *Osta*
had besieged *Bibrach*, an Imperial City not very well
fortified, and the Inhabitants being under the *Swede*'s
Protection, defended themselves as well as they could, but
were in great Danger, and sent several Expresses to the King
for Help.

The King immediately detaches a strong Body of Horse
and Foot, to relieve *Bibrach*, and would be the Commander

himself; I marched among the Horse, but the *Imperialists* saved us the Labour; for the News of the King's coming frighted away *Osta*, that he left *Bibrach*, and hardly looked behind him 'till he got up to the *Bodensee*, on the Confines of *Swisserland*.

At our Return from this Expedition, the King had the first News of *Wallestein*'s Approach, who on the Death of Count *Tilly*, being declared Generalissimo of the Emperor's Forces, had plaid the Tyrant in *Bohemia*, and was now advancing with 60000 Men, as they reported, to relieve the Duke of *Bavaria*.

The King therefore, in order to be in a Posture to receive this great General, resolves to quit *Bavaria*, and to expect him on the Frontiers of *Franconia*; and because he knew the *Norembergers*, for their Kindness to him, would be the first Sacrifice, he resolved to defend that City against him whatever it cost.

Nevertheless he did not leave *Bavaria* without a Defence; but on the one Hand he left Sir *John Bannier* with 10000 Men about *Ausburgh*, and the Duke of *Saxe-Weymar* with another like Army about *Ulme* and *Meningen*, with Orders so to direct their March, as that they might join him upon any Occasion in a few Days.

We encamped about *Noremberg* the Middle of *June*. The Army, after so many Detachments, was not above 19000 Men. The Imperial Army joined with the *Bavarian*, were not so numerous as was reported, but were really 60000 Men. The King, not strong enough to fight yet, as he used to say, was strong enough not to be forced to to fight, formed his Camp so under the Cannon of *Noremberg*, that there was no besieging the Town, but they must besiege him too; and he fortified his Camp in so formidable a Manner, that *Wallestein* never durst attack him. On the 30th of *June*, *Wallestein*'s Troops appeared, and on the 5th of *July*, encamped close by the King, and posted themselves not on the *Bavarian* Side, but between the King and his own Friends of *Schwaben*, and *Frankenland* in order to intercept his Provisions, and, as they thought, to starve him out of his Camp.

Here they lay to see, as it were, who could subsist longest; the King was strong in Horse, for we had full 8000 Horse and Dragoons in the Army, and this gave us great Advantage in the several Skirmishes we had with the Enemy. The Enemy had Possession of the whole Country, and had taken effectual Care to furnish their Army with Provisions; they placed their Guards in such excellent Order, to secure their Convoys, that their Waggons went from Stage to Stage as quiet as in a time of Peace, and were relieved every five Miles by Parties constantly posted on the Road. And thus the Imperial General sat down by us, not doubting but he should force the King either to fight his Way through, on very disadvantageous Terms, or to rise for want of Provisions, and leave the City of *Noremberg* a Prey to his Army; for he had vowed the Destruction of the City, and to make it a second *Magdeburg*.

But the King, who was not to be easily deceived, had countermined all *Wallestein*'s Designs; he had passed his Honour to the *Norembergers*, that he would not leave them, and they had undertaken to Victual his Army, and secure him from Want, which they did so effectually, that he had no Occasion to expose his Troops to any Hazard or Fatigues for Convoys or Forage on any Account whatever.

The City of *Noremberg* is a very rich and populous City; and the King being very sensible of their Danger, had given his Word for their Defence: And when they, being terrified at the Threats of the *Imperialists*, sent their Deputies to beseech the King to take care of them, he sent them Word, he would, and be besieged with them. They on the other Hand laid in such Stores of all Sorts of Provision, both for Men and Horse, that had *Wallestein* lain before it six Months longer, there would have been no Scarcity. Every private House was a Magazine, the Camp was plentifully supplied with all Manner of Provisions, and the Market always full, and as cheap as in Times of Peace. The Magistrates were so careful, and preserved so excellent an Order in the Disposal of all sorts of Provision, that no engrossing[1] of Corn could be practised; for the Prices were every Day directed at the Town-house: And if any Man offered to demand more Money for Corn, than the stated Price, he could not sell, because at the Town Store-house you might buy cheaper. Here are two Instances of good and bad Conduct; the City of *Magdeburgh* had been intreated by the King to settle Funds, and raise Money for their Provision and Security, and to have a sufficient Garrison to defend them, but they made Difficulties, either to raise Men for themselves, or to admit the King's Troops to assist them, for fear of the Charge of maintaining them; and this was the Cause of the City's Ruin.

The City of *Noremberg* open'd their Arms to receive the Assistance proferred by the *Swedes*, and their Purses to defend their Town, and Common Cause, and this was the saving them absolutely from Destruction. The rich Burghers and Magistrates kept open Houses, where the Officers of the Army were always welcome; and the Council of the City took such Care of the Poor, that there was no Complaining nor Disorders in the whole City. There is no doubt but it cost the City a great deal of Money; but I never saw a publick Charge borne with so much Chearfulness, nor managed with so much Prudence and Conduct in my Life. The City fed above 50000 Mouths every Day, including their own Poor, besides themselves; and yet when the King had lain thus 3 Months, and finding his Armies longer in coming up than he expected, asked the Burgrave how their Magazines held out? He answered, they desired his Majesty not to hasten things for them, for they could maintain themselves and him 12 Months longer, if there was Occasion. This Plenty kept both the Army and City in good Health, as well as in good Heart; whereas nothing was to be had of us but Blows; for we fetched nothing from without our Works, nor had no Business without the Line, but to interrupt the Enemy.

The Manner of the King's Encampment deserves a particular Chapter. He was a compleat Surveyor, and a Master in Fortification, not to be outdone by any Body. He had posted his Army in the Suburbs of the Town, and drawn Lines round the whole Circumference, so that he begirt the whole City with his Army; his Works were large, the Ditch deep, flanked with innumerable Bastions, Ravelins, Horn-works, Forts, Redoubts, Batteries and Pallisadoes, the incessant Work of 8000 Men for about 14 Days; besides that the King was adding some thing or other to it every Day; and the very Posture of his Camp was enough to tell a bigger Army than *Wallestein*'s, that he was not to be assaulted in his Trenches.

The King's Design appeared chiefly to be the Preservation of the City; but that was not all: He had three Armies acting abroad in three several Places; *Gustavus Horn* was on the *Mosel*, the Chancellor *Oxenstern* about *Mentz*, *Cologn*, and the *Rhine*, Duke *William* and Duke *Bernard*, together with General *Bannier* in *Bavaria*: And though he designed they should all join him, and had wrote to them all to that purpose, yet he did not hasten them, knowing that while he kept the main Army at Bay about *Noremberg*, they would without Opposition reduce those several Countries they were acting in to his Power. This occasioned his lying longer in the Camp at *Noremberg* than he would have done, and this occasioned his giving the *Imperialists* so many Alarms by his strong Parties of Horse, of which he was well provided, that they might not be able to make any considerable Detachments for the Relief of their Friends: And here he shewed his Mastership in the War; for by this means his Conquests went on as effectually as if he had been abroad himself.

In the mean Time, it was not to be expected two such Armies should lye long so near without some Action; the Imperial Army being Masters of the Field, laid the Country for 20 Miles round *Noremberg* in a manner desolate; what the Inhabitants could carry away had been before secured in such strong Towns as had Garrisons to protect them, and what was left, the hungry *Crabats* devoured, or set on Fire; but sometimes they were met with by our Men, who often paid them home for it. There had passed several small Rencounters between our Parties and theirs; and as it falls out in such Cases, sometimes one Side, sometimes the other, got the better; but I have observed there never was any Party sent out by the King's special Appointment, but always came home with Victory.

The first considerable Attempt, as I remember, was made on a Convoy of Ammunition: The Party sent out was commanded by a *Saxon* Collonel, and consisted of a 1000 Horse, and 500 Dragoons, who burnt above 600 Waggons, loaden with Ammunition and Stores for the Army, besides taking about 2000 Musquets which they brought back to the Army.

The latter end of *July* the King received Advice, that the *Imperialists* had formed a Magazine for Provision at a Town called *Freynstat*, 20 Miles from *Noremberg*. Hither all the Booty and Contributions raised in the *Upper Palatinate*, and Parts adjacent, was brought and laid up as in a Place of Security; a Garrison of 600 Men being placed to defend it; and when a Quantity of Provisions was got together, Convoys were appointed to fetch it off.

The King was resolved, if possible, to take or destroy this Magazine; and sending for Collonel *Dubalt*, a *Swede*, and a Man of extraordinary Conduct, he tells him his Design, and withal, that he must be the Man to put it in Execution, and ordered him to take what Forces he thought convenient. The Collonel, who knew the Town very well, and the Country about it, told his Majesty, he would attempt it with all his Heart; but he was affraid 'twould require some Foot to make the Attack; but we can't stay for that, says the King, you must then take some Dragoons with you, and immediately the King called for me. I was just coming up the Stairs, as the King's Page was come out to enquire for me; so I went immediately in to the King. Here is a Piece of hot Work for you, says the King, *Dubalt* will tell it you; go together and contrive it.

We immediately withdrew, and the Collonel told me the Design, and what the King and he had discoursed; that in his Opinion Foot would be wanted: But the King had declared there was no Time for the Foot to march, and had proposed Dragoons. I told him, I thought Dragoons might do as well; so we agreed to take 1600 Horse and 400 Dragoons. The King, impatient in his Design, came into the Room to us to know what we had resolved on, approved our Measures, gave us Orders immediately; and turning to me, you shall command the Dragoons, says the King, but *Dubalt* must be General in this Case, for he knows the Country. Your Majesty, said I, shall be always served by me in any Figure you please. The King wished us good Speed, and hurried us away the same Afternoon, in order to come to the Place in Time. We marched slowly on because of the Carriages we had with us, and came to *Freynstat* about One a Clock in the Night perfectly undiscover'd; the Guards were so negligent, that we came to the very Port before they had Notice of us, and a Serjeant with 12 Dragoons thrust in upon the Out-Centinels, and killed them without Noise.

Immediately Ladders were placed to the Half-Moon which defended the Gate, which the Dragoons mounted and carried in a trice, about 28 Men being cut in Pieces within. As soon as the Ravelin was taken, they burst open the Gate, at which I entered at the Head of 200 Dragoons, and seized the Drawbridge. By this Time the Town was in Alarm, and the Drums beat to Arms, but it was too late; for by the help of a Petard we broke open the Gate, and entered the Town. The Garrison made an obstinate Fight for about half an Hour, but our Men being all in, and 3 Troops of Horse dismounted coming to our Assistance with their Carabines, the Town was entirely mastered by Three of the Clock, and Guards set to prevent any Body running to give Notice to the Enemy. There were about 200 of the Garrison killed, and the rest taken Prisoners. The Town being thus secured, the Gates were opened, and Collonel *Dubalt* came in with the Horse.

The Guards being set, we entered the Magazine where we found an incredible Quantity of all sorts of Provision. There was 150 Tun of Bread, 8000 Sacks of Meal, 4000 Sacks of Oats, and of other Provisions in Proportion. We caused as much of it as could be loaded to be brought away in such Waggons and Carriages as we found, and set the rest on Fire, Town and all; we staid by it till we saw it past a Possibility of being saved, and then drew off with 800 Waggons, which we found in the Place, most of which we loaded with Bread, Meal and Oats. While we were doing this we sent a Party of Dragoons into the Fields, who met us again as we came out, with above a 1000 Head of Black Cattle, besides Sheep.

Our next Care was to bring this Booty home without meeting with the Enemy; to secure which, the Collonel immediately dispatch'd an Express to the King, to let him know of our Success, and to desire a Detachment might be made to secure our Retreat, being charged with so much Plunder.

And it was no more than Need; for tho' we had used all the Diligence possible to prevent any Notice, yet some body more forward than ordinary, had scap'd away and carried News of it to the *Imperial* Army. The General upon this bad News detaches Major General *Sparr*, with a Body of 6000 Men to cut off our Retreat. The King, who had Notice of this Detachment, marches out in Person with 3000 Men to wait upon General *Sparr*: All this was the Account of one Day; the King met General *Sparr* at the Moment when his Troops were divided, fell upon them, routed one Part of them, and the rest in a few Hours after; killed them a 1000 Men, and took the General Prisoner.

In the Interval of this Action, we came safe to the Camp with our Booty, which was very considerable, and would have supplied our whole Army for a Month. Thus we feasted at the Enemy's Cost, and beat them into the Bargain.

The King gave all the live Cattle to the *Norembergers*, who, tho' they had really no want of Provisions, yet fresh Meat was not so plentiful as such Provisions which were stored up in Vessels and laid by.

After this Skirmish, we had the Country more at Command than before, and daily fetch'd in fresh Provisions and Forage in the Fields.

The two Armies had now lain a long Time in sight of one another, and daily Skirmishes had considerably weakened them;[1] and the King beginning to be impatient, hastened the Advancement of his Friends to join him, in which also they were not backward; but having drawn together their Forces from several Parts, and all joined the Chancellor *Oxenstern*, News came the 15th of *August*, that they were in full March to join us; and being come to a small Town called *Brock*, the King went out of the Camp with about 1000 Horse to view them. I went along with the Horse, and the 21st of *August* saw the Review of all the Armies together, which were 30000 Men in extraordinary Equipage, old Soldiers, and commanded by Officers of the greatest Conduct and Experience in the World. There was the rich Chancellor of *Sweden* who commanded as General, *Gustavus Horn* and *John Bannier*, both *Swedes* and old Generals; Duke *William* and Duke *Bernard* of *Weymar*, the Landgrave of *Hesse Cassel*, the Palatine of *Birkenfelt*, and Abundance of Princes and Lords of the Empire.

The Armies being joined, the King who was now a Match for *Wallestein*, quits his Camp and draws up in Battalia before the *Imperial* Trenches; but the Scene was changed; *Wallestein* was no more able to fight now than the King was before; but keeping within his Trenches, stood upon his Guard. The King coming up close to his Works, plants Batteries, and cannonaded him in his very Camp.

The *Imperialists* finding the King press upon them, retreat into a woody Country about three Leagues, and taking Possession of an old ruin'd Castle, posted their Army behind it.

This old Castle[1] they fortified, and placed a very strong Guard there. The King having viewed the Place, tho' it was a very strong Post, resolved to attack it with the whole right Wing. The Attack was made with a great deal of Order and Resolution, the King leading the first Party on with Sword in Hand, and the Fight was maintained on both Sides with the utmost Gallantry and Obstinacy all the Day and the next Night too; for the Cannon and Musquet never gave over 'till the Morning; but the *Imperialists* having the Advantage of the Hill, of their Works and Batteries, and being continually relieved, and the *Swedes* naked, without Cannon or Works, the Post was maintained; and the King finding it would cost him too much Blood, drew off in the Morning.

This was the famous Fight at *Attembergh*, where the *Imperialists* boasted to have shewn the World the King of *Sweden* was not invincible. They call it the Victory at *Attembergh*; 'tis true, the King failed in his Attempt of carrying their Works, but there was so little of a Victory in it, that the *Imperial* General thought fit not to venture a second Brush, but to draw off their Army as soon as they could to a safer Quarter.[2]

I had no Share in this Attack, very few of the Horse being in the Action; but my Comerade, who was always among the *Scots* Voluntiers was wounded and taken Prisoner by the Enemy. They used him very civilly, and the King and *Wallestein* straining Courtesies with one another, the King released Major General *Sparr* without Ransom, and the *Imperial* General sent home Collonel *Tortenson* a *Swede*, and 16 Voluntier Gentlemen who were taken in the Heat of the Action, among whom my Captain was one.

The King lay 14 Days facing the *Imperial* Army, and using all the Stratagems possible to bring them to a Battle, but to no purpose; during which Time, we had Parties continually out, and very often Skirmishes with the Enemy.

I had a Command of one of these Parties in an Adventure, wherein I got no Booty, nor much Honour. The King had received Advice of a Convoy of Provisions which was to

come to the Enemy's Camp from the *Upper Palatinate*, and
having a great Mind to surprize them, he commanded us to
way-lay them with 1200 Horse, and 800 Dragoons. I had
exact Directions given me of the Way they were to come,
and posting my Horse in a Village a little out of the Road, I
lay with my Dragoons in a Wood, by which they were to
pass by break of Day. The Enemy appeared with their
Convoy, and being very wary, their Out-Scouts discovered
us in the Wood, and fired upon the Centinel I had posted in
a Tree at the Entrance of the Wood. Finding my self discovered, I would have retreated to the Village where my
Horse were posted, but in a Moment the Wood was skirted
with the Enemy's Horse, and a Thousand commanded
Musqueteers advanced to beat me out. In this Pickle I sent
away three Messengers one after another for the Horse, who
were within two Miles of me, to advance to my Relief; but
all my Messengers fell into the Enemy's Hands. 400 of my
Dragoons on foot, whom I had plac'd at a little Distance
before me, stood to their Work, and beat off two Charges of
the Enemy's Foot with some Loss on both Sides: Mean Time
200 of my Men fac'd about, and rushing out of the Wood,
broke through a Party of the Enemy's Horse who stood to
watch our coming out. I confess I was exceedingly surprized
at it, thinking those Fellows had done it to make their
Escape, or else were gone over to the Enemy; and my Men
were so discouraged at it, that they began to look about
which way to run to save themselves, and were just upon the
Point of disbanding to shift for themselves, when one of the
Captains called to me aloud to beat a Parle and Treat. I made
no Answer, but, as if I had not heard him, immediately gave
the Word for all the Captains to come together. The Consultation was but short, for the Musqueteers were advancing
to a third Charge, with Numbers which we were not likely
to deal with. In short, we resolved to beat a Parle, and demand Quarter, for that was all we could expect; when on a
sudden the Body of Horse I had posted in the Village being
directed by the Noise, had advanced to relieve me, if they

saw Occasion, and had met the 200 Dragoons who guided them directly to the Spot where they had broke thro', and all together fell upon the Horse of the Enemy who were posted on that Side, and mastering them before they could be relieved, cut them all to Pieces and brought me off. Under the Shelter of this Party, we made good our Retreat to the Village, but we lost above 300 Men, and were glad to make off from the Village too, for the Enemy were very much too strong for us.

Returning thence towards the Camp, we fell foul with 200 *Crabats* who had been upon the plundering Account: We made our selves some Amends upon them for our former Loss, for we shew'd them no Mercy; but our Misfortunes were not ended, for we had but just dispatch'd those *Crabats* when we fell in with 3000 *Imperial* Horse, who, on the Expectation of the aforesaid Convoy, were sent out to secure them.

All I could do, could not persuade my Men to stand their Ground against this Party; so that finding they would run away in Confusion, I agreed to make off, and facing to the Right, we went over a large Common at full Trot, 'till at last Fear, which always encreases in a Flight, brought us to a plain Flight, the Enemy at our Heels. I must confess I was never so mortified in my Life; 'twas to no Purpose to turn Head, no Man would stand by us, we run for Life, and a great many we left by the Way who were either wounded by the Enemy's Shot, or else could not keep Pace with us.

At last having got over the Common, which was near two Miles, we came to a Lane; one of our Captains, a *Saxon* by Country, and a Gentleman of a good Fortune alighted at the Entrance of the Lane, and with a bold Heart faced about, shot his own Horse, and called his Men to stand by him and defend the Lane. Some of his Men halted, and we rallied about 600 Men which we posted as well as we could, to defend the Pass; but the Enemy charged us with great Fury. The *Saxon* Gentleman, after defending himself with exceeding Gallantry and refusing Quarter, was killed upon the Spot: A *German* Dragoon as I thought him, gave me a rude Blow with the Stock of his Piece on the Side of my Head, and was just going to repeat it, when one of my Men shot him dead. I was so stunn'd with the Blow, that I knew nothing; but recovering, I found my self in the Hands of two of the Enemy's Officers, who offered me Quarter, which I accepted; and indeed, to give them their due, they used me very civilly. Thus this whole Party was defeated, and not above 500 Men got safe to the Army, nor had half the Number escaped, had not the *Saxon* Captain made so bold a Stand at the Head of the Lane.

Several other Parties of the King's Army revenged our Quarrel, and paid them home for it; but I had a particular Loss in this Defeat, that I never saw the King after; for tho' his Majesty sent a Trumpet to reclaim us as Prisoners the very next Day, yet I was not delivered, some Scruple happening about exchanging, 'till after the Battle of *Lutzen*, where that Gallant Prince lost his Life.

The Imperial Army rise from their Camp about eight or ten Days after the King had removed, and I was carried Prisoner in the Army 'till they sat down to the Siege of *Coburgh Castle*,[1] and then was left with other Prisoners of War, in the Custody of Collonel *Spezuter*, in a small Castle near the Camp called *Newstad*. Here we continued indifferent well treated, but could learn nothing of what Action the Armies were upon, 'till the Duke of *Friedland* having been beaten off from the Castle of *Coburgh*, marched into *Saxony*, and the Prisoners were sent for into the Camp, as was said, in order to be exchanged.

I came into the Imperial Leager at the Siege of *Leipsick*, and within three Days after my coming, the City was surrendred, and I got Liberty to lodge at my old Quarters in the Town upon my Parole.

The King of *Sweden* was at the Heels of the *Imperialists*; for finding *Wallestein* resolved to ruin the Elector of *Saxony*, the King had recollected as much of his divided Army as he could, and came upon him just as he was going to besiege *Torgau*.

As it is not my Design to write a History of any more of these Wars than I was actually concerned in, so I shall only note, that upon the King's Approach, *Wallestein* halted, and likewise called all his Troops together; for he apprehended the King would fall on him; and we that were Prisoners, fancied the *Imperial* Soldiers went unwillingly out; for the very Name of the King of *Sweden* was become terrible to them. In short, they drew all the Soldiers of the Garrison they could spare, out of *Leipsick*, sent for *Papenheim* again, who was gone but three Days before with 6000 Men on a private Expedition. On the 16th of *November*, the Armies met on the Plains of *Lutzen*; a long and bloody Battle was fought; the *Imperialists* were entirely routed and beaten, 12000 slain upon the Spot, their Cannon, Baggage and 2000 Prisoners taken, but the King of *Sweden* lost his Life, being killed at the Head of his Troops in the Beginning of the Fight.

It is impossible to describe the Consternation the Death of this conquering King struck into all the Princes of *Germany*; the Grief for him exceeded all Manner of human Sorrow: All People looked upon themselves as ruined and swallowed up; the Inhabitants of two Thirds of all *Germany* put themselves into Mourning for him; when the Ministers mentioned him in their Sermons or Prayers, whole Congregations would burst out into Tears: The Elector of *Saxony* was utterly inconsolable, and would for several Days walk about his Palace like a distracted Man, crying the Saviour of *Germany* was lost, the Refuge of abused Princes was gone; the Soul of the War was dead, and from that Hour was so hopeless of out-living the War, that he sought to make Peace with the Emperor.

Three Days after this mournful Victory, the *Saxons* recovered the Town of *Leipsick* by Stratagem. The Duke of *Saxony*'s Forces lay at *Torgau*, and perceiving the Confusion the *Imperialists* were in at the News of the Overthrow of their Army, they resolved to attempt the Recovery of the Town. They sent about 20 scattering Troopers who pretending themselves to be *Imperialists* fled from the Battle, were let in one by one, and still as they came in, they staid at the Court of Guard in the Port, entertaining the Souldiers with Discourse about the Fight, and how they escaped, and the like; 'till the whole Number being got in at a Watch Word, they fell on the Guard, and cut them all in Pieces; and immediately opening the Gate to three Troops of *Saxon* Horse, the Town was taken in a Moment.

It was a welcome Surprise to me, for I was at Liberty of Course; and the War being now on another Foot, as I thought, and the King dead, I resolved to quit the Service.

I had sent my Man, as I have already noted into *England*, in Order to bring over the Troops my Father had raised for the King of *Sweden*. He executed his Commission so well, that he landed with five Troops at *Embden*, in very good Condition; and Orders were sent them by the King, to join the Duke of *Lunenberg*'s Army; which thcy did at the Siege of *Boxtude*, in the Lower *Saxony*. Here by long and very sharp Service they were most of them cut off, and though they were several Times recruited, yet I understood there were not three full Troops left.

The Duke of *Saxe-Weymar*, a Gentleman of great Courage, had the Command of the Army after the King's Death, and managed it with so much Prudence, that all things were in as much Order as could be expected, after so great a Loss; for the *Imperialists* were every where beaten, and *Wallestein* never made any Advantage of the King's Death.

I waited on him at *Hailbron*, whither he was gone to meet the great Chancellor of *Sweden*, where I paid him my Respects, and desired he would bestow the Remainder of my Regiment on my Comerade the Captain, which he did with all the Civility and Readiness imaginable: So I took my Leave of him, and prepared to come for *England*.

I shall only note this, that at this Dyet, the Protestant

Princes of the Empire renewed their League[1] with one another, and with the Crown of *Sweden*, and came to several Regulations and Conclusions for the carrying on the War, which they afterwards prosecuted under the Direction of the said Chancellor of *Sweden*. But it was not the Work of a small Difficulty, nor of a short Time; and having been perswaded to continue almost two Years afterwards at *Frankfort*, *Hailbron*, and thereabout, by the particular Friendship of that noble wise Man, and extraordinary Statesman *Axell Oxenstern*, Chancellor of *Sweden*, I had Opportunity to be concerned in, and present at several Treaties of extraordinary Consequence, sufficient for a History, if that were my Design.

Particularly I had the Happiness to be present at, and have some Concern in the Treaty for the restoring the Posterity of the truly noble *Palsgrave* King of *Bohemia*. King *James* of *England* had indeed too much neglected the whole Family; and I may say with Authority enough, from my own Knowledge of Affairs, had nothing been done for them but what was from *England*, that Family had remained desolate and forsaken to this Day.

But that glorious King, whom I can never mention without some Remark of his extraordinary Merit, had left particular Instructions with his Chancellor to rescue the *Palatinate* to its rightful Lord, as a Proof of his Design to restore the Liberty of *Germany*, and reinstate the oppressed Princes who were subjected to the Tyranny of the House of *Austria*.

Pursuant to this Resolution, the Chancellor proceeded very much like a Man of Honour; and tho' the King of *Bohemia* was dead a little before, yet he carefully managed the Treaty, answered the Objections of several Princes, who, in the general Ruin of the Family, had reaped private Advantages, settled the Capitulations for the Quota of Contributions, very much for their Advantage, and fully reinstalled the Prince *Charles* in the Possession of all his Dominions in the *Lower Palatinate*, which afterwards was confirmed to him and his Posterity by the Peace of *West-Phalia*,[1] where all these bloody Wars were finished in a Peace, which has since been the Foundation of the *Protestants* Liberty, and the best Security of the whole Empire.

I spent two Years rather in wandring up and down, than travelling; for tho' I had no Mind to serve, yet I could not find in my Heart to leave *Germany*; and I had obtained some so very close Intimacies with the General Officers, that I was often in the Army, and sometimes they did me the Honour to bring me into their Councils of War.

Particularly, at that eminent Council before the Battle of *Nordlingen*,[2] I was invited to the Council of War, both by Duke *Bernard* of *Weymar*, and by *Gustavus Horn*. They were Generals of equal Worth, and their Courage and Experience had been so well, and so often tried, that more than ordinary Regard was always given to what they said. Duke *Bernard* was indeed the younger Man, and *Gustavus* had served longer under our Great Schoolmaster the King; but 'twas hard to judge which was the better General, since both had Experience enough, and shewn undeniable Proofs both of their Bravery and Conduct.

I am obliged, in the Course of my Relation, so often to mention the great Respect I often received from these great Men, that it makes me sometimes jealous, least the Reader may think I affect it as a Vanity. The Truth is, and I am ready to confess the Honours I received, upon all Occasions, from Persons of such Worth, and who had such an eminent Share in the greatest Action of that Age, very much pleased me; and particularly, as they gave me Occasions to see every thing that was doing on the whole Stage of the War: For being under no Command, but at Liberty to rove about, I could come to no *Swedish* Garrison or Party, but sending my Name to the commanding Officer I could have *the Word* sent me; and if I came into the Army, I was often treated as I was now at this famous Battle of *Nordlingen*.

But I cannot but say, that I always looked upon this particular Respect to be the Effect of more than ordinary

Regard the great King of *Sweden* always shewed me, rather than any Merit of my own; and the Veneration they all had for his Memory, made them continue to shew me all the Marks of a suitable Esteem.

But to return to the Council of War, the great, and indeed the only Question before us was, shall we give Battle to the *Imperialists*, or not? *Gustavus Horn* was against it, and gave, as I thought, the most invincible Arguments against a Battle that Reason could imagine.

First, They were weaker than the Enemy by above 5000 Men.

Secondly, The Cardinal Infant of *Spain*, who was in the *Imperial* Army with 8000 Men, was but there *en Passant*, being going from *Italy* to *Flanders*, to take upon him the Government of the *Low Countries*; and if he saw no Prospect of immediate Action, would be gone in a few Days.

Thirdly, They had two Reinforcements, one of 5000 Men, under the Command of Collonel *Cratz*, and one of 7000 Men under the Rhinegrave, who were just at Hand, the last within three Days March of them: And

Lastly, They had already saved their Honour, in that they had put 600 Foot into the Town of *Nordlingen*, in the Face of the Enemy's Army, and consequently the Town might hold out some Days the longer.

Fate rather than Reason certainly blinded the rest of the Generals against such Arguments as these. Duke *Bernard* and almost all the Generals were for Fighting, alledging, the Affront it would be to the *Swedish* Reputation, to see their Friends in the Town lost before their Faces.

Gustavus Horn stood stiff to his cautious Advice, and was against it; and I thought the Baron *D'Offkirk* treated him a little indecently; for being very warm in the Matter, he told them; *That if* Gustavus Adolphus *had been governed by such cowardly Council, he had never been Conqueror of half* Germany *in two Years. No*, replied old General *Horn*, very smartly, *But he had been now alive to have testified for me, that I was never taken by him for a Coward; and yet* says he, *the King was never for a Victory with a Hazard, when he could have it without.*

I was asked my Opinion, which I would have declined, being in no Commission; but they pressed me to speak. I told them, I was for staying at least till the Rhinegrave came up; who at least might, if Expresses were sent to hasten him, be up with us in 24 Hours. But *Offkirk* could not hold his Passion, and had not he been over-rul'd, he would have almost quarrelled with Marshal *Horn*. Upon which the old General, not to foment him, with a great deal of Mildness stood up, and spoke thus.

Come, Offkirk, says he, *I'll submit my Opinion to you and the Majority of our Fellow-Soldiers: We will fight, but upon my Word we shall have our Hands full.*

The Resolution thus taken, they attacked the *Imperial* Army. I must confess the Councils of this Day seemed as confused as the Resolutions of the Night.

Duke *Bernard* was to lead the Van of the Left Wing, and to post himself upon a Hill which was on the Enemy's Right without their Entrenchments; so that having secured that Post, they might level their Cannon upon the Foot, who stood behind the Lines, and relieved the Town at Pleasure. He marched accordingly by Break of Day, and falling with great Fury upon 8 Regiments of Foot which were posted at the Foot of the Hill, he presently routed them and made himself Master of the Post. Flushed with this Success, he never regards his own concerted Measures of stopping there, and possessing what he had got, but pushes on and falls in with the Main Body of the Enemy's Army.

While this was doing, *Gustavus Horn* attacks another Post on a Hill, where the *Spaniards* had posted and lodged themselves behind some Works they had cast up on the side of the Hill; here they defended themselves with extreme Obstinacy for five Hours, and at last obliged the *Swedes* to give it over with Loss. This extraordinary Gallantry of the *Spaniards* was the saving of the *Imperial* Army; for Duke *Bernard* having all this while resisted the frequent Charges of the *Imperialists*, and borne the Weight of two Thirds of their Army, was not able to stand any longer, but sending one Messenger in the Neck of another to *Gustavus Horn* for more Foot, he finding he could not carry his Point, had given it over, and was in full March to second the Duke. But now 'twas too late; for the King of *Hungary* seeing the Duke's Men as it were wavering, and having Notice of *Horn*'s wheeling about to second him, falls in with all his Force upon his Flank, and with his *Hungarian* Hussars, made such a furious Charge, that the *Swedes* could stand no longer.

The Rout of the Left Wing was so much the more unhappy, as it happened just upon *Gustavus Horn*'s coming up; for being pushed on with the Enemies at their Heels, they were driven upon their own Friends, who having no Ground, to open, and give them way, were trodden down by their own run-away Brethren. This brought all into the utmost Confusion. The *Imperialists* cried *Victoria*, and fell into the Middle of the Infantry with a terrible Slaughter.

I have always observed, 'tis fatal to upbraid an old experienced Officer with want of Courage. If *Gustavus Horn* had not been whetted with the Reproaches of the Baron *D'Offkirk*, and some of the other General Officers, I believe it had saved the Lives of a 1000 Men; for when all was thus lost, several Officers advised him to make a Retreat with such Regiments as he had yet unbroken; but nothing could perswade him to stir a Foot: But turning his Flank into a Front, he saluted the Enemy as they pass'd by him in Pursuit of the rest, with such terrible Volleys of small Shot, as cost them the Lives of Abundance of their Men.

The *Imperialists*, eager in the Pursuit, left him unbroken, till the *Spanish* Brigade came up and charged him: These he bravely repulsed with a great Slaughter, and after them a Body of Dragoons; till being laid at on every Side, and most of his Men killed, the brave old General, with all the rest who were left, were made Prisoners.

The *Swedes* had a terrible Loss here; for almost all their Infantry were killed or taken Prisoners. *Gustavus Horn* refused Quarter several times; and still those that attacked him were cut down by his Men, who fought like Furies, and by the Example of their General, behaved themselves like Lions. But at last, these poor Remains of a Body of the bravest Men in the World were forced to submit. I have heard him say, he had much rather have died than been taken, but that he yielded in Compassion to so many brave Men as were about him; for none of them would take Quarter till he gave his Consent.

I had the worst Share in this Battle that ever I had in any Action of my Life; and that was to be posted among as brave a Body of Horse as any in *Germany*, and yet not be able to succour our own Men; but our Foot were cut in Pieces (as it were) before our Faces; and the Situation of the Ground was such as we could not fall in. All that we were able to do, was to carry off about 2000 of the Foot, who running away in the Rout of the Left Wing, rallied among our Squadrons, and got away with us. Thus we stood till we saw all was lost, and then made the best Retreat we could to save our selves, several Regiments having never charged, nor fired a Shot; for the Foot had so embarassed themselves among the Lines and Works of the Enemy, and in the Vineyards and Mountains, that the Horse were rendered absolutely unserviceable.

The Rhinegrave had made such Expedition to join us, that he reached within three Miles of the Place of Action that Night, and he was a great Safeguard for us in rallying our dispersed Men, who else had fallen into the Enemy's Hands, and in checking the Pursuit of the Enemy.

And indeed, had but any considerable Body of the Foot made an orderly Retreat, it had been very probable they had given the Enemy a Brush that would have turned the Scale of Victory; for our Horse being whole, and in a manner untouched, the Enemy found such a Check in the Pursuit, that 1600 of their forwardest Men following too eagerly, fell in with the Rhinegrave's advanced Troops the next Day, and were cut in Pieces without Mercy.

This gave us some Satisfaction for the Loss, but it was

but small compared to the Ruin of that Day. We lost near 8000 Men upon the Spot, and above 3000 Prisoners, all our Cannon and Baggage, and 120 Colours. I thought I never made so indifferent a Figure in my Life, and so we thought all; to come away, lose our Infantry, our General, and our Honour, and never fight for it. Duke *Bernard* was utterly disconsolate for old *Gustavus Horn*; for he concluded him killed; he tore the Hair from his Head like a mad Man, and telling the Rhinegrave the Story of the Council of War, would reproach himself with not taking his Advice, often repeating it in his Passion, *'Tis I*, said he, *have been the Death of the bravest General* in Germany; would call himself Fool and Boy, and such Names, for not listening to the Reasons of an old experienced Soldier. But when he heard he was alive in the Enemy's Hands, he was the easier, and applied himself to the recruiting his Troops, and the like Business of the War; and it was not long before he paid the *Imperialists* with Interest.

I returned to *Frankfort au Main* after this Action, which happened the 17th of *August* 1634; but the Progress of the *Imperialists* was so great, that there was no staying at *Frankfort*. The Chancellor *Oxenstern* removed to *Magdeburg*, Duke *Bernard* and the Landgrave marched into *Alsatia*, and the *Imperialists* carried all before them, for all the rest of the Campaign: They took *Philipsburgh* by Surprize; they took *Ausburgh* by Famine, *Spire* and *Treves* by Sieges, taking the Elector Prisoner. But this Success did one Piece of Service to the *Swedes*, that it brought the *French* into the War[1] on their Side; for the Elector of *Treves* was their Confederate. The *French* gave the Conduct of the War to Duke *Bernard*. This, though the Duke of *Saxony* fell off, and fought against them, turned the Scale so much in their Favour, that they recovered their Losses, and proved a Terror to all *Germany*. The farther Accounts of the War I refer to the Histories of those Times, which I have since read with a great deal of Delight.

I confess, when I saw the Progress of the *Imperial* Army

after the Battle of *Nordlingen*, and the Duke of *Saxony* turning his Arms against them, I thought their Affairs declining; and giving them over for lost, I left *Frankfort*, and came down the Rhine to *Cologn*, and from thence into *Holland*.

I came to the *Hague* the 8th of *March* 1635, having spent three Years and a half in *Germany* and the greatest Part of it in the *Swedish* Army.

I spent some Time in *Holland* viewing the wonderful Power of Art which I observed in the Fortifications of their Towns, where the very Bastions stand on bottomless Morasses, and yet are as firm as any in the World. There I had the Opportunity to see the *Dutch* Army, and their famous General Prince *Maurice*.[1] 'Tis true, the Men behaved themselves well enough in Action, when they were put to it, but the Prince's way of beating his Enemies without Fighting, was so unlike the Gallantry of my Royal Instructer, that it had no manner of Relish with me. Our way in *Germany* was always to seek out the Enemy and fight him; and, give the *Imperialists* their due, they were seldom hard to be found, but were as free of their Flesh as we were.

Whereas Prince *Maurice* would lye in a Camp till he starved half his Men, if by lying there he could but starve two Thirds of his Enemies; so that indeed the War in *Holland* had more of Fatigues and Hardships in it, and ours had more of Fighting and Blows: Hasty Marches, long and unwholesome Encampments, Winter Parties, Counter-marching, Dodging, and Entrenching, were the Exercises of his Men, and often times killed him more Men with Hunger, Cold, and Diseases, than he could do with Fighting: Not that it required less Courage, but rather more; for a Soldier had at any time rather die in the Field *a la Coup de Mousquet*, than be starved with Hunger, or frozen to Death in the Trenches.

Nor do I think I lessen the Reputation of that Great General; for tis most certain he ruined the *Spaniard* more by spinning the War thus out in Length, than he could possibly have done by a swift Conquest: For had he, *Gustavus* like, with a Torrent of Victory dislodged the *Spaniard* of all the 12 Provinces in 5 Years, whereas he was 40 Years, a beating them out of 7, he had left them rich and strong at Home, and able to keep them in constant Apprehensions of a Return of his Power: Whereas, by the long Continuance of the War, he so broke the very Heart of the *Spanish* Monarchy, so absolutely and irrecoverably impoverished them, that they have ever since languished of the Disease, till they are fallen from the most powerful, to be the most despicable Nation in the World.

The prodigious Charge the King of *Spain* was at in losing the Seven Provinces, broke the very Spirit of the Nation; and that so much, that all the Wealth of their *Peruvian* Mountains have not been able to retrieve it; King *Philip* having often declared, that War, besides his Armada for invading *England*, had cost him 370 Millions of Ducats, and 4000000 of the best Soldiers in *Europe*; whereof, by an unreasonable *Spanish* Obstinacy, above Sixty Thousand lost their Lives before *Ostend*, a Town not worth a sixth Part, either of the Blood or Money it cost in a Siege of three Years; and which at last he had never taken, but that Prince *Maurice* thought it not worth the Charge of defending it any longer.

However, I say, their Way of fighting in *Holland* did not relish with me at all. The Prince lay a long time before a little Fort called *Shenkscans*,[1] which the *Spaniard* took by Surprize, and I thought he might have taken it much sooner. Perhaps it might be my Mistake; but I fancied my Heroe, the King of *Sweden*, would have carried it Sword in Hand, in Half the Time.

However it was, I did not like it; so in the latter End of the Year I came to the *Hague*, and took Shipping for *England*, where I arrived, to the great Satisfaction of my Father and all my Friends.

My Father was then in *London*, and carried me to kiss the King's Hand. His Majesty was pleased to received me very well, and to say a great many very obliging things to my Father upon my Account.

I spent my Time very retired from Court, for I was almost wholly in the Country; and it being so much different from my Genius, which hankered after a warmer Sport than Hunting among our *Welch* Mountains, I could not but be peeping in all the foreign Accounts from *Germany*, to see who and who was together. There I could never hear of a Battle, and the *Germans* being beaten, but I began to wish my self there. But when an Account came of the Progress of *John Bannier*, the *Swedish* General in *Saxony*, and of the constant Victories he had there over the *Saxons*, I could no longer contain my self, but told my Father this Life was very disagreeable to me; that I lost my Time here, and might to much more Advantage go into *Germany*, where I was sure I might make my Fortune upon my own Terms: That, as young as I was, I might have been a General Officer by this Time, if I had not laid down my Commission: That General *Bannier*, or the Marshal *Horn*, had either of them so much Respect for me, that I was sure I might have any thing of them: And that if he pleased to give me Leave, I would go for *Germany* again. My Father was very unwilling to let me go, but seeing me uneasy, told me, that if I was resolv'd, he would oblige me to stay no longer in *England* than the next Spring, and I should have his Consent.

The Winter following began to look very unpleasant upon us in *England*, and my Father used often to sigh at it; and would tell me sometimes, he was afraid we should have no need to send *Englishmen* to fight in *Germany*.

The Cloud that seemed to threaten most was from *Scotland*. My Father, who had made himself Master of the Arguments on both Sides, used to be often saying, he feared there was some about the King who exasperated him too much against the *Scots*, and drove things too high. For my part, I confess I did not much trouble my Head with the Cause; but all my Fear was, they would not fall out, and we should have no Fighting. I have often reflected since, that I

ought to have known better, that had seen how the most
flourishing Provinces of *Germany* were reduced to the most
miserable Condition that ever any Country in the World
was, by the Ravagings of Soldiers, and the Calamities of
War.

How much soever I was to blame, yet so it was, I had a
secret Joy at the News of the King's raising an Army, and
nothing could have with-held me from appearing in it; but
my Eagerness was anticipated by an Express the King sent
to my Father, to know if his Son was in *England*; and my
Father having ordered me to carry the Answer my self, I
waited upon his Majesty with the Messenger. The King
received me with his usual Kindness, and asked me if I was
willing to serve him against the *Scots*?

I answered, I was ready to serve him against any that his
Majesty thought fit to account his Enemies, and should
count it an Honour to receive his Commands. Hereupon his
Majesty offered me a Commission. I told him, I supposed
there would not be much Time for raising of Men; that if his
Majesty pleased I would be at the Rendezvous with as many
Gentlemen as I could get together, to serve his Majesty as
Voluntiers.

The Truth is, I found all the Regiments of Horse the
King designed to raise, were but two, as Regiments; the
rest of the Horse were such as the Nobility raised in their
several Counties, and commanded them themselves; and,
as I had commanded a Regiment of Horse abroad, it looked
a little odd to serve with a single Troop at home; and the
King took the thing presently. *Indeed 'twill be a Voluntier
War*, said the King, *for the Northern Gentry have sent me an
Account of above* 4000 *Horse they have already*. I bowed, and
told his Majesty I was glad to hear his Subjects were so
forward to serve him; so taking his Majesty's Orders to be
at *York*[1] by the End of *March*, I returned to my Father.

My Father was very glad I had not taken a Commission,
for I know not from what kind of Emulation[2] between the
Western and Northern Gentry. The Gentlemen of our Side

were not very forward in the Service; their Loyalty to the King in the succeeding Times made it appear it was not from any Disaffection to his Majesty's Interest or Person, or to the Cause; but this however made it difficult for me when I came home, to get any Gentleman of Quality to serve with me, so that I presented my self to his Majesty only as a Voluntier, with eight Gentlemen, and about 36 Countrymen well mounted and armed.

And as it proved, these were enough, for this Expedition ended in an Accommodation with the *Scots*; and they not advancing so much as to their own Borders, we never came to any Action; but the Armies lay in the Counties of *Northumberland* and *Durham*, eat up the Country, and spent the King a vast Sum of Money, and so this War ended, a Pacification[1] was made, and both Sides returned.

The Truth is, I never saw such a despicable Appearance of Men in Arms to begin a War, in my Life; whether it was that I had seen so many braver Armies abroad that prejudiced me against them, or that it really was so; for to me they seemed little better than a Rabble met together to devour, rather than fight for their King and Country. There was indeed a great Appearance of Gentlemen, and those of extraordinary Quality; but their Garb, their Equipages, and their Mein, did not look like War; their Troops were filled with Footmen and Servants, and wretchedly armed, God wot. I believe I might say, without Vanity, one Regiment of *Finland* Horse would have made Sport at beating them all. There were such Crouds of Parsons, (for this was a Church War in particular) that the Camp and Court was full of them; and the King was so eternally besieged with Clergymen of one sort or another, that it gave Offence to the chief of the Nobility.

As was the Appearance, so was the Service; the Army marched to the Borders, and the Head Quarter was at *Berwick* upon *Tweed*; but the *Scots* never appeared, no, not so much as their Scouts; whereupon the King called a Council of War, and there it was resolved to send the Earl of *Holland* with a Party of Horse into *Scotland*,[1] to learn some News of the Enemy; and truly the first News he brought us was, that finding their Army encamped about *Coldingham*, 15 Miles from *Berwick*, as soon as he appeared, the *Scots* drew out a Party to charge him, upon which most of his Men halted, I don't say run away, but 'twas next Door to it; for they could not be perswaded to fire their Pistols, and wheel off like Soldiers, but retreated in such a disorderly and shameful Manner, that had the Enemy but had either the Courage or Conduct to have followed them, it must have certainly ended in the Ruin of the whole Party.

THE SECOND PART

I CONFESS, when I went into Arms at the Beginning of this War, I never troubled my self to examine Sides: I was glad to hear the Drums beat for Soldiers; as if I had been a meer *Swiss*,[1] that had not car'd which Side went up or down, so I had my Pay. I went as eagerly and blindly about my Business, as the meanest Wretch that listed in the Army; nor had I the least compassionate Thought for the Miseries of my native Country, 'till after the Fight at *Edgehill*. I had known as much, and perhaps more than most in the Army, what it was to have an Enemy ranging in the Bowels of a Kingdom; I had seen the most flourishing Provinces of *Germany* reduced to perfect Desarts, and the voracious *Crabats*, with inhuman Barbarity, quenching the Fires of the plundered Villages with the Blood of the Inhabitants. Whether this had hardened me against the natural Tenderness which I afterwards found return upon me, or not, I cannot tell; but I reflected upon my self afterwards with a great deal of Trouble, for the Unconcernedness of my Temper at the approaching Ruin of my native Country.

I was in the first Army at *York*, as I have already noted, and I must confess, had the least Diversion there that ever I found in an Army in my Life; for when I was in *Germany* with the King of *Sweden*, we used to see the King with the General Officers every Morning on Horseback, viewing his Men, his Artillery, his Horses, and always something going forward: Here we saw nothing but Courtiers and Clergymen, Bishops and Parsons, as busy as if the Direction of the War had been in them; the King was seldom seen among us, and never without some of them always about him.

Those few of us that had seen the Wars, and would have made a short End of this for him, began to be very uneasy; and particularly a certain Nobleman took the Freedom to tell the King, that the Clergy would certainly ruin the Expedition; *the Case was this* he would ha' had the King have immediately marched into *Scotland*, and put the Matter to the Trial of a Battle; and he urged it every Day; and the King finding his Reasons very good, would often be of his Opinion; but next Morning he would be of another Mind.

This Gentleman was a Man of Conduct enough, and of unquestioned Courage, and afterwards lost his Life for the King. He saw we had an Army of young stout Fellows, numerous enough; and tho' they had not yet seen much Service, he was for bringing them to Action, that the *Scots* might not have time to strengthen themselves; nor they have time by Idleness and Sotting, *the Bane of Soldiers*, to make themselves unfit for any thing.

I was one Morning in Company with this Gentleman; and as he was a warm Man, and eager in his Discourse, a Pox of these Priests, says he, 'tis for them the King has raised this Army, and put his Friends to a vast Charge; and now we are come, they won't let us fight.

But I was afterwards convinced, the Clergy saw farther into the Matter than we did; they saw the *Scots* had a better Army than we had; bold and ready, commanded by brave Officers; and they foresaw, that if we fought, we should be beaten, and if beaten, they were undone. And 'twas very true, we had all been ruined, if we had engaged.

It is true, when we came to the Pacification which followed, I confess I was of the same Mind the Gentleman had been of; for we had better have fought, and been beaten, than have made so dishonourable a Treaty, without striking a Stroke. This Pacification seems to me to have laid the Scheme of all the Blood and Confusion which followed in the Civil

War; for whatever the King and his Friends might pretend to do by talking big, the *Scots* saw he was to be bullied into any thing, and that when it came to the Push, the Courtiers never cared to bring it to Blows.

I have little or nothing, to say as to Action, in this Mock-Expedition. The King was perswaded at last to march to *Berwick*; and as I have said already, a Party of Horse went out to learn News of the *Scots*, and as soon as they saw them, run away from them, bravely.

This made the *Scots* so insolent, that whereas before they lay encamped behind a River, and never shewed themselves, in a sort of modest Deference to their King, which was the Pretence of not being Aggressors or Invaders, only arming in their own Defence; now, having been invaded by the *English* Troops entring *Scotland*, they had what they wanted: And to shew it was not Fear that restrained them before, but Policy, now they came up in Parties to our very Gates, braving, and facing us every Day.

I had, with more Curiosity than Discretion, put my self as a Voluntier at the Head of one of our Parties of Horse, under my Lord *Holland*, when they went out to discover the Enemy; they went, they said, to see what the *Scots* were a-doing.

We had not marched far, but our Scouts brought Word, they had discovered some Horse, but could not come up to them, because a River parted them. At the Heels of these came another Party of our Men upon the Spur to us, and said the Enemy was behind, which might be true, for ought we knew; but it was so far behind, that no Body could see them; and yet the Country was plain and open for above a Mile before us: Hereupon we made a Halt, and indeed I was afraid 'twould have been an odd Sort of a Halt; for our Men began to look one upon another, as they do in like Cases, when they are going to break; and when the Scouts came galloping in, the Men were in such Disorder, that had but one Man broke away, I am satisfied they had all run for it.

I found my Lord *Holland* did not perceive it; but after

the first Surprize was a little over, I told my Lord what I had observed; and that unless some Course was immediately taken, they would all run at the first Sight of the Enemy. I found he was much concerned at it, and began to consult what Course to take, to prevent it. I confess 'tis a hard Question, how to make Men stand and face an Enemy, when Fear has possessed their Minds with an Inclination to run away: But I'll give that Honour to the Memory of that noble Gentleman, who tho' his Experience in Matters of War was small, having never been in much Service; yet his Courage made amends for it; for I dare say he would not have turned his Horse from an Army of Enemies, nor have saved his Life at the Price of running away for it.

My Lord soon saw, as well as I, the Fright the Men were in, after I had given him a Hint of it; and to encourage them, rode thro' their Ranks, and spoke chearfully to them, and used what Arguments he thought proper to settle their Minds. I remembered a Saying which I had heard old Marshal *Gustavus Horn* speak in *Germany*, If you find your Men faulter, or in Doubt, never suffer them to halt, but keep them advancing; for while they are going forward, it keeps up their Courage.

As soon as I could get Opportunity to speak to him, I gave him this as my Opinion. That's very well, says my Lord, but I am studying, says he, to post them so as that they can't run if they would; and if they stand but once to face the Enemy, I don't fear them afterwards.

While we were discoursing thus, Word was brought, that several Parties of the Enemies were seen on the farther Side of the River, upon which my Lord gave the Word to march, and as we were marching on, my Lord calls out a Lieutenant who had been an old Soldier, with only five Troopers whom he had most Confidence in; and having given him his Lesson, he sends him away; in a Quarter of an Hour, one of the five Troopers comes back galloping and hallowing, and tells us his Lieutenant had with his small Party beaten a Party of 20 of the Enemy's Horse over the River, and had secured the Pass, and desired my Lord would march up to him immediately.

'Tis a strange thing that Mens Spirits should be subjected to such sudden Changes, and capable of so much Alteration from Shadows of things. They were for running before they saw the Enemy; now they are in haste to be led on, and but that in raw Men we are obliged to bear with any thing, the Disorder in both was intolerable.

The Story was a premeditated Sham, and not a Word of Truth in it, invented to raise their Spirits, and cheat them out of their cowardly flegmatick Apprehensions, and my Lord had his End in it; for they were all on Fire to fall on: And I am perswaded, had they been led immediately into a Battle begun to their Hands, they would have laid about them like Furies; for there is nothing like Victory to flush a young Soldier. Thus while the Humour was high, and the Fermentation lasted, away we marched; and passing one of their great Commons which they call *Moors*, we came to the River, as he called it, where our Lieutenant was posted with his four Men; 'twas a little Brook fordable with Ease, and leaving a Guard at the Pass, we advanced to the Top of a small Ascent, from whence we had a fair View of the *Scots* Army, as they lay behind another River larger than the former.

Our Men were posted well enough, behind a small Enclosure, with a narrow Lane in their Front: And my Lord had caused his Dragoons to be placed in the Front to line the Hedges; and in this Posture he stood viewing the Enemy at a Distance. The *Scots* who had some Intelligence of our coming, drew out three small Parties, and sent them by different Ways to observe our Number; and forming a fourth Party, which I guessed to be about 600 Horse, advanced to the Top of the Plain, and drew up to face us, but never offered to attack us.

One of the small Parties making about 100 Men, one third Foot passes upon our Flank in View, but out of reach; and as they marched, shouted at us, which our Men better

pleased with that Work than with Fighting, readily enough
answered, and would fain have fired at them for the Pleasure
of making a Noise; for they were too far off to hit them.

I observed that these Parties had always some Foot with
them; and yet if the Horse galloped, or pushed on ever so
forward, the Foot were as forward as they, which was an
extraordinary Advantage.

Gustavus Adolphus that King of Soldiers, was the first that
I have ever observed found the Advantage of mixing small
Bodies of Musqueteers among his Horse; and had he had
such nimble strong Fellows as these, he would have prized
them above all the rest of his Men. These were those they
call *Highlanders*; they would run on Foot with their Arms,
and all their Acoutrements, and keep very good Order too,
and yet keep Pace with the Horse, let them go at what Rate
they would. When I saw the Foot thus interlined among the
Horse, together with the Way of ordering their flying Parties,
it presently occurred to my Mind, that here was some of our
old *Scots*, come home out of *Germany*, that had the ordering
of Matters; and if so, I knew we were not a Match for them.

Thus we stood facing the Enemy 'till our Scouts brought
us Word the whole *Scots* Army was in Motion, and in full
march to attack us; and though it was not true, and the Fear
of our Men doubled every Object, yet 'twas thought convenient to make our Retreat. The whole Matter was, that the
Scouts having informed them what they could, of our
Strength; the 600 were ordered to march towards us, and
three Regiments of Foot were drawn out to support the
Horse.

I know not whether they would have ventured to attack
us, at least before their Foot had come up; but whether they
would have put it to the Hazard or no, we were resolved not
to hazard the Trial, so we drew down to the Pass; and, as
retreating looks something like running away, especially
when an Enemy is at hand, our Men had much a-do to
make their Retreat pass for a March, and not a Flight; and,
by their often looking behind them, any Body might know

what they would have done if they had been pressed.

I confess, I was heartily ashamed when the *Scots* coming up to the Place where we had been posted, stood and shouted at us. I would have perswaded my Lord to have charged them, and he would have done it with all his Heart, but he saw it was not practicable; so we stood at gaze with them above 2 Hours, by which time their Foot were come up to them, and yet they did not offer to attack us. I never was so ashamed of my self in my Life; we were all dispirited, the *Scots* Gentlemen would come out single, within Shot of our Post, which in a time of War is always accounted a Challenge to any single Gentleman, to come out and exchange a Pistol with them, and no Body would stir; at last our old Lieutenant rides out to meet a *Scotchman* that came pickeering on his Quarter. This Lieutenant was a brave and a strong Fellow, had been a Soldier in the *Low Countries*; and though he was not of any Quality, only a meer Soldier, had his Preferment for his Conduct. He gallops bravely up to his Adversary, and exchanging their Pistols, the Lieutenant's Horse happened to be killed. The *Scotchman* very generously dismounts, and engages him with his Sword, and fairly masters him, and carries him away Prisoner; and I think this Horse was all the Blood was shed in that War.

The Lieutenants Name thus conquered was *English*, and as he was a very stout old Soldier, the Disgrace of it broke his Heart. The *Scotchman* indeed used him very generously; for he treated him in the Camp very courteously, gave him another Horse, and set him at Liberty, *gratis*. But the Man laid it so to Heart, that he never would appear in the Army, but went home to his own Country and died.

I had enough of Party-making, and was quite sick with Indignation at the Cowardice of the Men; and my Lord was in as great a Fret as I, but there was no Remedy; we durst not go about to retreat, for we should have been in such Confusion, that the Enemy must have discovered it: So my Lord resolved to keep the Post, if possible, and send to the King for some Foot. Then were our Men ready to fight with one another who should be the Messenger; and at last when a Lieutenant with 20 Dragoons was dispatched, he told us afterwards he found himself an Hundred strong before he was gotten a Mile from the Place.

In short, as soon as ever the Day declined, and the Dusk of the Evening began to shelter the Designs of the Men, they dropt away from us one by one; and at last in such Numbers, that if we had stayed till the Morning, we had not had 50 Men left, out of 1200 Horse and Dragoons.

When I saw how 'twas, consulting with some of the Officers, we all went to my Lord *Holland*, and pressed him to retreat, before the Enemy should discern the Flight of our Men; so he drew us off, and we came to the Camp the next Morning, in the shamefullest Condition that ever poor Men could do. And this was the End of the worst Expedition ever I made in my Life.

To fight and be beaten, is a Casualty common to a Soldier, and I have since had enough of it; but to run away at the Sight of an Enemy, and neither strike or be stricken, this is the very Shame of the Profession, and no Man that has done it, ought to shew his Face again in the Field, unless Disadvantages of Place or Number make it tolerable, neither of which was our Case.

My Lord *Holland* made another March a few Days after, in hopes to retrieve this Miscarriage; but I had enough of it, so I kept in my Quarters: And though his Men did not desert him as before, yet upon the Appearance of the Enemy, they did not think fit to fight, and came off with but little more Honour than they did before.

There was no need to go out to seek the Enemy after this; for they came, as I have noted, and pitched in Sight of us, and their Parties came up every Day to the very Out-works of *Berwick*; but no Body cared to meddle with them: And in this Posture things stood when the Pacification was agreed on by both Parties; which, like a short Truce, only gave both Sides Breath to prepare for a new War more ridiculously managed than the former. When the Treaty was so near a Conclusion, as that Conversation was admitted on both Sides, I went over to the *Scotch* Camp to satisfy my Curiosity, as many of our *English* Officers did also.[1]

I confess, the Soldiers made a very uncouth Figure, especially the *Highlanders*: The Oddness and Barbarity of their Garb and Arms seemed to have something in it remarkable.

They were generally tall swinging Fellows; their Swords were extravagantly, and I think insignificantly broad, and they carried great wooden Targets large enough to cover the upper part of their Bodies. Their Dress was as antique as the rest; a Cap on their Heads, called by them a Bonnet, long hanging Sleeves behind, and their Doublet, Breeches and Stockings, of a Stuff they called Plaid, striped a-cross red and yellow, with short Cloaks of the same. These Fellows looked, when drawn out, like a Regiment of *Merry Andrews* ready for *Bartholomew* Fair. They are in Companies all of a Name, and therefore call one another only by their Christian Names, as *Jemy*, *Jocky*, that is *John*; and *Sawny*, that is, *Alexander*, and the like. And they scorn to be commanded but by one of their own Clan or Family. They are all Gentlemen, and proud enough to be Kings. The meanest Fellow among them is as tenacious of his Honour, as the best Nobleman in the Country, and they will fight, and cut one another's Throats for every trifling Affront.

But to their own Clans or Lairds, they are the willingest and most obedient Fellows in Nature. Give them their due, were their Skill in Exercises and Discipline proportioned to their Courage, they would make the bravest Soldiers in the World. They are large Bodies, and prodigiously strong; and two Qualities they have above other Nations, *viz.* hardy to endure Hunger, Cold, and Hardships, and wonderfully swift of Foot. The latter is such an Advantage in the Field, that I know none like it; for if they conquer, no Enemy can escape them; and if they run, even the Horse can hardly overtake them. These were some of them, who, as I observed before, went out in Parties with their Horse.

There were three or four Thousand of these in the *Scots* Army, armed only with Swords and Targets; and in their Belts some of them had a Pistol, but no Musquets at that time among them.

But there were also a great many Regiments of disciplined Men, who by their carrying their Arms, looked as if they understood their Business, and by their Faces, that they durst see an Enemy.

I had not been Half an Hour in their Camp, after the Ceremony of giving our Names, and passing their Out-Guards and Main Guard was over, but I was saluted by several of my Acquaintance; and in particular, by one who led the *Scotch* Voluntiers at the Taking the Castle of *Openheim*, of which I have given an Account. They used me with all the Respect they thought due to me, on Account of old Affairs, gave me the Word, and a Sergeant waited upon me whenever I pleased to go abroad.

I continued 12 or 14 Days among them, till the Pacification was concluded; and they were ordered to march home. They spoke very respectfully of the King, but I found were exasperated to the last Degree at Arch-bishop *Laud* and the *English* Bishops, for endeavouring to impose the *Common-Prayer-Book* upon them; and they always talked with the utmost Contempt of our Soldiers and Army. I always waved the Discourse about the Clergy, and the Occasion of the War; but I could not but be too sensible what they said of our Men was true; and by this I perceived they had an universal Intelligence from among us, both of what we were doing, and what sort of People we were that were doing it; and they were mighty desirous of coming to Blows with us. I had an Invitation from their General,[1] but I declined it, lest I should give Offence. I found they accepted the Pacification as a thing not likely to hold, or that they did not design should hold; and that they were resolved to keep their Forces on Foot, notwithstanding the Agreement. Their whole Army was full of brave Officers, Men of as much Experience and Conduct as any in the World; and all Men who know any thing of the War, know good Officers presently make a good Army.

Things being thus huddled up, the *English* came back to *York*, where the Army separated, and the *Scots* went home to encrease theirs; for I easily foresaw, that Peace was the farthest thing from their Thoughts.

The next Year the Flame broke out again, the King draws his Forces down into the North, as before, and Expresses were sent to all the Gentlemen that had Commands, to be at the Place by the 15th of *July*. As I had accepted of no Command in the Army, so I had no Inclination at all to go; for I foresaw there would be nothing but Disgrace attend it. My Father observing such an Alteration in my usual Forwardness, asked me one Day, what was the Matter, that I, who used to be so forward to go into the Army, and so eager to run abroad to fight, now shewed no Inclination to appear when the Service of the King and Country called me to it? I told him, I had as much Zeal as ever for the King's Service, and for the Country too: But he knew a Soldier could not abide to be beaten; and being from thence a little more inquisitive, I told him the Observations I had made in the *Scots* Army, and the People I had conversed with there; and, Sir, says I, assure your self, if the King offers to fight them, he will be beaten; and I don't love to engage, when my Judgement tells me before-hand, I shall be worsted: And as I had foreseen, it came to pass; for the Scots resolving to proceed, never stood upon the Ceremony of Aggression, as before, but on the 20th of *August* they entered *England* with their Army.

However, as my Father desired, I went to the King's Army, which was then at *York*, but not gotten all together: The King himself was at *London*; but upon this News takes Post for the Army, and advancing a Part of his Forces, he posted the Lord *Conway* and Sir *Jacob Astley*, with a Brigade of Foot and some Horse at *Newborn*, upon the River *Tine*, to keep the *Scots* from passing that River.

The *Scots* could have passed the *Tine* without Fighting;

but to let us see that they were able to force their Passage, they fall upon this Body of Men; and notwithstanding all the Advantages of the Place, they beat them from the Post, took their Baggage and two Pieces of Cannon, with some Prisoners. Sir *Jacob Astley* made what Resistance he could; but the *Scots* charged with so much Fury, and being also over-powered, he was soon put into Confusion. Immediately the *Scots* made themselves Masters of *Newcastle*,[1] and the next Day of *Durham*, and laid those two Counties under intolerable Contributions.

Now was the King absolutely ruined; for among his own People the Discontents before were so plain, that had the Clergy had any Forecast, they would never have embroiled him with the *Scots*, till he had fully brought Matters to an Understanding at Home: But the Case was thus: The King, by the good Husbandry of Bishop *Juxon*, his Treasurer, had a Million of ready Money in his Treasury, and upon that Account having no need of a Parliament, had not called one in 12 Years; and perhaps had never called another, if he had not by this unhappy Circumstance been reduced to a Necessity of it; for now this ready Money was spent in two foolish Expeditions, and his Army appeared in a Condition not fit to engage the *Scots*; the Detatchment under Sir *Jacob Astley*, which were of the Flower of his Men, had been routed at *Newborn*, and the Enemy had Possession of two entire Counties.

All Men blamed *Laud* for prompting the King to provoke the *Scots*, a headstrong Nation, and zealous for their own Way of Worship; and *Laud* himself found too late the Consequences of it, both to the whole Cause and to himself; for the *Scots*, whose native Temper is not easily to forgive an Injury, pursued him by their Party in *England*, and never gave it over, till they laid his Head on the Block.

The ruined Country now clamoured in his Majesty's Ears with daily Petitions, and the Gentry of other Neighbour Counties cry out for Peace and a Parliament. The King, embarassed with these Difficulties, and quite empty of

Money, calls a Great Council[1] of the Nobility at *York*, and demands their Advice, which any one could have told him before, would be to call a Parliament.

I cannot, without Regret, look back upon the Misfortune of the King, who, as he was one of the best Princes in his personal Conduct that ever reigned in *England*, had yet some of the greatest Unhappinesses in his Conduct as a King, that ever Prince had, and the whole Course of his Life demonstrated it.

1. An impolitick Honesty. His Enemies called it Obstinacy: But as I was perfectly acquainted with his Temper, I cannot but think it was his Judgment, when he thought he was in the right to adhere to it as a Duty tho' against his Interest.

2. Too much Compliance when he was complying.

No Man but himself would have denied what at some-times he denied, and have granted what at other times he granted; and this Uncertainty of Counsel proceeded from two things.

1. The Heat of the Clergy, to whom he was exceedingly devoted, and for whom indeed he ruined himself.

2. The Wisdom of his Nobility.

Thus when the Counsel of his Priests prevailed, all was Fire and Fury; the *Scots* were Rebels, and must be subdued; and the Parliament's Demands were to be rejected as exorbitant; but whenever the King's Judgment was led by the grave and steady Advice of his Nobility and Counsellors, he was always enclined by them to temperate his Measures between the two Extremes: And had he gone on in such a Temper, he had never met with the Misfortunes which afterward attended him, or had so many Thousands of his Friends lost their Lives and Fortunes in his Service.

I am sure, we that knew what it was to fight for him, and that loved him better than any of the Clergy could pretend to, have had many a Consultation how to bring over our Master from so espousing their Interest, as to ruin himself for it; but 'twas in vain.

I took this Interval, when I sat still and only looked on,

to make these Remarks, because I remember the best Friends the King had were at this time of that Opinion. That 'twas an unaccountable Piece of Indiscretion, to commence a Quarrel with the *Scots*, a poor and obstinate People, for a Ceremony and Book of Church Discipline,[1] at a time when the King stood but upon indifferent Terms with his People at Home.

The Consequence was, it put Arms into the Hands of his Subjects to rebel against him; it embroiled him with his Parliament in *England*, to whom he was fain to stoop in a fatal and unusual Manner to get Money,[2] all his own being spent, and so to buy off the *Scots* whom he cou'd not beat off.

I cannot but give one Instance of the unaccountable Politicks of his Ministers. If they over-ruled this unhappy King to it, with Design to exhaust and impoverish him, they were the worst of Traytors; if not, the grossest of Fools. They prompted the King to equip a Fleet against the *Scots*, and to put on board it 5000 Land Men. Had this been all, the Design had been good, that while the King had faced the Army upon the Borders, these 5000 landing in the Firth of *Edinburgh* might have put that whole Nation into Disorder. But in Order to this, they advise the King to lay out his Money in fitting out the biggest Ships he had, and the Royal Sovereign, the biggest Ship the World had ever seen, which cost him no less than 100000 Pounds was now built, and fitted out for this Voyage.

This was the most incongruous and ridiculous Advice that could be given, and made us all believe we were betrayed, tho' we knew not by whom.

To fit out Ships of 100 Guns to invade *Scotland*, which had not one Man of War in the World, nor any open Confederacy with any Prince or State that had any Fleet! 'twas a most ridiculous thing. An Hundred Sail of *Newcastle* Colliers, to carry the Men with their Stores and Provisions, and ten Frigates of 40 Guns each, had been as good a Fleet as Reason, and the Nature of the thing could ha' made tolerable.

Thus things were carried on, 'till the King, beggar'd by the Mismanagement of his Counsels, and beaten by the *Scots*, was driven to the Necessity of calling a Parliament in *England*.

It is not my Design to enter into the Feuds and Brangles[1] of this Parliament. I have noted, by Observations of their Mistakes, who brought the King to this unhappy Necessity of calling them.

His Majesty had tried Parliaments upon several Occasions before, but never found himself so much embroiled with them but he could send them Home, and there was an End of it; but as he could not avoid Calling these, so they took Care to put him out of a Condition to dismiss them.

The *Scots* Army was now quartered upon the *English*. The Counties, the Gentry, and the Assembly of Lords at *York*, petitioned for a Parliament.

The *Scots* presented their Demands to the King, in which it was observed, that Matters were concerted between them and a Party in *England*; and I confess, when I saw that, I began to think the King in an ill Case; for as the *Scots* pretended Grievances, we thought, the King redressing those Grievances, they could ask no more; and therefore all Men advised the King to grant their full Demands. And whereas the King had not Money to supply the *Scots* in their March home, I know there were several Meetings of Gentlemen with a Design to advance considerable Sums of Money to the King to set him free, and in order to reinstate his Majesty, as before. Not that we ever advised the King to rule without a Parliament, but we were very desirous of putting him out of the Necessity of calling them, at least, just then.

But the Eighth Article[2] of the *Scots* Demands expressly required, That an *English* Parliament might be called to remove all Obstructions of Commerce, and to settle Peace, Religion and Liberty; and in another Article they tell the King, the 24th of *September* being the Time his Majesty appointed for the Meeting of the Peers, will make it too long e'er the Parliament meet.

And in another, That a Parliament was the only Way of settling Peace, and bringing them to his Majesty's Obedience.

When we saw this in the Army, 'twas time to look about. Every body perceived that the *Scots* Army would call an *English* Parliament; and whatever Aversion the King had to it, we all saw he would be obliged to comply with it; and now they all began to see their Error, who advised the King to this *Scotch* War.

While these things were transacting, the Assembly of the Peers meet at *York*; and by their Advice a Treaty was begun with the *Scots*. I had the Honour to be sent with the first Message which was in Writing.

I brought it, attended with a Trumpet, and a Guard of 500 Horse, to the *Scots* Quarters. I was stoped at *Darlington*, and my Errand being known, General *Lesly* sent a *Scots* Major and 50 Horse, to receive me, but would let neither my Trumpet or Guard set Foot within their Quarters. In this Manner, I was conducted to Audience in the Chapter-House at *Durham*, where a Committee of *Scots* Lords who attended the Army, received me very courteously, and gave me their Answer in Writing also.

'Twas in this Answer that they shewed at least to me their Design of embroiling the King with his *English* Subjects; they discoursed very freely with me, and did not order me to withdraw when they debated their private Opinions: They drew up several Answers but did not like them; at last, they gave me one which I did not receive; I thought it was too insolent to be born with, as near as I can remember, it was thus.

The Commissioners of Scotland *attending the Service in the Army, do refuse any Treaty in the City of* York.

One of the Commissioners who treated me with more Distinction than the rest, and discoursed freely with me, gave me an Opportunity to speak more freely of this than I expected.

I told them, if they would return to his Majesty an Answer fit for me to carry, or if they would say they would not treat at all, I would deliver such a Message: But I entreated them to consider the Answer was to their Sovereign, and to whom they made a great Profession of Duty and Respect; and at least they ought to give their Reasons, why they declined a Treaty at *York*; and to name some other Place, or humbly to desire his Majesty to name some other Place: But to send Word they would not treat at *York*, I could deliver no such Message, for when put into *English* it would signify, they would not treat at all.

I used a great many Reasons and Arguments with them on this Head: And at last, with some Difficulty, obtained of them to give the Reason, which was the Earl of *Strafford*'s having the chief Command at *York*, whom they declared their mortal Enemy, he having declared them Rebels in *Ireland*.

With this Answer I returned. I could make no Observation in the short time I was with them; for as I staid but one Night, so I was guarded as a close Prisoner all the while. I saw several of their Officers whom I knew, but they durst not speak to me; and if they would ha' ventured, my Guard would not ha' permitted them.

In this Manner I was conducted out of their Quarters to my own Party again, and having delivered my Message to the King, and told his Majesty the Circumstances, I saw the King receive the Account of the haughty Behaviour of the *Scots* with some Regret; however it was his Majesty's time now to bear, and therefore the *Scots* were comply'd with, and the Treaty appointed at *Rippon*;[1] where, after much Debate, several preliminary Articles were agreed on, as a Cessation of Arms, *Quarters and Bounds to the Armies*, *Subsistence to the* Scots *Army*, and the Residue of the Demands was referred to a Treaty at *London*, *&c.*

We were all amazed at the Treaty, and I cannot but remember we used to wish much rather we had been suffered to fight;[2] for tho' we had been worsted at first, the Power and Strength of the King's Interest which was not yet tried, must, in fine, ha' been too strong for the *Scots*: Whereas now we saw the King was for complying with any thing, and all his Friends would be ruined.

I confess, I had nothing to fear, and so was not much concerned; but our Predictions soon came to pass: For no sooner was this Parliament called, but Abundance of those who had embroiled their King with his People of both Kingdoms, like the Disciples, when their Master was betrayed to the *Jews, forsook him and fled*;[1] and now Parliament Tyranny began to succeed Church Tyranny, and we Soldiers were glad [to] see it at first: The Bishops trembled, the Judges went to Gaol; the Officers of the Customs were laid hold on; and the Parliament began to lay their Fingers on the great ones, particularly Arch-Bishop *Laud*, and the Earl of *Strafford*.[2] We had no great Concern for the first, but the last was a Man of so much Conduct and Gallantry, and so beloved by the Soldiers and principal Gentry of *England*, that every Body was touched with his Misfortune.

The Parliament now grew mad in their Turn, and as the Prosperity of any Party is the time to shew their Discretion, the Parliament shewed they knew as little where to stop as other People. The King was not in a Condition to deny any thing, and nothing could be demanded but they push'd it. They attainted the Earl of *Strafford*, and thereby made the King cut off his right Hand, to save his left, and yet not save it neither. They obtain another Bill, to empower them to sit during their own Pleasure, and after them, Triennial Parliaments to meet, whether the King call them or no; and Granting this compleated his Majesty's Ruin.

Had the House only regulated the Abuses of the Court, punished evil Counsellors, and restor'd Parliaments to their original and just Powers, all had been well; and the King, tho' he had been more than mortified, had yet reaped the Benefit of future Peace; for now the *Scots* were sent Home, after having eaten up two Counties, and received a prodigious Sum of Money to boot: And the King, tho' too late, goes in Person to *Edinburgh*, and grants them all they could desire, and more than they asked; but in *England*, the Desires of ours were unbounded, and drove at all Extremes.

They threw out the Bishops from sitting in the House, make a Protestation equivalent to the *Scotch* Covenant; and this done, print their Remonstrance.[1] This so provoked the King, that he resolves upon seizing some of the Members,[2] and in an ill Hour enters the House in Person to take them. Thus one imprudent thing on one Hand produced another of the other Hand, 'till the King was obliged to leave them to themselves, for fear of being mobbed into something or other unworthy of himself.

These Proceedings began to alarm the Gentry and Nobility of *England*; for however willing we were to have evil Counsellours removed, and the Government return to a settled and legal Course, according to the happy Constitution of this Nation, and might ha' been forward enough to have owned the King had been misled, and imposed upon to do things which he had rather had not been done; yet it did not follow, that all the Powers and Prerogatives of the Crown should devolve upon the Parliament, and the King in a Manner be deposed, or else sacrificed to the Fury of the Rabble.

The Heats of the House running them thus to all Extremes, and at last to take from the King the Power of the Militia,[3] which indeed was all that was left to make him any thing of a King, put the King upon opposing Force with Force; and thus the Flame of Civil War began.

However backward I was in engaging in the second Year's Expedition against the *Scots*, I was as forward now; for I waited on the King at *York*, where a gallant Company of Gentlemen as ever were seen in *England*, engaged themselves to enter into his Service; and here some of us formed our selves into Troops for the Guard of his Person.

The King having been waited upon by the Gentry of *Yorkshire*, and having told them his Resolution of erecting his Royal Standard, and received from them hearty Assurances of Support; dismisses them, and marches to *Hull*, where lay the Train of Artillery, and all the Arms and

Amunition belonging to the *Northern* Army which had been disbanded. But here the Parliament had been beforehand with his Majesty, so that when he came to *Hull*, he found the Gates shut, and Sir *John Hotham* the Governour upon the Walls, tho' with a great deal of seeming Humility and Protestations of Loyalty to his Person, yet with a positive Denial to admit any of the King's Attendants into the Town. If his Majesty pleased to enter the Town in Person with any reasonable Number of his Househould, he would submit, but would not be prevailed on to receive the King, as he would be received, with his Forces, tho' those Forces were then but very few.

The King was exceedingly provoked at this Repulse, and indeed it was a great Surprize to us all; for certainly never Prince began a War against the whole Strength of his Kingdom, under the Circumstances that he was in. He had not a Garrison, or a Company of Soldiers in his Pay, not a Stand of Arms, or a Barrel of Powder, a Musquet, Cannon or Mortar, not a Ship of all the Fleet, or Money in his Treasury to procure them; whereas the Parliament had all his Navy, and Ordinance, Stores, Magazines, Arms, Ammunition, and Revenue, in their Keeping. And this I take to be another Defect of the King's Counsel, and a sad Instance of the Distraction of his Affairs; that when he saw how all things were going to wreck, as it was impossible but he should see it, and 'tis plain he did see it, that he should not long enough before it came to Extremities, secure the Navy, Magazines, and Stores of War, in the Hands of his trusty Servants that would have been sure to have preserved them for his Use, at a Time when he wanted them.

It cannot be supposed, but the Gentry of *England*, who generally preserved their Loyalty for their Royal Master, and at last heartily shewed it, were exceedingly discouraged at first, when they saw the Parliament had all the Means of making War in their own Hands, and the King was naked and destitute either of Arms, or Ammunition, or Money to procure them.

Not but that the King, by extraordinary Application, recovered the Disorder the Want of these things had thrown him into, and supplied himself with all things needful.

But my Observation was this, had his Majesty had the Magazines, Navy, and Forts in his own Hand, the Gentry, who wanted but the Prospect of something to encourage them, had come in at first, and the Parliament being unprovided, would have been presently reduced to Reason.

But this was it that baulked the Gentry of *Yorkshire*, who went home again, giving the King good Promises, but never appeard for him, till by raising a good Army in *Shropshire* and *Wales*, he marched towards *London*, and they saw there was a Prospect of their being supported.

In this Condition the King erected his Standard at *Nottingham*, *August* the 22d 1642, and, I confess, I had very melancholy Apprehensions of the King's Affairs; for the Appearance to the Royal Standard was but small. The Affront the King had met with at *Hull*, had baulked and dispirited the Northern Gentry, and the King's Affairs looked with a very dismal Aspect. We had Expresses from *London* of the prodigious Success of the Parliament's Levies, how their Men came in faster than they could entertain them, and that Arms were delivered out to whole Companies listed together, and the like: And all this while the King had not got together a Thousand Foot, and had no Arms for them neither. When the King saw this, he immediately dispatches five several Messengers, whereof one went to the Marquess of *Worcester* into *Wales*; one went to the Queen, then at *Windsor*; one to the Duke of *Newcastle*, then Marquess of *Newcastle*, into the *North*; one into *Scotland*, and one into *France*, where the Queen soon after arrived to raise Money, and buy Arms, and to get what Assistance she could among her own Friends: Nor was her Majesty idle, for she sent over several Ships laden with Arms and Ammunition, with a fine Train of Artillery, and a great many very good Officers; and though one of the first fell into the Hands of the Parliament, with 300 Barrels of Powder and some

Arms, and 150 Gentlemen, yet most of the Gentlemen found Means, one Way or other, to get to us, and most of the Ships the Queen freighted arrived; and at last her Majesty came her self, and brought an extraordinary Supply, both of Men, Money, Arms, &c. with which she joined the King's Forces under the Earl of *Newcastle* in the *North*. Finding his Majesty thus bestirring himself to muster his Friends together, I ask'd him, if he thought it might not be for his Majesty's Service to let me go among my Friends, and his loyal Subjects about *Shrewsbury?* Yes, says the King, smiling, I intend you shall, and I design to go with you my self. I did not understand what the King meant then, and did not think it good Manners to enquire; but the next Day I found all things disposed for a March, and the King on Horseback by Eight of the Clock; when calling me to him, he told me I should go before, and let my Father and all my Friends know, he would be at *Shrewsbury* the *Saturday* following. I left my Equipages, and taking Post with only one Servant, was at my Father's the next Morning by Break of Day. My Father was not surprized at the News of the King's coming at all; for, it seems, he, together with the loyal Gentry of those Parts, had sent particularly to give the King an Invitation to move that Way, which I was not made privy to; with an Account what Encouragement they had there in the Endeavours made for his Interest. In short, the whole Country was entirely for the King, and such was the universal Joy the People shewed when the News of his Majesty's coming down was positively known, that all Manner of Business was laid aside, and the whole Body of the People seemed to be resolved upon the War.

As this gave a new Face to the King's Affairs, so I must own it filled me with Joy; for I was astonished before, when I considered what the King and his Friends were like to be exposed to. The News of the Proceedings of the Parliament, and their powerful Preparations were now no more terrible; the King came at the Time appointed, and having lain at my Father's House one Night, entered *Shrewsbury* in the

Morning. The Acclamations of the People, the Concourse of the Nobility and Gentry about his Person, and the Crouds which now came every Day in to his Standard, were incredible.[1]

The Loyalty of the *English* Gentry was not only worth Notice, but the Power of the Gentry is extraordinary visible in this Matter: The King, in about six Weeks time, which was the most of his Stay at *Shrewsbury*, was supplied with Money, Arms, Ammunition, and a Train of Artillery, and listed a Body of an Army upwards of 20000 Men.

His Majesty seeing the general Alacrity of his People, immediately issued out Commissions, and form'd Regiments of Horse and Foot; and having some experienced Officers about him, together with about 16 who came from *France*, with a Ship loaded with Arms and some Field-pieces which came very seasonably into the *Severn*; the Men were exercised, regularly disciplined, and quartered, and now we began to look like Soldiers. My Father had raised a Regiment of Horse at his own Charge, and compleated them, and the King gave out Arms to them from the Supplies which I mentioned came from Abroad. Another Party of Horse, all brave stout Fellows, and well mounted, came in from *Lancashire*, and the Earl of *Derby* at the Head of them. The *Welchmen* came in by Droves; and so great was the Concourse of People, that the King began to think of Marching, and gave the Command, as well as the Trust of Regulating the Army, to the brave Earl of *Lindsey*, as General of the Foot. The Parliament General being the Earl of *Essex*, two braver men, or two better Officers, were not in the Kingdom; they had both been old Soldiers, and had served together as Voluntiers, in the *Low Country* Wars, under Prince *Maurice*. They had been Comrades and Companions Abroad, and now came to face one another as Enemies in the Field.

Such was the Expedition used by the King and his Friends, in the Levies of this first Army, that notwithstanding the wonderful Expedition the Parliament made, the King was in the Field before them; and now the Gentry in other Parts of the Nation bestirred themselves, and siezed upon, and Garrisoned several considerable Places for the King. In the North, the Earl of *Newcastle* not only Garrisoned the most considerable Places, but even the general Possession of the North was for the King, excepting *Hull*, and some few Places, which the old Lord *Fairfax* had taken up for the Parliament. On the other Hand, entire *Cornwall*, and most of the Western Counties were the King's. The Parliament had their chief Interest in the South and Eastern Part of *England*, as *Kent*, *Surry*, and *Sussex*, *Essex*, *Suffolk*, *Norfolk*, *Cambridge*, *Bedford*, *Huntington*, *Hertford*, *Buckinghamshire*, and the other midland Counties. These were called, or some of them at least, the Associated Counties, and felt little of the War, other than the Charges; but the main Support of the Parliament was the City of *London*. The King made the Seat of his Court at *Oxford*, which he caused to be regularly fortified. The Lord *Say* had been here, and had Possession of the City for the Enemy, and was debating about fortifying it, but came to no Resolution, which was a very great Oversight in them; the Situation of the Place, and the Importance of it, on many Accounts, to the City of *London*, considered; and they would have retrieved this Error afterwards, but then 'twas too late; for the King made it the Head Quarter, and received great Supplies and Assistance from the Wealth of the Colleges, and the Plenty of the neighbouring Country. *Abingdon*, *Wallingford*, *Basing* and *Reading*, were all Garrisoned and fortified as Outworks to defend this as the Center. And thus all *England* became the Theater of Blood, and War was spread into every Corner of the Country, though as yet there was no Stroke struck. I had no Command in this Army; my Father led his own Regiment, and old as he was, would not leave his royal Master, and my elder Brother staid at home to support the Family. As for me, I rode a Voluntier in the royal Troop of Guards, which may very well deserve the Title of a royal Troop; for it was composed of young Gentlemen Sons of the Nobility and some of the prime Gentry of the Nation, and I think not a Person of so mean a Birth or Fortune as my self. We reckoned in this Troop Two and Thirty Lords, or who came afterwards to be such, and Eight and Thirty of younger Sons of the Nobility, five *French* Noblemen, and all the rest Gentlemen of very good Families and Estates.

And that I may give the due to their personal Valour, many of this Troop lived afterwards to have Regiments and Troops under their Command, in the Service of the King; many of them lost their Lives for him, and most of them their Estates: Nor did they behave unworthy of themselves in their first shewing their Faces to the Enemy, as shall be mentioned in its Place.

While the King remained at *Shrewsbury*, his loyal Friends bestirred themselves in several Parts of the Kingdom. *Goring* had secured *Portsmouth*; but being young in Matters of War, and not in Time relieved, though the Marquess of *Hertford* was marching to relieve him, yet he was obliged to quit the Place, and shipped himself for *Holland*, from whence he returned with Relief for the King, and afterwards did very good Service upon all Occasions, and so effectually cleared himself of the Scandal the hasty Surrender of *Portsmouth* had brought upon his Courage.

The chief Power of the King's Forces lay in three Places, in *Cornwall*, in *Yorkshire*, and at *Shrewsbury*: In *Cornwall*, Sir *Ralph Hopton*, afterwards Lord *Hopton*; Sir *Bevil Granvil* and Sir *Nicholas Slamming*, secured all the Country, and afterwards spread themselves over *Devonshire* and *Somersetshire*, took *Exeter* from the Parliament, fortified *Bridgwater*, and *Barnstable*, and beat Sir *William Waller* at the Battle of *Roundway Down*, as I shall touch at more particularly when I come to recite the Part of my own Travels that Way.

In the *North*, the Marquess of *Newcastle* secured all the Country, Garrisoned *York*, *Scarborough*, *Carlisle*, *Newcastle Pomfret*, *Leeds*, and all the considerable Places, and took the Field with a very good Army, though afterwards he proved more unsuccessful than the rest, having the whole Power of a Kingdom at his Back, the *Scots* coming in with an Army to the Assistance of the Parliament; which indeed was the general Turn of the Scale of the War; for had it not been for this *Scots* Army, the King had most certainly reduced the Parliament, at least to good Terms of Peace, in two Years time.

The King was the third Article: His Force at *Shrewsbury* I have noted already; the Alacrity of the Gentry filled him with Hopes, and all his Army with Vigour, and the 8th of *October* 1642, his Majesty gave Orders to march. The Earl of *Essex* had spent above a Month after his leaving *London* (for he went thence the 9th of *September*) in modelling and drawing together his Forces; his Rendezvous was at St. *Albans*, from whence he marched to *Northampton*, *Coventry*, and *Warwick*, and leaving Garrisons in them, he comes on to *Worcester*. Being thus advanced, he possesses *Oxford*, as I noted before, *Banbury*, *Bristol*, *Gloucester*, and *Worcester*, out of all which Places, except *Gloucester*, we drove him back to *London* in a very little while.

Sir *John Biron* had raised a very good Party of 500 Horse, most Gentlemen, for the King, and had possessed *Oxford*; but on the Approach of the Lord *Say* quitted it, being now but an open Town, and retreated to *Worcester*: From whence, on the Approach of *Essex*'s Army, he retreated to the King. And now all things grew ripe for Action, both Parties having secured their Posts, and settled their Schemes of the War, taken their Posts and Places as their Measures and Opportunities directed, the Field was next in their Eye, and the Soldiers began to enquire when they should fight; for as yet there had been little or no Blood drawn, and 'twas not long before they had enough of it; for I believe I may challenge all the Historians in *Europe* to tell me of any War in the World where, in the Space of four Years, there were so many pitched Battles, Sieges, Fights, and Skirmishes, as in this War; we never encamped or entrenched, never fortified the Avenues to our Posts, or lay fenced with Rivers and Defiles; here was no Leaguers in the Field, as at the

Story of *Noremberg*, neither had our Soldiers any Tents, or what they call heavy Baggage. 'Twas the general Maxim of this War, Where is the Enemy? Let us go and fight them: Or, on the other Hand, if the Enemy was coming, what was to be done? Why, what should be done? Draw out into the Fields, and fight them. I cannot say 'twas the Prudence of the Parties, and had the King fought less he had gained more: And I shall remark several times, when the Eagerness of Fighting was the worst Counsel, and proved our Loss. This Benefit however happened in general to the Country, that it made a quick, though a bloody End, of the War, which otherwise had lasted till it might have ruined the whole Nation.

On the 10th of *October* the King's Army was in full March, his Majesty Generalissimo, the Earl of *Lindsey* General of the Foot, Prince *Rupert* General of the Horse; and the first Action in the Field was by Prince *Rupert* and Sir *John Biron*. Sir *John* had brought his Body of 500 Horse, as I noted already, from *Oxford* to *Worcester*; the Lord *Say*, with a strong Party, being in the Neighbourhood of *Oxford*, and expected in the Town, Collonel *Sandys*, a hot Man, and who had more Courage than Judgment, advances with about 1500 Horse and Dragoons, with Design to beat Sir *John Biron* out of *Worcester*, and take Post there for the Parliament.

The King had notice that the Earl of *Essex* designed for *Worcester*, and Prince *Rupert* was ordered to advance with a Body of Horse and Dragoons, to face the Enemy, and bring off Sir *John Biron*. This his Majesty did to amuse[1] the Earl of *Essex*, that he might expect him that Way; whereas the King's Design was to get between the Earl of *Essex*'s Army and the City of *London*; and his Majesty's End was doubly answered; for he not only drew *Essex* on to *Worcester*, where he spent more Time than he needed, but he beat the Party into the Bargain.

I went Voluntier in this Party, and rid in my Father's Regiment; for though we really expected not to see the

Enemy, yet I was tired with lying still. We came to *Worcester* just as Notice was brought to Sir *John Biron*, that a Party of the Enemy was on their March for *Worcester*, upon which the Prince immediately consulting what was to be done, resolves to march the next Morning, and fight them.

The Enemy, who lay at *Pershore*,[1] about eight Miles from *Worcester*, and, as I believe, had no Notice of our March, came on very confidently in the Morning, and found us fairly drawn up to receive them: I must confess this was the bluntest downright Way of making War that ever was seen. The Enemy, who, in all the little Knowledge I had of War ought to have discovered our Numbers, and guessed by our Posture what our Design was, might equally have informed themselves, that we intended to attack them, and so might have secured the Advantage of a Bridge in their Front; but without any Regard to these Methods of Policy, they came on at all Hazards. Upon this Notice, my Father proposed to the Prince, to halt for them, and suffer ourselves to be attacked, since we found them willing to give us the Advantage: The Prince approved of the Advice, so we halted within View of a Bridge, leaving Space enough on our Front for about half the Number of their Forces to pass and draw up; and at the Bridge was posted about 50 Dragoons, with Orders to retire as soon as the Enemy advanced, as if they had been afraid. On the Right of the Road was a Ditch, and a very high Bank behind, where we had placed 300 Dragoons, with Orders to lye flat on their Faces till the Enemy had passed the Bridge, and to let fly among them as soon as our Trumpets sounded a Charge. No Body but Collonel *Sandys* would have been caught in such a Snare; for he might easily have seen, that when he was over the Bridge, there was not Room enough for him to fight in: But the Lord of Hosts was so much in their Mouths, *for that was the Word*[2] *for that Day*, that they took little heed how to conduct the Host of the Lord to their own Advantage.

As we expected, they appeared, beat our Dragoons from

the Bridge, and passed it: We stood firm in one Line with a Reserve, and expected a Charge; but Collonel *Sandys* shewing a great deal more Judgment than we thought he was Master of, extends himself to the Left, finding the Ground too streight, and began to form his Men with a great deal of Readiness and Skill; for by this time he saw our Number was greater than he expected: The Prince perceiving it, and foreseeing that the Stratagem of the Dragoons would be frustrated by this, immediately charges with the Horse, and the Dragoons at the same time standing upon their Feet, poured in their Shot upon those that were passing the Bridge: This Surprize put them into such Disorder, that we had but little Work with them; for though Collonel *Sandys* with the Troops next him sustained the Shock very well, and behaved themselves gallantly enough, yet the Confusion beginning in their Reer, those that had not yet passed the Bridge were kept back by the Fire of the Dragoons, and the rest were easily cut in Pieces. Collonel *Sandys* was mortally wounded and taken Prisoner, and the Crowd was so great, to get back, that many pushed into the Water; and were rather smothered than drowned. Some of them who never came into the Fight, were so frighted, that they never looked behind them, 'till they came to *Pershore*; and as we were afterwards informed, the Life-Guards of the General who had quartered in the Town, left it in Disorder enough, expecting us at the Heels of their Men.

If our Business had been to keep the Parliament Army from coming to *Worcester*, we had a very good Opportunity to have secured the Bridge at *Pershore*; but our Design lay another Way, as I have said, and the King was for drawing *Essex* on to the *Severn*, in hopes to get behind him, which fell out accordingly.

Essex, spurred by this Affront in the Infancy of their Affairs, advances the next Day, and came to *Pershore* time enough to be at the Funeral of some of his Men; and from thence he advances to *Worcester*.

We marched back to *Worcester* extremely pleased with

the good Success of our first Attack; and our Men were so flushed with this little Victory, that it put Vigour into the whole Army. The Enemy lost about 3000 Men, and we carried away near 150 Prisoners, with 500 Horses, some Standards and Arms, and among the Prisoners their Collonel, but he died a little after of his Wounds.

Upon the Approach of the Enemy, *Worcester* was quitted, and the Forces marched back to join the King's Army which lay then at *Bridgnorth*, *Ludlow*, and thereabout. As the King expected, it fell out; *Essex* found so much Work at *Worcester* to settle Parliament Quarters, and secure *Bristol*, *Gloucester*, and *Hereford*, that it gave the King a full Day's March of him; so the King having the Start of him, moves towards *London*; and *Essex*, nettled to be both beaten in Fight, and out-done in Conduct, decamps, and follows the King.

The Parliament, and the *Londoners* too, were in a strange Consternation at this Mistake of their General; and had the King, whose great Misfortune was always to follow precipitant Advices: Had the King, I say, pushed on his first Design, which he had formed with very good Reason, and for which he had been dodging with *Essex* eight or ten Days, *viz.* Of marching directly to *London*, where he had a very great Interest, and where his Friends were not yet oppressed and impoverished, as they were afterwards, he had turned the Scale of his Affairs: And every Man expected it; for the Members began to shift for themselves, Expresses were sent on the Heels of one another to the Earl of *Essex*, to hasten after the King, and if possible to bring him to a Battle. Some of these Letters fell into our Hands, and we might easily discover, that the Parliament were in the last Confusion at the Thoughts of our coming to *London*: Besides this, the City was in a worse Fright than the House, and the great moving[1] Men began to go out of Town. In short, they expected us, and we expected to come, but Providence for our Ruine had otherwise determined it.

Essex, upon News of the King's March, and upon Receipt

of the Parliament's Letters, makes long Marches after us, and on the 23d of *October* reaches the Village of *Keynton* in *Warwickshire*. The King was almost as far as *Banbury*, and there calls a Council of War. Some of the old Officers that foresaw the Advantage the King had, the Concern the City was in, and the vast Addition both to the Reputation of his Forces, and the Encrease of his Interest, it would be, if the King could gain that Point, urged the King to march on to *London*. Prince *Rupert*, and the fresh Collonells pressed for Fighting, told the King, it dispirited their Men to march with the Enemy at their Heels; that the Parliament Army was inferiour to him by 6000 Men, and fatigued with hasty Marching; that their Orders were to fight, he had nothing to do, but to post himself to Advantage, and receive them to their Destruction; that the Action near *Worcester* had let him know how easy it was to deal with a rash Enemy; and that 'twas a Dishonour for him, whose Forces were so much superior, to be pursued by his Subjects in Rebellion. These and the like Arguments prevailed with the King to alter his wiser Measures, and resolve to fight. Nor was this all, when a Resolution of fighting was taken, that Part of the Advice which they who were for fighting gave, as a Reason for their Opinion, was forgot, and instead of halting, and posting our selves to Advantage till the Enemy came up, we were ordered to march back, and meet them.

Nay, so eager was the Prince for fighting, that when from the Top of *Edgehill*, the Enemy's Army was descried in the Bottom between them and the Village of *Keynton*, and that the Enemy had bid us Defiance, by discharging three Cannons, we accepted the Challenge, and answering with two Shot from our Army, we must needs forsake the Advantages of the Hills, which they must have mounted under the Command of our Cannon, and march down to them into the Plain. I confess, I thought here was a great deal more Gallantry than Discretion; for it was plainly taking an Advantage out of our own Hands, and putting it into the Hands of the Enemy. An Enemy that *must fight*, may always be fought with to Advantage. My old Heroe, the Glorious *Gustavus Adolphus*, was as forward to fight as any Man of true Valour mixt with any Policy need to be, or ought to be; but he used to say, *An Enemy reduced to a Necessity of Fighting, is half Beaten.*

'Tis true, we were all but young in the War; the Souldiers hot and forward, and eagerly desired to come to Hands with the Enemy. But I take the more Notice of it here, because the King in this acted against his own Measures: For it was the King himself had laid the Design of getting the Start of *Essex*, and marching to *London*. His Friends had invited him thither, and expected him, and suffered deeply for the Omission; and yet he gave way to these hasty Counsels, and suffered his Judgment to be over-ruled by Majority of Voices; an Error, I say, the Kings of *Sweden* was never guilty of: For if all the Officers at a Council of War were of a different Opinion, yet unless their Reasons mastered his Judgment, their Votes never altered his Measures: But this was the Error of our good, but unfortunate Master, three times in this War, and particularly in two of the greatest Battles of the time, *viz.* this of *Edgehill*, and that of *Naseby*.

The Resolution for Fighting being published in the Army, gave an universal Joy to the Soldiers, who expressed an extraordinary Ardour for Fighting. I remember, my Father talking with me about it, asked me what I Thought of the approaching Battle: I told him, I Thought the King had done very well; for at that time I did not consult the Extent of the Design, and had a mighty Mind, like other rash People, to see it brought to a Day, which made me answer my Father as I did: But said I, Sir, *I Doubt there will be but indifferent Doings on both Sides, between two Armies both made up of fresh Men, that have never seen any Service.* My Father minded little what I spoke of that; but when I seemed pleased that the King had resolved to fight, he looked angrily at me, and told me he was sorry I could see no farther into things. I tell you, says he hastily, *If the King should kill, and take Prisoners, this whole Army, General and all, the Parliament will have the Victory; for we have lost more by slipping this Opportunity of getting into* London, *than we shall ever get by ten Battles.* I saw enough of this afterwards to convince me of the Weight of what my Father said, and so did the King too; but it was then too late, Advantages slipt in War are never recovered.

We were now in a full March to fight the Earl of *Essex*. It was on *Sunday* Morning the 24th of *October*, 1642, fair Weather over Head, but the Ground very heavy and dirty. As soon as we came to the Top of *Edgehill*, we discovered their whole Army. They were not drawn up, having had two Miles to march that Morning; but they were very busy forming their Lines, and posting the Regiments as they came up. Some of their Horse were exceedingly fatigued, having marched 48 Hours together; and had they been suffered to follow us three or four Days March farther, several of their Regiments of Horse would have been quite ruined, and their Foot would have been rendered unserviceable for the present. But we had no Patience.

As soon as our whole Army was come to the Top of the Hill, we were drawn up in Order of Battle: The King's Army made a very fine Appearance; and indeed they were a Body of gallant Men as ever appeared in the Field, and as well furnished at all Points: The Horse exceeding well accoutred, being most of them Gentlemen and Voluntiers; some whole Regiments serving without Pay. Their Horses very good and fit for Service as could be desired. The whole Army were not above 18000 Men, and the Enemy not a 1000 over or under, though we had been told they were not above 12000; but they had been reinforced with 4000 Men from *Northampton*.

The King was with the General, the Earl of *Lindsey*, in the Main Battle; Prince *Rupert* commanded the Right Wing, and the Marquess of *Hertford*, the Lord *Willoughby*, and several other very good Officers, the Left.

The Signal of Battle being given with two Cannon Shot, we marched in Order of Battalia down the Hill, being drawn up in two Lines with Bodies of Reserve; the Enemy advanced to meet us much in the same Form, with this Difference only, that they had placed their Cannon on their Right, and the King had placed ours in the Center, before, or rather between two great Brigades of Foot. Their Cannon began with us first, and did some Mischief among the Dragoons of our left Wing; but our Officers perceiving the Shot took the Men, and missed the Horses, ordered all to alight, and every Man leading his Horse, to advance in the same Order; and this saved our Men, for most of the Enemy's Shot flew over their Heads. Our Cannon made a terrible Execution upon their Foot for a Quarter of an Hour, and put them into great Confusion, till the General obliged them to halt, and changed the Posture of his Front, marching round a small rising Ground by which he avoided the Fury of our Artillery.

By this time the Wings were engaged, the King having given the Signal of Battle, and ordered the Right Wing to fall on. Prince *Rupert* who as is said, commanded that Wing, fell on with such Fury, and pushed the Left Wing of the Parliament Army so effectually, that in a Moment he filled all with Terror and Confusion: Comissary General *Ramsey*, a Scochman, a Low Country Soldier, and an experienced Officer, commanded their Left Wing; and though he did all that an expert Soldier, and a brave Commander could do, yet 'twas to no Purpose; his lines were immediately broken, and all overwhelmed in a trice: Two Regiments of Foot, whether as Part of the Left Wing, or on the Left of the Main Body, I know not, were disordered by their own Horse, and rather trampled to Death by the Horses, than beaten by our Men; but they were so entirely broken and disordered, that I do not remember that ever they made one Volley upon our Men; for their own Horse running away, and falling foul on these Foot, were so vigorously followed by our Men, that the Foot never had a Moment to rally, or look behind them. The Point of the left Wing of Horse were not so soon broken as the rest, and three Regiments of them stood firm for some Time: The dexterous Officers of the other Regiments taking the Opportunity, rallied a great many of their scattered Men behind them, and pieced in some Troops with those Regiments; but after two or three Charges, which a Brigade of our second Line following the Prince, made upon them, they also were broken with the rest.

I remember, that at the great Battle of *Leipsick*, the Right Wing of the *Imperialists* having fallen in upon the *Saxons* with like Fury to this, bore down all before them, and beat the *Saxons* quite out of the Field; upon which the Soldiers cried, *Victoria, Let us follow. No, no*, said the old General *Tilly, let them go, but let us beat the* Swedes *too, and then all's our own*.[1] Had Prince *Rupert* taken this Method, and instead of following the Fugitives, who were dispersed so effectually, that two Regiments would have secured them from rallying; I say, had he fallen in upon the Foot, or wheeled to the Left, and fallen in upon the Rear of the Enemy's Right Wing of Horse, or returned to the Assistance of the Left Wing of our Horse, we had gained the most absolute and compleat Victory that could be; nor had 1000 Men of the Enemy's Army got off: But this Prince, who was full of Fire, and pleased to see the Rout of the Enemy, pursued them quite to the Town of *Keynton*, where indeed he killed Abundance of their Men, *and some Time also was lost in plundering the Baggage:* But in the mean Time, the Glory and Advantage of the Day was lost to the King; for the right Wing of the Parliament Horse could not be so broken. Sir *William Balfour* made a desperate Charge upon the Point of the King's Left; and had it not been for two Regiments of Dragoons who were planted in the Reserve, had routed the whole Wing; for he broke through the first Line, and staggered the second, who advanced to their Assistance, but was so warmly received by those Dragoons, who came seasonably in, and gave their first Fire on Horseback, that his Fury was checked, and having lost a great many Men, was forced to wheel about to his own Men; and had the King had but three Regiments of Horse at hand, to have charged him, he had been routed. The rest of this

Wing kept their Ground, and received the first Fury of the Enemy with great Firmness; after which, advancing in their Turn, they were once Masters of the Earl of *Essex*'s Cannon. And here we lost another Advantage; for if any Foot had been at hand to support these Horse, they had carried off the Cannon, or turned it upon the main Battle of the Enemy's Foot; but the Foot were otherwise engaged. The Horse on this Side fought with great Obstinacy, and Variety of Success a great while. Sir *Philip Stapylton*, who commanded the Guards of the Earl of *Essex*, being engaged with a Party of our *Shrewsbury* Cavaliers, as we called them, was once in a fair way to have been cut off by a Brigade of our Foot, who being advanced to fall on upon the Parliament's main Body, flanked Sir *Philip*'s Horse in their way, and facing to the Left, so furiously charged him with their Pikes, that he was obliged to retire in great Disorder, and with the Loss of a great many Men and Horses.

All this while the Foot on both Sides were desperately engaged, and coming close up to the Teeth of one another with the clubbed Musquet and Push of Pike, fought with great Resolution, and a terrible Slaughter on both Sides, giving no Quarter for a great while; and they continued to do thus, till, as if they were tired, and out of Wind, either Party seemed willing enough to leave off, and take Breath. Those which suffered most were that Brigade which had charged Sir *William Stapylton*'s Horse, who being bravely engaged in the Front which the Enemy's Foot, were, on the sudden, charged again in Front and Flank, by Sir *William Balfour*'s Horse, and disordered, after a very desperate Defence. Here the King's Standard was taken, the Standard-bearer, Sir *Edward Varney*, being killed; but it was rescued again by Captain *Smith*, and brought to the King the same Night, for which the King Knighted the Captain.

This Brigade of Foot had fought all the Day, and had not been broken at last, if any Horse had been at Hand to support them: The Field began to be now clear, both Armies stood, as it were, gazing at one another, only the King, having rallied his Foot, seemed inclined to renew the Charge, and began to cannonade them, which they could not return, most of their Cannon being nailed while they were in our Possession, and all the Cannoniers killed or fled, and our Gunners did Execution upon Sir *William Balfour*'s Troops for a good while.

My Father's Regiment being in the Right with the Prince, I saw little of the Fight, but the Rout of the Enemy's Left, and we had as full a Victory there as we could desire, but spent too much Time in it; we killed about 2000 Men in that Part of the Action, and having totally dispersed them, and plundred their Baggage, began to think of our Fellows when 'twas too late to help them. We returned however victorious to the King, just as the Battle was over; the King asked the Prince what News? He told him he could give his Majesty a good Account of the Enemy's Horse; *ay by G—d, says a Gentleman that stood by me, and of their Carts too.* That word was spoken with such a Sense of the Misfortune, and made such an Impression in the whole Army, that it occasioned some ill Blood afterwards among us; and but that the King took up the Business, it had been of ill Consequence; for some Person who had heard the Gentleman speak it, informed the Prince who it was, and the Prince resenting it, spoke something about it in the hearing of the Party when the King was present: The Gentleman not at all surprized, told his Highness openly, he had said the Words; and though he owned he had no Disrespect for his Highness, yet he could not but say, if it had not been so, the Enemy's Army had been better beaten. The Prince replied something very disobliging; upon which the Gentleman came up to the King, and kneeling, humbly besought his Majesty to accept of his Commission, and to give him leave to tell the Prince, that whenever his Highness pleased, he was ready to give him Satisfaction. The Prince was exceedingly provoked, and as he was very passionate, began to talk very oddly, and without all Government of himself: The Gentleman, as bold as he, but much calmer, preserved his Temper, but maintained his

Quarrel; and the King was so concerned, that he was very much out of Humour with the Prince about it. However, his Majesty upon Consideration, soon ended the Dispute, by laying his Commands on them both to speak no more of it for that Day; and refusing the Comission from the Collonel, for he was no less, sent for them both next Morning in private, and made them Friends again.

But to return to our Story, we came back to the King timely enough to put the Earl of *Essex*'s Men out of all Humour of renewing the Fight; and as I observed before, both Parties stood gazing at one another, and our Cannon playing upon them, obliged Sir *William Balfour*'s Horse to wheel off in some Disorder, but they returned us none again; which, as we afterwards understood, was, as I said before, for want of both Powder and Gunners; for the Cannoniers and Firemen were killed, or had quitted their Train in the Fight, when our Horse had Possession of their Artillery; and as they had spiked up some of the Cannon, so they had carryed away 15 Carriages of Powder.

Night coming on, ended all Discourse of more fighting; and the King drew off and marched towards the Hills. I know no other Token of Victory which the Enemy had, than their lying in the Field of Battle all Night, which *they did* for no other Reason, than that having lost their Baggage and Provisions, they had no where to go; and which we *did not*, because we had good Quarters at Hand.

The Number of Prisoners, and of the slain, were not very unequal; the Enemy lost more Men, we most of Quality. Six Thousand Men on both Sides were killed on the Spot, whereof, when our Rolls were examined, we missed 2500. We lost our brave General the old Earl of *Lindsey*, who was wounded and taken Prisoner, and died of his Wounds; Sir *Edward Stradling*, Collonel *Lundsford*, Prisoners; and Sir *Edward Varney*, and a great many Gentlemen of Quality slain. On the other Hand, we carried off Collonel *Essex*, Collonel *Ramsey*, and the Lord St. *John*, who also died of his Wounds; we took five Ammunition Waggons, full of Powder, and brought off about 500 Horse in the Defeat of the Left Wing, with 18 Standards and Colours, and lost 17.

The Slaughter of the Left Wing was so great, and the Flight so effectual, that several of the Officers rid clear away, coasting round, and got to *London*, where they reported, that the Parliament Army was entirely defeated, all lost, killed, or taken, as if none but them were left alive to carry the News. This filled them with Consternation for a while; but when other Messengers followed, all was restored to Quiet again, and the Parliament cried up their Victory, and sufficiently mocked God and their General, with their publick Thanks for it. Truly, as the Fight was a Deliverance to them, they were in the right to give Thanks for it; but as to its being a Victory, neither Side had much to boast of, and they less a great deal than we had.

I got no Hurt in this Fight; and indeed we of the Right Wing had but little fighting; I think I discharged my Pistols but once, and my Carabin twice, for we had more Fatigue than Fight; the Enemy fled, and we had little to do but to follow and kill those we could overtake. I spoiled a good Horse, and got a better from the Enemy in his Room, and came home weary enough. My Father lost his Horse, and in the Fall was bruised in his Thigh by another Horse, treading on him, which disabled him for some Time, and, at his Request, by his Majesty's Consent, I commanded the Regiment in his Absence.

The Enemy received a Recruit of 4000 Men[1] the next Morning; if they had not, I believe they had gone back towards *Worcester*; but, encouraged by that Reinforcement, they called a Council of War, and had a long Debate whether they could attack us again? but notwithstanding their great Victory, they durst not attempt it, though this Addition of Strength made them superiour to us by 3000 Men.

The King indeed expected, that when these Troops joined them they would advance, and we were preparing to receive them at a Village called *Aino*, where the Head Quarter continued three or four Days; and had they really esteemed the first Day's Work a Victory, as they called it, they would have done it, but they thought not good to venture, but march away to *Warwick*, and from thence to *Coventry*. The King, to urge them to venture upon him, and come to a second Battle, sits down before *Banbury*, and takes both Town and Castle, and two entire Regiments of Foot, and one Troop of Horse, quit the Parliament Service, and take up their Arms for the King. This was done almost before their Faces, which was a better Proof of a Victory on our Side, than any they could pretend to. From *Banbury* we marched to *Oxford*; and now all Men saw the Parliament had made a great Mistake, *for they were not always in the right any more than we*, to leave *Oxford* without a Garrison. The King caused new regular Works to be drawn round it, and seven royal Bastions with Ravelins and Out-works, a double Ditch, Counterscarp and Covered Way; all which added to the Advantage of its Situation, made it a formidable Place, and from this Time it became our Place of Arms, and the Center of Affairs on the King's Side.

If the Parliament had the Honour of the Field, the King reaped the Fruits of the Victory; for all this Part of the Country submitted to him: *Essex*'s Army made the best of their Way to *London*, and were but in an ill Condition when they came there, especially their Horse.

The Parliament, sensible of this, and receiving daily Accounts of the Progress we made, began to cool a little in their Temper, abated of their first Rage, and voted an Address for Peace; and sent to the King, to let him know they were desirous to prevent the Effusion of more Blood, and to bring things to an Accommodation, or, as they called it, a *Right Understanding*.

I was now, by the King's particular Favour, summoned to the Councils of War, my Father continuing absent and ill; and now I began to think of the real Grounds, and which was more, of the fatal Issue of this War. I say, I now began it; for I cannot say that I ever rightly stated Matters in my own Mind before, though I had been enough used to Blood, and to see the Destruction of People, sacking of Towns, and plundering the Country; yet 'twas in *Germany*, and among Strangers; but I found a strange secret and unaccountable Sadness upon my Spirits to see this acting in my own native Country. It grieved me to the Heart, even in the Rout of our Enemies, to see the Slaughter of them; and even in the Fight, to hear a Man cry for Quarter in *English*, moved me to a Compassion which I had never been used to; nay, sometimes it looked to me as if some of my own Men had been beaten; and when I heard a Soldier cry, *O God, I am shot*, I looked behind me to see which of my own Troop was fallen. Here I saw my self at the cutting of the Throats of my Friends; and indeed some of my near Relations. My old Comerades and Fellow-soldiers in *Germany* were some *with us*, some *against us*, as their Opinions happened to differ in Religion. For my part, I confess I had not much Religion in me, at that time; but I thought Religion rightly practised on both Sides would have made us all better Friends; and therefore sometimes I began to think, that both the Bishops of our Side, and the Preachers on theirs, made Religion rather *the Pretence* than *the Cause* of the War; and from those Thoughts I vigorously argued it at the Council of War against marching to *Brentford*, while the Address for a Treaty of Peace[1] from the Parliament was in Hand; for I was for taking the Parliament by the Handle which they had given us, and entring into a Negotiation with the Advantage of its being *at their own Request*.

I thought the King had now in his Hands an Opportunity to make an honourable Peace; for this Battle at *Edgehill*, as much as they boasted of the Victory to hearten up their Friends, had sorely weakened their Army, and discouraged their Party too, which in Effect was worse as to their Army. The Horse were particularly in an ill Case, and the Foot greatly diminished; and the Remainder very sickly: But besides this, the Parliament, were greatly alarmed at the Progress we made afterward; and still fearing the King's surprizing them, had sent for the Earl of *Essex* to *London*, to defend them; by which the Country was as it were, deserted and abandoned, and left to be plundered; our Parties over-run all Places at Pleasure. All this while I considered, that whatever the Soldiers of Fortune meant by the War, our Desires were to suppress the exorbitant Power of a Party, to establish our King in his just and legal Rights; but not with a Design to destroy the Constitution of Government, and the Being of Parliament; and therefore I thought now was the Time for Peace, and there were a great many worthy Gentlemen in the Army of my Mind; and, had our Master had Ears to hear us, the War might have had an End here.

This Address for Peace was received by the King at *Maidenhead*, whither this Army was now advanced, and his Majesty returned Answer by Sir *Peter Killegrew*, that he desired nothing more, and would not be wanting on his Part. Upon this the Parliament name Commissioners, and his Majesty excepting against Sir *John Evelyn*, they left him out, and sent others; and desired the King to appoint his Residence near *London*, where the Commissioners might wait upon him. Accordingly the King appointed *Windsor* for the Place of Treaty, and desired the Treaty might be hastened.[1] And thus all things looked with a favourable Aspect, when one unlucky Action knocked it all on the Head, and filled both Parties with more implacable Animosities than they had before, and all Hopes of Peace vanished.

During this Progress of the King's Armies, we were always abroad with the Horse ravaging the Country, and plundering the Roundheads. Prince *Rupert*, a most active vigilant Party-man, and I must own, fitter for such than for a General, was never lying still, and I seldom stayed behind; for our Regiment being very well mounted, he would always send for us, if he had any extraordinary Design in Hand.

One time in particular he had a Design upon *Alisbury*, the Capital of *Buckinghamshire*; indeed our View at first was rather to beat the Enemy out of Town and demolish their Works, and perhaps raise some Contributions on the rich Country round it, than to Garrison the Place, and keep it;

for we wanted no more Garrisons, being Masters of the Field.

The Prince had 2500 Horse with him in this Expedition, but no Foot; the Town had some Foot raised in the Country by Mr. *Hambden*, and two Regiments of the Country Militia, whom we made light of, but we found they stood to their Tackle better than *well enough*. We came very early to the Town, and thought they had no Notice of us; but some false Brother had given them the Alarm and we found them all in Arms, the Hedges without the Town lined with Musqueteers, on that Side in particular where they expected us, and the two Regiments of Foot drawn up in View to support them, with some Horse in the Rear of all.

The Prince willing however to do some thing, caused some of his Horse to alight, and serve as Dragoons; and having broken a Way into the Enclosures, the Horse beat the Foot from behind the Hedges, while the rest who were alighted charged them in the Lane which leads to the Town. Here they had cast up some Works, and fired from their Lines very regularly, considering them as Militia only, the Governour encouraging them by his Example; so that finding without some Foot there would be no good to be done, we gave it over, and drew off; and so *Alisbury* scaped a scouring for that Time.

I cannot deny but these flying Parties of Horse committed great Spoil among the Country People; and sometimes the Prince gave a Liberty to some Cruelties which were not at all for the King's Interest; because it being still upon our own Country, and the King's own Subjects, whom, in all his Declarations, he protested to be careful of. It seemed to contradict all those protestations and Declarations, and served to aggravate and exasperate the Common People; and the King's Enemies made all the Advantages of it that was possible, by crying out of twice as many Extravagancies as were committed.

'Tis true, the King, who naturally abhorred such things, could not restrain his Men, no nor his Generals, so absolutely as he would have done. The War, on his Side, was very much *a la Voluntier*; many Gentlemen served him at their own Charge, and some paid whole Regiments themselves: Sometimes also the King's Affairs were straiter than ordinary, and his Men were not very well paid, and this obliged him to wink at their Excursions upon the Country, though he did not approve of them; and yet I must own, that in those Parts of *England* where the War was hottest, there never was seen that Ruin and Depopulation, Murthers, Ravishments, and Barbarities, which I have seen even among Protestant Armies abroad in *Germany*, and other foreign Parts of the World. And if the Parliament People had seen those things abroad, as I had, they would not have complained.

The most I have seen was plundering the Towns for Provisions, drinking up their Beer, and turning our Horses into their Fields, or Stacks of Corn; and sometimes the Soldiers would be a little rude with the Wenches; but alas! what was this to Count *Tilly*'s Ravages in *Saxony*? Or what was our taking of *Leicester* by Storm, where they cried out of our Barbarities, to the sacking of *New Brandenburgh*, or the taking of *Magdeburgh*? In *Leicester*, of 7 or 8000 People in the Town, 300 were killed; in *Magdeburgh*, of 25000 scarce 2700 were left, and the whole Town burnt to Ashes. I my self, have seen 17 or 18 Villages on Fire in a Day, and the People driven away from their Dwellings, like Herds of Cattle; the Men murthered, the Women stript; and, 7 or 800 of them together, after they had suffered all the Indignities and Abuses of the Soldiers, driven stark naked in the Winter through the great Towns, to seek Shelter and Relief from the Charity of their Enemies. I do not instance these greater Barbarities to justify lesser Actions, which are nevertheless irregular; but, *I do say*, that Circumstances considered, this War was managed with as much Humanity on both Sides as could be expected, especially also considering the Animosity of Parties.

But to Return to the Prince, he had not always the same Success in these Enterprizes, for sometimes we came short home. And I cannot omit one pleasant Adventure which happened to a Party of ours in one of these Excursions into *Buckinghamshire*. The Major of our Regiment was soundly beaten by a Party which, as I may say was led by a Woman; and, if I had not rescued him, I know not but he had been taken Prisoner by a Woman. It seems our Men had besieged some fortified House about *Oxfordshire*, towards *Tame*, and the House being defended by the Lady in her Husband's Absence, she had yielded the House upon a Capitulation; one of the Articles of which was, to march out with all her Servants, Soldiers, and Goods, and to be convey'd to *Tame*: Whether she thought to have gone no farther, or that she reckoned her self safe there, I know not; but my Major, with two Troops of Horse meets with this Lady and her Party, about five Miles from *Tame*, as we were coming back from our defeated Attack of *Alisbury*. We reckoned our selves in an Enemy's Country, and had lived a little at large, or at Discretion, *as 'tis called abroad*; and these two Troops with the Major, were returning to our Detachment from a little Village, where, at a Farmer's House, they had met with some Liquor, and truly some of his Men were so drunk they could but just sit upon their Horses. The Major himself was not much better, and the whole Body were but in a sorry Condition to fight. Upon the Road they meet this Party; the Lady having no Design of Fighting, and being as she thought under the Protection of the Articles, sounds a Parley, and desired to speak with the Officer. The Major *as drunk as he was*, could tell her, that by the Articles she was to be assured no farther than *Tame*, and being now five Miles beyond it, she was a fair Enemy, and therefore demanded to render themselves Prisoners. The Lady seemed surprized, but being sensible she was in the wrong, offered to compound for her Goods, and would have given him 300 l. and, I think, seven or eight Horses: The Major would certainly have taken it, if he had not been drunk; but he refused it, and gave threatening Words to her, blustering in Language which he thought proper to fright a Woman, *viz.* that he would cut them all to Pieces, and give no Quarter, *and the like*. The Lady, who had been more used to the Smell of Powder than he imagined, called some of her Servants to her, and consulting with them what to do, they all unanimously encouraged her to let them fight; told her, it was plain that the Commander was drunk, and all that were with him were rather worse than he, and hardly able to sit their Horses; and that therefore one bold Charge would put them all into Confusion. *In a Word*, she consented, and, as she was a Woman, they desired her to secure her self among the Waggons; but she refused, and told them bravely, she would take her Fate with them. *In short*, she boldly bad my Major Defiance, and that he might do his worst, since she had offered him fair, and he had refused it; her Mind was altered now, and she would give him nothing, and bad his Officer that parlied longer with her, be gone; so the Parly ended. After this, she gave him fair Leave to go back to his Men; but before he could tell his Tale to them, she was at his Heels, with all her Men, and gave him such a home Charge as put his Men into Disorder; and, being too drunk to rally, they were knocked down before they knew what to do with themselves; and, in a few Minutes more, they took to a plain Flight. But what was still worse, the Men, being some of them very drunk, when they came to run for their Lives, fell over one another, and tumbled over their Horses, and made such Work, that a Troop of Women might have beaten them all. In this Pickle, with the Enemy at his Heels, I came in with him, hearing the Noise; when I appeared, the Pursuers retreated, and, seeing what a Condition my People were in, and not knowing the Strength of the Enemy, I contented my self with bringing them off without pursuing the other; nor could I ever hear positively who this Female Captain was, We lost 17 or 18 of our Men, and about 30 Horses; but when the Particulars of the Story were told us, our Major was so laughed at by the whole Army, and laughed at every where, that he was ashamed to shew himself for a Week or a Fortnight after.

But, to return to the King; his Majesty, *as I observed*, was at *Maidenhead* addressed by the Parliament for Peace, and *Windsor* being appointed for the Place of Treaty, the Van of his Army lay at *Colebrook*. In the mean time, whether it were true, or only a Pretence, but it was reported the Parliament General had sent a Body of his Troops, with a Train of Artillery, to *Hammersmith*, in order to fall upon some part of our Army, or to take some advanced Post, which was to the Prejudice of our Men; whereupon the King ordered the Army to march, and, by the Favour of a thick Mist, came within half a Mile of *Brentford* before he was discovered. There were two Regiments of Foot, and about 600 Horse in the Town, of the Enemy's best Troops; these taking the Alarm, posted themselves on the Bridge at the West End of the Town. The King attacked them with a select Detachment of his best Infantry, and they defended themselves with incredible Obstinacy. I must own, I never saw *raw Men*, for they could not have been in Arms above four Months, act like them in my Life. *In short*, there was no forcing these Men; for, though two whole Brigades of our Foot, backed by our Horse, made five several Attacks upon them, they could not break them, and we lost a great many brave Men in that Action. At last, seeing the Obstinacy of these Men, a Party of Horse was ordered to go round from *Osterly*; and, entering the Town on the North Side, where, though the Horse made some Resistance, it was not considerable, the Town was presently taken. I led my Regiment through an Enclosure, and came into the Town nearer to the Bridge than the rest, by which Means I got first into the Town; but I had this Loss by my Expedition, that the Foot charged me before the Body was come up, and pouring in their Shot very furiously, my Men were but in an ill Case, and would not have stood much longer, if the rest of the Horse coming up the Lane had not found them other Employment. When the Horse were thus entered, they immediately dispersed the Enemy's Horse, who fled away towards *London*, and falling in Sword in Hand upon the

Rear of the Foot, who were engaged at the Bridge, they were all cut in Pieces, except about 200, who scorning to ask Quarter, desperately threw themselves into the River of *Thames*, where they were most of them drowned.

The Parliament, and their Party, made a great Outcry at this Attempt; that it was base and treacherous while in a Treaty of Peace; and that the King, having amused them with hearkening to a Treaty, designed to have seized upon their Train of Artillery first, and, after that, to have surprized both the City of *London* and the Parliament. And I have observed since, that our Historians note this Action as contrary to the Laws of Honour and Treaties; though as there was no Cessation of Arms agreed on, nothing is more contrary to the Laws of War than to suggest it.

That it was a very unhappy thing to the King and whole Nation, as it broke off the Hopes of Peace, and was the Occasion of bringing the *Scots* Army in upon us, I readily acknowledge; but that there was any thing dishonourable in it, I cannot allow: For though the Parliament had addressed to the King for Peace, and such Steps were taken in it, as before; yet, as I have said, there was no Proposals made on either Side for a Cessation of Arms; and all the World must allow, that in such Cases the War goes on in the Field, while the Peace goes on in the Cabinet. And if the War goes on, admit the King had designed to surprize the City or Parliament, or all of them, it had been no more than the Custom of War allows, and what they would have done by him, if they could. The Treaty of *Westphalia*,[1] or Peace of *Munster*, which ended the bloody Wars of *Germany*, was a Precedent for this. That Treaty was actually negotiating seven Years, and yet the War went on with all the Vigour and Rancour imaginable, even to the last: Nay, the very Time after the Conclusion of it, but before the News could be brought to the Army, did he that was afterwards King of *Sweden*, *Carolus Gustavus*, take the City of *Prague*, by Surprize, and therein an inestimable Booty. Besides, all the Wars of *Europe* are full of Examples of this Kind; and therefore I cannot see any Reason to blame the King for this Action as to the Fairness of it. Indeed as to the Policy of it, I can say little; but the Case was this, the King had a gallant Army, flushed with Success, and things hitherto had gone on very prosperously, both with his own Army and elsewhere; he had above 35000 Men in his own Army, including his Garrisons left at *Banbury*, *Shrewsbury*, *Worcester*, *Oxford*, *Wallingford*, *Abbingdon*, *Reading*, and Places adjacent. On the other Hand, the Parliament Army came back to *London* in but a very* sorry Condition; for what with their Loss *in their Victory*, *as they called it*, *at* Edgehill, their Sickness, and a hasty March to *London*, they were very much diminished; though at *London* they soon recruited them again. And this Prosperity of the King's Affairs might encourage him to strike this Blow, thinking to bring the Parliament to the better Terms, by the Apprehensions of the superior Strength of the King's Forces.

But *however it was*, the Success did not equally answer the King's Expectation; the vigorous Defence the Troops posted at *Brentford* made as above, gave the Earl of *Essex* Opportunity, with extraordinary Application, to draw his Forces out to *Turnham-Green*; and the exceeding Alacrity of the Enemy was such, that their whole Army appeared with them, making together an Army of 24000 Men, drawn up in View of our Forces, by 8 o' Clock the next Morning. The City Regiments were placed between the regular Troops, and all together offered us Battle, but we were not in a Condition to accept it. The King indeed was sometimes of the Mind to charge them, and once or twice ordered Parties to advance to begin to skirmish; but upon better Advice, altered his Mind; and indeed it was the wisest Counsel to defer the fighting at that Time. The Parliament Generals were as unfixed in their Resolutions on the other Side, as the King: Sometimes they sent out Parties, and then called them back

---

*Note, General *Ludlow*, in his Memoirs, p. 52.[1] says, their Men returned from *Warwick* to *London*, not like Men who had obtained a Victory, but like Men that had been beaten.

again. One strong Party, of near 3000 Men marched off towards *Acton*, with Orders to amuse us on that Side, but were counter-manded. Indeed I was of the Opinion, we might have ventured the Battle; for though the Parliament's Army were more numerous, yet the City Trained-Bands, which made up 4000 of their Foot, were not much esteemed, and the King was a great deal stronger in Horse than they; but the main Reason that hindred the Engagement, was want of Ammunition, which the King having duly weighed, he caused the Carriages and Cannon to draw off first, and then the Foot, the Horse continuing to face the Enemy till all was clear gone, and then we drew off too, and marched to *Kingston*, and the next Day to *Reading*.

Now the King saw his Mistake, in not continuing his March for *London*, instead of Facing about to fight the Enemy at *Edgehill*. And all the Honour we had gained in so many successful Enterprizes lay buried in this shameful Retreat from an Army of Citizens Wives: For, truly that Appearance at *Turnham-Green* was gay, but not great. There was as many Lookers on as Actors; the Crouds of Ladies, 'Prentices and Mob was so great, that when the Parties of our Army advanced, and, as they thought, to Charge, the Coaches, Horsemen, and Croud, that cluttered away, to be out of Harm's way, looked little better than a Rout: And I was perswaded a good home Charge from our Horse would have sent their whole Army after them; but so it was, that this Croud of an Army was to triumph over us, and they did it; for all the Kingdom was carefully informed how their dreadful Looks had frightened us away.

Upon our Retreat, the Parliament resent this Attack, which they called treacherous, and vote no Accommodation; but they considered of it afterwards, and sent six Commissioners to the King with Propositions; but the Change of the Scene of Action changed the Terms of Peace; and now they made Terms like Conquerors, petition him to desert his Army, and return to the Parliament, and the like. Had his Majesty, at the Head of his Army, with the full Reputation they had before, and in the Ebb of their Affairs, rested at *Windsor*, and commenced a Treaty, they had certainly made more reasonable Proposals; but now the Scabbard seemed to be thrown away on both Sides.

The rest of the Winter was spent in strengthening Parties, and Places also in fruitless Treaties of Peace, Messages, Remonstrances, and Paper War on both Sides, and no Action remarkable happened any where that I remember: Yet the King gained Ground every where, and his Forces in the *North* encreased under the Earl of *Newcastle*; also my Lord *Goring*, then only called Collonel *Goring*, arrived from *Holland*, bringing three Ships loaden with Arms and Ammunition, and Notice that the Queen was following with more. *Goring* brought 4000 Barrels of Gunpowder, and 20000 small Arms; all which came very seasonably, for the King was in great want of them, especially the Powder. Upon this Recruit the Earl of *Newcastle* draws down to *York*, and being above 16000 strong, made Sir *Thomas Fairfax* give Ground, and retreat to *Hull*.

Whoever lay still, Prince *Rupert* was always abroad, and I chose to go out with his Highness as often as I had Opportunity; for hitherto he was always successful. About this Time the Prince, being at *Oxford*, I gave him Intelligence of a Party of the Enemy who lived a little at large, too much for good Soldiers, about *Cirencester*: The Prince glad of the News, resolved to attack them, and though it was a wet Season, and the Ways exceeding bad, being in *February*,[1] yet we marched all Night in the Dark, which occasioned the Loss of some Horses and Men too, in Sloughs and Holes, which the Darkness of the Night had suffered them to fall into. We were a very strong Party, being about 3000 Horse and Dragoons, and coming to *Cirencester* very early in the Morning, to our great Satisfaction the Enemy were perfectly surprized, not having the least Notice of our March, which answered our End more Ways than one. However, the Earl of *Stamford*'s Regiment made some Resistance; but the Town having no Works to defend it, saving a slight Breast-

Work at the Entrance of the Road, with a Turn-pike, our Dragoons alighted, and forcing their Way over the Bellies of *Stamford*'s Foot, they beat them from their Defence, and followed them at their Heels into the Town. *Stamford*'s Regiment was entirely cut in Pieces, and several others, to the Number of about 800 Men, and the Town entered without any other Resistance. We took 1200 Prisoners, 3000 Arms, and the County Magazin, which at that [time] was considerable; for there was about 120 Barrels of Powder, and all things in Proportion.

I received the first Hurt I got in this War, at this Action; for having followed the Dragoons, and brought my Regiment within the Barricado which they had gained, a Musquet Bullet struck my Horse just in the Head; and that so effectually, that he fell down as dead as a Stone, all at once. The Fall plunged me into a Puddle of Water, and daubed me; and my Man having brought me another Horse, and cleaned me a little, I was just getting up, when another Bullet strook me on my left Hand, which I had just clapt on the Horse's Mane, to lift my self into the Saddle. The Blow broke one of my Fingers, and bruised my Hand very much, and it proved a very painful Hurt to me. For the present I did not much concern my self about it, but made my Man tye it up close in my Handkerchief, and led up my Men to the Market Place, where we had a very smart Brush with some Musqueteers who were posted in the Church-yard; but our Dragoons soon beat them out there, and the whole Town was then our own. We made no Stay here, but marched back with all our Booty to *Oxford*, for we knew the Enemy were very strong at *Gloucester*, and that way.

Much about the same Time, the Earl of *Northampton*, with a strong Party, set upon *Litchfield*, and took the Town, but could not take the Close; but they beat a Body of 4000 Men coming to the Relief of the Town, under Sir *John Gell* of *Darbyshire* and Sir *William Brereton* of *Cheshire*, and killing 600 of them, dispersed the rest.

Our second Campaign now began to open; the King

marched from *Oxford* to relieve *Reading*, which was besieged by the Parliament Forces; but Collonel *Fielding*, Lieutenant Governour, Sir *Arthur Ashton* being wounded, surrendred to *Essex* before the King could come up; for which he was tried by Martial Law, and condemned to die; but the King forbore to execute the Sentence. This was the first Town we had lost in the War; for still the Success of the King's Affairs was very encouraging. This bad News however was over-balanced by an Account brought the King at the same time, by an Express from *York*, that the Queen had landed in the *North*, and had brought over a great Magazin of Arms and Ammunition, besides some Men. Some time after this, her Majesty marching Southward to meet the King, joined the Army near *Edgehill*, where the first Battle was fought. She brought the King 3000 Foot, 1500 Horse and Dragoons, six Pieces of Cannon, 1500 Barrels of Powder, 12000 small Arms.

During this Prosperity of the King's Affairs, his Armies encreased mightily in the Western Counties also. Sir *William Waller* indeed commanded for the Parliament in those Parts too, and particularly in *Dorsetshire*, *Hampshire*, and *Berkshire*, where he carried on their Cause but too fast; but farther West, Sir *Nicholas Flamming*,[1] Sir *Ralph Hopton*, and Sir *Bevil Greenvil*, had extended the King's Quarters from *Cornwall* through *Devonshire*, and into *Somersetshire*, where they took *Exeter*, *Barnstable*, and *Biddiford*; and the first of these they fortified very well, making it a Place of Arms for the West, and afterwards it was the Residence of the Queen.

At last, the Famous Sir *William Waller*, and the King's Forces met, and came to a pitched Battle, where Sir *William* lost all his Honour again. This was at *Roundway-down*[2] in *Wiltshire*. *Waller* had engaged our *Cornish* Army at *Lansdown*, and in a very obstinate Fight had the better of them, and made them retreat to the *Devizes*. Sir *William Hopton* however having a good Body of Foot untouched, sent Expresses and Messengers one in the Neck of another to the

King for some Horse, and the King being in great Concern
for that Army, who were composed of the Flower of the
Cornish Men, commanded me to march with all possible
Secrecy, as well as Expedition, with 1200 Horse and Dragoons from *Oxford*, to join them. We set out in the Depth of
the Night, to avoid, if possible, any Intelligence being given
of our Rout, and soon joined with the *Cornish* Army, when
it was as soon resolved to give Battle to *Waller*; and, give
him his due, he was as forward to fight as we. As it is easy
to meet when both Sides are willing to be found, Sir *William
Waller* met us upon *Roundway-down*, where we had a fair
Field on both Sides, and Room enough to draw up our
Horse. In a Word, there was little Ceremony to the Work;
the Armies joined, and we charged his Horse with so much
Resolution, that they quickly fled, and quitted the Field; for
we over-matched him in Horse, and this was the entire
Destruction of their Army: For their Infantry, which out-
numbered ours by 1500, were now at our Mercy; some faint
Resistance they made, just enough to give us Occasion to
break into their Ranks with our Horse, where we gave Time
to our Foot to defeat others that stood to their Work: Upon
which they began to disband, and run every Way they could;
but our Horse having surrounded them, we made a fearful
Havock of them.

We lost not above 200 Men in this Action; *Waller* lost
above 4000 killed and taken, and as many dispersed that
never returned to their Colours: Those of Foot that escaped
got into *Bristol*, and *Waller*, with the poor Remains of his
routed Regiments, got to *London*; so that it is plain some run
East, and some run West, that is to say, they fled every Way
they could.

My going with this Detachment prevented my being at
the Siege of *Bristol*,[1] which Prince *Rupert* attacked much
about the same Time, and it surrendered in three Days. The
Parliament questioned Collonel *Nathaniel Fienns*, the Governor, and had him tried as a Coward by a Court Martial,
and condemned to die, but suspended the Execution also, as

the King did the Governor of *Reading*. I have often heard Prince *Rupert* say, they did Collonel *Fienns* wrong in that Affair; and that if the Collonel would have summoned him, he would have demanded a Passport of the Parliament, and have come up and convinced the Court, that Collonel *Fienns* had not misbehaved himself; and that he had not a sufficient Garrison to defend a City of that Extent; having not above 1200 Men in the Town, excepting some of *Waller*'s Runaways, most of whom were unfit for Service, and without Arms; and that the Citizens in general being disaffected to him, and ready on the first Occasion to open the Gates to the King's Forces, it was impossible for him to have kept the City; and *when I had farther informed them*, said the Prince, *of the Measures I had taken for a general Assault the next Day, I am confident I should have convinc'd them, that I had taken the City by Storm, if he had not surrendered.*

The King's Affairs were now in a very good Posture, and three Armies in the North, West, and in the Center, counted in the Musters above 70000 Men, besides small Garrisons and Parties abroad. Several of the Lords, and more of the Commons, began to fall off from the Parliament, and make their Peace with the King; and the Affairs of the Parliament began to look very ill. The City of *London* was their inexhaustible Support and Magazine, both for Men, Money, and all things necessary; and whenever their Army was out of Order, the Clergy of their Party in but one *Sunday* or two, would preach the young Citizens out of their Shops, the Labourers from their Masters, into the Army, and recruit them on a sudden: And all this was still owing to the Omission I first observed, of not marching to *London*, when it might have been so easily effected.

We had now another, or a fairer Opportunity, than before, but, as ill Use was made of it. The King, as I have observed, was in a very good Posture; he had three large Armies roving at large over the Kingdom. The *Cornish* Army, Victorious and Numerous, had beaten *Waller*, secured and fortified *Exeter*, which the Queen had made her Residence, and was there delivered of a Daughter, the Princess *Henrietta Maria*, afterwards Dutchess of *Orleans*, and Mother of the Dutchess Dowager of *Savoy*, commonly known in the *French* Stile by the Title of *Madam Royal*.[1] They had secured *Salisbury*, *Sherbon* Castle, *Weymouth*, *Winchester*, and *Basing-house*, and commanded the whole Country, except *Bridgewater* and *Taunton*, *Plymouth* and *Linn*; all which Places they held blocked up. The King was also entirely Master of all *Wales*, *Monmouthshire*, *Cheshire*, *Shropshire*, *Staffordshire*, *Worcestershire*, *Oxfordshire*, *Berkshire*, and all the Towns from *Windsor* up the *Thames* to *Cirencester*, except *Reading* and *Henly*; and of the whole *Severn*, except *Gloucester*.

The Earl of *Newcastle* had Garrisons in every strong Place in the *North*, from *Berwick* upon *Tweed*, to *Boston* in *Lincolnshire*, and *Newark* upon *Trent*, *Hull* only excepted, whither the Lord *Fairfax* and his Son Sir *Thomas* were retreated, their Troops being routed and broken, Sir *Thomas Fairfax* his Baggage with his Lady and Servants taken Prisoners, and himself hardly escaping.

And now a great Council of War was held in the King's Quarters, what Enterprize to go upon; and it happened to be the very same Day when the Parliament were in a serious Debate what should become of them, and whose Help they should seek? And indeed they had Cause for it; and had our Counsels been as ready and well grounded as theirs, we had put an End to the War in a Month's time.

In this Council the King proposed the Marching to *London*, to put an End to the Parliament, and encourage his Friends and loyal Subjects in *Kent*, who were ready to rise for him; and shewed us Letters from the Earl of *Newcastle*, wherein he offered to join his Majesty with a Detachment of 4000 Horse, and 8000 Foot, if his Majesty thought fit to march Southward, and yet leave Forces sufficient to guard the *North* from any Invasion. I confess, when I saw the Scheme the King had himself drawn for this Attempt, I felt an unusual Satisfaction in my Mind, from the Hopes that we might bring this War to some tolerable End; for I professed my self on all Occasions heartily weary of Fighting with Friends, Brothers, Neighbours, and Acquaintance: And I made no Question, but this Motion of the King's would effectually bring the Parliament to Reason.

All Men seemed to like the Enterprize but the Earl of *Worcester*, who on particular Views for securing the Country behind, as he called it, proposed the taking in the Town of *Gloucester* and *Hereford* first: He made a long Speech of the Danger of leaving *Massey*, an active, bold Fellow, with a strong Party in the Heart of all the King's Quarters, ready on all Occasions to sally out, and surprize the neighbouring Garrisons, as he had done *Sudley* Castle and others; and of the Ease and Freedom to all those Western Parts, to have them fully cleared of the Enemy. Interest presently backs this Advice, and all those Gentlemen whose Estates lay that way, or whose Friends lived about *Worcester*, *Shrewsbury*, *Bridgnorth*, or the Borders; and who, as they said, had heard the frequent Wishes of the Country to have the City of *Gloucester* reduced, fell in with this Advice, alledging the Consequence it was of for the Commerce of the Country, to have the Navigation of the *Severn* free, which was only interrupted by this one Town from the Sea up to *Shrewsbury* &c.

I opposed this, and so did several others: Prince *Rupert* was vehemently against it; and we both offered, with the Troops of the County, to keep *Gloucester* blocked up during the King's March for *London*, so that *Massey* should not be able to stir.

This Proposal made the Earl of *Worcester*'s Party more eager for the Siege than before; for they had no Mind to a Blockade, which would leave the Country to maintain the Troops all the Summer; and of all Men the Prince did not please them: For he having no extraordinary Character for Discipline, his Company was not much desired even by our Friends. Thus, *in an ill Hour* 'twas resolved to sit down before *Gloucester*. The King had a gallant Army of 28000

Men, whereof 11000 Horse, the finest Body of Gentlemen that ever I saw together in my Life; their Horses without Comparison, and their Equipages the finest and the best in the World, and their Persons *Englishmen*, which I think is enough to say of them.

According to the Resolution taken in the Council of War, the Army marched Westward, and sat down before *Gloucester* the Beginning of *August*. There we spent a Month to the least Purpose that ever Army did; our Men received frequent Affronts from the desperate Sallies of an inconsiderable Enemy. I cannot forbear reflecting on the Misfortunes of this Siege: Our Men were strangely dispirited in all the Assaults they gave upon the Place; there was something looked like Disaster and Mismanagement, and our Men went on with an ill Will, and no Resolution. The King despised the Place, and the King, to carry it Sword in Hand, made no regular Approaches, and the Garrison being desperate, made therefore the greater Slaughter. In this Work our Horse, who were so numerous and so fine, had no Employment: 2000 Horse had been enough for this Business, and the Enemy had no Garrison or Party within fourty Miles of us; so that we had nothing to do but look on with infinite Regret, upon the Losses of our Foot.

The Enemy made frequent and desperate Sallies, in one of which I had my Share. I was posted upon a Parade, or Place of Arms, with Part of my Regiment, and Part of Collonel *Goring*'s Regiment of Horse, in order to support a Body of Foot who were ordered to storm the Point of a Breast-work which the Enemy had raised to defend one of the Avenues to the Town. The Foot were beat off with Loss, as they always were; and *Massey* the Governor, not content to have beaten them from his Works, sallies out with near 400 Men, and falling in upon the Foot as they were rallying under the Cover of our Horse, we put our selves in the best Posture we could to receive them. As *Massey* did not expect, I suppose, to engage with any Horse, he had no Pikes with him, which encouraged us to treat him the more rudely; but as to desperate Men Danger is no Danger, when he found he must clear his Hands of us, before he could dispatch the Foot, he faces up to us, fires but one Volley of his small Shot, and fell to battering us with the Stocks of their Musquets, in such a manner, that one would have thought they had been mad Men.

We at first despised this way of Clubbing us, and charging through them, laid a great many of them upon the Ground; and in repeating our Charge, trampled more of them under our Horses Feet: And wheeling thus continually, beat them off from our Foot, who were just upon the Point of disbanding. Upon this they charged us again with their Fire, and at one Volley killed 33 or 34 Men and Horses; and had they had Pikes with them, I know not what we should have done with them: But at last charging through them again, we divided them; one Part of them being hemmed in between us and our own Foot, were cut in Pieces to a Man; the rest, as I understood afterwards, retreated into the Town, having lost 300 of their Men.

In this last Charge I received a rude Blow from a stout Fellow on Foot, with the But End of his Musquet, which perfectly stunned me, and fetched me off from my Horse; and had not some near me took Care of me, I had been trod to Death by our own Men: But the Fellow being immediately killed, and my Friends finding me alive, had taken me up, and carried me off at some Distance, where I came to my self again, after some time, but knew little of what I did or said that Night. This was the Reason why I say I afterwards understood the Enemy retreated; for I saw no more what they did then; nor indeed was I well of this Blow for all the rest of the Summer, but had frequent Pains in my Head, Dizzinesses and Swimming, that gave me some Fears the Blow had injured the Scull, but it wore off again; nor did it at all hinder my attending my Charge.

This Action, I think, was the only one that looked like a Defeat given the Enemy at this Siege; we killed them near 300 Men, as I have said, and lost about 60 of our Troopers.

All this Time, while the King was harrassing and weakening the best Army he ever saw together during the whole War, the Parliament Generals, or rather Preachers, were recruiting theirs; for the Preachers were better than Drummers to raise Voluntiers, zealously exhorting the *London* Dames to part with their Husbands, and the City to send some of their Trained Bands to join the Army for the Relief of *Gloucester*; and now they began to advance towards us.

The King hearing of the Advance of *Essex*'s Army, who by this time was come to *Alisbury*, had summoned what Forces he had within Call, to join him; and accordingly he received 3000 Foot from *Somersetshire*: And having batter'd the Town for 36 Hours, and made a fair Breach, resolves upon an Assault, if possible, to carry the Town before the Enemy came up. The Assault was begun about Seven in the Evening, and the Men boldly mounted the Breach; but after a very obstinate and bloody Dispute, were beaten out again by the besieged with great Loss.

Being thus often repulsed, and the Earl of *Essex*'s Army approaching, the King calls a Council of War, and proposed to fight *Essex*'s Army. The Officers of the Horse were for fighting; and without doubt we were superior to him both in Number and Goodness of our Horse, but the Foot were not in an equal Condition: And the Collonels of Foot representing to the King the Weakness of their Regiments, and how their Men had been bauked and disheartened at this cursed Siege, the graver Counsel prevailed, and it was resolved to raise the Siege, and retreat towards *Bristol*, till the Army was recruited. Pursuant to this Resolution, the 5th of *September*, the King having before sent away his heavy Cannon and Baggage, raised the Siege, and marched to *Berkley* Castle. The Earl of *Essex* came the next Day to *Birdlip Hills*; and understanding by Messengers from Collonel *Massey*, that the Siege was raised, sends a Recruit of 2500 Men into the City, and followed us himself with a great Body of Horse.

This Body of Horse shewed themselves to us once in a

large Field fit to have entertained them in; and our Scouts having assured us they were not above 4000, and had no Foot with them, the King ordered a Detachment of about the same Number to face them. I desired his Majesty to let us have two Regiments of Dragoons with us, which was then 800 Men in a Regiment, lest there might be some Dragoons among the Enemy, which the King granted; and accordingly we marched, and drew up in View of them. They stood their Ground, having, as they supposed, some Advantage of the manner they were posted in, and expected we would charge them. The King who did us the Honour to command this Party, finding they would not stir, calls me to him, and ordered me with the Dragoons, and my own Regiment, to take a Circuit round by a Village to a certain Lane, where in their Retreat they must have passed, and which opened to a small Common on their Flank, with Orders, if they engaged, to advance and charge them in the Flank. I marched immediately; but though the Country about there was almost all Enclosures, yet their Scouts were so vigilant, that they discovered me, and gave Notice to the Body; upon which their whole Party moved to the Left, as if they intended to charge me, before the King with his Body of Horse could come; but the King was too vigilant to be circumvented so; and therefore his Majesty perceiving this, sends away three Regiments of Horse to second me, and a Messenger before them, to order me to halt, and expect the Enemy, for that he would follow with the whole Body.

But before this Order reached me, I had halted for some time; for, finding my self discovered, and not judging it safe to be entirely cut off from the main Body, I stopt at the Village, and causing my Dragoons to alight, and line a thick Hedge on my Left. I drew up my Horse just at the Entrance into the Village opening to a Common; the Enemy came up on the Trot to charge me, but were saluted with a terrible Fire from the Dragoons out of the Hedge, which killed them near 100 Men. This being a perfect Surprize to them, they halted; and just at that Moment they received Orders from their main Body to retreat; the King at the same time appearing upon some small Heights in their Rear, which obliged them to think of retreating, or coming to a general Battle, which was none of their Design.

I had no Occasion to follow them, not being in a Condition to attack their whole Body; but the Dragoons coming out into the Common, gave them another Volley at a Distance, which reached them effectually; for it killed about 20 of them, and wounded more; but they drew off, and never fired a Shot at us, fearing to be enclosed between two Parties, and so marched away to their General's Quarters, leaving 10 or 12 more of their Fellows killed, and about 180 Horses. Our Men, after the Country Fashion, gave them a Shout at parting, to let them see we knew they were afraid of us.

However, this Relieving of *Gloucester* raised the Spirits as well as the Reputation of the Parliament Forces, and was a great Defeat to us; and from this time things began to look with a melancholy Aspect; for the prosperous Condition of the King's Affairs began to decline. The Opportunities he had let slip, were never to be recovered; and the Parliament, in their former Extremity, having voted an Invitation to the *Scots* to March to their Assistance, we had now new Enemies to encounter; and indeed there began the Ruine of his Majesty's Affairs; for the Earl of *Newcastle*, not able to defend himself against the *Scots* on his Rear, the Earl of *Manchester* in his Front, and Sir *Thomas Fairfax* on his Flank, was every where routed and defeated, and his Forces obliged to quit the Field to the Enemy.

About this Time it was that we first began to hear of one *Oliver Cromwell*, who, like a little Cloud, rose out of the East, and spread first into the North, 'till it shed down a Flood that overwhelmed the three Kingdoms.

He first was a private Captain of Horse, but now commanded a Regiment whom he armed *Cap-a-pee a la Cuirassier*; and joining with the Earl of *Manchester*, the first Action we heard of him, that made him any thing famous, was about *Grantham*,[1] where, with only his own Regiment, he defeated 24 Troops of Horse and Dragoons of the King's Forces: Then at *Gainsborough*, with two Regiments, his own of Horse, and one of Dragoons, where he defeated near 3000 of the Earl of *Newcastle*'s Men, killed Lieutenant General *Cavendish*, Brother to the Earl of *Devonshire*, who commanded them, and relieved *Gainsborough*; and though the whole Army came in to the Rescue, he made good his Retreat to *Lincoln*, with little Loss; and the next Week he defeated Sir *John Henderson*, at *Winsby*, near *Horn Castle*, with sixteen Regiments of Horse and Dragoons, himself having not half that Number, killed the Lord *Widdrington*,[2] Sir *Ingram Hopton*, and several Gentlemen of Quality.

Thus this Firebrand of War began to blaze, and he soon grew a Terror to the North; for Victory attended him like a Page of Honour, and he was scarce ever known to be beaten, during the whole War.

Now we began to reflect again on the Misfortune of our Master's Counsels: Had we marched to *London*, instead of besieging *Gloucester*, we had finished the War with a Stroke. The Parliament's Army was in a most despicable Condition, and had never been recruited, had we not given them a Month's time, which we lingered away at this fatal Town of *Gloucester*:[3] But 'twas too late to reflect; we were a disheartened Army, but we were not beaten yet, nor broken; we had a large Country to recruit in, and we lost no time, but raised Men apace. In the mean time his Majesty, after a short Stay at *Bristol*, makes back again towards *Oxford* with a part of the Foot, and all the Horse.

At *Cirencester* we had a Brush again with *Essex*; that Town owed us a shrewd Turn for having handled them coarsely enough before, when Prince *Rupert* seized the County Magazine. I happened to be in the Town that Night with Sir *Nicholas Crisp*,[4] whose Regiment of Horse quartered there with Collonel *Spencer*, and some Foot; my own Regiment was gone before to *Oxford*. About Ten at Night, a Party of *Essex*'s Men beat up our Quarters by Surprize,

just as we had served them before; they fell in with us, just
as People were going to Bed, and having beaten the Out-
Guards, were gotten into the Middle of the Town, before
our Men could get on Horseback. Sir *Nicholas Crisp* hearing
the Alarm, gets up, and with some of his Clothes on, and
some off, comes into my Chamber: We are all undone, *says
he*, the Roundheads are upon us. We had but little time to
consult; but being in one of the principal Inns in the Town,
we presently ordered the Gates of the Inn to be shut, and
sent to all the Inns where our Men were quartered, to do
the like, with Orders, if they had any Back-doors, or Ways
to get out, to come to us. By this means however we got so
much time as to get on Horseback, and so many of our Men
came to us by Back-ways, that we had near 300 Horse in the
Yards and Places behind the House; and now we began to
think of Breaking out by a Lane which led from the back
Side of the Inn; but a new Accident determined us another,
though a worse Way. The Enemy being entered, and our
Men cooped up in the Yards of the Inns, Collonel *Spencer*
the other Collonel, whose Regiment of Horse lay also in the
Town, had got on Horseback before us, and engaged with
the Enemy, but being over-powered, retreated fighting, and
sends to Sir *Nicholas Crisp* for Help. Sir *Nicholas* moved to
see the Distress of his Friend, turning to me, says he *What
can we do for him?* I told him, I thought 'twas time to help
him, if possible; upon which, opening the Inn Gates, we
sallied out in very good Order, about 300 Horse; and
several of the Troops from other parts of the Town joining
us, we recovered Collonel *Spencer*, and charging home, beat
back the Enemy to their main Body: But finding their Foot
drawn up in the Church-yard, and several Detachments
moving to charge us, we retreated in as good Order as we
could. They did not think fit to pursue us, but they took all
the Carriages which were under the Convoy of this Party,
and loaden with Provisions and Ammunition, and above
500 of our Horse. The Foot shifted away as well as they
could: Thus we made off in a shattered Condition towards

Farrington, and so to *Oxford*, and I was very glad my Regiment was not there.

We had small Rest at *Oxford*, or indeed any where else; for the King was marched from thence, and we followed him. I was something uneasy at my Absence from my Regiment, and did not know how the King might resent it, which caused me to ride after them with all Expedition. But the Armies were engaged that very Day at *Newberry*, and I came in too late. I had not behaved my self so as to be suspected of a wilful Shunning the Action; but a Collonel of a Regiment ought to avoid Absence from his Regiment in time of Fight, be the Excuse never so just, as carefully as he would a Surprize in his Quarters. The *Truth is*, 'twas an Error of my own, and owing to two Days Stay I made at the *Bath*, where I met with some Ladies who were my Relations: And this is far from being an Excuse; for if the King had been a *Gustavus Adolphus*, I had certainly received a Check for it.

This Fight was very obstinate, and could our Horse have come to Action as freely as the Foot, the Parliament Army had suffered much more; for we had here a much better Body of Horse than they, and we never failed beating them where the Weight of the Work lay upon the Horse.

Here the City Train-Bands, of which there was two Regiments, and whom we used to despise, fought very well: They lost one of their Collonels,[1] and several Officers in the Action; and I heard our Men say, they behaved themselves as well as any Forces the Parliament had.

The Parliament cried Victory here too, *as they always did*; and indeed where the Foot were concerned they had some Advantage; but our Horse defeated them evidently. The King drew up his Army in Battalia, in Person, and faced them all the next Day, inviting them to renew the Fight; but they had no Stomach to come on again.

It was a kind of a Hedge Fight, for neither Army was drawn out in the Field; if it had, 'twould never have held from six in the Morning to ten at Night: But they fought for Advantages; sometimes one Side had the better, sometimes another. They fought twice through the Town, in at one End, and out at the other; and in the Hedges and Lanes, with exceeding Fury. The King lost the most Men, his Foot having suffered for want of the Succour of their Horse, who on two several Occasions, could not come at them. But the Parliament Foot suffered also, and two Regiments were entirely cut in Pieces, and the King kept the Field.

Essex, the Parliament General, had the Pillage of the dead, and left us to bury them; for while we stood all Day to our Arms, having given them a fair Field to fight us in, their Camp Rabble stript the dead Bodies, and they not daring to venture a second Engagement with us, marched away towards *London*.

The King Lost in this Action the Earls of *Carnarvon* and *Sunderland*, the Lord *Falkland*, a *French* Marquess,[1] and some very gallant Officers, and about 1200 Men. The Earl of *Carnarvon* was brought into an Inn in *Newberry*, where the King came to see him. He had just Life enough to speak to his Majesty, and died in his Presence. The King was exceedingly concerned for him, and was observed to shed Tears at the Sight of it. We were indeed all of us troubled for the Loss of so brave a Gentleman, but the Concern our royal Master discovered, moved us more than ordinary. Every body endeavoured to have the King out of the Room, but he would not stir from the Bed Side, till he see all Hopes of Life was gone.

The indefatigable Industry of the King, his Servants and Friends, continually to supply and recruit his Forces, and to harrass and fatigue the Enemy, was such, that we should still have given a good Account of the War had the *Scots* stood neuter. But bad News came every Day out of the North; as for other Places, Parties were always in Action: Sir *William Waller* and Sir *Ralph Hopton* beat one another by Turns, and Sir *Ralph* had extended the King's Quarters from *Launceston* in *Cornwall* to *Farnham* in *Surry*, where he gave Sir *William Waller* a Rub, and drove him into the Castle.

But in the North, the Storm grew thick, the *Scots* advanced to the Borders, and entered *England* in Confederacy with the Parliament, against their King; for which the Parliament requited them afterwards as they deserved.

Had it not been for this *Scotch* Army, the Parliament had easily been reduced to Terms of Peace: But after this they never made any Proposals fit for the King to receive. Want of Success before had made them differ among themselves: *Essex* and *Waller* could never agree; the Earl of *Manchester* and the Lord *Willoughby* differed to the highest Degree; and the King's Affairs went never the worse for it. But this Storm in the North ruined us all; for the *Scots* prevailed in *Yorkshire*, and being joined with *Fairfax*, *Manchester*, and *Cromwell*, carried all before them; so that the King was obliged to send Prince *Rupert* with a Body of 4000 Horse, to the Assistance of the Earl of *Newcastle*, where that Prince finished the Destruction of the King's Interest, by the rashest and unaccountablest Action in the World, of which I shall speak in its Place.

Another Action of the King's, though in it self no greater a Cause of Offence than the calling the *Scots* into the Nation, gave great Offence in general, and even the King's own Friends disliked it; and was carefully improved by his Enemies to the Disadvantage of the King, and of his Cause.

The Rebels in *Ireland* had, ever since the bloody Massacre of the Protestants, maintained a War against the *English*, and the Earl of *Ormond* was General and Governour for the King. The King finding his Affairs pinch him at home, sends Orders to the Earl of *Ormond* to consent to a Cessation of Arms[1] with the Rebels, and to ship over certain of his Regiments hither to his Majesty's Assistance. '*Tis true*, the *Irish* had deserved to be very ill treated by the *English*; but while the Parliament pressed the King with a cruel and unnatural War at home, and called in an Army out of *Scotland* to support their Quarrel with their King, I could never be convinced, that it was such a dishonourable Action for the King to suspend the Correction of his *Irish* Rebels, 'till he was in a Capacity to do it with Safety to himself; or to delay any farther Assistance to preserve himself at home; and the Troops he recalled being his own, it was no Breach of his Honour to make use of them, since he now wanted them for his own Security, against those who fought against him at home.

But the King was perswaded to make one Step farther; and that, I confess, was unpleasing to us all; and some of his best and most faithful Servants took the Freedom to speak plainly to him of it; and that was bringing some Regiments of the *Irish* themselves over. This cast, as we thought an *Odium* upon our whole Nation, being some of those very Wretches who had dipt their Hands in the innocent Blood of the Protestants, and with unheard of Butcheries, had massacred so many Thousands of *English* in cool Blood.

Abundance of Gentlemen forsook the King upon this Score; and seeing they could not brook the Fighting in Conjunction with this wicked Generation, came into the Declaration of the Parliament, and making Composition for their Estates, lived retired Lives all the rest of the War, or went abroad.

But as Exigences and Necessities oblige us to do things which at other times we would not do, and is, as to Man, some Excuse for such things; so I cannot but think the Guilt and Dishonour of such an Action must lye, very much of it, at least, at their Doors, who drove the King to these Necessities and Distresses by calling in an Army of his own Subjects whom he had not injured, but had complied with them in every thing, to make War upon him without any Provocation.

As to the Quarrel between the King and his Parliament, there may something be said on both Sides; and the King saw Cause himself, to disown and dislike some things he had done, which the Parliament objected against, such as levying Money without Consent of Parliament, Infractions on their Privileges, *and the like*: Here I say, was some room for an Argument at least, and Concessions on both Sides were needful to come to a Peace; but for the *Scots*, all their Demands had been answered, all their Grievances had been redressed, they had made Articles with their Sovereign, and he had performed those Articles; their capital Enemy Episcopacy was abolished; they had not one thing to demand of the King which he had not granted: And therefore they had no more Cause to take up Arms against their Sovereign, than they had against the *Grand Senior*. But it must for ever lye against them as a Brand of Infamy, and as a Reproach on their Whole Nation that, *purchased by the Parliament's Money*, they sold their *Honesty*, and rebelled against their King *for Hire*; and it was not many years before, as I have said already, they were fully paid the Wages of their Unrighteousness, and chastised for their Treachery by the very same People whom they thus basely assisted: Then they would have retrieved it, if it had not been too late.

But I could not but accuse this Age of Injustice and Partiality, who while they reproached the King for his Cessation of Arms with the *Irish* Rebels, and not prosecuting them with the utmost Severity, though he was constrained by the Necessities of the War to do it, could yet, at the same time, justify the *Scots* taking up Arms in a Quarrel they had no Concern in, and against their own King, with whom they had articled and capitulated, and who had so punctually complied with all their Demands, that they had no Claim upon him, no Grievances to be redressed, no Oppression to cry out of, nor could ask any thing of him which he had not granted.

But as no Action in the World is so vile, but the Actors can cover with some specious Pretence, so the *Scots* now passing into *England*, publish a Declaration to justify their Assisting the Parliament: To which I shall only say, in my Opinion, it was no Justification at all; for admit the Parliament's Quarrel had been never so just, it could not be just in them to aid them, because 'twas against their own King too, to whom they had sworn Allegiance, or at least had crowned him; and thereby had recognized his Authority:

For if Male-Administration be, according to *Prynn*'s
Doctrine, or according to their own *Buchanan*, a sufficient
Reason for Subjects to take up Arms against their Prince,
the Breach of his Coronation Oath being supposed to dissolve
the Oath of Allegiance, which *however I cannot believe*; yet
this can never be extended to make it lawful, that because
a King of *England* may, by Male-Administration discharge
the Subjects of *England* from their Allegiance, that therefore
the Subjects of *Scotland* may take up Arms against the King
of *Scotland*, he having not infringed the Compact of Government as to them, and they having nothing to complain of for
themselves: Thus I thought their own Arguments were
against them, and Heaven seemed to concur with it; for
although they did carry the Cause for the *English* Rebels,
yet the most of them left their Bones here in the Quarrel.

But what signifies Reason to the Drum and the Trumpet.
The Parliament had the supream Argument with those Men,
(*viz.*) the Money; and having accordingly advanced a good
round Sum, upon Payment of this, (*for the* Scots *would not
stir a Foot without it*) they entred *England* on the 15th of
January 1643[4], with an Army of 12000 Men, under the
Command of old *Lesley* now Earl of *Leven*, an old Soldier
of great Experience, having been bred to Arms from a
Youth in the Service of the Prince of *Orange*.

The *Scots* were no sooner entred *England*, but they were
joined by all the Friends to the Parliament Party in the
North; and first, Collonel *Grey*, Brother to the Lord *Grey*,
joined them with a Regiment of Horse, and several out of
Westmorland and *Cumberland*, and so they advanced to
Newcastle, which they summoned to surrender. The Earl of
Newcastle, who rather saw, than was able to prevent this
Storm, was in *Newcastle*, and did his best to defend it; but
the *Scots* encreased by this time to above 20000, lay close
Siege to the Place, which was but meanly fortified; and
having repulsed the Garrison upon several Sallies, and
pressing the Place very Close; after a Siege of 12 Days, or
thereabouts, they enter the Town Sword in Hand. The Earl

of *Newcastle* got away, and afterwards gathered what Forces together he could; but not strong enough to hinder the *Scots* from advancing to *Durham* which he quitted to them, nor to hinder the Conjunction of the *Scots* with the Forces of *Fairfax*, *Manchester*, and *Cromwell*. Whereupon the Earl seeing all things thus going to wreck, he sends his Horse away, and retreats with his Foot into *York*, making all necessary Preparations for a vigorous Defence there, in case he should be attacked, which he was pretty sure of, as indeed afterwards happened. *York* was in a very good Posture of Defence: The Fortifications very regular, and exceeding strong; well furnished with Provisions, and had now a Garrison of 12000 Men in it. The Governour under the Earl of *Newcastle* was Sir *Thomas Glemham*, a good Souldier, and a Gentleman brave enough.

The *Scots*, as I have said, having taken *Durham*, *Tinmouth* Castle and *Sunderland*, and being joined by Sir *Thomas Fairfax*, who had taken *Selby*, resolve, with their united Strength, to besiege *York*; but when they came to view the City, and saw a Plan of the Works, and had Intelligence of the Strength of the Garrison, they sent Expresses to *Manchester* and *Cromwell* for Help, who came on, and join them with 9000, making together about 30000 Men, rather more than less.

Now had the Earl of *Newcastle*'s repeated Messengers convinced the King, that it was absolutely necessary to send some Forces to his Assistance, or else all would be lost in the North. Whereupon Prince *Rupert* was detached with Orders first to go into *Lancashire*, and relieve *Latham-House*, defended by the brave Countess of *Derby*; and then taking all the Forces he could collect in *Cheshire*, *Lancashire*, and *Yorkshire*, to march to relieve *York*.

The Prince marched from *Oxford* with but three Regiments of Horse, and one of Dragoons, making in all about 2800 Men. The Collonels of Horse were Collonel *Charles Goring*, the Lord *Biron*, and my self; the Dragoons were of Collonel *Smith*. In our March we were joined by a Regiment of Horse from *Banbury*, one of Dragoons from *Bristol*, and three Regiments of Horse from *Chester*: So that when we came into *Lancashire*, we were about 5000 Horse and Dragoons. These Horse we received from *Chester*, were those who having been at the Siege of *Nantwich*, were obliged to raise the Siege by Sir *Thomas Fairfax*; and the Foot having yielded, the Horse made good their Retreat to *Chester*, being about 2000; of whom three Regiments now joined us.

We received also 2000 Foot from *West-Chester*, and 2000 more out of *Wales*; and with this Strength we entered *Lancashire*. We had not much time to spend, and a great deal of Work to do.

Bolton and *Leverpool* felt the first Fury[1] of our Prince: At *Bolton* indeed he had some Provocation; for here we were like to be beaten off. When first the Prince came to the Town, he sent a Summons to demand the Town for the King, but received no Answer but from their Guns, commanding the Messenger to keep off at his Peril. They had raised some Works about the Town, and having by their Intelligence, learnt that we had no Artillery, and were only a flying Party, *so they called us*, they contemned the Summons, and shewed themselves upon their Ramparts ready for us. The Prince was resolved to humble them, if possible, and takes up his Quarters close to the Town. In the Evening he orders me to advance with one Regiment of Dragoons, and my Horse to bring them off, if Occasion was, and to post my self as near as possibly I could to the Lines, yet so as not to be discovered; and at the same time having concluded what Part of the Works to fall upon, he draws up his Men on two other Sides, as if he would Storm them there; and on a Signal I was to begin the real Assault on my Side, with my Dragoons. I had got so near the Town with my Dragoons, making them creep upon their Bellies a great way, that we could hear the Soldiers talk on the Walls, that we could hear the Soldiers talk on the Walls, when the Prince believing one Regiment would be too few, sends me Word, that he had ordered a Regiment of Foot to help, and that I should not discover my self till they were come up to me. This broke our Measures; for the March of this Regiment was discovered by the Enemy, and they took the Alarm. Upon this I sent to the Prince, to desire he would put off the Storm for that Night, and I would answer for it the next Day; but the Prince was impatient, and sent Orders we should fall on as soon as the Foot came up to us. The Foot marching out of the Way, missed us, and fell in with a Road that leads to another Part of the Town; and being not able to find us, make an Attack upon the Town themselves; but the Defendants being ready for them, received them very warmly, and beat them off with great Loss. I was at a Loss now what to do; for hearing the Guns, and by the Noise knowing it was an Assault upon the Town, I was very uneasy to have my Share in it; but as I had learnt under the King of *Sweden* punctually to adhere to the Execution of Orders; and my Orders being to lye still till the Foot came up with me; I would not stir if I had been sure to have done never so much Service; but however to satisfy my self, I sent to the Prince to let him know that I continued in the same Place expecting the Foot, and none being yet come, I desired farther Orders. The Prince was a little amazed at this, and finding there must be some Mistake, came galloping away in the Dark to the Place, and drew off the Men, which was no hard Matter, for they were willing enough to give it over.

As for me, the Prince ordered me to come off so privately, as not to be discovered, if possible, which I effectually did; and so we were baulked for that Night. The next Day the Prince fell on upon another Quarter with three Regiments of Foot, but was beaten off with Loss; and the like a third time. At last, the Prince, *resolved to carry it*, doubled his Numbers, and renewing the Attack with fresh Men, the Foot entred the Town over their Works, killing in the first Heat of the Action, all that came in their way; some of the Foot at the same time letting in the Horse; and so the Town was entirely won. There was about 600 of the Enemy killed, and we lost above 400 in all which was owing to the foolish Mistakes we made. Our Men got some Plunder here, which the Parliament made a great Noise about; but it was their due, and they bought it dear enough.

Leverpool did not cost us so much, nor did we get so much by it, the People having sent their Women and Children, and best Goods on board the Ships in the Road; and as we had no Boats to board them with, we could not get at them. Here, as at *Bolton*, the Town and Fort was taken by Storm, and the Garrison were many of them cut in Pieces, which by the way was their own Faults.

Our next Stop was *Latham-House*, which the Countess of *Derby* had gallantly defended above 18 Weeks, against the Parliament Forces; and this Lady not only encouraged her Men by her chearful and noble Maintenance of them, but by Examples of her own undaunted Spirit, exposing her self upon the Walls in the midst of the Enemy's Shot, would be with her Men in the greatest Dangers; and she well deserved our Care of her Person; for the Enemy were prepaired to use her very rudely if she fell into their Hands.

Upon our Approach, the Enemy drew off; and the Prince not only effectually relieved this vigorous Lady, but left her a good Quantity of all Sorts of Ammunition, three great Guns, 500 Arms, and 200 Men, commanded by a Major, as her extraordinary Guard.

Here the Way being now opened, and our Success answering our Expectation, several Bodies of Foot came in to us from *Westmoreland*, and from *Cumberland*; and here it was that the Prince found Means to surprize the Town of *Newcastle upon Tyne*,[1] which was recovered for the King, by the Management of the Mayor of the Town, and some loyal Gentlemen of the County, and a Garrison placed there again for the King.

But our main Design being the Relief of *York*, the Prince advanced that Way a-pace, his Army still increasing; and being joined by the Lord *Goring* from *Richmondshire* with 4000 Horse, which were the same the Earl of *Newcastle* had sent away when he threw himself into *York* with the Infantry. We were now 18000 effective Men, whereof 10000 Horse and Dragoons; so the Prince, full of Hopes, and his Men in good Heart, boldly marched directly for *York*.

The *Scots*, as much surprized at the taking of *Newcastle*, as at the coming of their Enemy, began to enquire which Way they should get home, if they should be beaten; and calling a Council of War, they all agreed to raise the Siege. The Prince, who drew with him a great Train of Carriages charged with Provision and Ammunition, for the Relief of the City, like a wary General, kept at a Distance from the Enemy, and fetching a great Compass about, brings all safe into the City, and enters into *York*[1] himself with all his Army.

No Action of this whole War had gained the Prince so much Honour, or the King's Affairs so much Advantage as this, had the Prince but had the Power to have restrained his Courage after this, and checked his fatal Eagerness for Fighting. Here was a Siege raised, the Reputation of the Enemy justly slurred, a City relieved and furnished, with all things necessary in the Face of an Army superior in Number by near 10000 Men, and commanded by a Triumvirate of Generals *Leven*, *Fairfax* and *Manchester*. Had the Prince but remembered the Proceeding of the great Duke of *Parma* at the Relief of *Paris*,[2] he would have seen the relieving the City was his Business; 'twas the Enemy's Business to fight, if possible, 'twas his to avoid it; for, having delivered the City, and put the Disgrace of raising the Siege upon the Enemy, he had nothing farther to do, but to have waited till he had seen what Course the Enemy would take, and taken his farther Measures from their Motion.

But *the Prince*, a continual Friend to precipitant Counsels, would hear no Advice: I entreated him not to put it to the Hazard; I told him, that he ought to consider if he lost the Day, he lost the Kingdom, and took the Crown off from the King's Head. I put him in mind that it was impossible those three Generals should continue long together; and that if they did, they would not agree long in their Counsels: Which would be as well for us as their separating. 'Twas plain *Manchester* and *Cromwell* must return to the associated Counties, who would not suffer them to stay, for fear the King should attempt them; That he could subsist well enough, having *York* City and River at his Back; but the *Scots* would eat up the Country, make themselves odious, and dwindle away to nothing, if he would but hold them at Bay a little; other General Officers were of the same Mind; but all I could say, or they either, to a Man deaf to any thing but his own Courage, signified nothing.[1] He would draw out and fight, there was no perswading him to the contrary, unless a Man would run the Risque of being upbraided with being a Coward, and afraid of the Work. The Enemy's Army lay on a large Common, called *Marston-Moor*, doubtful what to do: Some were for fighting the Prince, the *Scots* were against it, being uneasy at having the Garrison of *Newcastle* at their Backs; but the Prince brought their Councils of War to a Result; for he let them know, they must fight him, whether they would or no; for the Prince being, *as before*, 18000 Men, and the Earl of *Newcastle* having joined him with 8000 Foot out of the City, were marched in Quest of the Enemy, had entered the Moor in View of their Army, and began to draw up in Order of Battle; but the Night coming on, the Armies only viewed each other at a Distance for that time. We lay all Night upon our Arms, and with the first of the Day were in Order of Battle; the Enemy was getting ready, but part of *Manchester*'s Men were not in the Field, but lay about three Miles off, and made a hasty March to come up.

The Prince his Army was exceedingly well managed; he himself commanded the Left Wing, the Earl of *Newcastle* the Right Wing; and the Lord *Goring*, as General of the Foot, assisted by Major General *Porter*, and Sir *Charles Lucas*, led the main Battle. I had prevailed with the Prince, according to the Method of the King of *Sweden*, to place some small Bodies of Musqueteers in the Intervals of his Horse, in the Left Wing, but could not prevail upon the Earl of *Newcastle* to do it in the Right; which he afterwards repented. In this Posture we stood facing the Enemy, expecting they would advance to us, which at last they did; and the Prince began the Day by saluting them with his Artillery, which being placed very well, galled them terribly for a Quarter of an Hour; they could not shift their Front, so they advanced the hastier to get within our great Guns, and consequently out of their Danger, which brought the Fight the sooner on.

The Enemy's Army was thus ordered; Sir *Thomas Fairfax* had the Right Wing, in which was the *Scots* Horse, and the Horse of his own and his Father's Army; *Cromwell* led the Left Wing, with his own and the Earl *Manchester*'s Horse, and the three Generals *Lesley*, old *Fairfax*, and *Manchester*, led the main Battle.

The Prince, with our Left Wing, fell on first, and, with his usual Fury, broke, like a Clap of Thunder, into the Right Wing of the *Scots* Horse, led by Sir *Thomas Fairfax*; and, as nothing could stand in his Way, he broke through and through them, and entirely routed them, pursuing them quite out of the Field. Sir *Thomas Fairfax*, with a Regiment of Lances, and about 500 of his own Horse, made good the Ground for some time; but our Musqueteers, which, as I said, were placed among our Horse were such an unlooked for sort of an Article in a Fight among the Horse, that those Lances, which otherwise were brave Fellows, were mowed down with their Shot, and all was put into Confusion. Sir *Thomas Fairfax* was wounded in the Face, his Brother killed, and a great Slaughter was made of the *Scots*, to whom I confess we shewed no Favour at all.

While this was doing on our Left, the Lord *Goring* with the main Battle charged the Enemy's Foot, and particularly one Brigade commanded by Major General *Porter*, being mostly Pikemen, not regarding the Fire of the Enemy, charged with that Fury in a close Body of Pikes, that they overturned all that came in their Way, and breaking into the Middle of the Enemy's Foot, filled all with Terror and Confusion, insomuch that the three Generals thinking all had been lost, fled, and quitted the Field.

But Matters went not so well with that *always Unfortunate* Gentleman the Earl of *Newcastle*, and our Right Wing of Horse; for *Cromwell* charged the Earl of *Newcastle* with a powerful Body of Horse; and though the Earl, and those about him, did what Men could do, and behaved themselves with all possible Gallantry, yet there was no withstanding *Cromwell's* Horse; but, like Prince *Rupert*, they bore down all before them; and now the Victory was wrung out of our Hands by our own gross Miscarriage; for the Prince, as 'twas his Custom, too eager in the Chase of the Enemy, was gone, and could not be heard of: The Foot in the Center, the Right Wing of the Horse being routed by *Cromwell*, was left, and without the Guard of his Horse; *Cromwell* having routed the Earl of *Newcastle*, and beaten him quite out of the Field, and Sir *Thomas Fairfax* rallying his dispersed Troops, they fall all together upon the Foot. General Lord *Goring*, like himself, fought like a Lion, but, forsaken of his Horse, was hemmed in on all Sides, and overthrown; and an Hour after this, the Prince returning too late to recover his Friends, was obliged with the rest to quit the Field to Conquerors.

This was a fatal Day to the King's Affairs, and the Risque too much for any Man in his Wits to run; we lost 4000 Men on the Spot, 3000 Prisoners, amongst whom was Sir *Charles Lucas*, Major General *Porter*, Major General *Telier*, and about 170 Gentlemen of Quality. We lost all our Baggage, 25 Pieces of Cannon, 300 Carriages, 150 Barrels of Powder, and 10000 Arms.

The Prince got into *York* with the Earl of *Newcastle*, and a great many Gentlemen, and 7 or 8000 of the Men, as well Horse as Foot.

I had but very course Treatment in this Fight; for returning with the Prince from the Pursuit of the Right Wing, and finding all lost, I halted with some other Officers, to consider what to do: At first we were for making our Retreat in a Body, and might have done so well enough, if we had known what had happened, before we saw our selves in the Middle of the Enemy; for Sir *Thomas Fairfax*, who had got together his scattered Troops, and joined by some of the Left Wing, knowing who we were, charged us with great Fury. 'Twas not a Time to think of any thing but getting away, or dying upon the Spot; the Prince kept on in the Front, and Sir *Thomas Fairfax*, by this Charge cut off about three Regiments of us from our Body; but bending his main Strength at the Prince, left us, as it were, behind him, in the Middle of the Field of Battle. We took this for the only Opportunity we could have to get off, and joining together, we made cross the Place of Battle in as good Order as we could, with our Carabines presented. In this Posture we passed by several Bodies of the Enemy's Foot, who stood with their Pikes charged to keep us off; but they had no Occasion, for we had no Design to meddle with them, but to get from them. Thus we made a swift March, and thought our selves pretty secure, but our Work was not done yet; for, on a sudden, we saw our selves under a Necessity of Fighting our Way through a great Body of *Manchester*'s Horse, who came galloping upon us over the Moor. They had as, we suppose, been pursuing some of our broken Troops, which were fled before, and seeing us, they gave us a home Charge. We received them as well as could, but pushed to get through them, which at last we did with a considerable Loss to them. However, we lost so many Men, either killed or separated from us, (for all could not follow the same Way) that of our three Regiments we could not be above 400 Horse together, when we got quite clear, and these were mixt Men, some of one Troop and Regiment, some of another. Not that I believe many of us were killed in the last Attack; for we had plainly the better of the Enemy; but our Design being to get off, some shifted for themselves one Way, and some another, in the best Manner they could, and as their several Fortunes guided them. 400 more of this Body, as I afterwards understood, having broke through the Enemy's Body another Way, kept together, and got into *Pontfract* Castle, and 300 more, made Northward, and to *Skippon*, where the Prince afterwards fetched them off.

Those few of us that were left together, with whom I was, being now pretty clear of Pursuit, halted, and began to enquire who and who we were, and what we should do; and on a short Debate, I proposed we should make to the first Garrison of the King's that we could recover; and that we should keep together, lest the Country People should insult us upon the Roads. With this Resolution we pushed on Westward for *Lancashire*; but our Misfortunes were not yet at an End: We travelled very hard, and got to a Village upon the River *Wharf*, near *Wetherby*. At *Wetherby* there was a Bridge, but we understood that a Party from *Leeds* had secured the Town and the Post, in order to stop the flying Cavaliers; and that 'twould be very hard to get through there; though, as we understood afterwards, there were no Soldiers there but a Guard of the Townsmen. In this Pickle we consulted what Course to take; to stay where we were till Morning, we all concluded would not be safe; some advised to take the Stream with our Horses; but the River, which is deep, and the Current strong, seemed to bid us have a care what we did of that Kind, especially in the Night. We resolved, therefore to refresh our selves and our Horses, *which indeed is more than we did*, and go on till we might come to a Ford or Bridge, where we might get over. Some Guides we had, but they either were foolish or false; for after we had rid eight or nine Miles, they plunged us into a River, at a Place they called a Ford, but 'twas a very ill one; for most of our Horses swam, and seven or eight were lost, but we saved the Men; however, we got all over.

We made bold with our first Convenience to trespass upon the Country for a few Horses, where we could find them, to remount our Men, whose Horses were drowned, and continued our March; but being obliged to refresh our selves

at a small Village on the Edge of *Bramham-moor*, we found
the Country alarmed by our taking some Horses, and we
were no sooner got on Horseback in the Morning, and
entering on the Moor, but we understood we were pursued
by some Troops of Horse: There was no Remedy but we
must pass this Moor; and though our Horses were exceedingly
tired, yet we pressed on upon a round Trot, and recovered
an enclosed Country on the other Side, where we halted.
And here, Necessity putting us upon it, we were obliged to
look out for more Horses, for several of our Men were dismounted, and others Horses disabled by carrying double,
those who lost their Horses getting up behind them; but we
were supplied by our Enemies against their Will.

The Enemy followed us over the Moor, and we having
a woody enclosed Country about us, where we were, I
observed by their moving, they had lost Sight of us; upon
which I proposed concealing our selves till we might judge
of their Numbers. We did so, and lying close in a Wood,
they past hastily by us, without skirting or searching the
Wood, which was what on another Occasion they would not
have done. I found they were not above 150 Horse, and
considering, that to let them go before us, would be to alarm
the Country, and stop our Design; I thought, since we might
be able to deal with them, we should not meet with a better
Place for it, and told the rest of our Officers my Mind, which
all our Party presently, (for we not had Time for a long
Debate) agreed to. Immediately upon this I caused two Men
to fire their Pistols in the Wood, at two different Places, as
far asunder as I could. This I did to give them an Alarm,
and amuse them; for being in the Lane, they would otherwise have got through before we had been ready, and I
resolved to engage them there, as soon as 'twas possible.
After this Alarm, we rushed out of the Wood, with about
100 Horse, and charged them on the Flank in a broad Lane,
the Wood being on their Right. Our Passage into the Lane
being narrow, gave us some Difficulty in our getting out;
but the Surprize of the Charge did our Work; for the

Enemy thinking we had been a Mile or two before, had not
the least Thoughts of this Onset, till they heard us in the
Wood, and then they who were before could not come back.
We broke into the Lane just in the Middle of them, and by
that means divided them; and facing to the Left, charged
the Rear. First our dismounted Men, which were near 50,
lined the Edge of the Wood, and fired with their Carabines
upon those which were before, so warmly, that they put
them into a great Disorder: Mean while 50 more of our
Horse from the farther Part of the Wood shewed themselves
in the Lane upon their Front; this put them of the foremost
Party into a great Perplexity, and they began to face about,
to fall upon us who were engaged in the Rear: But their
facing about in a Lane where there was no Room to wheel,
and one who understands the Manner of wheeling a Troop
of Horse, must imagine, put them into a great Disorder. Our
Party in the Head of the Lane taking the Advantage of this
Mistake of the Enemy, charged in upon them, and routed
them entirely. Some found means to break into the Enclosures
on the other Side of the Lane, and get away. About 30 were
killed, and about 25 made Prisoners, and 40 very good
Horses were taken; all this while not a Man of ours was lost,
and not above seven or eight wounded. Those in the Rear
behaved themselves better; for they stood our Charge with
a great deal of Resolution, and all we could do, could not
break them; but at last our Men who had fired on Foot
through the Hedges at the other Party, coming to do the like
here, there was no standing it any longer. The Rear of them
faced about, and retreated out of the Lane, and drew up in
the open Field to receive and rally their Fellows. We killed
about 17 of them, and followed them to the End of the Lane,
but had no mind to have any more fighting than needs must;
our Condition at that time not making it proper, the Towns
round us being all in the Enemy's Hands, and the Country
but indifferently pleased with us; however, we stood facing
them till they thought fit to march away. Thus we were
supplied with Horses enough to remount our Men, and

pursued our first Design of getting into *Lancashire*. As for our Prisoners, we let them go off on Foot.

But the Country being by this time alarmed, and the Rout of our Army every where known, we foresaw Abundance of Difficulties before us; we were not strong enough to venture into any great Towns, and we were too many to be concealed in small ones. Upon this we resolved to halt in a great Wood about three Miles beyond the Place, where we had the last Skirmish, and sent out Scouts to discover the Country, and learn what they could, either of the Enemy, or of our Friends.

Any Body may suppose we had but indifferent Quarters here, either for our selves or for our Horses; but however, we made shift to lye here two Days and one Night. In the interim I took upon me, with two more, to go to *Leeds* to learn some News; we were disguised like Country Ploughmen; the Clothes we got at a Farmer's House, which for that particular Occasion we plundered; and I cannot say no Blood was shed in a Manner too rash, and which I could not have done at another Time; but our Case was desperate, and the People too surly, and shot at us out the Window, wounded one Man and shot a Horse, which we counted as great a Loss to us as a Man, for our Safety depended upon our Horses. Here we got Clothes of all Sorts enough for both Sexes, and thus dressing my self up *a la Paisant*, with a white Cap on my Head, and a Fork on my Shoulder, and one of my Comerades in the Farmer's Wife's Russet Gown and Petticoat, like a Woman; the other with an old Crutch like a lame Man, and all mounted on such Horses as we had taken the Day before from the Country. Away we go to *Leeds* by three several Ways, and agreed to meet upon the Bridge. My pretended Country Woman acted her Part to the Life, though the Party was a Gentleman of good Quality of the Earl of *Worcester*'s Family, and the Cripple did as well he; but I thought my self very awkward in my Dress, which made me very shy, especially among the Soldiers. We passed their Centinels and Guards at *Leeds* unobserved, and put up our Horses at several Houses in the Town, from whence we went up and down to make our Remarks.[1] My Cripple was the fittest to go among the Soldiers, because there was less Danger of being pressed:[2] There he informed himself of the Matters of War, particularly that the Enemy sat down again to the Siege of *York*; that flying Parties were in Pursuit of the Cavaliers; and there he heard that 500 Horse of the Lord *Manchester*'s Men had followed a Party of Cavaliers over *Bramham Moor*; and, that entering a Lane, the Cavaliers, who were 1000 strong, fell upon them, and killed them all but about 50. This, though it was a Lie, was very pleasant to us to hear, knowing it was our Party, because of the other part of the Story, which was thus; that the Cavaliers had taken Possession of such a Wood, where they rallied all the Troops of their flying Army; that they had plundered the Country as they came, taking all the Horses they could get; that they had plundered Goodman *Thompson*'s House, which was the Farmer I mentioned, and killed Man, Woman and Child; and that they were about 2000 strong.

My other Friend in Woman's Clothes got among the good Wives at an Inn, where she set up her Horse, and there she heard the same sad and dreadful Tidings; and that this Party was so strong, none of the neighbouring Garrisons durst stir out; but that they had sent Expresses to *York* for a Party of Horse to come to their Assistance.

I walked up and down the Town, but fancied my self so ill disguised, and so easy to be known, that I cared not to talk with any Body. We met at the Bridge exactly at our Time, and compared our Intelligence, found it answered our End of coming, and that we had nothing to do but to get back to our Men; but my Cripple told me, he would not stir still he bought some Victuals: So away he hops with his Crutch, and buys four or five great Pieces of Bacon, as many of hung Beef, and two or three Loaves; and, borrowing a Sack at the Inn (which I suppose he never restored,) he loads his Horse, and, getting a large Leather

Bottle, he filled that of *Aquavitæ* instead of small Beer; my Woman Comerade did the like. I was uneasy in my Mind, and took no Care but to get out of Town; however, we all came off well enough; but 'twas well for me that I had no Provisions with me, as you will hear presently. We came, as I said, into the Town by several Ways, and so we went out; but about three Miles from the Town we met again exactly where we had agreed: I being about a Quarter of a Mile from the rest, I meets three Country Fellows on Horseback; one had a long Pole on his Shoulder, another a Fork, the third no Weapon at all, that I saw; I gave them the Road very orderly, being habited like one of their Brethren; but one of them stopping short at me, and looking earnestly, calls out, *Hark thee, Friend*, says he, in a broad North Country Tone, *whar hast thou thilk Horse?* I must confess I was in the utmost Confusion at the Question, neither being able to answer the Question, nor to speak in his Tone; so I made as if I did not hear him, and went on. *Na, but ye's not gang soa*, says the Boor, and comes up to me, and takes hold of the Horse's Bridle to stop me; at which, vexed at Heart that I could not tell how to talk to him, I reached him a great Knock on the Pate with my Fork, and fetched him off of his Horse, and then began to mend my Pace. The other Clowns, though it seems they knew not what the Fellow wanted, pursued me, and, finding they had better Heels than I, I saw there was no Remedy but to make use of my Hands, and faced about. The first that came up with me was he that had no Weapons, so I thought I might parley with him; and, speaking as Country like as I could, I asked him what he wanted? *Thou'st knaw that soon*, says *Yorkshire, and Ise but come at thee. Then keep awa' Man*, said I, *or Ise brain thee.* By this Time the third Man came up, and the Parley ended; for he gave me no Words but laid at me with his long Pole, and that with such Fury, that I began to be doubtful of him: I was loath to shoot the Fellow, though I had Pistols under my grey Frock, as well for that the Noise of a Pistol might bring more People in, the Village

being on our Rear; and also because I could not imagine
what the Fellow meant, or would have; but at last finding
he would be too many for me with that long Weapon, and a
hardy strong Fellow, I threw my self off of my Horse, and
running in with him, stabbed my Fork into his Horse; the
Horse being wounded, staggered a while, and then fell
down, and the Booby had not the Sense to get down in time,
but fell with him; upon which, giving him a knock or two
with my Fork, I secured him. The other, by this Time, had
furnished himself with a great Stick out of a Hedge, and,
before I was disingaged from the last Fellow, gave me two
such Blows, that if the last had not missed my Head, and hit
me on the Shoulder, I had ended the Fight and my Life
together. 'Twas time to look about me now, for this was a
mad Man; I defended my self with my Fork, but 'twould
not do; at last, in short, I was forced to Pistol him, and get
on Horseback again, and, with all the Speed I could make
get away to the Wood to our Men.

If my two Fellow Spies had not been behind, I had never
known what was the Meaning of this Quarrel of the three
Countrymen, but my Cripple had all the Particulars; for he
being behind us, as I have already observed, when he came
up to the first Fellow, who began the Fray, he found him
beginning to come to himself; so he gets off, and pretends
to help him, and sets him up upon his Breech, and being a
very merry Fellow, talked to him, *Well and what's the
Matter now*, says he to him, *ah wae's me*, says the Fellow,
I is killed: Not quite Mon, says the Cripple. *O that's a fau
Thief*, says he, and thus they parlied. My Cripple got him
on's Feet, and gave him a Dram of his *Aquavitæ* Bottle,
and made much of him, in order to know what was the
Occasion of the Quarrel. Our disguised Woman pitied the
Fellow too, and together they set him up again upon his
Horse, and then he told him that that Fellow was got upon
one of his Brother's Horses who lived at *Wetherby*: They
said the Cavaliers stole him, but 'twas like such Rogues;
no Mischief could be done in the Country, but 'twas the

poor Cavaliers must bear the Blame, and the like; and thus they jogged on till they came to the Place where the other two lay. The first Fellow they assisted as they had done t'other, and gave him a Dram out of the Leather Bottle; but the last Fellow was past their Care; so they came away: For when they understood that 'twas my Horse, they claimed, they began to be affraid that their own Horses might be known too, and then they had been betraid in a worse Pickle than I, and must have been forced to have done some Mischief or other to have got away.

I had sent out two Troopers to fetch them off, if there was any Occasion; but their Stay was not long, and the two Troopers saw them at a Distance coming towards us, so they returned.

I had enough of going for a Spy, and my Companions had enough of staying in the Wood; for other Intelligences agreed with ours, and all concurred in this, that it was time to be going; however, this Use we made of it, that while the Country thought us so strong we were in the less Danger of being attacked, though in the more of being observed; but all this while we heard nothing of our Friends, till the next Day. We heard Prince *Rupert*, with about 1000 Horse, was at *Skipton*, and from thence marched away to *Westmoreland*.

We concluded now we had two or three Days time good; for, since Messengers were sent to *York* for a Party to suppress us, we must have at least two Days March of them, and therefore all concluded we were to make the best of our Way; early in the Morning therefore we decamped from those dull Quarters; and as we marched through a Village, we found the People very civil to us, and the Women cried out, *God bless them, 'tis pity the Roundheads should make such Woork with such brave Men*, and the like. Finding we were among our Friends, we resolved to halt a little and refresh our selves; and, indeed, the People were very kind to us, gave us Victuals and Drink, and took Care of our Horses. It happened to be my Lot to stop at a House where the good

Woman took a great deal of Pains to provide for us; but I observed the good Man walked about with a Cap upon his Head, and very much out of Order, I took no great Notice of it, being very sleepy, and having asked my Landlady to let me have a Bed, I lay down and slept heartily: When I waked I found my Landlord on another Bed groaning very heavily.

When I came down Stairs, I found my Cripple talking with my Landlady; he was now out of his Disguise, but we called him Cripple still; and the other, who put on the Woman's Clothes, we called Goody *Thompson*. As soon as he saw me, he called me out, *Do you know*, says he *the Man of the House you are quartered in? No, not I*, says I. *No, so I believe, nor they you*, says he, *if they did, the good Wife would not have made you a Posset, and fetched a white Loaf for you. What do you mean*, says I. *Have you seen the Man* says he? *Seen him*, says I, *yes, and heard him too; the Man's Sick, and groans so heavily*, says I, *that I could not lye upon the Bed any longer for him. Why, this is the poor Man*, says he, *that you knocked down with your Fork Yesterday, and I have had all the Story out yonder at the next Door*. I confess it grieved me to have been forced to treat one so roughly who was one of our Friends, but to make some amends, we contrived to give the poor Man his Brother's Horse; and my Cripple told him a formal Story, that he believed the Horse was taken away from the Fellow by some of our Men; and, if he knew him again, if 'twas his Friend's Horse, he should have him. The Man came down upon the News, and I caused six or seven Horses, which were taken at the same time, to be shewn him; he immediately chose the right; so I gave him the Horse, and we pretended a great deal of Sorrow for the Man's Hurt; and that we had not knocked the Fellow on the Head as well as took away the Horse. The Man was so over-joyed at the Revenge he thought was taken on the Fellow, that we heard him groan no more. We ventured to stay all Day at this Town, and the next Night, and got Guides to lead us to *Blackstone Edge*, a Ridge of Mountains which part this Side of *Yorkshire* from *Lancashire*. Early in the Morning we marched, and kept our Scouts very carefully out every Way, who brought us no News for this Day; we kept on all Night, and made our Horses do Penance for that little Rest they had, and the next Morning we passed the Hills, and got into *Lancashire*, to a Town called *Littlebury*; and from thence to *Rochedale*, a little Market-Town. And now we thought our selves safe as to the Pursuit of Enemies from the Side of *York*; our Design was to get to *Bolton*, but all the County was full of the Enemy in flying Parties, and how to get to *Bolton* we knew not. At last we resolved to send a Messenger to *Bolton*; but he came back and told us, he had with lurking and hiding, tried all the Ways that he thought possible, but to no Purpose; for he could not get into the Town. We sent another, and he never returned; and some time after we understood he was taken by the Enemy. At last one got into the Town, but brought us Word, they were tired out with constant Alarms, had been straitly blocked up, and every Day expected a Siege, and therefore advised us either to go Northward, where Prince *Rupert*, and the Lord *Goring* ranged at Liberty; or to get over *Warrington* Bridge, and so secure our Retreat to *Chester*. This double Direction divided our Opinions; I was for getting into *Chester*, both to recruit my self with Horses and with Money, both which I wanted, and to get Refreshment, which we all wanted; but the major Part of our Men were for the North. First they said, there was their General, and 'twas their Duty to the Cause, and the King's Interest obliged us to go where we could do best Service; and there was their Friends, and every Man might hear some News of his own Regiment, for we belonged to several Regiments; besides, all the Towns to the Left of us, were possessed by Sir *William Brereton*, *Warrington* and *Northwich*, Garrisoned by the Enemy, and a strong Party at *Manchester*; so that 'twas very likely we should be beaten and dispersed before we could get to *Chester*. These Reasons, and especially the last, determined us for the North, and we had resolved to march the next Morning, when other Intelligence brought us to more speedy Resolutions. We kept our Scouts continually abroad, to bring us Intelligence of the Enemy, whom we expected on our Backs, and also to keep an Eye upon the Country; for as we lived upon them something at large, they were ready enough to do us any ill Turn, as it lay in their Power.

The first Messenger that came to us, was from our Friends at *Bolton*, to inform us, that they were preparing at *Manchester* to attack us: One of our Parties had been as far as *Stockport*, on the Edge of *Cheshire*, and was pursued by a Party of the Enemy, but got off by the Help of the Night. Thus all things looking black to the South, we had resolved to march Northward in the Morning, when one of our Scouts from the Side of *Manchester* assured us, Sir *Thomas Middleton*, with some of the Parliament Forces, and the Country Troops, making above 1200 Men, were on their March to attack us, and would certainly beat up our Quarters that Night. Upon this Advice we resolved to be gone; and getting all things in Readiness, we began to march about two Hours before Night: And having gotten a trusty Fellow for a Guide, a Fellow that we found was a Friend to our Side, he put a Project into my Head, which saved us all for that time; and that was, to give out in the Village, that we were marched back to *Yorkshire*, resolving to get into *Pontfract* Castle; and accordingly he leads us out of the Town the same way we came in; and taking a Boy with him, he sends the Boy back just at Night, and bad him say he saw us go up the Hills at *Blackstone-Edge*; and it happened very well; for this Party were so sure of us, that they had placed 400 Men on the Road to the Northward, to intercept our Retreat that Way, and had left no Way for us, as they thought, to get away, but back again.

About Ten a Clock at Night, they assaulted our Quarters, but found we were gone; and being informed which way, they followed upon the Spur, and travelling all Night, being Moon-Light, they found themselves the next Day about

15 Miles East, just out of their Way; for we had by the Help of our Guide, turned short at the Foot of the Hills, and through blind, untrodden Paths, and with Difficulty enough, by Noon the next Day, had reached almost 25 Miles North near a Town called *Clithero*. Here we halted in the open Field, and sent out our People to see how things were in the Country. This Part of the Country almost unpassable, and walled round with Hills, was indifferent quiet, and we got some Refreshment for our selves, but very little Horsemeat, and so went on; but we had not marched far before we found our selves discovered; and the 400 Horse sent to lye in wait for us as before, having understood which way we went, followed us hard; and by Letters to some of their Friends at *Preston*, we found we were beset again. Our Guide began now to be out of his Knowledge, and our Scouts brought us Word, the Enemy's Horse was posted before us, and we knew they were in our Rear. In this Exigence, we resolved to divide our small Body, and so amusing them, at least one might get off, if the other miscarried. I took about 80 Horse with me, among which were all that I had of our own Regiment, amounting to above 32, and took the Hills to-wards *Yorkshire*. Here we met with such unpassable Hills, vast Moors, Rocks, and stony Ways, as lamed all our Horses, and tired our Men; and sometimes I was ready to think we should never be able to get over them, till our Horses failing, and Jack-boots being but indifferent things to travel in, we might be starved before we should find any Road, or Towns, (for Guide we had none) but a Boy who knew but little, and would cry, when we asked him any Questions. I believe neither Men nor Horses ever passed in some Places where we went, and for 20 Hours we saw not a Town nor a House, excepting sometimes from the Top of the Mountains, at a vast Distance. I am perswaded we might have encamped here, if we had had Provisions, till the War had been over, and have met with no Disturbance; and I have often wondered since, how we got into such horrible Places, as much as how got out. That which was worse to

us than all the rest, was, that we knew not where we were
going, nor what Part of the Country we should come into,
when we came out of those desolate Craggs. At last, after a
terrible Fatigue, we began to see the Western Parts of *Yorkshire*, some few Villages, and the Country at a Distance,
looked a little like *England*; for I thought before it looked
like old *Brennus* Hill,[1] which the *Grisons* call the Grandfather
of the *Alps*. We got some Relief in the Villages, which
indeed some of us had so much need of, that they were
hardly able to sit their Horses, and others were forced to
help them off, they were so faint. I never felt so much of the
Power of Hunger in my Life; for having not eaten in 30
Hours, I was as ravenous as a Hound; and if I had had a
Piece of Horseflesh, I believe I should not have had Patience
to have staid Dressing it, but have fallen upon it raw, and
have eaten it as greedily as a *Tartar*.

However, I eat very cautiously, having often seen the
Danger of Mens eating heartily after long Fasting. Our next
Care was to enquire our Way. *Hallifax*, they told us, was on
our right; there we durst not think of going; *Skippon* was
before us, and there we knew not how it was; for a Body of
3000 Horse, sent out by the Enemy in Pursuit of Prince
Rupert, had been there but two Days before, and the Country
People could not tell us, whether they were gone, or no:
And *Manchester*'s Horse, which were sent out after our
Party, were then at *Hallifax*, in Quest of us, and afterwards
marched into *Cheshire*. In this Distress we would have hired
a Guide, but none of the Country People would go with us;
for the Roundheads would hang them, they said, when they
came there. Upon this I called a Fellow to me, *Harke ye
friend*, says I, *dost thee know the Way so as to bring us into*
Westmoreland, *and not keep the great Road from* York? *Ay
merry*, says he, *I ken the Ways weel enou ; and you would go
and guide us*, said I, *but that you are afraid the Roundheads
will hang you? Indeed would I*, says the Fellow. *Why then*,
says I, *thou hadst as good be hanged by a Roundhead as a
Cavalier ; for if thou wilt not go, I'll hang thee just now. Na*,

and ye serve me soa, says the Fellow, *Ise ene gang with ye; for I care not for Hanging; and ye'l get me a good Horse, Ise gang and be one of ye, for I'll nere come heame mere.* This pleased us still better, and we mounted the Fellow; for three of our Men died that Night with the extreme Fatigue of the last Service.

Next Morning, when our new Trooper was mounted and cloathed, we hardly knew him; and this Fellow led us by such Ways, such Wildernesses, and yet with such Prudence, keeping the Hills to the left, that we might have the Villages to refresh our selves, that without him, we had certainly either perished in those Mountains, or fallen into the Enemy's Hands. We passed the great Road from *York* so critically as to time, that from one of the Hills he shewed us a Party of the Enemy's Horse, who were then marching into *Westmoreland.* We lay still that Day, finding we were not discovered by them; and our Guide proved the best Scout that we could have had; for he would go out ten Miles at a time, and bring us in all the News of the Country: Here he brought us word, that *York*[1] was surrendered upon Articles, and that *Newcastle,* which had been surprized by the King's Party, was besieged by another Army of *Scots* advanced to help their Brethren.

Along the Edges of those vast Mountains we past with the Help of our Guide, till we came into the Forest of *Swale;* and finding our selves perfectly concealed here, for no Soldier had ever been here all the War, nor perhaps would not, if it had lasted 7 Years; we thought we wanted a few Days Rest, at least for our Horses, so we resolved to halt, and while we did so, we made some Disguises, and sent out some Spies into the Country; but as here were no great Towns, nor no Post Road, we got very little Intelligence. We rested four Days, and then marched again; and indeed having no great Stock of Money about us, and not very free of that we had, four Days was enough for those poor Places to be able to maintain us.

We thought our selves pretty secure now; but our chief

Care was how to get over those terrible Mountains; for having passed the great Road that leads from *York* to *Lancaster*, the Craggs, the farther Northward we looked, look'd still the worse, and our Business was all on the other Side. Our Guide told us, he would bring us out, if we would have Patience, which we were obliged to, and kept on this slow March, till he brought us to *Stanhope*, in the County of *Durham*; where some of *Goring*'s Horse, and two Regiments of Foot, had their Quarters: This was 19 Days from the Battle of *Marston-Moor*. The Prince who was then at *Kendal* in *Westmoreland*, and who had given me over as lost, when he had News of our Arrival, sent an Express to me, to meet him at *Appleby*. I went thither accordingly, and gave him an Account of our Journey, and there I heard the short History of the other Part of our Men, whom we parted from in *Lancashire*. They made the best of their way North; they had two resolute Gentlemen who commanded; and being so closely pursued by the Enemy, that they found themselves under a Necessity of Fighting, they halted, and faced about, expecting the Charge. The Boldness of the Action made the Officer who led the Enemy's Horse (which it seems were the County Horse only) afraid of them; which they perceiving, taking the Advantage of his Fears, bravely advance, and charge them; and, though they were above 200 Horse, they routed them, killed about 30 or 40, got some Horses, and some Money, and pushed on their March Night and Day; but coming near *Lancaster*, they were so way-laid and pursued, that they agreed to separate, and shift every Man for himself; many of them fell into the Enemy's Hands; some were killed attempting to pass through the River *Lune*; some went back again, six or seven got to *Bolton*, and about 18 got safe to Prince *Rupert*.

The Prince was in a better Condition hereabouts than I expected; he and my Lord *Goring*, with the Help of Sir *Marmaduke Langdale*, and the Gentlemen of *Cumberland*, had gotten a Body of 4000 Horse, and about 6000 Foot; they had retaken *Newcastle*, *Tinmouth*, *Durham*, *Stockton*, and several Towns of Consequence from the *Scots*, and might have cut them out Work enough still, if that base People, resolved to engage their whole Interest to ruine their Sovereign, had not sent a second Army of 10000 Men, under the Earl of *Calender*, to help their first. These came and laid Siege to *Newcastle*, but found more vigorous Resistance now than they had done before.

There were in the Town Sir *John Morley*, the Lord *Crawford*, Lord *Rea*, and *Maxwell*, *Scots*; and old Soldiers, who were resolved their Countrymen should buy the Town very dear if they had it; and had it not been for our Disaster at *Marston-Moor*, they had never had it; for *Calender*, finding he was not able to carry the Town, sends to General *Leven* to come from the Siege of *York* to help him.

Mean time the Prince forms a very good Army, and the Lord *Goring*, with 10000 Men shews himself on the Borders of *Scotland*, to try if that might not cause the *Scots* to recal their Forces; and, I am perswaded had he entered *Scotland*, the Parliament of *Scotland* had recalled the Earl of *Calender*, for they had but 5000 Men left in Arms to send against him; but they were loath to venture.

However, this Effect it had, that it called the *Scots* Northward again, and found them Work there for the rest of the Summer, to reduce the several Towns in the Bishoprick of *Durham*.

I found with the Prince the poor Remains of my Regiment, which when joined with those that had been with me, could not all make up three Troops, and but two Captains, three Lieutenants, and one Cornet; the rest were dispersed, killed, or taken Prisoners.

However, with those, which we still called a Regiment, I joined the Prince, and after having done all we could on that Side, the *Scots* being returned from *York*, the Prince returned through *Lancashire* to *Chester*.

The Enemy often appeared and alarmed us, and once fell on one of our Parties, and killed us about a hundred Men; but we were too many for them to pretend to fight us, so we came to *Bolton*, beat the Troops of the Enemy near *Warrington*, where I got a Cut with a Halbard in my Face, and arrived at *Chester* the beginning of *August*.

The Parliament, upon their great Success in the North, thinking the King's Forces quite broken, had sent their General *Essex* into the West, where the King's Army was commanded by Prince *Maurice*, Prince *Rupert*'s elder Brother, but not very strong; and the King being, as they supposed, by the Absence of Prince *Rupert*, weakened so much as, that he might be checked by Sir *William Waller*, who, with 4500 Foot, and 1500 Horse, was at that Time about *Winchester*, having lately beaten Sir *Ralph Hopton*. Upon all these Considerations, the Earl of *Essex* marches Westward.

The Forces in the West being too weak to oppose him, every thing gives way to him, and all People expected he would besiege *Exeter*, where the Queen was newly lying in, and sent a Trumpet to desire he would forbear the City, while she could be removed; which he did, and passed on Westward, took *Tiverton*, *Biddeford*, *Barnstable*, *Lanceston*, relieved *Plymouth*, drove Sir *Richard Greenvil* up into *Cornwall*, and followed him thither, but left Prince *Maurice* behind him with 4000 Men about *Barnstable* and *Exeter*. The King, in the mean time, marches from *Oxford* into *Worcester*, with *Waller* at his Heels; at *Edgehill* his Majesty turns upon *Waller*, and gave him a Brush, to put him in mind of the Place; the King goes on to *Worcester*, sends 300 Horse to relieve *Durley* Castle, besieged by the Earl of *Denby*, and sending Part of his Forces to *Bristol*, returns to *Oxford*.

His Majesty had now firmly resolved to march into the West, not having yet any Account of our Misfortunes in the North. *Waller* and *Middleton* way-lay the King at *Cropedy* Bridge: The King assaults *Middleton* at the Bridge; *Waller*'s Men were posted with some Cannon to guard a Pass; *Middleton*'s Men put a Regiment of the King's Foot to the Rout, and pursued them: *Waller*'s Men, willing to come in for the Plunder, a thing their General had often used them to, quit their Post at the Pass, and their great Guns, to have Part in the Victory. The King coming in seasonably to the Relief of his Men, routs *Middleton*, and at the same time sends a Party round, who clapt in between Sir *William Waller*'s Men and their great Guns, and secured the Pass and the Cannon too.

The King took three Collonels, besides other Officers, and about 300 Men Prisoners, with eight great Guns, 19 Carriages of Ammunition, and killed about 200 Men.

Waller lost his Reputation in this Fight, and was exceedingly slighted ever after, even by his own Party; but especially by such as were of General *Essex*'s Party, between whom and *Waller* there had been Jealousies and Misunderstandings for some time.

The King, about 8000 strong, marched on to *Bristol*, where Sir *William Hopton* joined him; and from thence he follows *Essex* into *Cornwall*; *Essex* still following *Greenvil*, the King comes to *Exeter*, and joining with Prince *Maurice*, resolves to pursue *Essex*; and now the Earl of *Essex* began to see his Mistake, being cooped up between two Seas, the King's Army in his Rear, the Country his Enemy, and Sir *Richard Greenvil* in his Van.

The King, who always took the best Measures, when he was left to his own Counsel, wisely refuses to engage, though superior in Number, and much stronger in Horse. *Essex* often drew out to fight, but the King fortifies, takes the Passes and Bridges, Plants Cannon, and secures the Country to keep off Provisions, and continually streightens their Quarters, but would not fight.

Now *Essex* sends away to the Parliament for Help, and they write to *Waller*, and *Middleton*, and *Manchester*, to follow, and come up with the King in his Rear; but some were too far off, and could not, as *Manchester* and *Fairfax*; others made no Haste, as having no mind to it, as *Waller* and *Middleton*, and if they had, it had been too late.

At last the Earl of *Essex* finding nothing to be done, and

unwilling to fall into the King's Hands, takes Shipping, and leaves his Army to shift for themselves. The Horse, under Sir *William Balfour*, the best Horse-Officer, and, without Comparison, the bravest in all the Parliament Army, advanced in small Parties, as if to Skirmish, but following in with the whole Body, being 3500 Horse, broke through, and got off. Though this was a Loss to the King's Victory, yet the Foot were now in a Condition so much the worse. Brave old *Skippon* proposed to fight through with the Foot and die, as he called, it, like *English* Men, with Sword in Hand; but the rest of the Officers shook their Heads at it; for, being well paid, they had at present no Occasion for dying.

Seeing it thus, they agreed to treat, and the King grants them Conditions, upon laying down their Arms,[1] to march off free. This was too much; had his Majesty but obliged them upon Oath not to serve again for a certain Time, he had done his Business; but this was not thought of; so they passed free, only disarmed, the Soldiers not being allowed so much as their Swords.

The King gained by this Treaty 40 Pieces of Cannon, all of Brass, 300 Barrels of Gunpowder, 9000 Arms, 8000 Swords, Match and Bullet in Proportion, 200 Waggons, 150 Colours and Standards, all the Bag and Baggage of the Army, and about 1000 of the Men listed in his Army. This was a compleat Victory without Bloodshed; and, had the King but secured the Men from serving but for six Months, it had most effectually answered the Battle of *Marston-Moor*.

As it was, it infused new Life into all his Majesty's Forces and Friends, and retrieved his Affairs very much; but especially it encouraged us in the North, who were more sensible of the Blow received at *Marston-Moor*, and of the Destruction the *Scots* were bringing upon us all.

While I was at *Chester*, we had some small Skirmishes with Sir *William Brereton*. One Morning in particular Sir *William* drew up, and faced us, and one of our Collonels of Horse observing the Enemy to be not, as he thought, above

200, desires Leave of Prince *Rupert* to attack them with the like Number, and accordingly he sallied out with 200 Horse. I stood drawn up without the City with 800 more, ready to bring him off, if he should be put to the worst, which happened accordingly; for, not having discovered neither the Country nor the Enemy as he ought, Sir *William Brereton* drew him into an Ambuscade; so that before he came up with Sir *William*'s Forces, near enough to charge, he finds about 300 Horse in his Rear: Though he was surprized at this, yet, being a Man of a ready Courage, he boldly faces about with 150 of his Men, leaving the other 50 to face Sir *William*. With this small Party, he desperately charges the 300 Horse in his Rear, and putting them into Disorder, breaks through them, and, had there been no greater Force, he had cut them all in Pieces. Flushed with this Success, and loath to desert the 50 Men he had left behind, he faces about again, and charges through them again, and with these two Charges entirely routs them. Sir *William Brereton* finding himself a little disappointed, advances, and falls upon the 50 Men just as the Collonel came up to them; they fought him with a great deal of Bravery, but the Collonel being unfortunately killed in the first Charge, the Men gave Way, and came flying all in Confusion, with the Enemy at their Heels. As soon as I saw this, I advanced, according to my Orders, and the Enemy, as soon as I appeared, gave over the Pursuit. This Gentleman, as I remember, was Collonel *Morough*; we fetched off his Body, and retreated into *Chester*.

The next Morning the Prince drew out of the City with about 1200 Horse and 2000 Foot, and attacked Sir *William Brereton* in his Quarters. The Fight was very sharp for the time, and near 700 Men, on both Sides, were killed; but Sir *William* would not put it to a general Engagement, so the Prince drew off, contenting himself to have insulted him in his Quarters.

We now had received Orders from the King to join him; but I representing to the Prince the Condition of my

Regiment, which was now 100 Men, and, that being within 25 Miles of my Father's House, I might soon recruit it, my Father having got some Men together already, I desired Leave to lye at *Shrewsbury* for a Month, to make up my Men. Accordingly having obtained his Leave, I marched to *Wrexham*, where, in two Days time I got 20 Men, and so on to *Shrewsbury*. I had not been here above 10 Days, but I received an Express to come away with what Recruits I had got together, Prince *Rupert* having positive Orders to meet the King by a certain Day. I had not mounted 100 Men, though I had listed above 200, when these Orders came; but leaving my Father to compleat them for me, I marched with those I had, and came to *Oxford*.

The King, after the Rout of the Parliament Forces in the West, was marched back, took *Barnstable*, *Plympton*, *Lanceston*, *Tiverton*, and several other Places, and left *Plymouth* besieged by Sir *Richard Greenvil*, met with Sir *William Waller* at *Shaftsbury*, and again at *Andover*, and boxed him at both Places, and marched for *Newberry*. Here the King sent for Prince *Rupert* to meet him, who with 3000 Horse made long Marches to join him; but the Parliament having joined their three Armies together, *Manchester* from the North, *Waller* and *Essex*, the Men being cloathed and armed, from the West, had attacked the King, and obliged him to fight the Day, before the Prince came up.

The King had so posted himself, as that he could not be obliged to fight but with Advantage; the Parliament's Forces being superior in Number, and therefore, when they attacked him, he galled them with his Cannon, and declining to come to a general Battle, stood upon the Defensive, expecting Prince *Rupert* with the Horse.[1]

The Parliament's Forces had some Advantage over our Foot, and took the Earl of *Cleveland* Prisoner; but the King, whose Foot were not above one to two, drew his Men under the Cannon of *Dennington* Castle, and having secured his Artillery and Baggage, made a Retreat with his Foot in very good Order, having not lost in all the Fight above 300 Men, and the Parliament as many: We lost five Pieces of Cannon and took two, having repulsed the Earl of *Manchester*'s Men on the North Side of the Town, with considerable Loss.

The King, having lodged his Train of Artillery and Baggage in *Dennington* Castle, marched the next Day for *Oxford*; there we joined him with 3000 Horse, and 2000 Foot. Encouraged with this Reinforcement, the King appears upon the Hills on the North-west of *Newberry*, and faces the Parliament Army. The Parliament having too many Generals as well as Soldiers, they could not agree whether they should fight or no. This was no great Token of the Victory they boasted of; for they were now twice our Number in the whole, and their Foot three for one. The King stood in Battalia all Day, and finding the Parliament Forces had no Stomach to engage him, he drew away his Cannon and Baggage out of *Dennington* Castle, in View of their whole Army, and marched away to *Oxford*.

This was such a false Step of the Parliament's Generals, that all the People cried shame of them: The Parliament appointed a Committee to enquire into it. *Cromwell* accused *Manchester*, and he *Waller*, and so they laid the Fault upon one another. *Waller* would have been glad to have charged it upon *Essex*; but as it happened he was not in the Army, having been taken ill some Days before; but, as it generally is when a Mistake is made, the Actors fall out among themselves, so it was here. No doubt it was as false a Step as that of *Cornwall*, to let the King fetch away his Baggage and Cannon in the Face of three Armies, and never fire a Shot at them.

The King had not above 8000 Foot in his Army, and they above 25000: 'Tis true, the King had 8000 Horse, a fine Body, and much superior to theirs; but the Foot might, with the greatest Ease in the World, have prevented the removing the Cannon, and in three Days time have taken the Castle, with all that was in it.

Those Differences produced their Self-denying Ordinance,[1] and the putting by most of their old Generals, as *Essex*, *Waller*, *Manchester*, and the like; and Sir *Thomas Fairfax*, a terrible Man in the Field, though the mildest of Men out of it, was voted to have the Command of all their Forces, and *Lambert* to take the Command of Sir *Thomas Fairfax's* Troops in the North, old *Skippon* being Major General.

This Winter was spent on the Enemy's Side in modelling, as they called it, their Army;[2] and, on our Side, in recruiting ours, and some petty Excursions. Amongst the many Addresses, I observed one from *Sussex* or *Surrey*, complaining of the Rudeness of their Soldiers, and particularly of the ravishing of Women, and the murthering of Men; from which I only observed, that there were Disorders among them, as well as among us, only with this Difference, that they, for Reasons I mentioned before, were under Circumstances to prevent it better than the King: But I must do the King's Memory that Justice, that he used all possible Methods, by Punishment of Soldiers, charging, and sometimes entreating, the Gentlemen not to suffer such Disorders and such Violences in their Men; but it was to no Purpose for his Majesty to attempt it, while his Officers, Generals, and Great Men, winked at it; for the Licentiousness of the Soldier is supposed to be approved by the Officer, when it is not corrected.

The Rudeness of the Parliament Soldiers began from the Divisions among their Officers; for, in many Places, the Soldiers grew so out of all Discipline, and so unsufferably rude, that they in particular refused to march when Sir *William Waller* went to *Weymouth*. This had turned to good Account for us, had these cursed *Scots* been out of our way, but they were the Staff of the Party; and now they were daily sollicited to march Southward, which was a very great Affliction to the King, and all his Friends.

One Booty the King got at this time, which was a very seasonable Assistance to his Affairs, (*viz.*) a great Merchant Ship richly laden at *London*, and bound to the *East-Indies*, was, by the Seamen, brought into *Bristol*, and delivered up to the King. Some Merchants in *Bristol* offered the King 40000 l. for her, which his Majesty ordered should be accepted, reserving only 30 great Guns for his own Use.

The Treaty at *Uxbridge* now was begun, and we that had been well beaten in the War, heartily wished the King would come to a Peace; but we all foresaw the Clergy would ruine it all. The Commons were for Presbytery, and would never agree the Bishops should be restored; the King was willinger to comply with any thing than this, and we foresaw it would be so; from whence we used to say among our selves, *That the Clergy was resolved if there should be no Bishop, there should be no King*.

This Treaty at *Uxbridge* was a perfect War between the Men of the Gown, ours was between those of the Sword; and I cannot but take Notice how the Lawyers, Statesmen, and the Clergy of every Side bestirred themselves, rather to hinder than promote the Peace.

There had been a Treaty at *Oxford* some time before, where the Parliament insisting that the King should pass a Bill to abolish Episcopacy, quit the Militia, abandon several of his faithful Servants to be exempted from Pardon, and making several other most extravagant Demands. Nothing was done, but the Treaty broke off, both Parties being rather farther exasperated, than inclined to hearken to Conditions.

However, soon after the Success in the West, his Majesty, to let them see that Victory had not puffed him up so as to make him reject the Peace, sends a Message to the Parliament, to put them in Mind of Messages of like Nature which they had slighted; and to let them know, that notwithstanding he had beaten their Forces, he was yet willing to hearken to a reasonable Proposal for putting an End to the War.

The Parliament pretended the King, in his Message, did not treat with them as a legal Parliament, and so made Hesitations; but after long Debates and Delays they agreed to draw up Propositions for Peace to be sent to the King. As this Message was sent to the Houses about *August*, I think they made it the middle of *November* before they brought the Propositions for Peace; and, when they brought them, they had no Power to enter either upon a Treaty, or so much as Preliminaries for a Treaty, only to deliver the Letter, and receive an Answer.

However, such were the Circumstances of Affairs at this Time, that the King was uneasy to see himself thus treated, and take no Notice of it: The King returned an Answer to the Propositions, and proposed a Treaty by Commissioners which the Parliament appointed.

Three Months more were spent in naming Commissioners. There was much Time spent in this Treaty, but little done; the Commissioners debated chiefly the Article of Religion, and of the Militia; in the latter they were very likely to agree, in the former both Sides seemed too positive. The King would by no Means abandon Episcopacy, nor the Parliament Presbytery; for both in their Opinion were *Jure Divino*.[1]

The Commissioners finding this Point hardest to adjust, went from it to that of the Militia; but the Time spinning out, the King's Commissioners demanded longer Time for the Treaty; the other sent up for Instructions, but the House refused to lengthen out the Time.

This was thought an Insolence upon the King, and gave all good People a Detestation of such haughty Behaviour; and thus the Hopes of Peace vanished,[2] both Sides prepared for War with as much Eagerness as before.

The Parliament was employed at this Time in what they called a Modelling their Army; that is to say, that now the Independent Party beginning to prevail; and, as they outdid all the others in their Resolution of carrying on the War to all Extremities, so they were both the more vigorous and more politick Party in carrying it on.

Indeed the War was after this carried on with greater Annimosity than ever, and the Generals pushed forward with a Vigour, that, as it had something in it unusual, so it told us plainly from this Time, whatever they did before, they now pushed at the Ruine even of Monarchy it self.

All this while also the War went on, and though the Parliament had no settled Army, yet their Regiments and Troops were always in Action; and the Sword was at work in every Part of the Kingdom.

Among an infinite Number of Party Skirmishings and Fights this Winter, one happened which nearly concerned me, which was the Surprize of the Town and Castle of *Shrewsbury*. Collonel *Mitton*, with about 1200 Horse and Foot, having Intelligence with some People in the Town, on a *Sunday* Morning early broke into the Town, and took it, Castle and all. The Loss for the Quality, more than the Number, was very great to the King's Affairs. They took there 15 Pieces of Cannon, Prince *Maurice*'s Magazine of Arms and Ammunition, Prince *Rupert*'s Baggage, above 50 Persons of Quality and Officers: There was not above 8 or 10 Men killed on both Sides; for the Town was surprized, not stormed.[1] I had a particular Loss in this Action; for, all the Men and Horses my Father had got together for the recruiting my Regiment, were here lost and dispersed; and, which was the worse, my Father happening to be then in the Town, was taken Prisoner, and carried to *Beeston* Castle in *Cheshire*.

I was quartered all this Winter at *Banbury*, and went little abroad; nor had we any Action till the latter end of *February*, when I was ordered to march to *Leicester* with Sir *Marmaduke Langdale*, in order, as we thought, to raise a Body of Men in that County and *Staffordshire*, to join the King.

We lay at *Daventry* one Night, and continuing our March to pass the River above *Northampton*, that Town being possessed by the Enemy, we understood a Party of *Northampton* Forces were abroad, and intended to attack us: Accordingly in the Afternoon our Scouts brought us Word, the Enemy were quartered in some Villages on the Road to *Coventry*; our Commander thinking it much better to set upon them in their Quarters, than to wait for them in the

Field, resolves to attack them early in the Morning, before they were aware of it. We refreshed our selves in the Field for that Day, and getting into a great Wood near the Enemy, we stayed there all Night, till almost break of Day, without being discovered.

In the Morning very early we heard the Enemy's Trumpets sound to Horse; this roused us to look abroad; and, sending out a Scout, he brought us Word a Party of the Enemy was at Hand. We were vexed to be so disappointed, but finding their Party small enough to be dealt with, Sir *Marmaduke* ordered me to charge them with 300 Horse and 200 Dragoons, while he at the same Time entered the Town. Accordingly I lay still till they came to the very Skirt of the Wood where I was posted, when I saluted them with a Volley from my Dragoons out of the Wood, and immediately shewed my self with my Horse on their Front, ready to charge them; they appeared not to be surprized, and received our Charge with great Resolution; and, being above 400 Men, they pushed me vigorously in their Turn, putting my Men into some Disorder. In this Extremity I sent to order the Dragoons to charge them in the Flank, which they did with great Bravery, and the other still maintained the Fight with desperate Resolution. There was no want of Courage in our Men on both Sides; but our Dragoons had the Advantage, and at last routed them, and drove them back to the Village. Here Sir *Marmaduke Langdale* had his Hands full too; for my firing had alarmed the Towns adjacent, that when he came into the Town, he found them all in Arms; and, contrary to his Expectation, two Regiments of Foot, with about 500 Horse more. As Sir *Marmaduke* had no Foot, only Horse and Dragoons, this was a Surprize to him; but he caused his Dragoons to enter the Town, and charge the Foot, while his Horse secured the Avenues of the Town.

The Dragoons bravely attacked the Foot, and Sir *Marmaduke* falling in with his Horse, the Fight was obstinate and very bloody, when the Horse that I had routed came flying into the Street of the Village, and my Men at their Heels. Immediately I left the Pursuit, and fell in with all my Force to the Assistance of my Friends, and, after an obstinate Resistance, we routed the whole Party; we killed about 700 Men, took 350, 27 Officers, 100 Arms, all their Baggage, and 200 Horses, and continued our March to *Harborough*, where we halted to refresh our selves.

Between *Harborough* and *Leicester* we met with a Party of 800 Dragoons of the Parliament Forces. They found themselves too few to attack us, and therefore to avoid us, they had gotten into a small Wood; but perceiving themselves discovered, they came boldly out, and placed themselves at the Entrance into a Lane, lining both Sides of the Hedges with their Shot. We immediately attacked them, beat them from their Hedges, beat them into the Wood, and out of the Wood again, and forced them at last to a down right *Run-away*, on Foot, among the Enclosures, where we could not follow them, killed about 100 of them, and took 250 Prisoners, with all their Horses, and came that Night to *Leicester*. When we came to *Leicester*, and had taken up our Quarters, Sir *Marmaduke Langdale* sent for me to sup with him, and told me, that he had a secret Commission in his Pocket, which his Majesty had commanded him not to open 'till he came to *Leicester*; that now he had sent for me to open it together, that we might know what it was we were to do, and to consider how to do it; so pulling out his sealed Orders, we found we were to get what Force we could together, and a certain Number of Carriages with Ammunition which the Governour of *Leicester* was to deliver us, and a certain Quantity of Provision, especially Corn and Salt, and to relieve *Newark*. This Town had been long besieged: The Fortifications of the Place, together with its Situation, had rendered it the strongest Piece in *England*; And, as it was the greatest Pass in *England*, so it was of vast Consequence to the King's Affairs. There was in it a Garrison of brave old rugged Boys, Fellows, that, like Count *Tilly's Germans*, had Iron Faces, and they had defended themselves with extraordinary Bravery a great while, but were reduced to an exceeding Streight for want of Provisions.

Accordingly we received the Ammunition and Provision, and away we went for *Newark*; about *Melton Mowbray*, Collonel *Roseter* set upon us, with above 3000 Men; we were about the same Number, having 2500 Horse, and 800 Dragoons. We had some Foot, but they were still at *Harborough*, and were ordered to come after us.

Roseter, like a brave Officer, as he was, charged us with great Fury, and rather outdid us in Number, while we defended our selves with all the Eagerness we could, and withal gave him to understand we were not so soon to be beaten as he expected. While the Fight continued doubtful; especially on our Side, our People, who had charge of the Carriages and Provisions, began to enclose our Flanks with them, as if we had been marching; which, though it was done without Orders, had two very good Effects, and which did us extraordinary Service. First, it secured us from being charged in the Flank, which *Roseter* had twice attempted; and, Secondly, it secured our Carriages from being plundered, which had spoiled our whole Expedition. Being thus enclosed, we fought with great Security; and though *Roseter* made three desperate Charges upon us, he could never break us. Our Men received him with so much Courage, and kept their Order so well, that the Enemy finding it impossible to force us, gave it over, and left us to pursue our Orders. We did not offer to chase them, but contented enough to have repulsed and beaten them off, and our Business being to relieve *Newark*, we proceeded.

If we are to reckon by the Enemy's usual Method, we got the Victory, because we kept the Field, and had the Pillage of their Dead; but otherwise, neither Side had any great Cause to boast. We lost about 150 Men, and near as many hurt; they left 170 on the Spot, and carried off some. How many they had wounded we could not tell; we got 70 or 80 Horse, which helped to remount some of our Men that had lost theirs in the Fight. We had, however, this Disadvantage, that we were to march on immediately after this Service; the Enemy only to retire to their Quarters, which was but hard by. This was an Injury to our wounded Men, who we were after obliged to leave at *Belvoir* Castle, and from thence we advanced to *Newark*.

Our Business at *Newark* was to relieve the Place, and this we resolved to do, whatever it cost, though, at the same Time, we resolved not to fight, unless we were forced to it. The Town was rather blocked up than besieged; the Garrison was strong, but ill provided; we had sent them word of our coming to them, and our Orders to relieve them, and they proposed some Measures for our doing it. The chief Strength of the Enemy lay on the other Side of the River; but they having also some Notice of our Design, had sent over Forces to strengthen their Leaguer on this Side. The Garrison had often surprized them by Sallies, and indeed had chiefly subsisted for some time by what they brought in on this Manner.

Sir *Marmaduke Langdale*, who was our General for the Expedition, was for a general Attempt to raise the Siege; but I had perswaded him off of that: First, Because if we should be beaten, as might be probable, we then lost the Town. Sir *Marmaduke* briskly replied, *A Soldier ought never to suppose he shall be beaten. But, Sir,* says I, *you'll get more Honour by relieving the Town, than by beating them: One will be a Credit to your Conduct, as the other will be to your Courage; and, if you think you can beat them, you may do it afterward, and then if you are mistaken, the Town is nevertheless secured, and half your Victory gained.*

He was prevailed with to adhere to this Advice, and accordingly we appeared before the Town about two Hours before Night. The Horse drew up before the Enemy's Works; the Enemy drew up within their Works, and seeing no Foot, expected when our Dragoons would dismount and attack them. They were in the right to let us attack them, because of the Advantage of their Batteries and Works, if that had been our Design; but, as we intended only to amuse them, this Caution of theirs effected our Design; for, while we thus faced them with our Horse, two Regiments of Foot, which came up to us but the Night before, and was all the Infantry we had, with the Waggons of Provisions, and 500 Dragoons, taking a Compass clean round the Town, posted themselves on the lower Side of the Town by the River. Upon a Signal the Garrison agreed on before, they sallied out at this very Juncture, with all the Men they could spare, and dividing themselves in two Parties, while one Party moved to the Left to meet our Relief, the other Party fell on upon Part of that Body which faced us. We kept in Motion, and upon this Signal advanced to their Works, and our Dragoons fired upon them; and the Horse wheeling and counter-marching often, kept them continually expecting to be attacked. By this Means the Enemy were kept employed, and our Foot with the Waggons, appearing on that Quarter where they were least expected, easily defeated the advanced Guards, and forced that Post, where entring the Leaguer, the other Part of the Garrison, who had sallied that way, came up to them, received the Waggons, and the Dragoons entered with them into the Town. That Party which we faced on the other Side of the Works; knew nothing of what was done till all was over; the Garrison retreated in good Order, and we drew off, having finished what we came for without fighting.

Thus we plentifully stored the Town with all things wanting, and with an Addition of 500 Dragoons to their Garrison; after which we marched away without fighting a Stroke. Our next Orders were to relieve *Pontfract* Castle, another Garrison of the King's, which had been besieged ever since a few Days after the Fight at *Marston-Moor*, by the Lord *Fairfax*, Sir *Thomas Fairfax*, and other Generals in their Turn.

By the Way, we were joined with 800 Horse out of *Derbyshire*, and some Foot, so many as made us, about 4500 Men in all.

Collonel *Forbes*, a *Scotchman*, commanded at the Siege,

in the Absence of the Lord *Fairfax*; the Collonel had sent to my Lord for more Troops, and his Lordship was gathering his Forces to come up to him; but he was pleased to come too late. We came up with the Enemy's Leaguer about Break of Day, and having been discovered by their Scouts, they, with more Courage than Discretion, drew out to meet us. We saw no Reason to avoid them, being stronger in Horse than they; and though we had but a few Foot, we had 1000 Dragoons, which helped us out. We had placed our Horse and Foot throughout in one Line, with two Reserves of Horse, and between every Division of Horse, a Division of Foot, only that on the Extremes of our Wings, there were two Parties of Horse on each Point by themselves, and the Dragoons in the Center, on Foot. Their Foot charged us home, and stood with Push of Pike a great while; but their Horse charging our Horse and Musqueteers, and being closed on the Flanks with those two extended Troops on our Wings, they were presently disordered, and fled out of the Field. The Foot thus deserted, were charged on every Side, and broken. They retreated still fighting, and in good Order, for a while; but the Garrison sallying upon them at the same Time, and being followed close by our Horse, they were scattered, entirely routed, and most of them killed. The Lord *Fairfax* was come with his Horse as far as *Ferribridge*, but the Fight was over; and all he could do was to rally those that fled, and save some of their Carriages, which else had fallen into our Hands. We drew up our little Army in Order of Battle the next Day, expecting the Lord *Fairfax* would have charged us; but his Lordship was so far from any such Thoughts, that he placed a Party of Dragoons, with Orders to fortify the Pass at *Ferribridge*, to prevent our falling upon him in his Retreat, which he needed not have done; for, having raised the Siege of *Pontfract*, our Business was done, we had nothing to say to him, unless we had been strong enough to stay.

We lost not above 30 Men in this Action, and the Enemy 300, with about 150 Prisoners, one Piece of Cannon, all their

Ammunition, 1000 Arms, and most of their Baggage, and Collonel *Lambert* was once taken Prisoner, being wounded, but got off again.

We brought no Relief for the Garrison, but the Opportunity to furnish themselves out of the Country, which they did very plentifully. The Ammunition taken from the Enemy was given to them, which they wanted, and was their Due, for they had siezed it in the Sally they made, before the Enemy was quite defeated.

I cannot omit taking Notice, on all Occasions, how exceeding serviceable this Method was of posting Musqueteers in the Intervals, among the Horse, in all this War: I perswaded our Generals to it, as much as possible, and I never knew a Body of Horse beaten that did so; yet I had great Difficulty to prevail upon our People to believe it, though it was taught me by the greatest General in the World, (viz.) the King of *Sweden*. Prince *Rupert* did it at the Battle *Marston-Moor*; and had the Earl of *Newcastle* not been obstinate against it in his Right Wing, as I observed before, the Day had not been lost. In discoursing this with Sir *Marmaduke Langdale*, I had related several Examples of the Serviceableness of these small Bodies of Firemen, and, with great Difficulty, brought him to agree, telling him, I would be answerable for the Success; but, after the Fight, he told me plainly he saw the Advantage of it, and would never fight otherwise again, if he had any Foot to place. So having relieved these two Places, we hastened, by long Marches, through *Derbyshire*, to join Prince *Rupert* on the Edge of *Shropshire* and *Cheshire*. We found Collonel *Roseter* had followed us at a Distance, ever since the Business at *Melton Mowbray*, but never cared to attack us, and we found he did the like still. Our General would fain have been doing with him again, but we found him too shy. Once we laid a Trap for him at *Dove-Bridge*, between *Derby* and *Burton upon Trent*, the Body being marched two Days before; 300 Dragoons were left to guard the Bridge, as if we were afraid he should fall upon us. Upon this we marched, as I said, on to *Burton*, and, the next Day, fetching a Compass round, came to a Village near *Titbury* Castle, whose Name I forgot, where we lay still expecting our Dragoons would be attacked.

Accordingly the Collonel, strengthned with some Troops of Horse from *Yorkshire*, comes up to the Bridge, and finding some Dragoons posted, advances to charge them: The Dragoons immediately get a Horseback, and run for it, as they were ordered; but the old Lad was not to be caught so; for he halts immediately at the Bridge, and would not come over till he had sent three or four flying Parties abroad, to discover the Country. One of these Parties fell into our Hands, and received but coarse Entertainment. Finding the Plot would not take, we appeared, and drew up in View of the Bridge but he would not stir: So we continued our March into *Cheshire*, where we joined Prince *Rupert*, and Prince *Maurice*, making together a fine Body, being above 8000 Horse and Dragoons.

This was the best and most successful Expedition I was in during this War. 'Twas well concerted, and executed with as much Expedition and Conduct as could be desired, and the Success was answerable to it: And indeed, considering the Season of the Year (for we set out from *Oxford* the latter end of *February*) the Ways bad, and the Season wet, it was a terrible March of above 200 Miles, in continual Action, and continually dodged and observed by a vigilant Enemy, and at a Time when the North was over-run by their Armies, and the *Scots* wanting Employment for their Forces; yet in less than 23 Days, we marched 200 Miles, fought the Enemy in open Field four Times, relieved one Garrison besieged, and raised the Siege of another, and joined our Friends at last in Safety.

The Enemy was in great Pain for Sir *William Brereton* and his Forces, and Expresses rid Night and Day to the *Scots* in the North, and to the Parties in *Lancashire*, to come to his Help. The Prince, who used to be rather too forward to fight than otherwise, could not be perswaded to make use of this Opportunity, but loitered, if I may be allowed to say so, till the *Scots*, with a Brigade of Horse and 2000 Foot, had joined him; and then 'twas not thought proper to engage them.

I took this Opportunity to go to *Shrewsbury* to visit my Father, who was a Prisoner of War there, getting a pass from the Enemy's Governour. They allowed him the Liberty of the Town, and sometimes to go to his own House, upon his Parole, so that his Confinement was not very much to his personal Injury; but this, together with the Charges he had been at in raising the Regiment, and above 20000 l. in Money and Plate, which at several Times he had lent, or given rather, to the King, had reduced our Family to very ill Circumstances; and now they talked of cutting down his Woods.

I had a great deal of Discourse with my Father on this Affair; and finding him extremely concerned, I offered to go to the King, and desire his Leave to go to *London*, and treat about his Composition,[1] or to render my self a Prisoner in his stead, while he went up himself. In this Difficulty I treated with the Governour of the Town, who very civilly offered me his Pass to go for *London*, which I accepted; and waiting on Prince *Rupert*, who was then at *Worcester*, I acquainted him with my Design. The Prince was unwilling I should go to *London*; but told me, he had some Prisoners of the Parliament's Friends in *Cumberland*, and he would get an Exchange for my Father. I told him, if he would give me his Word for it, I knew I might depend upon it, otherwise there was so many of the King's Party in their Hands, that his Majesty was tired with Sollicitations for Exchanges; for we never had a Prisoner but there was ten Offers of Exchanges for him. The Prince told me, I should depend upon him; and he was as good as his Word quickly after.

While the Prince lay at *Worcester* he made an Incursion into *Herefordshire*, and having made some of the Gentlemen Prisoners, brought them to *Worcester*; and though it was an Action which had not been usual, they being Persons not in Arms, yet the like being my Father's Case, who was really not in Commission, nor in any Military Service, having resigned his Regiment three Years before to me, the Prince insisted on exchanging them for such as the Parliament had in Custody in like Circumstances. The Gentlemen seeing no Remedy, sollicited their own Case at the Parliament, and got it passed in their behalf; and by this Means my Father got his Liberty; and, by the Assistance of the Earl of *Denbigh*, got Leave to come to *London* to make a Composition, as a Delinquent, for his Estate. This they charged at 7000 l. but by the Assistance of the same noble Person, he got off for 4000 l. Some Members of the Committee moved very kindly, that my Father should oblige me to quit the King's Service; but that, as a thing which might be out of his Power, was not insisted on.

The Modelling the Parliament Army took them up all this Winter, and we were in great Hopes the Divisions which appeared amongst them might have weakened their Party; but when they voted Sir *Thomas Fairfax* to be General, I confess I was convinced the King's Affairs were lost and desperate. Sir *Thomas*, abating the Zeal of his Party, and the mistaken Opinion of his Cause, was the fittest Man amongst them to undertake the Charge: He was a compleat General, strict in his Discipline, wary in Conduct, fearless in Action, unwearied in the Fatigue of the War, and withal, of a modest, noble, generous Disposition. We all aprehended Danger from him, and heartily wished him of our own Side; and the King was so sensible, though he would not discover it, that when an Account was brought him of the Choice they had made, he replied, *he was sorry for it; he had rather it had been any Body than he.*

The first Attempts of this new General and new Army were at *Oxford*, which, by the Neighbourhood of a numerous Garrison in *Abingdon*, began to be very much streightned for Provisions; and the new Forces under *Cromwell* and *Skippon*, one Lieutenant General, the other Major General to *Fairfax*, approaching with a Design to block it up, the King left the

Place, supposing his Absence would draw them away, as it soon did.

The King resolving to leave *Oxford*, marches from thence with all his Forces, the Garrison excepted, with Design to have gone to *Bristol*, but the Plague was in *Bristol*, which altered the Measures, and changed the Course of the King's Designs, so he marched for *Worcester* about the beginning of *June* 1645. The Foot with a Train of 40 Pieces of Cannon, marching into *Worcester*, the Horse stayed behind some time in *Gloucestershire*.

The first Action our Army did, was to raise the Siege of *Chester*; Sir *William Brereton* had besieged it, or rather blocked it up, and when his Majesty came to *Worcester*, he sent Prince *Rupert*, with 4000 Horse and Dragoons, with Orders to join some Foot out of *Wales*, to raise the Siege; but Sir *William* thought fit to withdraw, and not stay for them, and the Town was freed without fighting. The Governour took Care in this Interval to furnish himself with all things necessary for another Siege; and, as for Ammunition and other Necessaries, he was in no Want.

I was sent with a Party into *Staffordshire*, with Design to intercept a Convoy of Stores coming from *London*, for the Use of Sir *William Brereton*; but they having some Notice of the Design, stopt, and went out of the Road to *Burton upon Trent*, and so I missed them; but that we might not come back quite empty, we attacked *Hawkesly* House, and took it, where we got good Booty, and brought 80 Prisoners back to *Worcester*.[1] From *Worcester* the King advanced into *Shropshire*, and took his Head Quarters at *Bridgenorth*. This was a very happy March of the King's, and had his Majesty proceeded, he had certainly cleared the North once more of his Enemies, for the Country was generally for him. At his advancing so far as *Bridgenorth*, Sir *William Brereton* fled up into *Lancashire*; the *Scots* Brigades who were with him retreated into the North, while yet the King was above 40 Miles from them, and all things lay open for Conquest. The new Generals, *Fairfax* and *Cromwell*, lay about *Oxford* preparing as if they would besiege it, and gave the King's Army so much Leisure, that his Majesty might have been at *Newcastle* before they could have been half Way to him. But Heaven, when the Ruine of a Person or Party is determined, always so infatuates their Counsels, as to make them instrumental to it themselves.

The King let slip this great Opportunity, as some thought, intending to break into the Associated Counties, of *Northampton*, *Cambridge*, *Norfolk*, where he had some Interests forming. What the Design was, we knew not, but the King turns Eastward, and Marches into *Leicestershire*, and having treated the Country but very indifferently, as having deserved no better of us, laid Siege to *Leicester*.

This was but a short Siege; for the King, resolving not to lose Time, fell on with his great Guns, and having beaten down their Works, our Foot entered, after a vigorous Resistance, and took the Town by Storm. There was some Blood shed here, the Town being carried by Assault; but it was their own Faults; for after the Town was taken, the Soldiers and Townsmen obstinately fought us in the Market-Place; insomuch that the Horse was called to enter the Town to clear the Streets. But this was not all; I was commanded to advance with these Horse, being three Regiments, and to enter the Town; the Foot, who were engaged in the Streets, crying out, *Horse, Horse*. Immediately I advanced to the Gate, for we were drawn up about Musquet Shot from the Works, to have supported our Foot, in Case of a Sally. Having siezed the Gate, I placed a Guard of Horse there, with Orders to let no Body pass in or out, and dividing my Troops, rode up by two Ways towards the Market-Place; the Garrison defending themselves in the Market-Place, and in the Church-yard, with great Obstinancy, killed us a great many Men; but, as soon as our Horse appeared, they demanded Quarter, which our Foot refused them in the first Heat, as is frequent in all Nations, in like Cases; 'till at last, they threw down their Arms, and yielded at Discretion; and then I can testify to the World, that fair Quarter was given them. I am the more particular in this Relation, having been an Eye-witness of the Action, because the King was reproached in all the publick Libels, with which those Times abounded, for having put a great many to Death, and hanged the Committee of the Parliament, and some *Scots*, in cold Blood, which was a notorious Forgery; and as I am sure there was no such thing done, so I must acknowledge I never saw any Inclination in his Majesty to Cruelty, or to act any thing which was not practised by the General Laws of War, and by Men of Honour in all Nations.

But the Matter of Fact, in Respect to the Garrison, was as I have related; and, if they had thrown down their Arms sooner, they had had Mercy sooner; but it was not for a conquering Army, entered a Town by Storm, to offer Conditions of Quarter in the Streets.

Another Circumstance was, that a great many of the Inhabitants, both Men and Women, were killed, which is most true; and the Case was thus: The Inhabitants, to shew their over-forward Zeal to defend the Town, fought in the Breach; nay, the very Women, to the Honour of the *Leicester* Ladies, if they like it, officiously did their Parts; and after the Town was taken, and when, if they had had any Brains in their Zeal, they would have kept their Houses, and been quiet, they fired upon our Men out of their Windows, and from the Tops of their Houses, and threw Tiles upon their Heads; and I had several of my Men wounded so, and 7 or 8 killed. This exasperated us to the last Degree; and, finding one House better manned than ordinary, and many Shot fired at us out of the Windows, I caused my Men to attack it, resolved to make them an Example for the rest; which they did, and breaking open the Doors, they killed all they found there, without Distinction; and I appeal to the World if they were to blame. If the Parliament Committee, or the *Scots* Deputies were here, they ought to have been quiet, since the Town was taken; but they began with us, and, I think, brought it upon themselves. This is the whole Case, so far as came within my Knowledge, for which his Majesty was so much abused.

We took here Collonel *Gray* and Captain *Hacker*, and about 300 Prisoners, and about 300 more were killed.[1] This was the last Day of *May* 1645.

His Majesty having given over *Oxford* for lost, continued here some Days, viewed the Town, ordered the Fortifications to be augmented, and prepares to make it the Seat of War. But the Parliament, rouzed at this Appearance of the King's Army, order their General to raise the Siege of *Oxford*, where the Garrison had, in a Sally, ruined some of their Works, and killed them 150 Men, taking several Prisoners, and carrying them with them into the City; and orders him to march towards *Leicester*, to observe the King.

The King had now a small, but gallant Army, all brave tried Soldiers, and seemed eager to engage the new-modelled Army; and his Majesty, hearing that Sir *Thomas Fairfax* having raised the Siege of *Oxford*, advanced towards him, fairly saves him the Trouble of a long March, and meets him half Way.

The Army lay at *Daventry*, and *Fairfax* at *Towcester*, about 8 Miles off. Here the King sends away 600 Horse, with 3000 Head of Cattle,[2] to relieve his People in *Oxford*; the Cattle he might have spared better than the Men. The King having thus victualled *Oxford*, changes his Resolution of fighting *Fairfax*, to whom *Cromwell* was now joined with 4000 Men,[3] or was within a Day's March, and marches Northward. This was unhappy Counsel, because late given: Had we marched Northward at first, we had done it; but thus it was. Now we marched with a triumphing Enemy at our Heels, and at *Naseby* their advanced Parties attacked our Rear. The King, upon this, alters his Resolution again, and resolves to fight, and at Midnight calls us up at *Harborough* to come to a Council of War. Fate and the King's Opinion determined the Council of War; and 'twas resolved to fight. Accordingly the Van, in which was Prince *Rupert*'s Brigade of Horse, of which my Regiment was a Part, countermarched early in the Morning.

By five a Clock in the Morning,[1] the whole Army, in Order of Battle, began to descry the Enemy from the rising Grounds, about a Mile from *Naseby*, and moved towards them. They were drawn up on a little Ascent in a large Common Fallow Field, in one Line extended from one Side of the Field to the other, the Field something more than a Mile over, our Army in the same Order, in one Line, with the Reserves.

The King led the main Battle of Foot, Prince *Rupert* the Right Wing of the Horse, and Sir *Marmaduke Langdale* the Left. Of the Enemy *Fairfax* and *Skippon* led the Body, *Cromwell* and *Roseter* the Right, and *Ireton* the Left. The Numbers of both Armies so equal, as not to differ 500 Men, save that the King had most Horse by about 1000, and *Fairfax* most Foot by about 500. The Number was in each Army about 18000 Men.

The Armies coming close up, the Wings engaged first. The Prince with his Right Wing charged with his wonted Fury, and drove all the Parliament's Wing of Horse, one Division excepted, clear out of the Field. *Ireton*, who commanded this Wing, give him his due, rallied often, and fought like a Lion; but our Wing bore down all before them, and pursued them with a terrible Execution.

Ireton seeing one Division of his Horse left, repaired to them, and keeping his Ground, fell foul of a Brigade of our Foot, who coming up to the Head of the Line, he like [a] mad Man charges them with his Horse: But they with their Pikes tore him to Pieces; so that this Division was entirely ruined. *Ireton* himself thrust through the Thigh with a Pike, wounded in the Face with a Halberd, was unhorsed and taken Prisoner.

Cromwell, who commanded the Parliament's Right Wing, charged Sir *Marmaduke Langdale* with extraordinary Fury; but he an old tried Soldier, stood firm, and received the Charge with equal Gallantry, exchanging all their Shot,

Carabines and Pistols, and then fell on Sword in Hand. *Roseter* and *Whaley* had the better on the Point of the Wing, and routed two Divisions of Horse, pushing them behind the Reserves, where they rallied, and charged again, but were at last defeated; the rest of the Horse now charged in the Flank retreated fighting, and were pushed behind the Reserves of Foot.

While this was doing, the Foot engaged with equal Fierceness, and for two Hours there was a terrible Fire. The King's Foot backed with gallant Officers, and full of Rage at the Rout of their Horse, bore down the Enemy's Brigade led by *Skippon.* The old Man wounded, bleeding retreats to their Reserves. All the Foot, except the General's Brigade, were thus driven into the Reserves, where their Officers rallied them, and bring them on to a fresh Charge; and here the Horse having driven our Horse about a Quarter of a Mile from the Foot, face about, and fall in on the Rear of the Foot.

Had our Right Wing done thus, the Day had been secured; but Prince *Rupert* according to his Custom, following the flying Enemy, never concerned himself with the Safety of those behind; and yet he returned sooner than he had done in like Cases too. At our Return we found all in Confusion, our Foot broken, all but one Brigade, which though charged in Front, Flank and Rear, could not be broken, till Sir *Thomas Fairfax* himself came up to the Charge with fresh Men, and then they were rather cut in Pieces then beaten; for they stood with their Pikes charged every Way to the last Extremity.

In this Condition, at the Distance of a Quarter of a Mile, we saw the King rallying his Horse, and preparing to renew the Fight; and our Wing of Horse coming up to him, gave him Opportunity to draw up a large Body of Horse, so large, that all the Enemy's Horse facing us, stood still and looked on, but did not think fit to charge us, till their Foot, who had entirely broken our main Battle, were put into Order again, and brought up to us.

The Officers about the King advised his Majesty rather to draw off; for, since our Foot were lost, it would be too much Odds to expose the Horse to the Fury of their whole Army, and would but be sacrificing his best Troops, without any Hopes of Success.

The King, though with great Regret, at the Loss of his Foot, yet seeing there was no other Hope, took this advice, and retreated in good Order to *Harborough*, and from thence to *Leicester*.[1]

This was the Occasion of the Enemy having so great a Number of Prisoners; for the Horse being thus gone off, the Foot had no Means to make their Retreat, and were obliged to yield themselves. Commissary General *Ireton* being taken by a Captain of Foot, makes the Captain his Prisoner, to save his Life, and gives him his Liberty for his Courtesy before.

Cromwell and *Roseter*, with all the Enemy's Horse, followed us as far as *Leicester*, and killed all that they could lay hold on straggling from the Body, but durst not attempt to charge us in a Body. The King expecting the Enemy would come to *Leicester*, removes to *Ashby de la Zouch*, where we had some Time to recollect our selves.

This was the most fatal Action of the whole War; not so much for the Loss of our Cannon, Ammunition, and Baggage, of which the Enemy boasted so much, but as it was impossible for the King ever to retrieve it: The Foot, the best that ever he was Master of, could never be supplied; his Army in the West was exposed to certain Ruin, the North over-run with the *Scots*; *in short*, the Case grew desperate, and the King was once upon the Point of bidding us all disband, and shift for our selves.

We lost in this Fight not above 2000 slain, and the Parliament near as many, but the Prisoners were a great Number; the whole Body of Foot being, as I have said, dispersed, there were 4500 Prisoners, besides 400 Officers, 2000 Horses, 12 Pieces of Cannon, 40 Barrels of Powder, all the King's Baggage, Coaches, most of his Servants, and his

Secretary, with his Cabinet of Letters, of which the Parliament made great Improvement, and, basely enough caused his private Letters between his Majesty and the Queen, her Majesty's Letters to the King, and a great deal of such Stuff to be printed.[1]

After this fatal Blow, being retreated, as I have said, to *Ashby de la Zouch* in *Leicestershire*, the King ordered us to divide; his Majesty, with a Body of Horse, about 3000, went to *Litchfield*, and through *Cheshire* into North *Wales* and Sir *Marmaduke Langdale*, with about 2500 went to *Newark*.

The King remained in *Wales* for several Months; and though the Length of the War had almost drained that Country of Men, yet the King raised a great many Men there, recruited his Horse Regiments, and got together six or seven Regiments of Foot, which seemed to look like the Beginning of a New Army.

I had frequent Discourses with his Majesty in this low Ebb of his Affairs, and he would often wish he had not exposed his Army at *Naseby*. I took the Freedom once to make a Proposition to his Majesty, which if it had taken Effect, I verily believe would have given a new Turn to his Affairs; and that was, at once to slight all his Garrisons in the Kingdom, and give private Orders to all the Soldiers in every Place, to join in Bodies, and meet at two General Rendezvous, which I would have appointed to be, one at *Bristol*, and one at *Westchester*. I demonstrated how easily all the Forces might reach these two Places; and both being strong and wealthy Places, and both Sea-Ports, he would have a free Communication by Sea, with *Ireland*, and with his Friends abroad; and having *Wales* entirely his own, he might yet have an Opportunity to make good Terms for himself, or else have another fair Field with the Enemy.

Upon a fair Calculation of his Troops in several Garrisons and small Bodies dispersed about, I convinced the King, by his own Accounts, that he might have two compleat Armies, each of 25000 Foot, 8000 Horse, and 2000 Dragoons; that the Lord *Goring* and the Lord *Hopton* might Ship all their Forces, and come by Sea in two Tides, and be with him in a shorter Time than the Enemy could follow.

With two such Bodies he might face the Enemy, and make a Day of it; but now his Men were only sacrificed, and eaten up by Piece-meal in a Party-War, and spent their Lives and Estates to do him no Service: That if the Parliament garrisoned the Towns and Castles he should quit, they would lessen their Army, and not dare to see him in the Field; and if they did not, but left them open, then 'twould be no Loss to him, but he might possess them as often as he pleased.[1]

This Advice I pressed with such Arguments, that the King was once going to dispatch Orders for the doing it; but to be irresolute in Counsel, is always the Companion of a declining Fortune; the King was doubtful, and could not resolve till it was too late.

And yet, though the King's Forces were very low, his Majesty was resolved to make one Adventure more, and it was a strange one; for, with but a Handful of Men he made a desperate March, almost 250 Miles in the Middle of the whole Kingdom, compassed about with Armies and Parties innumerable, traversed the Heart of his Enemy's Country, entered their associated Counties, where no Army had ever yet come, and in spight of all their victorious Troops facing and following him, alarmed even *London* it self, and returned safe to *Oxford*.

His Majesty continued in *Wales* from the Battle at *Naseby* till the 5th or 6th *August*, and till he had an Account from all parts of the Progress of his Enemies, and the Posture of his own Affairs.

Here he found, that the Enemy being hard pressed in *Somersetshire* by the Lord *Goring*, and Lord *Hopton*'s Forces, who had taken *Bridgewater*, and distressed *Taunton*, which was now at the Point of Surrender, they had ordered *Fairfax* and *Cromwell*, and the whole Army to march Westward, to relieve the Town; which they did, and *Goring*'s

Troops were worsted, and himself wounded at the Fight at *Langport*.

The *Scots*, who were always the dead Weight upon the King's Affairs, having no more Work to do in the North, were, at the Parliament's Desire, advanced Southward, and then ordered away towards South *Wales*, and were set down to the Siege of *Hereford*. Here this famous *Scotch* Army spent several Months in a fruitless Siege, ill provided of Ammunition, and worse with Money; and having sat near three Months before the Town, and done little but eaten up the Country round them; upon the repeated Accounts of the Progress of the Marquess of *Montrose* in that Kingdom, and pressing Instances of their Countrymen, they resolved to raise their Siege, and go home to relieve their Friends.

The King, who was willing to be rid of the *Scots*, upon good Terms; and therefore to hasten them, and least they should pretend to push on the Siege to take the Town first, gives it out, that he was resolved with all his Forces to go into *Scotland*, and join *Montrose*; and so having secured *Scotland*, to renew the War from thence.

And accordingly his Majesty marches Northwards, with a Body of 4000 Horse; and, had the King really done this, and with that Body of Horse marched away, (for he had the Start of all his Enemies, by above a Fortnight's March) he had then had the fairest Opportunity for a general Turn of all his Affairs, that he ever had in all the latter Part of this War: For *Montrose*, a gallant daring Soldier, who from the least Shadow of Force in the farthest Corner of his Country, had, rowling like a Snow Ball, spread all over *Scotland*, was come into the South Parts, and had summoned *Edinburgh*, frighted away their Statesmen, beaten their Soldiers at *Dundee* and other Places, and Letters and Messengers in the Heels of one another, repeated their Cries to their Brethren in *England*, to lay before them the sad Condition of the Country, and to hasten the Army to their Relief. The *Scots* Lords of the Enemy's Party fled to *Berwick*, and the Chancellor of *Scotland* goes himself to General *Lesly*, to press him for help.

In this Extremity of Affairs *Scotland* lay, when we marched out of *Wales*. The *Scots* at the Siege of *Hereford* hearing the King was gone Northward with his Horse, conclude he was gone directly for *Scotland*, and immediately send *Lesly* with 4000 Horse and Foot to follow, but did not yet raise the Siege.

But the King still irresolute, turns away to the Eastward, and comes to *Litchfield*, where he shewed his Resentments[1] at Collonel *Hastings*, for his easy Surrender of *Leicester*.

In this March the Enemy took Heart; we had Troops of Horse on every Side upon us, like Hounds started at a fresh Stag. *Lesly*, with the *Scots*, and a strong Body followed in our Rear, Major General *Points*, Sir *John Gell*, Collonel *Roseter*, and others, in our Way; they pretended to be 10000 Horse, and yet never durst face us. The *Scots* made one Attempt upon a Troop which stayed a little behind, and took some Prisoners; but when a Regiment of our Horse faced them, they retired. At a Village near *Litchfield*, another Party of about 1000 Horse attacked my Regiment; we were on the left of the Army, and, at a little too far a Distance. I happened to be with the King at that time, and my Lieutenant Collonel with me; so that the Major had Charge of the Regiment; he made a very handsome Defence, but sent Messengers for speedy Relief; we were on a March, and therefore all ready, and the King orders me a Regiment of Dragoons and 300 Horse, and the Body halted to bring us off, not knowing how strong the Enemy might be. When I came to the Place I found my Major hard layed to, but fighting like a Lion; the Enemy had broke in upon him in two Places, and had routed one Troop, cutting them off from the Body, and had made them all Prisoners. Upon this I fell in with the 300 Horse, and cleared my Major from a Party who charged him in the Flank; the Dragoons immediately lighting, one Party of them comes up on my Wing, and saluting the Enemy with their Musquets, put them to a stand; the other Party of Dragoons wheeling to the Left, endeavoured to get behind them. The Enemy perceiving they should be over-powered, retreated in as good Order as they could, but left us most of our Prisoners, and about 30 of their own. We lost about 15 of our Men, and the Enemy about 40, chiefly by the Fire of our Dragoons in their Retreat.

In this Posture we continued our March; and though the King halted at *Litchfield*, which was a dangerous Article, having so many of the Enemy's Troops upon his Hands, and this Time gave them Opportunity to get into a Body; yet the *Scots*, with their General *Lesly*, resolving for the North, the rest of the Troops were not able to face us, till having ravaged the Enemy's Country through *Staffordshire*, *Warwick*, *Leicester*, and *Nottinghamshire*, we came to the Leaguer before *Newark*.

The King was once more on the Mind to have gone into *Scotland*, and called a Council of War to that Purpose; but then it was resolved by all Hands, that it would be too late to attempt it; for the *Scots* and Major General *Pointz* were before us, and several strong Bodies of Horse in our Rear; and there was no venturing now, unless any Advantage presented to rout one of those Parties which attended us.

Upon these and like Considerations we resolved for *Newark*; on our Approach the Forces which blocked up that Town drew off, being too weak to oppose us; for the King was now above 5000 Horse and Dragoons, besides 300 Horse and Dragoons he took with him from *Newark*.

We halted at *Newark* to assist the Garrison, or give them Time rather to furnish themselves from the Country with what they wanted, which they were very diligent in doing; for in two Days time they filled a large Island which lies under the Town, between the two Branches of the *Trent*, with Sheep, Oxen, Cows and Horses, an incredible Number; and our Affairs being now something desperate, we were not very nice in our Usage of the Country; for really if it was not with a Resolution, both to punish the Enemy and enrich our selves, no Man can give any rational Account why this desperate Journey was undertaken.

'Tis certain the *Newarkers*, in the Respite they gained by our coming, got above 50000 l. from the Country round them, in Corn, Cattle, Money, and other Plunder.

From hence we broke into *Lincolnshire*, and the King lay at *Belvoir* Castle, and from *Belvoir* Castle to *Stamford*. The Swiftness of our March was a terrible Surprize to the Enemy; for our Van being at a Village on the great Road called *Stilton*, the Country People fled into the Isle of *Ely*, and every Way, as if all was lost. Indeed our Dragoons treated the Country very coarsly; and all our Men in general made themselves rich. Between *Stilton* and *Huntingdon* we had a small Bustle with some of the Association Troops[1] of Horse, but they were soon routed, and fled to *Huntingdon*, where they gave such an Account of us to their Fellows, that they did not think fit to stay for us, but left their Foot to defend themselves as well as they could.

While this was doing in the Van, a Party from *Burleigh* House, near *Stamford*, the Seat of the Earl of *Exeter*, pursued four Troops of our Horse, who straggling towards *Peterborough*, and committing some Disorders there, were surprized before they could get into a Posture of Fighting; and encumbered, as I suppose, with their Plunder, they were entirely routed, lost most of their Horses, and were forced to come away on Foot; but finding themselves in this Condition, they got into a Body in the Enclosures, and in that Posture turning Dragoons, they lined the Hedges, and fired upon the Enemy with their Carabines. This way of Fighting, though not very pleasant to Troopers, put the Enemy's Horse to some Stand, and encouraged our Men to venture into a Village, where the Enemy had secured 40 of their Horse; and boldly charging the Guard, they beat them off and recovered those Horses; the rest made their Retreat good to *Wandsford* Bridge; but we lost near 100 Horses, and about 12 of our Men taken Prisoners.

The next Day the King took *Huntington*; the Foot which

were left in the Town, as I observed by their Horse, had posted themselves at the Foot of the Bridge, and fortified the Pass, with such Things as the Haste and Shortness of the Time would allow; and in this Posture they seemed resolute to defend themselves. I confess, had they in Time planted a good Force here, they might have put a full Stop to our little Army; for the River is large and deep, the Country on the left marshy, full of Drains and Ditches, and unfit for Horse, and we must have either turned back, or took the Right Hand into *Bedfordshire*; but here not being above 400 Foot, and they forsaken of their Horse, the Resistance they made was to no other Purpose than to give us Occasion to knock them in the Head, and plunder the Town.

However, they defended the Bridge, as I have said, and opposed our Passage. I was this Day in the Van, and our Forelorn having entered *Huntington* without any great Resistance till they came to the Bridge, finding it barricaded, they sent me Word; I caused the Troops to halt, and rid up to the Forelorn, to view the Countenance of the Enemy, and found by the Posture they had put themselves in, that they resolved to sell us the Passage as dear as they could.

I sent to the King for some Dragoons, and gave him Account of what I observed of the Enemy, and that I judged them to be 1000 Men; for I could not particularly see their Numbers. Accordingly the King ordered 500 Dragoons to attack the Bridge, commanded by a Major; the Enemy had 200 Musqueteers placed on the Bridge, their Barricade served them for a Breast-work on the Front, and the low Walls on the Bridge served to secure their Flanks: Two Bodies of their Foot were placed on the opposite Banks of the River, and a Reserve stood in the High-way on the Rear. The Number of their Men could not have been better ordered, and they wanted not Courage answerable to the Conduct of the Party. They were commanded by one *Bennet*, a resolute Officer, who stood in the Front of his Men on the Bridge with a Pike in his Hand.

Before we began to fall on, the King ordered to view the River, to see if it was no where passable, or any Boat to be had; but the River being not fordable, and the Boats all secured on the other Side, the Attack was resolved on, and the Dragoons fell on with extraordinary Bravery. The Foot defended themselves obstinately, and beat off our Dragoons twice; and though *Bennet* was killed upon the Spot, and after him his Lieutenant,[1] yet their Officers relieving them with fresh Men, they would certainly have beat us all off, had not a venturous Fellow, one of our Dragoons thrown himself into the River, swum over, and, in the midst of a Shower of Musquet Bullets, cut the Rope which tied a great flat-bottom Boat, and brought her over: With the Help of this Boat, I got over 100 Troopers first, and then their Horses, and then 200 more without their Horses; and with this Party fell in with one of the small Bodies of Foot that were posted on that Side, and having routed them, and after them the Reserve which stood in the Road, I made up to the other Party; they stood their Ground, and having rallied the Run-aways of both the other Parties, charged me with their Pikes, and brought me to a Retreat; but by this time the King had sent over 300 Men more, and they coming up to me, the Foot retreated. Those on the Bridge finding how 'twas and having no Supplies sent them, as before, fainted, and fled; and the Dragoons rushing forward, most of them were killed; about 150 of the Enemy were killed, of which all the Officers at the Bridge, the rest run away.

The Town suffered for it; for our Men left them little of any thing they could carry. Here we halted, and raised Contributions, took Money of the Country, and of the open Towns, to exempt them from Plunder. Twice we faced the Town of *Cambridge*, and several of our Officers advised his Majesty to storm it; but having no Foot, and but 1200 Dragoons, wiser Heads diverted him from it; and, leaving *Cambridge* on the left, we marched to *Wooburn*, in *Bedfordshire*, and our Parties raised Money all over the County quite into *Hertfordshire*, within 5 Miles of St. *Alban*'s.

The swiftness of our March, and Uncertainty which Way we intended, prevented all possible Preparation to oppose us, and we met with no Party able to make Head against us. From *Wooburn* the King went through *Buckingham* to *Oxford*; some of our Men straggling in the Villages for Plunder, were often picked up by the Enemy; but in all this long March we did not loose 200 Men, got an incredible Booty, and brought 6 Waggons loaden with Money, besides 2000 Horses, and 3000 Head of Cattle into *Oxford*.

From *Oxford* his Majesty moves again into *Gloucestershire* having left about 1500 of his Horse at *Oxford*, to scour the Country, and raise Contributions, which they did as far as *Reading*.

Sir *Thomas Fairfax* was returned from taking *Bridgewater*, and was sat down before *Bristol*, in which Prince *Rupert* commanded with a strong Garrison, 2500 Foot and 1000 Horse. We had not Force enough to attempt any thing there; but the *Scots*, who lay still before *Hereford*, were afraid of us, having before parted with all their Horse under Lieutenant General *Lesly*, and but ill stored with Provisions; and, if we came on their Backs, were in a fair way to be starved, or made to buy their Provisions at the Price of their Blood.

His Majesty was sensible of this, and had we had but 10 Regiments of Foot, would certainly have fought the *Scots*; but we had no Foot, or so few as was not worth while to march them. However, the King marched to *Worcester*, and the *Scots* apprehending they should be blocked up, immediately raised the Siege, pretending it was to go help their Brethren in *Scotland*, and away they marched Northwards.

We picked up some of their Stragglers, but they were so poor, had been so ill paid, and so harrassed at the Siege, that they had neither Money nor Clothes; and the poor Soldiers fed upon Apples and Roots, and eat the very green Corn as it grew in the Fields, which reduced them to a very sorry Condition of Health,[1] for they died like People infected with the Plague.

'Twas now debated whether we should yet march for

Scotland, but two Things prevented. 1. The Plague was broke out there, and Multitudes died of it, which made the King backward, and the Men more backward. 2. The Marquess of *Montrose* having routed a whole Brigade of *Lesly*'s best Horse, and carried all before him, wrote to his Majesty, that he did not now want Assistance, but was in Hopes in a few Days to send a Body of Foot into *England*, to his Majesty's Assistance. This over Confidence of his was his Ruine; for, on the contrary, had he earnestly pressed the King to have marched, and fallen in with his Horse, the King had done it, and been absolutely Master of *Scotland* in a Fortnight's time; but *Montrose* was too confident, and defied them all, till at last they got their Forces together, and *Lesly*, with his Horse out of *England*, and worsted him in two or three Encounters, and then never left him till they drove him out of *Scotland*.

While his Majesty stayed at *Worcester* several Messengers came to him from *Cheshire* for Relief, being exceedingly streightened by the Forces of the Parliament: In order to which, the King marched, but *Shrewsbury* being in the Enemy's Hands, he was obliged to go round by *Ludlow*, where he was joined by some Foot out of *Wales*. I took this Opportunity to ask his Majesty's Leave to go by *Shrewsbury* to my Father's, and taking only two Servants, I left the Army two Days before they marched.

This was the most Unsoldier-like Action that ever I was guilty of, to go out of the Army to pay a Visit, when a Time of Action was just at Hand; and, though I protest I had not the least Intimation, no not from my own Thoughts, that the Army would engage, at least before they came to *Chester*, before which I intended to meet them; yet it looked so ill, so like an Excuse, or a Sham of Cowardice, or Disaffection to the Cause, and to my Master's Interest, or something I know not what, that I could not bear to think of it, nor never had the Heart to see the King's Face after it.

From *Ludlow* the King marched to relieve *Chester*; *Poyntz*, who commanded the Parliament's Forces, follows the King, with Design to join with the Forces before *Chester*, under Collonel *Jones*, before the King could come up. To that End *Poyntz* passes through *Shrewsbury* the Day that the King marched from *Ludlow*; yet the King's Forces got the Start of him, and forced him to engage: Had the King engaged him but three Hours sooner, and consequently farther off from *Chester*, he had ruined him; for *Poyntz*'s Men not able to stand the Shock of the King's Horse, gave Ground, and would in half an Hour more been beaten out of the Field; but Collonel *Jones*, with a strong Party from the Camp, which was within two Miles, comes up in the Heat of the Action, falls on in the King's Rear, and turned the Scale of the Day: The Body was, after an obstinate Fight defeated, and a great many Gentlemen of Quality killed and taken Prisoners; the Earl of *Litchfield* was of the Number of the former, and 67 Officers of the latter, with 1000 others.

The King with about 500 Horse got into *Chester*,[1] and from thence into *Wales*, whither all that could get away made up to him as fast as they could, but in a bad Condition.[2]

This was the last Stroke they struck, the rest of the War was nothing but taking all his Garrisons from him, one by one, till they finished the War, with the captivating his Person, and then, for want of other Business, fell to fighting with one another.

I was quite disconsolate at the News of this last Action, and the more because I was not there; my Regiment was wholly dispersed, my Lieutenant Collonel, a Gentleman of a good Family, and a near Relation to my Mother, was Prisoner, my Major and three Captains killed, and most of the rest Prisoners.

The King, hopeless of any considerable Party in *Wales*, *Bristol* being surrendered, sends for Prince *Rupert* and Prince *Maurice*, who came to him. With them, and the Lord *Digby*, Sir *Marmaduke Langdale*, and a great Train of Gentlemen, his Majesty marches to *Newark* again, leaves a Thousand Horse with Sir *William Vaughan*, to attempt the

Relief of *Chester*, in doing whereof he was routed the second time by *Jones* and his Men, and entirely dispersed.[1]

The chief Strength the King had in these Parts was at *Newark*, and the Parliament were very earnest with the *Scots* to march Southward, and to lay Siege to *Newark*; and while the Parliament pressed them to it, and they sat still, and delayed it, several Heats began, and some ill blood between them, which afterwards broke out into open War. The *English* reproached the *Scots* with pretending to help them, and really hindering their Affairs. The *Scots* returned, that they come to fight for them, and are left to be starved, and can neither get Money nor Clothes. At last they came to this, the *Scots* will come to the Siege, if the Parliament will send them Money, but not before: However, as People sooner agree in doing ill, than in doing well, they came to Terms, and the *Scots* came with their whole Army to the Siege of *Newark*.

The King, foreseeing the Siege, calls his Friends about him, tells them, he sees his Circumstances are such, that they can help him but little, nor he protect them, and advises them to separate. The Lord *Digby*, with Sir *Marmaduke Langdale*, with a strong Body of Horse, attempt to get into *Scotland*, to join with *Montrose*, who was still in the Highlands, though reduced to a low Ebb; but these Gentlemen are fallen upon on every Side and routed, and at last being totally broken and dispersed, they fly to the Earl of *Derby*'s Protection in the Isle of Man.[2]

Prince *Rupert*, Prince *Maurice*, Collonel *Gerrard*, and above 400 Gentlemen, all Officers of Horse, lay their Commissions down, and siezing upon *Wooton* House for a Retreat, make Proposals to the Parliament to leave the Kingdom, upon their Parole not to return again in Arms against the Parliament,[3] which was accepted, though afterwards the Princes declined it. I sent my Man Post to the Prince to be included in this Treaty, and for Leave for all that would accept of like Conditions, but they had given in the List of their Names, and could not alter it.

This was a sad Time; the poor Remains of the King's Fortunes went every where to wreck; every Garrison of the Enemy was full of the Cavalier Prisoners, and every Garrison the King had was beset with Enemies, either blocked up or besieged. *Goring* and the Lord *Hopton* were the only Remainders of the King's Forces, which kept in a Body, and *Fairfax* was pushing them with all imaginable Vigour with his whole Army, about *Exeter*, and other Parts of *Devonshire* and *Cornwall*.

In this Condition the King left *Newark* in the Night, and got to *Oxford*. The King had in *Oxford* 8000 Men, and the Towns of *Banbury*, *Farrington*, *Dunnington* Castle, and such Places as might have been brought together in 24 Hours, 15 or 20000 Men, with which if he had then resolved to have quitted the Place, and collected the Forces in *Worcester*, *Hereford*, *Lichfield*, *Ashby de la Zouch*, and all the small Castles and Garrisons he had thereabouts, he might have had near 40000 Men, might have beaten the *Scots* from *Newark*, Collonel *Jones* from *Chester*, and all, before *Fairfax* who was in the West, could be able to come to their Relief, and this his Majesty's Friends in North *Wales* had concerted; and, in order to it, Sir *Jacob Ashby* gathered what Forces he could, in our Parts, and attempted to join the King at *Oxford*, and to have proposed it to him; but Sir *Jacob* was entirely routed at *Stow on the Would*, and taken Prisoner, and of 3000 Men not above 600 came to *Oxford*.

All the King's Garrisons dropt one by one; *Hereford* which had stood out against the whole Army of the *Scots* was surprized by six Men and a Lieutenant dressed up for Country Labourers, and a Constable pressed to work, who cut the Guards in Pieces, and let in a Party of the Enemy.[1]

Chester was reduced by Famine, all the Attempts the King made to relieve it being frustrated.

Sir *Thomas Fairfax* routed the Lord *Hopton* at *Torrington*, and drove him to such Extremities, that he was forced up into the farthest Corner of *Cornwall*. The Lord *Hopton* had a gallant Body of Horse with him of nine Brigades, but no Foot; *Fairfax*, a great Army.

Heartless, and tired out with continual ill News, and ill Success, I had frequent Meetings with some Gentlemen, who had escaped from the Rout of Sir *William Vaughan*, and we agreed upon a Meeting at *Worcester* of all the Friends we could get, to see if we could raise a Body fit to do any Service; or, if not, to consider what was to be done. At this Meeting we had almost as many Opinions as People; our Strength appeared too weak to make any Attempt, the Game was too far gone in our Parts to be retrieved; all we could make up did not amount to above 800 Horse.

'Twas unanimously agreed not to go into the Parliament as long as our Royal Master did not give up the Cause; but in all Places, and by all possible Methods, to do him all the Service we could. Some proposed one thing, some another; at last we proposed getting Vessels to carry us to the Isle of *Man* to the Earl of *Derby*, as Sir *Marmaduke Langdale*, Lord *Digby*, and others had done. I did not foresee any Service it would be to the King's Affairs, but I started a Proposal, that marching to *Pembrook* in a Body, we should there sieze upon all the Vessels we could, and embarking our selves, Horses, and what Foot we could get, cross the *Severn* Sea, and land in *Cornwall* to the Assistance of Prince *Charles*, who was in the Army of the Lord *Hopton*, and where only there seemed to be any Possibility of a Chance for the remaining part of our Cause.

This Proposal was not without its Difficulties, as how to get to the Sea-side, and, when there, what Assurance of Shipping. The Enemy, under Major General *Langhorn* had over-run *Wales*, and 'twould be next to impossible to effect it.

We could never carry our Proposal with the whole Assembly; but however, about 200 of us resolved to attempt it, and Meeting being broke up without coming to any Conclusion, we had a private Meeting among our selves to effect it.

We dispatched private Messengers to *Swanzey* and *Pembrook*, and other Places; but they all discouraged us from the Attempt that way, and advised us to go higher towards North *Wales*, where the King's Interest had more Friends, and the Parliament no Forces. Upon this we met, and resolved, and having sent several Messengers that Way, one of my Men provided us two small Vessels in a little Creek near *Harlegh* Castle, in *Merionethshire*. We marched away with what Expedition we could, and embarked in the two Vessels accordingly. It was the worst Voyage sure that ever Man went; for first, we had no Manner of Accommodation for so many People, Hay for our Horses we got none, or very little, but good Store of Oats, which served us for our own Bread as well as Provender for the Horses.

In this Conditions we put off to Sea, and had a fair Wind all the first Night, but early in the Morning a sudden Storm drove us within two or three Leagues of *Ireland*. In this Pickle Sea-Sick, our Horses rouling about upon one another, and our selves stifled for want of Room, no Cabins nor Beds, very cold Weather, and very indifferent Diet, we wished our selves ashore again a thousand times; and yet we were not willing to go on Shore in *Ireland*, if we could help it; for the Rebels having Possession of every Place, that was just having our Throats cut at once. Having rouled about at the Mercy of the Winds all Day, the Storm ceasing in the Evening, we had fair Weather again, but Wind enough, which being large, in two Days and a Night we came upon the Coast of *Cornwall*, and, to our no small Comfort, landed the next Day at St. *Ives* in the County of *Cornwall*.

We rested our selves here, and sent an Express to the Lord *Hopton*, who was then in *Devonshire*, of our Arrival, and desired him to assign us Quarters, and send us his farther Orders. His Lordship expressed a very great Satisfaction at our Arrival, and left it to our own Conduct to join him as we saw convenient.

We were marching to join him, when News came, that

Fairfax had given him an entire Defeat at *Torrington*. This was but the old Story over again; we had been used to ill News a great while, and 'twas the less Surprize to us.

Upon this News we halted at *Bodmin*, till we should hear farther; and it was not long before we saw a Confirmation of the News before our Eyes; for the Lord *Hopton*, with the Remainder of his Horse, which he had brought off at *Torrington* in a very shattered Condition, retreated to *Lanceston*, the first Town in *Cornwall*, and hearing that *Fairfax* pursued him, came on to *Bodmin*. Hither he summoned all the Troops which he had left, which when he had got together, were a fine Body indeed of 5000 Horse, but few Foot but what were at *Pendennis*, *Barnstable*, and other Garrisons; these were commanded by the Lord *Hopton*; the Lord *Goring* had taken shipping for *France*, to get Relief, a few Days before.

Here a Grand Council of War was called, and several things were proposed, but as it always is in Distress, People are most irresolute, so 'twas here: Some were for breaking through by Force, our Number being superiour to the Enemy's Horse. To fight them with their Foot would be Desperation, and ridiculous; and to retreat, would but be to coop up themselves in a narrow Place, where at last they must be forced to fight upon Disadvantage, or yield at Mercy. Others opposed this as a desperate Action, and without Probability of Success; and all were of different Opinions: I confess, when I saw how things were, I saw 'twas a lost Game, and I was for the Opinion of breaking through, and doing it now, while the Country was open and large, and not being forced to it when it must be with more Disadvantage; but nothing was resolved on, and so we retreated before the Enemy. Some small Skirmishes there happened near *Bodmin*, but none that were very considerable.

'Twas the 1st of *March* when we quitted *Bodmin*, and quartered at large at *Columb*, *St. Denis* and *Truro*, and the Enemy took his Quarters at *Bodmin*, posting his Horse at the Passes from *Padstow* on the North, to *War-bridge*

Lestithel and *Foy*, spreading so from Sea to Sea, that now breaking through was impossible. There was no more Room for Counsel; for unless we had Ships to carry us off, we had nothing to do but when we were fallen upon, to defend our selves, and sell Victory as dear as we could to the Enemies.

The Prince of *Wales* seeing the Distress we were in, and loath to fall into the Enemy's Hands, ships himself on board some Vessels at *Falmouth*, with about 400 Lords and Gentlemen; and, as I had no Command here, to oblige my Attendance, I was once going to make one; but my Comerades, whom I had been the principal Occasion of bringing hither, began to take it ill, that I would leave them, and so I resolved we would take our Fate together.

While thus we had nothing before us but a Soldier's Death, a fair Field, and a strong Enemy, and People began to look one upon another: The Soldiers asked how their Officers looked, and the Officers asked how their Soldiers looked, and every Day we expected to be our last, when unexpectedly the Enemy's General sent a Trumpet to *Truro* to my Lord *Hopton* with a very handsom Gentleman-like Offer.

That since the General could not be ignorant of his present Condition, and that the Place he was in could not afford him Subsistance or Defence; and especially considering that the State of our Affairs were such, that if we should escape from thence, we could not remove to our Advantage, he had thought good to let us know, *That if we would deliver up our Horses and Arms, he would, for avoiding the Effusion of Christian Blood, or the putting any unsoldiery Extremities upon us, allow such honourable and safe Conditions, as were rather better than our present Circumstances could demand, and such as should discharge him to all the World, as a Gentleman, as a Soldier, and as a Christian.*

After this followed the Conditions he would give us, which were as follows, (*viz.*) *That all the Soldiery, as well* English *as Foreigners, should have Liberty to go beyond the Seas, or to their own Dwellings, as they pleased; and to such as shall chuse to live at home, Protection for their Liberty, and from all Violence, and plundering of Soldiers, and to give them Bag and Baggage, and all their Goods, except Horses and Arms.*

That for Officers in Commission, and Gentlemen of Quality, he would allow them Horses for themselves and one Servant, or more, suitable to their Quality, and such Arms as are suitable to Gentlemen of such Quality travelling in Times of Peace; and such Officers as would go beyond Sea, should take with them their full Arms and Number of Horses as are allowed in the Army to such Officers.[1]

That all the Troopers should receive on the Delivery of their Horses, 20s. a Man, to carry them home; and the General's Pass and Recommendation to any Gentleman who desires to go to the Parliament to settle the Composition for their Estates.

Lastly, A very honourable Mention of the General, and Offer of their Mediation to the Parliament, to treat him as a Man of Honour, and one who has been tender of the Country, and behaved himself with all the Moderation and Candor that could be expected from an Enemy.

Upon the unexpected Receipt of this Message, a Council of War was called, and the Letter read; no Man offered to speak a Word; the General moved it, but every one was loath to begin.

At last, an old Collonel starts up, and asked the General what he thought might occasion the writing this Letter? The General told him, *he could not tell*; but he could tell he was sure of one thing, that he knew what was not the Occasion of it (*viz.*) That is, not any want of Force in their Army to oblige us to other Terms. Then a Doubt was started, whether the King and Parliament were not in any Treaty, which this Agreement might be prejudicial to.

This occasioned a Letter to my Lord *Fairfax*, wherein our General returning the Civilities, and neither accepting nor refusing his Proposal, put it upon his Honour, whether there was not some Agreement or Concession between his Majesty and the Parliament, in order to a General Peace, which this

Treaty might be prejudicial to, or thereby be prejudicial to us.

The Lord *Fairfax* ingenuously declared, he had heard the King had made some Concessions, and he heartily wished he would make such as would settle the Kingdom in Peace, that *Englishmen* might not wound and destroy one another; *but that he declared he knew of no Treaty commenced, nor any Thing past which could give us the least Shadow of hope for any Advantage in not accepting his Conditions.* At last telling us, *That though he did not insult over our Circumstances, yet if we thought fit, upon any such Supposition, to refuse his Offers, he was not to seek in his Measures.*[1]

And it appeared so, for he immediately advanced his Forlorns, and dispossessed us of two advanced Quarters, and thereby streightened us yet more.

We had now nothing to say, but treat, and our General was so sensible of our Condition, that he returned the Trumpet with a safe Conduct for Commissioners at 12 a Clock that Night; upon which a Cessation of Arms was agreed[2] on, we quitting *Truro* to the Lord *Fairfax*, and he left St. *Allan*'s to us to keep our head Quarter.

The Conditions were soon agreed on, we disbanded nine full Brigades of Horse, and all the Conditions were observed with the most Honour and Care by the Enemy that ever I saw in my Life.

Nor can I omit to make very honourable Mention of this noble Gentleman, though I did not like his Cause; but I never saw a Man of a more pleasant, calm, courteous, down-right, honest Behaviour in my Life; and, for his Courage and personal Bravery in the Field, that we had felt enough of. No Man in the World had more Fire and Fury in him while in Action, or more Temper and Softness out of it. In short, and I cannot do him greater Honour, he exceedingly came near the Character of my Foreign Heroe *Gustavus Adolphus*, and in my Account, is, of all the Soldiers in *Europe*, the fittest to be reckoned in the second Place of Honour to him.

I had particular Occasion to see much of his Temper in all this Action, being one of the Hostages given by our General for the Performance of the Conditions, in which Circumstance the General did me several times the Honour to send to me to dine with him; and was exceedingly pleased to discourse with me about the Passages of the Wars in *Germany*, which I had served in; he having been at the same time in the *Low Countries*, in the Service of Prince *Maurice*; but I observed if at any time my Civilities extended to Commendations of his own Actions, and especially to comparing him to *Gustavus Adolphus*, he would blush like a Woman, and be uneasy, declining the Discourse, and in this he was still more like him.

Let no Man scruple my honourable Mention of this noble Enemy, since no Man can suspect me of favouring the Cause he embarked in, which I served as heartily against as any Man in the Army; but I cannot conceal extraordinary Merit for its being placed in an Enemy.

This was the End of our making War; for now we were all under Parole never to bear Arms against the Parliament; and though some of us did not keep our Word, yet I think a Soldier's Parole ought to be the most sacred in such Case, that a Soldier may be the easier trusted at all Times upon his Word.

For my Part I went home fully contented, since I could do my Royal Master no better Service, that I had come off no worse.

The Enemy going now on in a full Current of Success, and the King reduced to the last Extremity, and *Fairfax*, by long Marches, being come back within five Miles of *Oxford*; his Majesty loath to be cooped up in a Town which could on no Account hold long out, quits the Town in a Disguise, leaving Sir *Thomas Glemham* Governour, and being only attended with Mr. *Ashburnham* and one more,[1] rides away to *Newark* and there fatally committed himself to the Honour and Fidelity of the *Scots*, under General *Leven*.

There had been some little Bickering between the Parliament and the *Scots* Commissioners, concerning the Propositions which the *Scots* were for a Treaty with the King upon, and the Parliament refused it. The Parliament, upon all Proposals of Peace, had formerly invited the King to come and throw himself upon the Honour, Fidelity and Affection of his Parliament; and now the King from *Oxford* offering to come up to *London*, on the Protection of the Parliament for the Safety of his Person, they refused him, and the *Scots* differed from them in it, and were for a personal Treaty.

This, in our Opinion, was the Reason which prompted the King to throw himself upon the Fidelity of the *Scots*, who really by their Infidelity had been the Ruine of all his Affairs, and now, by their perfidious Breach of Honour and Faith with him, will be virtually and mediately the Ruine of his Person.

The *Scots* were, as all the Nation besides them was, surprized at the King's coming among them; the Parliament began very high with them, and send an Order to General *Leven* to send the King to *Warwick* Castle; but he was not so hasty to part with so rich a Prize. As soon as the King came to the General, he signs an Order to Collonel *Ballasis*, the Governour of *Newark*, to surrender it, and immediately the *Scots* decamp homewards, carrying the King in the Camp with them, and marching on, a House was ordered to be provided for the King at *Newcastle*.

And now the Parliament saw their Error, in refusing his Majesty a Personal Treaty, which if they had accepted, (their Army was not yet taught the way of huffing their Masters,) the Kingdom might have been settled in Peace. Upon this the Parliament send to General *Leven* to have his Majesty not *be sent*, which was their first Language, but *be suffered to come to* London, to treat with his Parliament; before it was, *Let the King be sent to* Warwick *Castle*; now 'tis, *To let his Majesty come to* London *to treat with his People*.

But neither one or the other would do with the *Scots*; but

we who knew the *Scots* best, knew that there was *one Thing* would do with them, if the other would not, and that was Money; and therefore our Hearts aked for the King.

The *Scots*, as I said, had retreated to *Newcastle* with the King, and there they quartered their whole Army at large upon the Country; the Parliament voted they had no farther Occasion for the *Scots*,[1] and desired them to go home about their Business. I do not say it was in these Words, but in whatsoever good Words their Messages might be expressed, this and nothing less was the *English* of it. The *Scots* reply, by setting forth their Losses, Damages, and Dues, the Substance of which was, *Pay us our Money, and we will be gone, or else we won't stir.* The Parliament call for an Account of their Demands, which the *Scots* give in, amounting to a Million; but, according to their Custom, and especially finding that the Army under *Fairfax* inclined gradually that Way, fall down to 500000 l. and at last to four; but all the while this is transacting, a separate Treaty is carried on at *London* with the Commissioners of *Scotland*, and afterwards at *Edinburgh*, by which it is given them to understand, that whereas upon Payment of the Money, the *Scots* Army is to march out of *England*, and to give up all the Towns and Garrisons which they hold in this Kingdom, so they are to take it for granted, that 'tis the meaning of the Treaty, that they shall leave the King in the Hands of the *English* Parliament.

To make this go down the better, the *Scotch* Parliament, upon his Majesty's Desire to go with their Army into *Scotland*, send him for Answer, that it cannot be for the Safety of his Majesty or of the State, to come into *Scotland*, not having taken the Covenant, and this was carried in their Parliament but by two Voices.

The *Scots* having refused his coming into *Scotland*, as was concerted between the two Houses, and their Army being to march out of *England*, the delivering up the King became a Consequence of the Thing unavoidable, and of Necessity.

His Majesty thus deserted of those into whose Hands he

had thrown himself, took his Leave[1] of the *Scots* General at *Newcastle*, telling him only, in few Words, this sad Truth, *That he was Bought and Sold*.[2] The Parliament Commissioners received him at *Newcastle* from the *Scots*, and brought him to *Holmby* House, in *Northamptonshire*; from whence, upon the Quarrels and Feuds of Parties, he was fetched by a Party of Horse, commanded by one Cornet *Joyce*, from the Army, upon their mutinous Rendezvous at *Triplow-Heath*; and, after this, suffering many Violences, and Varieties of Circumstances among the Army, was carried to *Hampton-Court*, from whence his Majesty very readily made his Escape; but not having Notice enough to provide effectual Means for his more effectual Deliverance was obliged to deliver himself to Collonel *Hammond* in the Isle of *Wight*. Here, after some very indifferent Usage, the Parliament pursued a farther Treaty with him, and all Points were agreed but two. The entire Abolishing Episcopacy, which the King declared to be against his Conscience, and his Coronation Oath; and the Sale of the Church-Lands, which he declared, being most of them Gifts to God and the Church, by Persons deceased, his Majesty thought could not be alienated without the highest Sacrilege, and if taken from the Uses to which they were appointed by the Wills of the Donors, ought to be restored back to the Heirs and Families of the Persons who bequeathed them.

And these two Articles so stuck with his Majesty, that he ventured his Fortune and Royal Family, and his own Life for them: However, at last, the King condescended so far in these, that the Parliament voted his Majesty's Concessions to be sufficient to settle and establish the Peace of the Nation.

This Vote discovered the bottom of all the Counsels which then prevailed; for the Army, who knew if Peace were once settled, they should be undone, took the Alarm at this, and clubbing together in Committees and Councils, at last brought themselves to a Degree of Hardness above all that ever this Nation saw; for, calling into Question the Proceedings of their Masters who employed them, they immediately fall to Work upon the Parliament, remove Collonel *Hammond*, who had the Charge of the King, and used him honourably, place a new Guard upon him, dismiss the Commissioners, and put a Stop to the Treaty; and, following their Blow, march to *London*, place Regiments of Foot at the Parliament House Door, and, as the Members came up, sieze upon all those whom they had down in a List as Promoters of the Settlement and Treaty, and would not suffer them to sit; but the rest, who being of their own Stamp, are permitted to go on, carry on the Designs of the Army, revive their Votes of Non-Addresses to the King, and then, upon the Army's Petition, to bring all Delinquents to Justice; the Masque was thrown off, the Word all is declared to be meant the King, as well as every Man else they pleased. 'Tis too sad a Story, and too much a Matter of Grief to me, and to all good Men, to renew the Blackness of those Days, when Law and Justice was under the Feet of Power; the Army ruled the Parliament, the private Officers their Generals, the common Soldiers their Officers, and Confusion was in every Part of the Government: In this Hurry they sacrificed their King, and shed the Blood of the *English* Nobility without Mercy.

The History of the Times will supply the Particulars which I omit, being willing to confine my self to my own Accounts and Observations; I was now no more an Actor, but a melancholly Observator of the Misfortunes of the Times. I had given my Parole not to take up Arms against the Parliament, and I saw nothing to invite me to engage on their Side; I saw a World of Confusion in all their Counsels, and I always expected that in a Chain of Distractions, as it generally fals out, the last Link would be Destruction; and though I pretended to no Prophecy, yet the Progress of Affairs have brought it to pass, and I have seen Providence, who suffered, for the Correction of this Nation, the Sword to govern and devour us, has at last brought Destruction *by the Sword*,[1] upon the Head of most of the Party who first drew it.

If together with the brief Account of what Concern I had

in the Active Part of the War, I leave behind me some of my
own Remarks and Observations, it may be pertinent enough
to my Design, and not unuseful to Prosperity.

1. I observed by the Sequel of Things, that it may be some
Excuse to the first Parliament, who began this War, to say
that they manifested their Designs were not aimed at the
Monarchy, nor their Quarrel at the Person of the King;
because, when they had him in their Power, though against
his Will, they would have restored both his Person and
Dignity as a King, only loading it with such Clogs of the
People's Power as they at first pretended to, (*viz.*) the
Militia, and Power of naming the great Officers at Court,
and the like; which Powers, it was never denied, had been
stretched too far in the Beginning of this King's Reign, and
several things done illegally, which his Majesty had been
sensible of, and was willing to rectify; but they having
obtained the Power by Victory, resolved so to secure themselves, as that whenever they laid down their Arms, the King
should not be able to do the like again: And thus far they
were not to be so much blamed, and we did not, on our own
Part, blame them, when they had obtained the Power, for
parting with it on good Terms.

But when I have thus far advocated for the Enemies, I
must be very free to state the Crimes of this Bloody War, by
the Events of it. 'Tis manifest there were among them, from
the Beginning, a Party who aimed at the very Root of the
Government, and at the very thing which they brought to
pass, *viz.* The deposing and murthering of their Sovereign;
and, as the Devil is always Master where Mischief is the
Work, this Party prevailed, turned the other out of Doors,
and over-turned all that little Honesty that might be in the
first Beginning of this unhappy Strife.

The Consequence of this was, the Presbyterians saw their
Error when it was too late, and then would gladly have
joined the Royal Party, to have suppressed this new Leaven,
which had infected the Lump; and this is very remarkable,
that most of the first Champions of this War, who bore the

Brunt of it; when the King was powerful and prosperous, and when there was nothing to be got by it but Blows, first or last, were so ill used by this Independant powerful Party, who tripped up the Heels of all their Honesty, that they were either forced, by ill Treatment, to take up Arms on our Side, or suppressed and reduced by them. In this the Justice of Providence seemed very conspicuous, that these having pushed all things by Violence against the King, and by Arms and Force brought him to their Will, were at once both robbed of the End, their Church-Government, and punished for drawing their Swords against *their Masters*, by *their own Servants* drawing the Sword against them; and God, in his due Time, punished the others too: And, what was yet farther strange, the Punishment of this Crime of making War against their King, singled out those very Men, both in the Army and in the Parliament, who were the greatest Champions of the Presbyterian Cause in the Council, and in the Field. Some Minutes too of Circumstances I cannot forbear observing, though they are not very material, as to the Fatality and Revolutions of Days and Times.

A *Roman* Catholick Gentleman of *Lancashire*, a very religious Man in his way, who had kept a Calculate of Times, and had observed mightily the Fatality of Times, Places and Actions, being at my Father's House, was discoursing once upon the just Judgment of God in dating his Providences, so as to signify to us his Displeasure at particular Circumstances; and, among an infinite Number of Collections he had made, these were some which I took particular Notice of, and from whence I began to observe the like.

   1. That King *Edward* the VIth died the very same Day of the same Month in which he caused the Altar to be taken down, and the Image of the Blessed Virgin in the Cathedral of St. *Paul*'s.

   2. That *Cranmer* was burnt at *Oxford* the same Day and Month that he gave King *Henry* the VIIIth Advice to Divorce his Queen *Catherine*.

3. That Queen *Elizabeth* died the same Day and Month that she resolved, in her Privy Council, to behead the Queen of Scots.

4. That King *James* died the same Day that he published his Book against *Bellarmine*.

5. That King *Charles*'s long Parliament, which ruined him, began the very same Day and Month which that Parliament began, that at the Request of his Predecessor robbed the *Roman* Church of all her Revenues, and suppressed Abbies and Monasteries.

How just his Calculations were, or how true the Matter of Fact, I cannot tell, but it put me upon the same in several Actions and Successes of this War.

And I found a great many Circumstances, as to Time and Action, which befel both his Majesty and his Parties first.

Then others which befel the Parliament and Presbyterian Faction which raised the War.

Then the Independant Tyranny which succeeded and supplanted the first Party.

Then the *Scots*, who acted on both Sides.

Lastly, The Restoration and Re-establishment of the Loyalty and Religion of our Ancestors.

1. For King *Charles* the First; 'tis observable that the Charge against the Earl of *Strafford*, a thing which his Majesty blamed himself for all the Days of his Life, and at the Moment of his last Suffering, was first read in the Lords House on the 30th of *January*, the same Day of the Month six Year that the King himself was brought to the Block.

2. That the King was carried away Prisoner from *Newark*, by the *Scots*, *May* 10, the same Day six Year that, against his Conscience and Promise, he passed the Bill of Attainder against the loyal noble Earl of *Strafford*.

3. The same Day seven Year that the King entered the House of Commons for the five Members, which all his Friends blamed him for, the same Day the Rump voted

bringing his Majesty to Tryal, after they had set by the Lords for not agreeing to it, which was the 3d of *January* 1648.

4. The 12th of *May* 1646, being the Surrender of *Newark*, the Parliament held a Day of Thanksgiving and Rejoicing, for the Reduction of the King and his Party, and finishing the War, which was the same Day five Year that the Earl of *Strafford* was beheaded.

5. The Battle of *Naseby*, which ruin'd the King's Affairs, and where his Secretary and his Office was taken, was the 14th of *June* the same Day and Month the first Commission was given out by his Majesty to raise Forces.

6. The Queen voted a Traytor by the Parliament the 3d of *May*, the same Day and Month she carried the Jewels into *France*.

7. The same Day the King defeated *Essex* in the West, his Son King *Charles* II. was defeated at *Worcester*.

8. Arch-bishop *Laud*'s House at *Lambeth* assaulted by the Mob, the same Day of the same Month that he advised the King to make War upon the *Scots*.

9. Impeached the 15th of *December* 1640, the same Day Twelve-month that he ordered the Common-Prayer-Book of *Scotland* to be printed, in order to be imposed upon the *Scots*, from which all our Troubles began.

But many more, and more strange, are the critical Junctures of Affairs in the Case of the Enemy, or at least more observed by me.

1. Sir *John Hotham*, who repulsed his Majesty and refused him Admittance into *Hull* before the War, was siezed at *Hull* by the same Parliament for whom he had done it, the same 10th Day of *August* two Years that he drew the first Blood in that War.

2. *Hambden* of *Buckinghamshire* killed the same Day one Year that the Mob Petition from *Bucks* was presented to the King about him, as one of the five Members.

3. Young Captain *Hotham* executed the 1st of *January*,

the same Day that he assisted Sir *Thomas Fairfax* in the
first Skirmish with the King's Forces at *Bramham-Moor*.

4. The same Day and Month, being the 6th of *August*
1641, that the Parliament voted to raise an Army against the
King, the same Day and Month, *Anno* 1648, the Parliament
were assaulted and turned out of Doors by that very Army,
and none left to sit but who the Soldiers pleased, which were
therefore called the *Rump*.

5. The Earl of *Holland* deserted the King, who had made
him General of the Horse, and went over to the Parliament,
and the 9th of *March* 1641, carried the Commons reproach-
ing Declaration to the King; and afterwards taking up Arms
for the King against the Parliament, was beheaded by them
the 9th of *March* 1648, just seven Years after.

6. The Earl of *Holland* was sent to by the King to come
to his Assistance and refused, the 11th of *July* 1641, and that
very Day seven Years after was taken by the Parliament at
St. Needs.

7. Collonel *Massey* defended *Gloucester* against the King,
and beat him off the 5th of *September* 1643, was after taken
by *Cromwell*'s Men fighting for the King, on the 5th of
September 1651, two or three Days after the Fight at
Worcester.

8. *Richard Cromwell* resigning because he could not help
it, the Parliament voted a free Commonwealth, without a
single Person or House of Lords; this was the 25th of *May*
1658; the 25th of *May* 1660 the King landed at *Dover*, and
restored the Government of a single Person and House of
Lords.

9. *Lambert* was proclaimed a Traytor by the Parliament,
April the 20th, being the same Day he proposed to *Oliver
Cromwell* to take upon him the Title of King.

10. *Monk* being taken Prisoner at *Nantwich* by Sir
Thomas Fairfax, revolted to the Parliament, the same Day
nineteen Years he declared for the King, and thereby
restored the Royal Authority.

11. The Parliament voted to approve of Sir *John Hotham*'s

repulsing the King at *Hull*, the 28th of *April* 1642; the 28th of *April* 1660, the Parliament first debated in the House the restoring the King to the Crown.

12. The Agitators of the Army formed themselves into a Cabal, and held their first Meeting to sieze on the King's Person, and take him into their Custody from *Holmby*, the 28th of *April* 1647; the same Day 1660, the Parliament voted the Agitators to be taken into Custody, and committed as many of them as could be found.

13. The Parliament voted the Queen a Traytor for assisting her Husband the King, *May* the 3d 1643; her Son King *Charles* II. was presented with the Votes of Parliament to restore him, and the Present of 50000 l. the 3d of *May* 1660.

14. The same Day the Parliament passed the Act for Recognition of *Oliver Cromwell*, *October* the 13th 1654, *Lambert* broke the Parliament and set up the Army 1659, *October* the 13th.

Some other Observations I have made, which as not so pertinent I forbear to publish, among which I have noted the Fatality of some Days to Parties, as,

The 2d of *September*, the Fight at *Dunbar*; the Fight at *Worcester;* the Oath against a single Person past; *Oliver's* first Parliament called: For the Enemy.

The 2d of *September*, *Essex* defeated in *Cornwall*; *Oliver* died; City Works demolished: For the King.

The 29th of *May*, Prince *Charles* born; *Leicester* taken by Storm; King *Charles* II. restored: Ditto.

Fatality of Circumstances in this unhappy War, as,

1. The *English* Parliament call in the *Scots*, to invade their King, and are invaded themselves by the same *Scots*, in Defence of the King whose Case, and the Design of the Parliament the *Scots* had mistaken.

2. The *Scots*, who unjustly assisted the Parliament to

conquer their lawful Sovereign, contrary to their Oath of Allegiance, and without any Pretence on the King's Part, are afterwards absolutely conquered and subdued by the same Parliament they assisted.

3. The Parliament, who raised an Army to depose their King, deposed by the very Army they had raised.

4. The Army broke three Parliaments, and are at last broke by a free Parliament and all they had done by the Military Power, undone at once by the Civil.

5. Abundance of the Chief Men, who by their fiery Spirits involved the Nation in a Civil War, and took up Arms against their Prince, first or last met with Ruine or Disgrace from their own Party.

1. Sir *John Hotham* and his Son, who struck the first Stroke, both beheaded or hanged by the Parliament.

2. Major General *Massey* three times taken Prisoner by them, and once wounded at *Worcester*.

3. Major General *Langhorn*. 4. Collonel *Poyer*: And, 5. Collonel *Powell*, changed Sides, and at last taken, could obtain no other Favour than to draw Lots for their Lives; Collonel *Poyer* drew the Dead Lot, and was shot to Death.

6. Earl of *Holland*, who, when the House voted who should be reprieved, Lord *Goring*, who had been their worst Enemy, or the Earl of *Holland*, who, excepting one Offence, had been their constant Servant, voted *Goring* to be spared, and the Earl to die.

7. The Earl of *Essex*, their first General.

8. Sir *William Waller*.

9. Lieutenant General *Ludlow*.

10. The Earl of *Manchester*.

All disgusted and voted out of the Army, though they had stood the first Shock of the War, to make way for the new Model of the Army, and introduce a Party.

In all these Confusions I have observed two great Errors, one of the King, and one of his Friends.

Of the King, that when he was in their Custody, and at

their Mercy, he did not comply with their Propositions of Peace before their Army, for want of Employment, fell into Heats and Mutinies; that he did not at first grant the *Scots* their own Conditions, which, if he had done, he had gone into *Scotland*; and then, if the *English* would have fought the *Scots* for him, he had a Reserve of his loyal Friends, who would have had Room to have fallen in with the *Scots* to his Assistance, who were after dispersed and destroyed in small Parties attempting to serve him.

While his Majesty, remained at *Newcastle*, the Queen wrote to him, perswading him to make Peace upon any Terms; and in Politicks her Majesty's Advice was certainly the best: For, however low he was brought by a Peace, it must have been better than the Condition he was then in.

The Error I mention of the King's Friends was this, that after they saw all was lost, they could not be content to sit still, and reserve themselves for better Fortunes, and wait the happy Time when the Divisions of the Enemy would bring them to certain Ruin; but must hasten their own Miseries by frequent fruitless Risings, in the Face of a victorious Enemy, in small Parties, and I always found these Effects from it.

1. The Enemy, who were always together by the Ears, when they were let alone, were united and reconciled when we gave them any Interruption; as particularly, in the Case of the first Assault the Army made upon them, when Collonel *Pride*, with his Regiment garbled[1] the House, as they called it, at that Time, a fair Opportunity offered; but it was omitted till it was too late: That Insult upon the House had been attempted the Year before, but was hindered by the little Insurrections of the Royal Party, and the sooner they had fallen out, the better.

2. These Risings being desperate, with vast Disadvantages, and always suppressed, ruined all our Friends; the Remnants of the Cavaliers were lessened, the stoutest and most daring were cut off, and the King's Interest exceedingly weakened, there not being less than Thirty Thousand of his

best Friends cut off in the several Attempts made at *Maid-stone*, *Colchester*, *Lancashire*, *Pembrook*, *Pontfract*, *Kingston*, *Preston*, *Warrington*, *Worcester*, and other Places. Had these Men all reserved their Fortunes to a Conjunction with the *Scots*, at either of the Invasions they made into this Kingdom, and acted with the Conduct and Courage they were known Masters of, perhaps neither of those *Scots* Armies had been defeated.

But the Impatience of our Friends ruin'd all; for my Part, I had as good a Mind to put my Hand to the Ruine of the Enemy as any of them, but I never saw any tolerable Appearance of a Force able to match the Enemy, and I had no Mind to be beaten, and then hanged. Had we let them alone, they would have fallen into so many Parties and Factions, and so effectually have torn one another to Pieces, that which soever Party had come to us, we should, with them, have been too hard for all the rest.

This was plain by the Course of Things afterwards, when the Independant Army had ruffled the Presbyterian Parliament, the Soldiery of that Party made no Scruple to join us, and would have restored the King with all their Hearts, and many of them did join us at last.

And the Consequence, though late, ended so; for they fell out so many times, *Army* and *Parliament*, *Parliament* and *Army*, and alternately pulled one another down so often, till at last the Presbyterians, who began the War, ended it; and, to be rid of their Enemies, rather than for any Love to the Monarchy, restored King *Charles* the Second, and brought him in on the very Day that they themselves had formerly resolved the Ruine of his Father's Government, being the 29th of *May*, the same Day 20 Year that the private Cabal in *London* concluded their Secret League with the *Scots*, to embroil his Father King *Charles* the First.

APPENDIX

I. EXTRACTS FROM

The Swedish Intelligencer

The Battell of Leipsich
i. 121–25

Upon the fatall seaventh of *September* therefore being Wednesday, [Tilly] with 44000 brave men, in goodly order of battell first takes the field; which was upon a fayre plaine or heath (about a mile from *Leipsich*) called *Gods Aker*: sayd to be the very same place, wher the Emperor *Charles* the 5 heretofore overthrew the Duke of *Saxony*. *Tilly* like a prudent General, being carefull for all advantages, had placed himselfe upon a little hill thereabouts, (where the place of execution is,) having a wood also to hide his men, and for their retreate . . .

The King of *Sweden* having prepared his Army by prayers unto God, and encouragements to his men the day before, upon the same Wednesday morning before day, he advances from *Dieben* towards the place of battell. His owne Troupes were some 18000: and the Duke of *Saxonie*, together with the Marquis of *Brandenburg* some 20000 or 22000 . . .

Being now ready to come unto the Shocke; the Battels were thus ordered, *Tilly* made choice of the ancient order, to fight in great square bodies, himselfe leading now the right wing, the Duke of *Holsteyn* the left, and the Count of *Furstenburg* the *Battaile*. The King dividing his men into many smaller bodies; takes the right wing to himselfe, committing the left unto the Duke of *Saxonie* and his men: the wings of either battaile, tooke up two *English* miles in length . . . The fight was about 12 a clocke, first begun with their Canon, for that purpose placed before every division. Their roare made the very earth to tremble, and men to groane their last; for two houres together: about which time, the Generall *Tilly* drawing out of the wood, passes by the Kings wing, (which had also gotten one end of the same wood) and set amaine upon the Duke of *Saxonie*. Two charges the *Saxons* endured well enough: but the Enemie having direction to laye hardest upon the Dukes owne Guards (amongst whom himselfe fought;) they not able longer to endure it, begin to give ground a little. The rest of the *Saxons* now perceiving their Duke, and bravest men thus to retyre, thinke all lost; and all in confusion away they flie, leaving 3 Canons to the mercy of the Enemie; and pillaging their owne wagons by the way: that so they might at least seeme to be Conquerors; in carrying home spoiles of the warres, though not of their Enemies. Yet all fled not; for the Lord *Arnheym* (Field-Marshall to the Duke, and an old Souldier) together with Colonel *Bindauff*, *Done*, and *Vitz-thimb*, with their 4 Regiments, bravely yet stood unto it. *Steinau*, a Colonell of Horse, was with 4 Cornets taken prisoner by the Enemie; who at length perceiving the Kings partie to prevaile, brake through the Enemie, and assisted his owne side. The *Imperialists* now seeing the *Saxons* flying, cry *Victoria*, *Victoria*, *follow*, *follow*, *follow*: but the old Lad their Generall quickly countermaunded that; saying, *Let them goe, wee shall overtake them time enough: but let us beate the* Swede *too, and then all* Germany *is our owne*. In this medlie, *Furstenberg* with his old Regiment of *Italian* Horse, having charged quite thorow the *Saxons*, was now comming upon the *Swedens* backe: which they perceiving, with such resolution second his charge, and follow their owne, that they chase him almost an *English* mile from the place, so utterly cutting off & dispersing the whole Regiment, that they could not recover it all that battell: and here perchance himselfe was slaine . . .

By this time the King having notice of the Duke of *Saxonies* leaving the field, and that *Tilly* was ready to charge his battaile: presently drawes out 2000 commaunded Muskettiers of the brave *Scottish* Nation led by Colonel *Havord*, they having some 2000 horse upon their flancks: to stave off the enemie a while. The *Scots* ordering themselves in severall small *battagliaes*, about 6 or 700 in a body, presently now double their rankes, making their files then but 3 deepe (the discipline of the King of *Sweden* being, never to march above 6 deepe) this done, the formost rancke falling on their knees; the second stooping forward; and the third rancke standing right up; and all giving fire together, they powred so much lead at one instant in amongst the enemies horse, that their rankes were much broken with it . . . *Tilly* came, and conjoyned himselfe unto the valiant Baron of *Cronenberg*. This bold Baron and his Regiment serving in the right wing, had 4 times in those 4 houres, charged the Kings Forces: and hee at last, when no more could be done, bravely carried away his Generall, in the midst of his owne (now flying) Troupes . . .

Had the King had but 3 houres more of day light, scarcely had 1000 Enemies come off alive: but the darkenes which was safest for them to flie, being not so for him to pursue; the joyfull retreate is sounded, and the chace given over for that night.

ii. 11–16

The King thus in possession of the Towne, could not yet thinke himselfe Master of it; so long as the Castle of *Marienburg* (for so is it called) could at pleasure beate it about his eares. This peece is mounted upon so high a hill, as was to be commanded from no other ground: it having the Towne below at the foote of it. And as strongly was it fortified by Art, as advantageously situated by nature. The hill is a maine rocke; whereof one side is craggie and barren, and the other covered with vines: the whole tope of the little mountaine being crowned with the Castle, and with the ditches and out-works of it. Nor wanted here any inward fortifications; 800 or 1000 fighting men, being therein Garrison. And as for victuals, money and Ammunition, *Troy* it selfe was not better provided for its ten yeares siege, then this Fort was . . .

All that night and the next two dayes, did the Ordnance thunder from the Castle; & for as long a time were the garrison kept in continuall Action and Alarmes: a *besieged enemy* being like an *unmade Hawke*, to be *reclaymed* with *watching*. The *Trenches* or *Lines* being finished, the King commands Sir *John Hamilton* and Sir *Iames Ramsye* to fall on with their Regiments: for if a Fort be to be *stormed*, or any desperate peice of service to be set upon; the *Scottish* have hitherto had the honour and the danger, to be the first men that are put upon such a businesse. This *Halfe-moone* therefore upon the vineyards side, right before the bridge (which was over the moate of the Castle) doe the *Scottish* now full resolutely fall upon: the defendants likewise for two houres together (as 'tis said) as stoutly fighting for their worke . . .

An inestimable masse of treasure, which lay hid in a Cave or cleft of the Rocke. The chiefe of the slaine and prisoners, were rifled and stripped by the conquerors: and the Castle for one houre, permitted to the pillage: where an unvaluable booty was obtained by the Souldiers. Here was found about 34 peices of brasse Ordnance; some of which had the *Palsgrave Frederickes* Armes upon them. Many a hundred wayne-load of wine there was: with Ammunition, and some kind of victuals for the Bishops Court, enough (if it would have kept) for 20 yeares provision for such a garrison . . . A Palace it was, for any Prince in *Christendome*: which having beene something defaced by the Cannon, the King caused to be forthwith repaired; and with new fortifications to be made much the stronger. The Towne redeemed itself from pillaging, by the payment of 4 tunne of Gold; or of 300000 *Florens*, as others reckon it: So that the King and his Souldiers, never went so rich away from any place. Here was found a princely stable of goodly Horses; with which the King was very much delighted.

ii. 46–47

Wee left the King lately marching towards *Oppenheim*: where he yet lay, within Canon-shot (almost) of the very walls of it. Summons had already been given unto the towne: which, upon the taking of the Fort, sends out their keyes, and yeelds gladly enough unto his Majesty: and for that they knew him to be a friend unto the Prince Elector their Lord and Master, they receive in a garrison of 200 *Scots* unto them. These 200, were all (or almost all) that were left of Sir *Iames Ramsyes* Regiment: himselfe lay yet at *Wurtsburg* to be cured of his wound, which there (as we told you) he received. Upon an hill, a little above the edge of the towne, was there a large vast Castle with a garrison of 600 or 700 men in it; which yet stood out against the King. There having been 107 boates found under the Towne wall, upon the river; of these the King sends over enow, to fetch *Winckles* Regiment first, and *Hepburnes* after him: with the Cannon, baggage and Cavallery last of all. The streame carrying downe *Hepburn* and *Winckle* something lower then the towne; they upon their landing advance up the hill, to meete the Kings Forces: whom they now saw standing in faire *Battaglia*, ready to give a generall assault upon the Castle. And now those 200 *Scots* that had beene put into the towne at the yeelding of it; fall immediately thereupon to *Storme* the said Castle at the townport which is betwixt the Castle and the Towne. The *Scots* fell in with such a tempest and resolution, that they instantly force the garrison into the inner port; they *Storming* in together with them: so that by that time the King was ready to assault on one side, and *Hepburn* on the other; they meete (to their great admiration,) divers of the garrison that had already leapt over the walls, throwne away their Armes, and crying *Quarter*; as the rest also now did, that had not yet gotten out of the Castle.

ii. 76–82

Upon Thursday Febr. 16. he first sets forward to *Creutzenach* . . . The first view the King tooke of the Towne, was upon the lowest side; and where he had thought to have begun: but that he found so well fortified with Outworkes, Seconds, and Retreats, one worke within another, that he call'd them the *Divels workes*. He quickly discovered, that there was no attempting that way: yea judged by the best souldiours it was, that it could not have beene a businesse of lesse than a fortnight or three weekes time, to have mastered all these works, and so to have come at the Towne. Altering his course therefore, and deviding his little Army into two parts, hee by faire day light brings them on by another side, and lodges them within Musket shot, or 150 pases of the very walles: yea Lieftenant Colonell *George Douglasse* (a brave souldiour then newly come up to the King) having first runne his lines, sets himselfe downe with some three hundred men, (the most of them being the same *Scottish* that had *stormed Oppenheim* Castle even in the very Port. Here lay *Douglasse* all the night following: notwithstanding the place were so hot, that the enemy kill'd him some 47 men, with their shooting upon him; both from the walles, and Port above him . . .

Colonel *Winckle* commanding in Chiefe over the foot; three Captaines of his Regiment with some 350 men, and divers *English* and *French* Gentlemen voluntiers, came first into the breach: among all which, my Lord *Craven*, Lieftenant-Colonell *Talbot*, Master *Robert Marsham* and Master *Henry Wind*, marched in the first File. The Hill was so steepe where they approached, that the enemy by darting downe of Partisans and Halberts, casting downe of great stones, flinging of Fire-brands, and rowling downe of great pieces of Timber, forced the assay-lants unto a retreate . . . The King, (then at the Foote of the Hill) perceiving his men to be beaten off; call them *Pultrons*, and all to be-cowardied them: presently commanding the skaling-ladders to be in another place, set unto the Rampier of the *Ravelin*. And heere his Majesty having taken notice of the valour of my Lord *Craven*, in a familiar and encouraging manner claps him upon the Shoulder, bidding him to goe on againe. The young Lord did so: and was the very first man, that gained up to the top; where he valiantly came to push of pike with the enemy: himself receiving an honorable wound with the thrust of an Halbert in his thigh; which was not found to be dangerous. Those of our *English* Gentlemen before named, behaved them-selves right couragiously; being next unto my Lord *Craven*, and in the very heate of the danger. And this was the manner of the fight, for two houres together almost; the defendants bearing themselves like tall Souldiours. At last, the *High-Dutch* being in mutiny with the *Wallons* and *Burgundians*, (who were resolved to defend the place) one of the enemies began to speake of Quarter, and of Termes of yeelding: which the Lord *Craven* (who was still the formest man) wisely apprehending; reaches out his hand unto one of the enemies Captaines, and undertooke upon his honour to bring him to the King. The enemies Muskets hereupon gave over playing.

ii. 142–47

The place resolved upon, was betwixt *Rain* and *Thierhaubten*; just upon a point of land: made so, by the crooking or bending of the River. The ground on the Kings side, was a pikes length higher banckt, and playner withall, then that on *Tillyes*: which was both lower, and wooddy. There was a tryall made first of all, to lay a floate-bridge; but the River would not endure that: for notwithstanding it be not above thirty or forty paces over at the most, yet by reason of the straight course of it, the streame sets very swift and violent.

All the materials being now prepared; the King about nine at night, upon the fourth of *Aprill*, advances some 1000 *Commanded men*, unto the place aforesaid. Two houres after, they begin to worke a *running Trench* round about the crooked banke of the River, that the Muskettiers out of that, might with more security give fire into the Wood on the other side of the River. This *Line* or *Trench*, had a great Battery at each end of it, for halfe and quarter Cannon: together with many lesser *Battereyes* betweene, all along about the *Point*, for the smaller field pieces to play upon: which were every-where intermingled with Muskettiers also. Whilest the Pioners are thus a working, the King in divers other places (both above it and below) gives false fires and Alarms, both with Muskets and smaller fielding peeces, for to amuse the enemy; that till the morning they could not imagine where to find him.

By sixe on the Thursday morning, Aprill 5. was this worke finished, the Cannon mounted, the Arches or Tressels for the bridge, with the planckes and other materialls, all brought; and ready to be laide into the River. These Tressels, were to have great stones or weights tyed unto their legges, to sinke them withall; and were to be no longer, then to reach just unto the bottome of the River, so that the planckes were to lye even almost with the very Water. The longest Tressels were about foure yards long: which were for the channell of the River. By that time it was day-light, General *Tilly* begins to perceive the Kings designe, and falls to worke against him in the Wood: whose Pioners when the King heard chopping downe the trees, he gave order immediately unto his men, to give them a *Salvee* or a *Good morrow* (as he cald it) both with their Cannon and their Muskets. About 8 a clocke the same morning, the King in two small Boats that he had, send over the *Swedes* and *Fins* his Pioners and Carpenters, unto the other side of the River. The designe was, to have them make up a small *Halfe-moone*, with a *Stocket* or *Pallisadoe* unto it: which should both answer that small worke that *Tilly* had made for his Muskettiers to lodge in, almost right before the said point of the River: and to cover the Bridge withall, from the greater shot: which this *Halfe-moone* still latched. The *Fins* and *Swedes* laboured upon the worke, and made good the place; till that about 4 a clock in the afternoone, both it was finished and they relieved.

The King all this while, is diligent in laying over his bridge, and *Tilly* as busie to raise up Batteryes to beate it downe againe. The King himselfe stird not all that night, nor the next day, from the very end of the bridge: nor the King of *Bohemia* from him, for the most part. *Tilly* upon the edge of the thicket, close unto the River, raises up a *Trench* first, to lodge his Muskettiers in, as we told you: and about Musket shot further within the wood, gives order for the making of a very great *Worke*: that if the King should put over his bridge, he might by power of that *Worke*, and by cutting downe of the trees about it; have beene able (at least) to have hindred his further passage. The small and great shot, goe off incessantly on both sides all this while; and they continue thus with extreme hot execution upon one another, till about eleven a clocke at noone the same day. About which time, the General *Altringer* with the shot of a Field-peece (which grased upon his temples) was spoyled and carryed off in the Duke of *Bavariaes* owne Coach . . .

The *Bavarian* Captaines found this so hot a service; that *Tilly* himselfe was enforced to come up to the point, and into the very face of the danger, to give directions: where within halfe an houre after *Altringers* mis-chance; he also received a Musket shot in the thigh a little above the knee, which prooved a mortall wound unto him. This fatall accident of this brave old Generall, did so amaze, not the Common souldiours alone, but the Duke of *Bavaria* himselfe also; (who now staid behind in the groave with the Infantery:) that so soone as ever the sad news was brought unto him, notwithstanding he were *Generalissimo* over the whole Forces; yet he instantly tooke horse upon it, posted with all speed into *Ingolstat*; not staying so much as to give order, either for the continuing of the begun designe, or for the marching away of the army.

Tilly being carryed off, and the Duke gone: the afternoone is spent on the Kings side, as the forenoone had beene; which was with uncessant thunders and volleyes of small and great shot. Among the *Bavarians*, those that understood of the spoyling of their two Generalls, and the flight of the Duke, by degrees and disorder, they one after another retreated from their Charge: whilest others that knew not of it, stoutly maintained the encounter. Little dreamt the King of it all this while: whose men still continue their working. By foure in the afternoone, is the bridge finisht: as 2 houres after, the little *Halfe-moone* and *Pallisadoe* also are, on the other side of the water before the end of the bridge. This done, the Kings owne Company of his *Life-guards* is sent over the bridge, for the manning of the *Halfe-moone*; for feare the enemy should have fallen upon it. In the beginning of the night, other of the *Bavarians* begin to retire, and to draw off their Ordnance; and that in such haste, that they forgot to command off their *Out-guards*, which lay all along upon the side of the River.

The next morning, the King sends over a Partee of some thirty *Scottish* Muskettiers commanded by Captaine *Forbes*, to see what the *Bavarians* were doing in the Wood; for that he had lately heard no more of them. Here could *Forbes* find but two *Horse-Sentryes* upon the edge of the Wood; whom he tooke prisoners: who, when they were brought unto the King, protested that they were ignorant of the retreate of the rest of their fellowes.

But to returne a little backe. The King not knowing of *Tillyes* wounding, or the Dukes fleeing; durst not adventure that evening to put his forces over the bridge: but spends the rest of the night in drawing up his army before it. This being done, order is given unto the Infantery or foote, to march over in the first place: and of all them Sir *Iohn Hepburn* with his *Brigade* was to have the honor of the *Vant-guard*; The King understanding by *Forbes* of this great and unhoped for newes; he alters thereupon all his former intended resolution: commanding the next morning, Aprill sixth, 500 Horse first, and 300 more after them, to passe over into the *Bavarian* forsaken Quarters. The first 500 being advanced thorow the Wood, and into the plaine beyond it; there cut downe a many of the *Bavarian* straglers, that had beene too slow in following of their fellowes. Some other *Swedish* troopes are instantly also commanded towards *Rain*; which though *Tilly* had left reasonably well fortified, yet this former feare amongst his party, made it nothing so resistable to the *Swedish*. They presently entring the Towne, find some wagons, and many horses, ready laden with the enemies goods; which are made good booty: but the Towne paying 30000 dollars to the King, are freed from pillaging. This was the first Towne, that the King tooke in *Bavaria*. There was it understood, that both the Duke of *Bavaria*, and the two wounded Generalls, parted the night before towards *Newburg*; whither they first retired: and from thence with as many of their Army as were then comme to them, unto *Ingolstat*.

To returne to the King and his *Leaguer*. The rest of that Fryday, Aprile sixth, is spent in the marching over of more Horse, and of three *Brigades* of *Infantery*: together with most of the Artillery. The Infantery already marcht over, encampt that night upon the edge of the plaine, a little without the Wood: the rest that were left behind, sitting downe just before the bridge.

And now for that such as are skilled in the Arts of war, will desire to be satisfied with the *reason*, as well as to heare the *successe* of the *Action* (in which oftentimes *Chance* may have as great a share, as *Wisedome*:) we will therefore affoard them a briefe discourse upon the Kings great *Iudgement*, as well as we have done the relation of his fortune.

The reason of the Kings putting over his bridge at this place was, that hee might have the better conveniency, both by flanckering it on either side to defend it from the annoyance of the enemy; and that being as it was, just upon the Point: it could not be touched by *Tillyes* batteryes, which were on each hand of the bridge, though he very often removed his Cannon to that purpose. For notwithstanding *Tilly* had (with as much judgement and advantage as possibly might be) raised his Batteryes, not cloase unto the Rivers side, but at a distance from the banke: yet were all his shot so kept off by the round and sudden shouldering away of the banke of the River at either end, that his Ordnance could not possibly come to beare upon the bridge: but that either the bullets fell short and were latcht by the little *Half-moone*, or hill upon the high banke above the bridge; or else flew quite over the whole leaguer. As for the raising of a Battery right before the face of the point; that could not *Tilly* on the sudden come to doe: for besides that he was hindered by the wood; the fury of the Kings both small and great shot, would at so neere a distance have spoild him as many men, as had adventured upon the service: and the Kings Batteryes being first up, would not suffer *Tilly* to mount any of his Cannon right before him.

And yet for all this, there appeares to be more then a humane direction in it: seeing the King was made constant against all the minds and judgements of his greatest Commanders. For when the day before, he asked the advice of his ablest Generalls; and they, notwithstanding they saw him so farre already engaged in the action, as he could not come off with his honor; had freely (all of them) professed their utter dislike of the designe: yet did the King plainely tell them, that he continued against all their reasons, constant unto his owne purpose. Yea, there appeares not onely a more then humane *direction*, but a *benediction* also, in the easinesse of the attaining of the passage: which very much exceeded all the Kings owne hopes of it. For when the day before

he perceived *Tilly* to begin to worke against him; he apprehended
so much danger in his owne designe, that should he loose but
2000 men in winning of his passage, he should thinke (as he
confessed) that he had made a thrifty purchase of his entrance
into *Bavaria*. When the next day (in like manner) that himself
being marcht over with the Horse, had with his owne eyes
perceived how sufficiently *Tilly* was providing to entertaine him;
he blest himselfe for his good successe in it: saying to the King
of *Bohemia*, and divers of his Commanders then about him; *That
this dayes actions was neere of as great a consequence, as that of
Leipsich* . . .

And yet, for all this, had not the King escaped so cheape, as
with the lives of two thousand brave men; had not *He* that
directed *Davids sling-stone* into *Goliahs* forehead, guided one
bullet unto *Altringers* forehead, and another into *Tillyes* thigh-
bone; had not this brave old Count beene thus spoyled, the King
had found but an unfriendly well-come into *Bavaria*, from the
second and greater *Worke*, which *Tilly* had laboured upon, from
sixe in the morning to eleven, but not yet finished. That worke,
I meane, which is before mentioned in the wood.

ii. 166–69

About Aprill 27, are *Gustave Horn* and Sir *Iohn Hepburn*, sent
with 3000 Horse and 5000 Foote; to take in *Landshut*: a very
dainty little Towne upon the River *Iser* (though the glory of it
be chiefly in two Streets) some eight *English* miles to the North-
East of *Mosburg*. At the first comming of the *Swedish* forces
before the walls, one of their Lieftenants of a troope of Horse,
with some few others of his Cornet, were shot from an Ambush
in the gardens . . .

The Towne paid 100000 Dollars to the King for its ransome;
and gave *Gustavus Horn* 20000 besides, for a gratuity . . .

Upon Munday in the forenoone, May 7th, the King shewed
himself in faire Battaglia before [Munich]: although by that time
he were come within a *Dutch* mile: the Deputies had againe met
him, and there presented the towne keyes unto him, with a
promise of 300000 Dollars . . .

The next day, the King went to see the Magazine and Armories;
where great store of armes and ammunition were found, but no
Ordnance; at which the King not a little wondering; espied by

and by divers of the carriages; by which he guessed, as the truth was, that the peeces were buried under-ground. These *dead ones* (as he cald them) he caused the Boores with ropes and leavers, to raise up without a miracle. There were 140 faire Peeces of brasse Ordnance; and in one, 30000 pieces of gold, said to be found. Among the rest, were 12 eminent ones; by the Duke called the 12 *Apostles*: though surely the *Apostles* were never such *Sonnes of Thunder*. Some peeces had the *Palsgraves* Armes upon them; which caused the King of *Bohemia* both to sigh and smile, at the sight of them. But the *Kunst-Cammer*, or *Chamber of Rarities*, was the thing that affoorded most entertainment: where the beholders admired rather, then lookt upon, the incomparable varieties and curiosities, both of *Art* and *Nature* . . .

iii. 17–23

The King, towards the 20. of *July*, hearing of a Convoye of *Walensteins*, that was to come out of the nether parts of *Austria* towards his Leaguer: sends out Colonel *Wippenherst*, with a Partee of 800. Horse, and as many Dragooners; to cut off that Convoye. With these 1600 did *Wippenherst* light upon 800. wagons laden with ammunition, and with Gunnes especially: which he destroyed.

About the 27. of *July*, a Partee of *Swedish* Horse, tooke one Captaine *Darmis* prisoner, amongst other Free-booters. He being examined by the King upon his oath, confessed that *Walensteins* great Magazine of victuals was at *Freyenstat*: which was the place appointed for whatsoever came from *Ratisbone*, and the *Upper Palatinate*, untill it were sent for to the Leaguer; which, within 3. or 4. dayes, a strong Convoye was about to goe for. The advantage of this opportunity, the King thought worth the taking: resolving with the first to send either to bring away the provisions, or to destroy that which was to feede his enemies . . .

The leader that the King made choise of to doe the feate, was Colonell *Dubatell*: whom *Walenstein* had lately taken prisoner, and againe released; as we before told you, The Colonel knew the Countrey thereabouts, perfectly well: for it was not farre from thence, that he was taken prisoner. The troopes appointed to goe with him, I find to be 14. Cornets of Horse, some troopes of Dragooners, and 2. Wagons laden with Petards, Storming or Skaling ladders, &c. With these, comes he unto *Karnbergh* first;

2 *Dutch* miles from *Freyenstat*. His season and march he so proportioned, as that he might be before the towne he went unto, before day-light, upon the Munday morning *July* 30. He did so: and found most of the souldiers and townesmen, very securely sleeping: for who would have suspected, that the King of *Swedens* smaller Army, being beseiged as it were, by two greater; durst have presumed to send twenty miles off to surprize *Freyenstat*.

Dubatel, at his first comming before the Towne; surprises some drowsie Sentinells: and hangs 2. Petards upon the Sally-port. These not blowing open the gate, as he expected; he fearing the noyse of their going off, would send in the Alarme into the Towne; claps his skaling ladders to the naked and un-man'd walls; which he mounts and enters. Other Petards being by this time put to worke, had forced open the gate; and made an easie passage that way, for the residue of the *Swedish*. They thus gotten in, cut in pieces those few souldiers, which they found either sleeping or unprovided, upon the next Courts of Guard, and whosoever else, offered to make resistance. Having thus mastered all opposition, they make towards the Towne-Hall; which was the Magazine or Store-house they came thither for. There were in it, at this present, 200000. pound weight of bread; great store of Meale, Corne, salt, and other provisions; sufficient for 2 moneths victuals for *Walensteins* whole Army. For the bringing of all this unto the Emperiall Leaguer, were there 1000 Wagons provided: many of them already prest, and some laden, or, not yet unladen, upon the Market place. Many hundred head both of small and great Catell, were likewise found about the towne: which were to be driven alive unto the Imperiall Army. Of these provisions, the *Swedish* first of all choosing out so much, as they thought themselves well able to carry away: set fire immediately unto the Magazine . . . Twelve hundred Sheepe and Oxen, with 500 horses, they also driving away with them . . .

Some of the Imperial souldiers (it seemes) so soone as the *Swedes* were gotten into the towne; went Post with the newes of it unto *Walenstein*. Which he hearing of; immediately the same day dispatches the Sergeant-Major Generall of his Foot; towards *Freyenstat*: either to save the residue; or to cut off *Dubatell* in his comming home againe. It was Colonell *Sparre* that was now sent . . .

The King of *Sweden* to prevent such a matter, and the better to secure the retreate unto *Dubatel*; goes himselfe out the same day, before *Dubatel* was comme home with a selected Partee of some 2000. commanded men, towards the said *Freyenstat* . . .

Not many charges passed betwixt the King and the enemies Horse; but that the face of the skirmish began to be altered: insomuch that the Imperiall Horse and *Crabats*; were (to be briefe) quite rowted and defeated . . . *Sparre* himself was taken prisoner: 600 of his men, were slaine upon the place: and divers more drowned and buried alive, in the river and moorish places, thorow which they thought to have escaped . . .

After this victory, there (for a while) passed nothing of moment, between the two Armies. The pettier skirmishes betweene commanded Partees abroad, or the continued night-alarmes upon one anothers Camps or Guards at home; I list not to stand upon.

iii. 39–44

Wallenstein perceiving the Kings intention, he the better to assure his Cannon and Ammunition; retired himselfe into the Forest called *Altemberg*: which belongeth unto the Marquesse of *Onspach*. Here could he make use, likewise, of a certaine old Fortresse; which had beene a Lodge, (or some such like thing) in the younger dayes of it. Here, likewise, did he very strongly entrench himselfe; and barricadoed up all the wayes, by cutting downe the trees round about him. The hill was high, and very steepe: craggie withall, and bushie; so that it was an impossible thing (almost) to be taken from an enemy, that had any courage to dispute it . . .

And now began the conflict, for the winning and defending of that old Castle; which proved a medlye of 10 houres long, on both sides. Many a brave Gentleman, here lost his life; many a Cavalier was here wounded: and not a few taken prisoners. The King led on his men, with his sworde drawne in his hand: and the *Swedish*, as if to show the enemy how little they dreaded any thing, that they could doe unto them; and how much they despised danger: exposed themselves all naked unto the enemies shot; having not so much as any one Trench or Earth cast up, to shelter them. In this equipage, runne they close unto the enemies Works and Batteries: stoutly and manfully, fall they upon them; and with the courage of undaunted spirit, doe they rush into the danger. But the Imperialists as full of resolution, made a most stout resistance unto the *Swedish*. For having the advantage, both of the higher ground, of their owne Trenches and Batteries already before hand there cast up: and having the wals of the old Castle to retreate unto, and to shelter their fresh supplies in: they maintained it with extremity confidence . . .

Thus at length, the *Swedes* seeing no good to be done upon it: were enforced to quit the danger; the most of them withdrawing themselves, unto the foote of the Mountaine . . . The *Swedish*, for all their magnanimous undertakings, could not drive the Imperialists to the retreat; or beate up their Quarters: nor could they, much lesse, compell the Kings forces to give it over.

II. EXTRACTS FROM WHITELOCKE'S
Memorials

i. 398

. . . having several times attempted the taking of Shrewsbury, but failed therein, on the last Lord's-day about twelve hundred horse and foot, under colonel Mitton, marched to Shrewsbury, and unexpectedly entered and surprised the town and castle.

They took there eight knights and baronets, forty colonels, majors, captains, and others of quality, and two hundred others, prisoners, one captain and five soldiers slain, fifteen pieces of ordnance taken, store of arms and ammunition, prince Maurice's magazine, divers carriages, bag and baggage of the prince's.

i. 441

The king's forces having made their batteries stormed Leicester; those within made stout resistance, but some of them betrayed one of the gates; the women of the town laboured in making up the breaches, and in great danger.

The king's forces having entered the town, had a hot encounter in the market-place; and many of them were slain by shot out of the windows. That they gave no quarter, but hanged some of the committee, and cut others in pieces. Some letters said that the kennels ran down with blood.

That colonel Gray the governor and captain Hacker were wounded and taken prisoners, and very many of the garrison put to the sword, and the town miserably plundered.

i. 446–48

Fairfax sent out Ireton with a flying party of horse, who fell upon a party of the king's rear quartered in Naseby town, took many prisoners, some of the prince's lifeguard, and Langdale's brigade.

This gave such an alarm to the whole army, that the king at midnight leaves his own quarters, and for security hastens to Harborough, where the van of his army was quartered, raiseth prince Rupert, and calls a council of war.

There it was resolved (and chiefly by prince Rupert's eagerness, old commanders being much against it) to give battle: and because Fairfax had been so forward, they would no longer stay for him, but seek him out. Fairfax was come from Gilborough to Gilling, and from thence to Naseby, where both armies drawn up in battalia faced each other.

The king commanded the main body of his army, prince Rupert and prince Maurice the right wing, sir Marmaduke Langdale the left, the earl of Lindsey and the lord Ashley the right hand reserve, the lord Bard and sir George L'Isle the left reserve.

Of the parliament's army Fairfax and Skippon commanded the main body, Cromwell the right wing, with whom was Rosseter, and they both came in but a little before the fight: Ireton commanded the left wing, the reserves were brought up by Rainsborough, Hammond, and Pride.

Prince Rupert began, and charged the parliament's left wing with great resolution; Ireton made gallant resistance, but at last was forced to give ground, he himself being run through the thigh with a pike and into the face with a halberd, and his horse shot under him, and himself taken prisoner.

Prince Rupert follows the chase almost to Naseby town, and in his return summoned the train, who made no other answer but by their firelocks; he also visited the carriages, where was good plunder, but his long stay so far from the main body was no small prejudice to the king's army.

In the mean time Cromwell charged furiously on the king's left wing, and got the better, forcing them from the body, and, prosecuting the advantage, quite broke them and their reserve.

During which, the main bodies had charged one another with incredible fierceness, often retreating and rallying, falling in together with the but-ends of their muskets, and coming to hand blows with their swords.

Langdale's men having been in some discontent before, did not in this fight behave themselves as they used to do in others, as their own party gave it out of them; yet they did their parts, and the rest of the king's army, both horse and foot, performed their duties with great courage and resolution, both commanders and soldiers.

Some of the parliament horse having lingered a while about pillage, and being in some disadvantage, Skippon perceiving it, brought up his foot seasonably to their assistance, and in this charge (as himself related it to me) was shot in the side.

Cromwell coming in with his victorious right wing, they all charged together upon the king, who, unable to endure any longer, got out of the field towards Leicester.

Prince Rupert, who now too late returned from his improvident eager pursuit, seeing the day lost, accompanied them in their flight, leaving a complete victory to the parliamentarians, who had the chase of them for fourteen miles, within two miles of Leicester; and the king finding the pursuit so hot, left that town, and hastes to Litchfield.

This battle was won and lost as that of Marston-Moor, but proved more destructive to the king and his party; and it was exceeding bloody, both armies being very courageous and numerous, and not five hundred odds on either side.

It was fought in a large fallow field, on the north-west side of Naseby, about a mile broad, which space of ground was wholly taken up.

i. 495

Letters from the Scots army before Hereford inform of their proceedings at the leaguer; of their want of money, ammunition, and provisions; that the country will bring in none, and the Scots soldiers feed upon apples, peas, and green wheat, which is unwholesome.

i. 518

. . . the king with about five thousand horse and foot, advanced to relieve Chester; major-general Pointz pursued close after the king, and within two miles of Chester engaged with the king's whole body, was at the first worsted, but made good his ground upon the retreat.

In the meantime colonel Jones, with five hundred horse, and adjutant-general Louthian, came from the leaguer before Chester to the assistance of Pointz, giving notice of their coming by shooting off two great guns; and by that time Pointz had rallied his forces; then Pointz in the front and Jones in the rear charged, and utterly routed the king's whole body.

The king, with about three hundred horse, fled into Chester; and the pursuit was so violent, that he immediately left the town and fled into Wales: the rest of his party were utterly dispersed, killed, and taken.

In the fight and pursuit were slain the lord Bernard, earl of Litchfield, and one other lord, two knights, one colonel, with above four hundred more officers and soldiers.

There were taken prisoners eleven colonels, most of them knights, seven lieutenant-colonels, five majors, about forty other officers, and one thousand common soldiers.

i. 531

Letters from colonel Rossiter, informed that prince Rupert, prince Maurice, col. Gerrard, the lord Hawley, sir Richard Willis, and about four hundred other gentlemen of quality (the meanest whereof was a captain,) had laid down their commissions, deserted the king, and betook themselves to Wotton-house, fourteen miles from Newark, where they stood upon their guard.

They subscribed a declaration, that if they may obtain from the parliament a pass to go beyond sea, they will engage upon their honour and oath never to return to take up arms against the parliament, . . .

i. 549

Letters from colonel Birch informed the particulars of the taking of Hereford:

That he hired six men, and put them in the form of labourers, and a constable with them, with a warrant to bring these men to work in the town; that in the night he lodged these men within three-quarters musket-shot of the town, and an hundred-and-fifty firelocks near them; and himself with the foot and colonel Morgan with the horse came up in the night after them, and cut

off all intelligence from coming to the town, so that they were
never discovered.

That one night they came too short, but the next night, with
careful spies and scouts, they carried on the business; and in the
morning, upon letting down the drawbridge, the six countrymen
and the constable went with their pickaxes and spades to the
bridge;

That the guard beginning to examine them, they killed three
of the guard, and kept the rest in play till the firelocks came up
to them, and then made it good till the body came up, who
entered the town with small loss, and became masters of it.

i. 584–87

Sir Thomas Fairfax sent a summons to the lord Hopton to lay
down arms, to prevent effusion of blood . . . A trumpet came with
an answer from the lord Hopton to sir Thomas Fairfax's summons, implying a willingness to end the business of the west
without more bloodshed, but desires to know whether the king
and parliament be not near to a conclusion of a peace; that he,
being intrusted, may be careful of the king's honour; . . . Sir
Thomas Fairfax and the lord Hopton agreed upon these articles:

That the lord Hopton's army should presently be disbanded,
and his horse, arms, and ammunition, artillery, bag and baggage,
delivered up to sir Thomas Fairfax.

Officers to have their horses, and troopers 20s. a man, strangers
to have passes to go beyond sea, and English to go to their homes.

EXPLANATORY NOTES

ABBREVIATIONS

Ludlow, *Memoirs* *The Memoirs of Edmund Ludlow, 1625–72*, ed. C. H. Firth, 2 vols., 1894.

Swed. Int. *The Swedish Intelligencer*, printed for Nathaniel Butter and Nicolas Bourne, Pt. I, 1632; Pt. II, 1632; Pt. III, 1633.

Whitelocke *Memorials of the English Affairs* by Bulstrode Whitelock(e), new edn., 4 vols, 1853.

PART I

Page 3. (1) *late glorious Successor:* Charles XII of Sweden, killed in action at Frederikshald on 30 November 1718.

(2) *extraordinary History . . . Clarendon:* Edward Hyde's *History of the Rebellion and Civil Wars in England*, Oxford, 1702–4.

Page 8. *House:* a common Oxford term for 'College'. Unlikely to mean Christ Church now particularized as '*the* House'.

Page 10. *Match . . . Spain:* the proposal for a marriage between the Prince of Wales, later Charles I, and Princess Maria, Infanta of Spain, was made in 1617, suspended in 1618, and abortively resumed in 1623. War between England and Spain broke out in 1625 and was not brought to an end until 1630. Meanwhile England also became embroiled with France and attempted to relieve the Huguenots besieged in La Rochelle. Peace with France came in 1629. Consequently, at the time of the Cavalier's conversation—1628/9—it is not obvious what war his father expected to occur in the future 'between the King of England and the Spaniard', or indeed elsewhere in Europe, since England was currently engaged in hostilities.

Page 11. *Fielding:* Defoe possibly derived the name from his extensive reading of the *Swedish Intelligencer*, where (iii. 32) a marginal note reads: 'All this . . . received I from Lieutenant-Colonell *Terret*, Captaine *Feilding*, and Captaine *Legg*, then present in the Action'.

Page 12. *Pistoles:* from *c.* 1600 applied to a Spanish coin (worth 80–90p.), and after 1640 to the *louis d'or* issued by Louis XIII. Defoe probably intended the latter.

Page 14. (1) *Lieutenant-General . . . Roy:* see Introduction p. x. From this point to p. 31 Defoe relies largely on Le Clerc's *Life of Richlieu*, trans. Tom Brown, 1695, i. 330–55.

(2) *Manage:* skilful handling.

Page 15. *English had done it:* cf. Ludlow, *Memoirs*, i. 11–12. (An account of the siege of La Rochelle (1628) is given in a memoir of great interest to Defoe: *Memoirs of the Sieur De Pontis*, trans. Charles Cotton, 1694, i. vii.)

Page 18. *We stayed in Paris* (*p. 16*) . . . *times:* Defoe's interpolation into the material borrowed from Le Clerc.

Page 19. (1) *a State Broil:* see Introduction p. xi.
   (2) *Paix:* possibly should read '*Pain*'.

Page 28. (1) *The Duke de Momorency* (p. 25). . . . *Saluces:* cf. Le Clerc, op. cit., i. 344–45: 'The Army of Mareschals *de la Force* and *Schomberg* being very much enfeebled by Desertions, and by Sicknesses, required of necessity to be reinforced with a new body of an Army, and the Conduct thereof was given to the Duke of *Montmorency*, and the Marquis *d'Effiat*. It was composed of ten thousand Foot, and a thousand Horse, and to joyn the other Army they were to hazard a battle against the Troops of *Savoy*, commanded by the Prince *Thoiras*. The French being to pass a Defile, the Savoyards staid till all were passed, but the Rear-Guard, which they charged and put them presently into confusion; but the two French Generals having caused some of their Troops to turn back, they defeated the Savoyards, and laid near two thousand Men on the ground. A few days after they took the City of *Saluces*, by composition, which made the Duke of *Savoy* much perplexed. Being come to *Savigliano*, with design to repair the loss by a new Combat, because he was superior in Horse, he received the news of the taking of *Mantua*, which as much rejoyced him as it afflicted the French.'
   (2) *This put . . . Prince:* cf. Le Clerc, op. cit., i. 345: 'The French Generals having understood the Death of *Charles Emanuel*, deliberated whether they should go to *Casal*, whilst the courage of the Savoyards was abated by the Death of their Prince.'
   (3) *Plague:* the attack of the plague suffered by the Cavalier was doubtless prompted by Le Clerc's report (op. cit., i. 355) of the French king's being given over 'for lost without retrieve' from the same cause. But Defoe's long-standing concern with the plague must not be overlooked; it was to lead to his *Journal of the Plague Year* in 1722. Louis Landa, in his edition of the *Journal*, 1969, pp. x–xiv, documents this concern. The Cavalier suffered from ordinary bubonic plague with the 'bubo' in the neck (see Landa, pp. 76, 200).

Page 29. (1) *a Truce:* Treaty of Regensburg, 13 October 1630.
   (2) *Proverb:* first recorded use 1576 (M. P. Tilley, *Dictionary of Proverbs*, 1950, s. 822).

Page 31. (1) *League:* Treaty of Bärwalde, 23 January 1631.
   (2) *took . . . Stetin:* 20 July 1630.
   (3) *Gust:* relish or enjoyment.

Page 35. (1) *English Ambassador:* Sir Peter Wyche (*d.* 1643), ambassador at Constantinople 1627–41.
   (2) *related . . . Mecklenburgh:* through his grandfather, Gustav Vasa.

Page 36. *Treaty:* on 22 June 1631.

Page 38. *Seigensius:* no person of this name, exercising the influence Defoe ascribes to him, has been traced. The Duke of Saxony did place great confidence in a Lutheran minister—Matthias Hoë von Hoenëgg (1580–1645)—who urged him to defy the Emperor at Leipzig. If Defoe had Hoë in mind it is difficult to explain his use of 'Seigensius' in view of his historical accuracy elsewhere.

Page 43. *Tilly:* he had joined Pappenheim at the siege of Magdeburg in April 1631.

Page 44. Administrator of Magdenburgh : Christian William, a prince of the electoral house of Brandenburg (*Swed. Int.*, i. 110).

Page 51. English Ambassador : Sir Robert Anstruther.

Page 54. near Torgau : actually at Düben on 5 September 1631.

Page 56. Touch : trial

Page 59. Field : at Breitenfeld.

Page 62. The next Day (p. 59). . . . *General :* see App. I, *Swed. Int.*, i. 121–25.

Page 64. The Darkness . . . Order : see App. I, *Swed. Int.*, i. 121–25.

Page 65. Crabats : obsolete form of Croats or Croatians.

Page 66. light of : plundered

Page 67. Rix-dollars : silver coins (value 11–23p.) current *c.* 1600–1850 in various European countries.

Page 70. (1) *removed*: Gustavus had marched out of Erfurt on 26 September.
   (2) *that Day :* 30 September.

Page 73. The King was before (p. 71). . . . *see :* see App. I, *Swed. Int.*, ii. 11–16.

Page 80. (1) *The Castle at Oppenheim* (p. 79). . . . *own :* see App. I, *Swed. Int.*, ii. 46–7.
   (2) *capitulated :* on 12 December.
   (3) *Queen :* Marie Eleonora actually joined him at Hanau on 22 January 1632.

Page 82. Neuport : Prince Maurice of Nassau won one of his most famous victories at Nieuport in July 1600.

Page 83. The taking of (p. 82). . . . *surrendered :* see App. I, *Swed. Int.*, ii. 76–82.

Page 88. Serjeant of Dragoons : Gustavus in fact made a personal reconnaissance of the situation; he exchanged badinage with Tilly's sentries across the river (M. Roberts, *Gustavus Adolphus*, 1953–8, ii. 700); but the part played by the sergeant is Defoe's invention.

Page 89. Tale of a Tub : an apocryphal story.

Page 93. The King having (p. 89). . . . *Ausburg :* see App. I, *Swed. Int.*, ii. 142–47.

Page 96. Here the King . . . aforesaid : the King narrowly escaped with his life on both 19 and 20 April 1632 at the siege of Ingolstadt; Tilly died in the city on 20th (Roberts, op. cit., ii. 701, 704).

Page 97. The Army having . . . again : see App. I, *Swed. Int.*, ii. 166–69.

Page 100. engrossing : monopolizing.

Page 105. The first considerable (p. 102). . . . *them*: see App. I, *Swed. Int.*, iii. 17–23.

Page 106. (1) *old Castle :* the Alte Feste.
   (2) *The Imperialists finding* (p. 105). . . . *Quarter :* see App. I, *Swed. Int.*, iii. 39–44.

Page 109. *Coburgh Castle :* Coburg capitulated on 28 September 1632.

Page 112. *League :* At Heilbronn, April 1633, the treaty with Sweden created the League of Heilbronn for the defence of the Protestant Cause in the Empire.

Page 113. (1) *West-Phalia :* the Peace, ending the Thirty Years War, was signed on 24 October 1648.
  (2) *Nordlingen :* the battle was fought on 5–6 September 1634.

Page 118. *French into the War :* Bernard, Duke of Saxe-Weimar, and the remnant of the Heilbronn League negotiated the Treaty of Paris with Richelieu; it was signed on 1 November 1634.

Page 119. *Prince Maurice :* the Cavalier could not have seen him in 1635; Maurice died in 1625.

Page 120. *Shenkscans :* it was Prince Maurice's brother, Prince Frederick Henry (1584–1647) who took Schenkenschanz in 1635.

Page 122. (1) *York :* Charles I reached York on 30 March 1639.
  (2) *Emulation :* ambitious rivalry.

Page 123. *Pacification :* by the Pacification of Berwick, 19 June 1639, both armies agreed to disband.

Page 124. *to send the Earl* (p. 123). . . . *Scotland :* the incident Defoe describes— accurately in broad outline—occurred on 3 June 1639

PART II

Page 125. *a meer Swiss :* a mercenary.

Page 133. *I went over . . . also :* for corroborative evidence see *Hist. MSS Comm.*, 12th Report, App. IV, pp. 514–15.

Page 134. *their General :* Alexander Leslie, later Earl of Leven.

Page 136. *Newcastle :* the city was evacuated by Conway; Leslie entered it on 30 August 1640.

Page 137. *Great Council :* it met at York on 24 September 1640. Before it broke up at the end of October writs had gone out for a new parliament.

Page 138. (1) *a Ceremony and . . . Discipline :* a new Book of Canons had been ordered to replace John Knox's *Book of Discipline ;* the new Book of Common Prayer (1637) brought the order of worship in the Scottish church into line with that of England.
  (2) *Money :* Charles had ruled England for eleven years without a Parliament, raising enough revenue for peace-time by non-Parliamentary taxes (such as ship money); when confronted by the Scottish invasion he could not go on in that way. He had to summon Parliament to raise revenue to pay the Scots' occupation costs; he had therefore to accept the Commons' attack on all his past methods of government.

Page 139. (1) *Brangles:* wrangles.

(2) *Eighth Article:* alone among early historians of the Civil War, Whitelocke (i. 104) numbers this article as '8'.

Page 141. (1) *Treaty appointed at Rippon:* despite Secord's inference to the contrary (*Robert Drury's Journal*, 1961, p. 113), this is historically correct. See John Rushworth, *Historical Collection of Private Passages of State*, 1680, II. ii. 1291, 1293.

(2) *We were all ... fight:* cf. Whitelocke, i. 106.

Page 142. (1) *forsook ... fled:* Matt. 26: 56.

(2) *Laud, and ... Strafford:* Laud was impeached in December 1640 (executed on 10 January 1645); Strafford, attainted by the Commons in April 1641, was executed on 12 May.

Page 143. (1) *Remonstrance:* the Grand Remonstrance which recalled every act in Charles's reign that had offended his subjects, was passed by the Commons on 23 November 1641.

(2) *seizing some of the Members:* Charles made his abortive attempt to seize the five M.P.s on 4 January 1642.

(3) *Power of the Mititia:* when Charles refused his consent to the Militia Bill—which placed all armed forces under the direct control of Parliament—the Commons, in March 1642, issued the Militia Ordinance on their own authority.

Page 147. *The Acclamations ... incredible:* cf. Clarendon, *History*, vi. 29.

Page 151. *amuse:* mislead.

Page 152. (1) *The Enemy ... at Pershore:* Ludlow, *Memoirs*, i. 40–1 was probably Defoe's chief source for the incident he recounts.

(2) *Word:* password.

Page 154. *moving:* influential.

Page 159. *Victoria, Let us ... own:* see App. I, *Swed. Int.*, i. 121–25.

Page 163. *4000 Men:* cf. Ludlow, *Memoirs*, i. 45.

Page 165. *Address for ... Peace:* the two sides agreed on a 'cessation of arms' in early November 1642 while preliminaries for a peace conference were discussed. Prince Rupert, believing the truce had come to an end, attacked Brentford on 12 November.

Page 166. *Upon this the. ... hastened:* cf. Whitelocke, i. 189.

Page 172 *Treaty of Westphalia:* since it was not signed until 1648 it could not form a precedent for an action in 1642.

Page 173. *Memoirs, p. 52:* ed. C. H. Firth, i. 46.

Page 175. *February:* Cirencester was attacked on 2 February 1643.

Page 177. (1) *Sir Nicholas Flamming:* probably a compositor's error for 'Slanning'. No contemporary or modern authority records 'Flamming'; all attribute his alleged activity to Slanning.

(2) *Roundway-down:* on 13 July 1643.

Page 178. Siege of Bristol: 23–26 July 1643.

Page 180. delivered of . . . Royal: the daughter was actually named Henrietta Anne (1644–70); her mother was Henrietta Maria (1609–69). Whitelocke had made the same error (i. 205). The Cavalier's knowledge of her later titles is anachronistic.

Page 187. (1) *about Grantham:* on 13 May 1643.

(2) *killed . . . Widdrington:* Defoe here repeats Ludlow's error (*Memoirs*, i. 58). Widdrington's title was not conferred until after the battle of Winceby; he died following the battle of Wigan, 1651.

(3) *Had we marched. . . . of Gloucester:* cf. Whitelocke, i. 213.

(4) *with Sir Nicholas Crisp:* Defoe follows Whitelocke, i. 213–14, in asserting that Crisp was present at this encounter. In fact, though Crisp's regiment was captured to a man at Cirencester on 15 September 1643, he was not with it; he had been involved in a quarrel which led to a duel and was thus absent.

Page 189. one of their Collonels: perhaps 'colonel Tucker' whom Whitelocke mentions (i. 215).

Page 190. a French Marquess: Ludlow is the only contemporary source for this detail (*Memoirs*, i. 56).

Page 191. Cessation of Arms: agreed on 15 September 1643.

Page 196. Bolton . . . first Fury: Defoe follows Whitelocke, i. 275, in giving three events in unhistorical order. The relief of the Countess of Derby at Lathom House (not Rupert's achievement) was nearly simultaneous with the capture of Bolton on 28 May 1644; Liverpool was then taken, followed in July by the seizure of York.

Page 198. surprize . . . Tyne: historically untrue.

Page 199. (1) *fetching . . . York:* cf. Whitelocke, i. 275: 'The prince fetching a compass about with his army got into York.'

(2) *Duke of Parma . . . Paris:* Alessandro Farnese, duke of Parma (1545–92) relieved Paris in 1590.

Page 200. I entreated him not (p. 199) *. . .. nothing:* the Cavalier's wisdom may have derived from Ludlow, *Memoirs*, i. 98–9.

Page 208. (1) *Remarks:* observations.

(2) *pressed:* conscripted into military service.

Page 216. Brennus Hill: perhaps one of the summits (almost permanently covered in snow) near the Brenner Pass; the name is no longer used.

Page 217. York: surrendered on 16 July 1644.

Page 222. laying down their Arms: at Fowey on 1 September 1644. Much of the detail of the King's victory and its consequences derives from Whitelocke, i. 302–3.

Page 224. declining to come . . . Horse: cf. Whitelocke, i. 321.

Page 226. (1) *Self-denying Ordinance:* 'an Ordinance appointing, That no Member of either House, during the Time of this War, shall have or execute any Office or Command, Military or Civil', *Journal of the House of Commons*, 11 December 1644.

(2) *modelling ... their Army:* reforming the organization and discipline of the parliamentary army; the 'New Model Army' was effectively in being by April 1645.

Page 228. (1) *The King would ... Divino:* cf. Whitelocke, i. 390: 'government by bishops was *jure divino* ... the government of the Church by presbyteries was *jure divino.*'

(2) *Hopes of Peace vanished:* negotiations were abandoned on 22 February 1645.

Page 229. *the Surprize of the town ... stormed:* see App. II, Whitelocke, i. 398.

Page 238. *Composition:* the discharging of his liabilities.

Page 240. *we attacked Hawkesly ... Worcester:* cf. Whitelocke, i. 437: 'the king's party took Hawkesley-house ... and carried the garrison, being eighty prisoners, to Worcester.'

Page 243 (1) *Siege to Leicester* (p. 241). ... *killed:* see App. II, Whitelocke i. 441. See also J. Wilshere and S. Green, *The Siege of Leicester—1645* (Leicester, 1970).

(2) *3000 Head of Cattle:* cf. Whitelocke, i. 446.

(3) *Fairfax, to whom ... Men:* cf. Whitelocke, i. 444.

Page 244. *in the Morning:* 14 June 1645.

Page 246. *at Naseby their* (p. 243). ... *Leicester:* see App. II, Whitelocke, i. 446–48.

Page 247. *to be printed:* within a month of the victory at Naseby, *The King's Cabinet Opened, or certain packets of secret letters* was published. A copy of it was probably owned by Defoe; see *The Libraries of Daniel Defoe and Phillip Farewell* ed. H. Heidenreich (Berlin, 1970), item 1420 b.

Page 248. *I took the freedom* (p. 247). ... *pleased:* the source of the Cavalier's wisdom may have been Clarendon, *History*, ix. 42, 67.

Page 250. *showed his Resentments:* by placing Hastings (then Lord Loughborough) under arrest.

Page 252. *Association Troops:* in December 1642 Parliament had ordered groups of counties to associate for mutual defence. One such group was the Eastern Counties Association to which Huntingdonshire and Leicestershire were added in 1643. The troops provided by this Association are referred to here.

Page 254. *They were commanded* (p. 253) ... *Lieutenant:* cf. Whitelocke, i. 500: 'some resistance made at the bridge by captain Bennet with his foot, till he, his lieutenant, and many of his men were slain.'

Page 255 *they were so poor ... Health:* see App. II, Whitelocke, i. 495.

Page 257. (1) *got into Chester:* on 23 September 1645.

(2) *From Ludlow* (p. 256) ... *Condition:* see App. II, Whitelocke, i. 518.

Page 258. (1) *leaves a Thousand* (p. 257) ... *dispersed:* cf. Whitelocke, i. 532–33.

(2) *The Lord Digby ... Man:* cf. Whitelocke, i. 531–32.

(3) *Prince Rupert ... Parliament:* see App. II, Whitelocke, i. 531.

Page 259. *Hereford which had ... Enemy:* see App. II, Whitelocke, i. 549.

Page 264. when unexpectedly the Enemy's General (p. 263) . . . .*to such Officers:* see App. II, Whitelocke, i. 584–87.

Page 265. (1) *not to seek in his Measures:* not lacking in other action he could take.
(2) *Cessation of Arms was agreed:* on 13 March 1646.

Page 266. quits the Town . . . more: cf. Whitelocke, ii. 13: 'the king was escaped out of Oxford in disguise with Mr. John Ashburnham and one more.' Charles's unnamed companion was his chaplain, Michael Hudson; they left Oxford on 26 April 1646.

Page 268. voted they . . . Scots: cf. Whitelocke, ii. 22.

Page 269. (1) *took his Leave:* on 28 January 1647.
(2) *That he was Bought and Sold:* cf. Whitelocke, ii. 111: 'some reported he used the expression, *that he was bought and sold.*'

Page 270. by the Sword: cf. Matt. 26: 52.

Page 278. garbled: cleansed or purged ('Pride's Purge', December 1648).

GLOSSARY OF MILITARY TERMS

Articles, upon: on conditions

Bastion: a projecting part of a fortification, consisting of an earthwork in the form of an irregular pentagon
battalia, in: in order of battle
breastwork: a defensive parapet of breast height
burgrave: a town governor

Comisado: a night attack
carabine: a fire-arm used by mounted soldiers
counterscarp: the outer wall of a ditch which supports the covered way in a fortified system
crupper, on the: in the rear; close behind
cuirassier: a horse soldier wearing body armour

Fireman: one who uses firearms
flying party: a detachment organized for rapid forays
forelorn: a storming party
furniture: a set of harness and ornamental or defensive trappings for a horse

Halberd: a combination of spear and battle-axe
half-moon: a defensive outwork resembling a bastion with a crescent-shaped gorge
hornwork: an outwork consisting of two demi-bastions connected by a wall and joined to the main work by two parallel wings

Leaguer: a military camp, especially one engaged in a siege; or an investing force
light, to: to dismount
list, to: to enlist

Nail, to: to spike (make unserviceable) a cannon

Parle, to beat a: to call for an informal conference with an enemy, under truce, for the discussion of terms
partizan: an infantry weapon consisting of a long-handled spear, the blade having one or more lateral cutting projections
petard: an explosive device used to breach a wall or gate
pickeer, to: to reconnoitre or scout
piece: a fortified place, or stronghold
port: a gate or gateway of a walled town, or the town itself

Ravelin: an outwork consisting of two embankments which form a salient angle, constructed in front of a fortified position

redoubt: a small defensive position made in a bastion of a permanent fortification

reformado: an officer left without command owing to the reforming of his company; he retained his rank and pay

ride post, to: to ride with post-horses, hence with great haste

Scout, to be upon the: to act as a spy

Trained band: a trained company of citizen soldiery

traverse: a defensive barricade thrown across a line of approach

Yield at discretion, to: to surrender unconditionally

BIOGRAPHICAL INDEX

The page reference records the first appearance of the person named.

Brereton, Sir William (1604–61), Parl. commander in Cheshire and neighbouring counties, 176.

Buchanan, George (1506–82), in *De Jure Regni* (1579) expounded influential theory of limited monarchy and the right of people to elect kings, 194.

Calender, Earl of: James Livingstone, 1st Earl of Callander (*d.* 1674), Parl. commander; assisted Scots in northern counties, 219.

Carnarvon, Earl of: Robert Dormer, 1st Earl (*d.* 1643), Roy. officer; fought at Edgehill and Cirencester; killed at Newbury, 190.

Catherine, Queen (1485–1536), first queen of Henry VIII, 272.

Cavendish, Lieut.-Gen.: Charles Cavendish (1620–43), Roy. Gen.; seized Grantham 1643; defeated by Cromwell at Gainsborough and killed by his capt.-lieut., on 28 July 1643, 187.

Charles I, King of Great Britain (1600–49), 3.

Charles, Prince (1630–85), Prince of Wales (1638) and later Charles II, 260.

Charles Louis, Prince (1617–80); see Bohemia, King of.

Clarendon, Earl of: Edward Hyde, 1st Earl (1609–74), adviser to Charles I; later Lord Chancellor to Charles II; historian of Civil Wars, 3.

Cleveland, Earl of: Thomas Wentworth 1st Earl (1591–1667), Roy. Col. of horse; prisoner of war 1644–48, 224.

Colalto, Count de: Rambaldo XIII, Count of Collalto (1575–1630), Field Marshall and Imperial Chamberlain; commander in war of Mantuan succession, 29.

Conway, Lord: Edward, 2nd Viscount (1594–1655), Gen. of horse against Scots, 1640; defeated at Newburn, August 1640, 135.

Cranmer, Thomas (1489–1556), Archbp. of Canterbury and chief author of the English liturgy; burnt as a heretic under Mary I, 272.

Cratz, Col.: Johann Philipp Cratz (*d.* 1635), Imperial commander, made Field Marshall under Tilly (*Swed. Int.*, ii. 118); deserted to Swedes, 1633; captured at Nördlingen, Sept. 1634; executed in Vienna for high treason, 114.

Craven, William, 1st Earl (1606–97), served with Gustavus 1632–33; later attached to court of Elizabeth ex-Queen of Bohemia; returned to England 1660, 81.

Crawford, Lord: Ludovic Lindsay, 16th Earl (1600–52), Roy. commander at Edgehill and Marston Moor; captured at Newcastle, Oct. 1644, 219.

Crisp, Sir Nicholas (1599?–1666): wealthy merchant and customs farmer; regt. he raised captured at Cirencester, Sept. 1643, 187.

Cromwell, Oliver (1599–1658), fought at Edgehill 1642; Lieut.-Gen. 1644; largely responsible for remodelling Parl. army and for 'Self-denying Ordinance'; later Lord Protector, 1653, 186.

Cromwell, Richard (1626–1712), son of above; Lord Protector 1658, 275.

Cronenburgh, Baron: Adam Philip, Count von Cronberg (*d.* 1634), Col. of horse in Imperial army 1630; Maj.-Gen. 1632, 62.

Cullembach, Col.: Moritz Pensen von Caldenbach (d. 1631), Swedish commander; led cavalry regt. at Leipzig where he was killed, 62.

D'Effiat, Maréchal: Antoine Coiffier de Ruzé, Marquis D'Effiat (1581–1632), Marshall of France and superintendent of finances, 24.

De la Force, Maréchal: Jacques-Nompar de Caumont, Duc de La Force (1558–1652), Marshall of France, 24.

Denby, Earl of: Basil Fielding, 2nd Earl of Denbigh (1608?–1675), Col. of Parl. horse; promoted Maj.-Gen.; one of the commissioners to the King, 1644, 220.

Derby, Earl of: James Stanley, 7th Earl (1607–51, Roy. commander in the North,